HEAVEN ON EARTH

Book Four
THE POWER OF FOUR

HEAVEN ON EARTH

D.A. HENNEMAN

ISBN-13: 9781735360249

Content Editor: Jennifer Meltzer
Copy Editor: Alexa Nussio
Book & Cover Design: Sumo Design
Cover photos © Getty Images

Manufactured in the United States of America
First Edition: December 2020
Published by: Saray Books LLC

TO LEIGH

My dearest hope is that you found your happily ever after, and it gave you the wings you needed to fly. Here's to the memories...

1

The music from Tara Varela's flute drifted down the hillside and into the valley below near the monument where she worked. It had been her grandmother's heritage which had brought her to Crazy Horse Memorial all those years ago. It was her love of the Black Hills of South Dakota that compelled her to finish her degree and stay there as a park ranger.

The Lakota people were proud of their heritage and were wonderful stewards to the earth and Her creatures. The view from Tara's afternoon perch overlooked the construction of the lower part of the mountain, far away from the proud face of the honored leader. Not much happened in the winter months, although tourists from all over the world still visited daily.

While the monument was impressive to her for many reasons, the amount of work to be completed was unfathomable. After decades of construction, Crazy Horse's face and the top of his pointing arm were the only things finished. However, the more she learned about the passion of the late sculptor, Korczak Ziolkowski, and his family's continued work, the more she knew she was in the right place.

Another sour note, and Tara began again. She was still learning the correct movements for a song her co-worker, Paytah, had played at lunch recently. It had a Celtic vibe, unlike most of the music they heard day in and day out. Tara had been surprised to find it was from the soundtrack of *Lord of the Rings* and had watched the movie with new eyes. Much like the scenes they were played in, the haunting notes filled her heart with longing and hope. She had been trying to perfect the melody ever since.

On the days the notes came easily, the lyrics were sung in her mind in a rich baritone, unlike the woman on the soundtrack. The elder, Mato, had always said that notes strung together in a tune weren't as important as the music of her heart. With the recent addition of the man's voice to her rendition of the tune, she wondered if playing from her heart was starting to mess with her head.

Running steps and rustling stopped her mid-blow, and she turned to look up the hillside path. A frantic young woman ran up to her, with fresh cuts on her face and muddied clothes.

"I need your help," she panted.

Tara had already risen to her feet, her flute and musings forgotten at the base of the tree. "What's wrong? Are you hurt?" In a few steps, she met the woman on the path and did a once-over for injuries.

The woman shook her head, sucking in large gulps of breath as she tried to slow her breathing. "Not me. My boyfriend." She waved up the path then turned to start back the way she came. "He's hurt."

The woman was winded, with a few superficial scratches, but otherwise looked fine. She was just frantic. Panic came off her in waves. It increased Tara's heartrate and made her ill. She sent the woman calming thoughts.

"Can you take me to him?" Tara's question was logical, since she wasn't sure how familiar the stranger was with the area. The woman looked as though she may have run a few miles.

"Yes." The woman nodded.

The sun had already been blocked by the great mountain — another hour, and it would be gone entirely. She noted the woman was dressed properly for hiking. She had gear on her belt but no backpack, which made sense if she had been in a hurry to find someone. Tara gave her a directional nod and started to move.

The woman turned and ran ahead on the path. Tara kept up the quick pace while she pulled out her cellphone and lifted the privacy settings that shared her location. She hit Paytah's contact next and started a text, tapping the microphone symbol allowing her to do voice-to-text.

Hiker found me at my usual spot and needs help. Says her boyfriend is injured and we are on route. Location shared, follow with a med kit and blankets. She kept walking behind the woman as she waited for a response. The three dots signifying it was coming stopped with Paytah's reply.

Will be 10 minutes behind you.

Tara was comforted by the knowledge she had backup coming, especially since she only carried a small flashlight and first aid kit on her util-
ity belt. From the way the woman was behaving, the injuries might need
more than the bandages and gauze she had handy. Between her supplies
and the woman's, they should be able to provide enough aid until help
arrived. She hoped the couple had a lantern, it would be dark soon.

Tara picked up her pace, causing the woman to walk quicker. Moving
up the hillside was probably much slower going than the way down had
been. "How long were you running before you found me," she asked.

"About 15 minutes," the woman responded. "Was about this pace. I
didn't want to slip. It took me about 6 or 7 minutes to find you."

"Okay good. I've called for help. They are right behind us. My name
is Tara, by the way."

"Maggie," the woman said as she glanced over to Tara, who had caught
up to her. They were practically walking side by side. "My boyfriend's
name is Brent."

"Before we get there, can you tell me what happened?"

"We were hiking back to our campsite, and Brent's foot slipped into
a fox hole. He fell forward, and I heard it snap." Maggie's voice cracked.
"I managed to slow the bleeding, but it's broken. It pushed through his
skin." She covered her mouth with her hand.

Tara gave Maggie's arm a quick squeeze. Sounded bad, it would be
tricky to move him. Maybe they could find some branches along the way
to serve as a splint. Tara took her phone out again and sent another text
to Paytah.

Possible compound fracture, bring the gurney.

Her response came quickly. **Got it. On the way.**

"My co-worker will come with no less than two other people. We will
be able to get Brent help."

"Thank you so much, Tara. I'm so glad I heard your music on my way
to the Visitor Center. It was the only place I could think of where I would
find someone."

"We have a hospital nearby so once we get him off the mountain, they
should be able to secure his break for transport."

"I think it's right up here through these trees."

Tara squinted beyond the tree line to determine where Maggie's boyfriend was sitting. She spied him across the clearing, his body unmoving,

eyes wide and locked on something to his left. Tara saw it then and grasped Maggie's arm to pull her back and down into a crouching position. Maggie attempted to pull away in confusion, crouching down beside Tara after her fierce whisper.

"You need to stay here, and keep quiet," Tara said. "Don't move."

"Oh my God, I see it," Maggie whispered. She had hardly taken a breath since crouching down beside Tara. Their eyes were all locked in the same direction, and while the boyfriend was closest to it, it wouldn't take more than a few seconds for the mountain lion to make it to their location if it chose to do so.

Tara scooted closer to the clearing, leaving Maggie behind her by a foot or two. It was enough of a movement to attract the animal's attention. Its gaze locked on Tara as it adjusted its powerful body to face hers. She could hear Maggie's slight intake in breath, but otherwise, she was as silent as an evergreen. Tara slowly put her arms out on either side, her hands splayed with palms forward. The mountain lion bared its fangs with a sharp hiss, remaining completely still.

She couldn't think of anything else to do. The idea came as a mental flash to her mind, much like some of the other things she had been shown in the past few months. Going with her gut in these types of situations took her in the right direction her entire life — but much more so lately. Besides, it worked at home on her cat, Misty.

Tara took a deep breath and pushed her thoughts out in front of her, directing her intention at the large cat a few feet away from the injured man.

Peace. No Harm. Friend.

FOOD.

Interesting. The animal formed words along with the images, just like she received from Misty. The response wasn't angry, nor did it feel urgent. This animal wasn't starving but had merely come across something that smelled like blood. Tara felt the waves of curiosity coming from the beast. If the animal had truly been hungry, Brent would have already been attacked.

Not Food. Friend.

The mountain lion's head tipped to the side, much like Misty did when Tara spoke aloud to her. Her best friend, Brooke, had seen how attached Tara was to her cat and had left her behind when she moved away. Tara and Misty had their communication down to a science, but this was next level. It was only because they spoke to each other this way, Tara had even thought to attempt it with the wild feline. Words were always sent with images when she spoke to her cat. It seemed like now it worked on other animals as well.

Calm. Peace.

"Unbelievable," Maggie whispered in awe. Tara could only imagine what it must look like to her. After all, Tara had now lowered herself to her knees, and the cat had shifted its muscular body, so it was facing her fully.

FRIEND.

Tara smiled as the large cat started a rumbling purr and stopped twitching its tail. Its ears were up in a relaxed position, and it was waiting for her response. Just a conversation between two friends.

Yes. Friend.

The cat relaxed even further, rolling to its side and resting its head on the forest floor. It wasn't leaving, but Tara decided it was safe enough to approach. She needed to get the cat to leave before the others arrived. It would be a shame to tranquilize it. She knew Paytah would have the necessary tools in her kit, especially at this time of night.

Moving.

The cat watched, unblinking, as Tara stood in place with her arms still splayed at her sides. Maggie muttered under her breath, and Tara glanced back with a shake of her head to quiet her. She needed to concentrate and couldn't worry that Maggie would draw any undue attention to herself.

Tara took a step forward and paused, glancing over to Brent, who was no longer staring the mountain lion's way. He was still sitting against the tree, but his head was slumped forward chin to chest. He must have passed out from the pain. At least she hoped. Another step forward, and her attention was back on the large cat who gave her more and more of a Misty vibe as she continued to communicate with it.

SCRATCH.

The words that came to her were more visual than actual words. Pictures pushed into her mind by the cat, showed it rubbing itself across a tree stump and wrestling with its siblings. The images flickered by, like an old black and white movie. The words formed after images were shown, allowing her to know what the mountain lion truly wanted.

She was now within a couple feet of the animal, which rolled over on its back and showed its belly to her. The cat was young, probably just old enough to be without its mother. She supposed that was part of the reason it was so easy to communicate with. It hadn't had much human interaction, so its level of fear was minimal. Tara took the final few steps toward the cat and placed her hand on its chest. She could feel the rumble of the purr as she started to fill the feline's request.

As she rubbed her fingertips across the mountain lion's fur, she pushed more thoughts its way.

More humans coming. Cat must hide.

The large cat raised up and looked at her, cocking its head.

Tara continued to rub and pushed another message. *Cat must hide.* She pulled her hand off its belly and pushed one more message.

Man needs help.

The mountain lion understood and as Tara stood and took a step back, it rose to its feet and gave its great body a shake. The wet debris dropped from its fur. It stepped toward Tara and rubbed itself along her legs, practically knocking her over with its force. Even though it was young, it had to be over a hundred pounds. She reached down and rubbed the top of its head before giving it her final thought.

My friend. Cat hide.

HIDE.

Tara pointed toward the woods, and the animal gave one last look at her before turning and loping in that direction. The mountain lion was gone with a whisper, but Tara knew it wouldn't go far. It made her wonder if it would run into any other hikers, but she couldn't worry about that now. Its curiosity would keep it nearby and watching, but it would heed her warning. Of that, she was sure.

As she crossed over to Brent, the sound of running steps came to Tara. Within seconds, a distraught Maggie crouched down beside her boyfriend. Her hands reached out then pulled back, shaking in the process.

Tara always gave folks something to do when she was trying to give aid. She found it was a good idea; it kept them out of her space. Besides, for her next bit, she didn't want Maggie around. Taking a quick inventory of the situation, Tara gave Maggie some instruction.

"I need you to find a branch, something straight and about two feet long. We might need it for the break."

With wide eyes, Maggie nodded and hurried into the tree line to fulfill Tara's request. Tara turned back to Brent and saw the gentle rise and fall of his chest. He was still unconscious. Time to assess the damage.

It looked like a compound fracture, although it was hard to see the injury with the amount of blood that had congealed near the wound. Brent's pulse was strong, his breathing steady. She was glad he was out of it, as panicked people never made the best patients.

From first glance, the two hikers had completed the right steps to deal with the wound. They had used his leather belt as a tourniquet, wrapping it twice around before using the notches to secure it. It staunched the flow of blood to the site and seemed to have done the trick.

She cut the leg of his pants open with her knife to better see the break. The bone protruded from Brent's muddy knee, and she decided cleaning the wound would be the best place to start. Her backup would be there shortly.

Tara unzipped her first aid kit and dumped out the meager contents, opting for the plain gauze to get most of the mud off before using the alcohol wipes. The tune she had been playing earlier came to mind, and soon she was humming the notes.

The melody soothed her. Tara concentrated on the injury, thankful Brent was still unconscious during the sting of alcohol on his open wound. Her fingers tingled, and she wondered if she had scratched them earlier on the bark of the tree she had been sitting beneath. When she looked down to check them for cuts, they were glowing white.

"I found this," Maggie's voice said from behind her. Tara internally jumped, her shoulders following suit for a brief second. When she looked at her hands again, the glow was gone.

Maggie handed her a branch about two inches in diameter, with only a slight bend in the middle.

"This will be perfect. Do you have a flashlight? I'm having a hard time seeing what I'm doing."

"I have one here, but weren't you just using one?"

"Tara," a voice called out from behind them.

"Over here," she responded, thankful she didn't need to answer Maggie's question. "Go see if they need help. I'm not sure what they've brought with them."

"Okay." Maggie nodded and hurried out of the clearing, down the path that led to the Memorial. Tara heard snatches of their conversation as Maggie brought them up to speed.

Tara picked up her supplies and shoved them back into her pack, securing it on her belt. She took the blanket Brent had been using to cover himself and folded it up, laying the makeshift pillow next to him. By the time she stood up and attempted to shift Brent into a prone position, Paytah was at her side.

"I was just going to lay him down, so we can slide him onto the gurney," Tara explained.

"Don't worry about that," a deep voice said. Tara glanced up and saw Paytah's boyfriend, Robert, and another employee she didn't know carrying the supplies. "We can take it from here. How long has he been unconscious?"

"Just after we arrived," Tara answered. "Less than five minutes."

"Good," the other man responded. "What's his name?"

"Brent," Maggie replied. She gathered their belongings and zipped them into backpacks.

Tara watched as the man who came with Robert gave aid to the hiker. She was impressed by his muscular arms. He had a lot of tattoos, which wasn't normally her thing, but on him, they looked good.

The man snapped a packet in his fingers and waved it under Brent's nose, causing him to wake with a start. Tara and Paytah helped Robert finish the set up on the gurney.

"Brent, I'm Tyler and this is Rob. The ladies are Paytah and…"

"Tara," she added quickly.

Tyler continued his aid without missing a beat. "We all work at the Crazy Horse Memorial. We're here to get you to the hospital."

Brent nodded. He was awake, but his eyes were glazed. The waves of pain that came from him made Tara nauseous. As she mentally pulled on the red threads of agony coming from his body, her stomach churned, but it seemed to be helping him. She imagined absorbing as much as she could, pulling it deep into her body and as far away from him as possible. Tara channeled her healing energy to Brent, just like her Grandmother had taught her and Mato's teachings had reinforced. When Rob and Tyler moved him to the gurney, Brent's breathing seemed much less shallow. His voice came out in not much more than a whisper.

"Babe?"

"I'm right here," Maggie responded. The emotion in her voice breaking, but she needed to hold it together just a little while longer. Tara gathered a ball of positive energy and kept her hands behind her back until she reached Maggie. With a brush to her shoulders, Tara passed the energy to the woman as she slid the weight of the backpacks from them.

"I'll carry this for you."

Maggie's shoulders relaxed, the relief reflecting in her gratitude filled eyes. "Thank you all so much."

A rumble of thunder sounded in the distance, with a flash of lightning not far behind.

"Don't thank us yet," Rob quipped. "We still need to get our asses off this mountain. The storm is coming."

"Let's do this," Tyler said.

"I'll lead the way with Maggie," Paytah offered. "Tara, you can follow behind the men."

"Ready when you are," Tara answered.

As they left the clearing, Tara glanced back and did a quick sweep with her flashlight. The luminescent glow from a set of eyes made her jump.

FRIEND.

She pushed a message to the mountain lion with a smile as she hurried behind the group.

Yes, friend.

2.

In a land separated from ours by dimensions and magick, Theo stood near the tree where he lived, stretching the cramped state of his back. He had been content to sing along with the music that came to him each night of his lonely existence, but it had been silenced. He waited for its return until his ass grew numb and his fingers were chilled. Neither the music, nor the feathery voice that would sometimes hum the tune, could be heard. He looked forward to that voice, a soothing balm to his soul, but tonight's concert was cut short. The music's abrupt halt irritated him.

It had been nearly a century since he had seen another soul, and he grew weary of his solitude. With only his books and experiments to keep him entertained, he spent most of his time keeping the tree where he lived from dying. He wasn't having much luck. The toxins from the long-kept secret he was sentenced to hide were seeping to the surface of the tree. Like oozing wounds on skin, the putrid magick was no longer held by the ancient runic symbols he carved in the bark. They now glowed green and without a dryad to protect it, the tree was suffering. It was only a matter of time before the last of the evil was released.

He ran his hands along the rough bark, the glowing symbols cool beneath his touch. The toxic magick had drained his remaining elemental powers long ago and, over time, had broken free of the prison he had built for it. There were days he wasn't sure why he remained. It was evident most of the magick had already made its way out into the world he vowed to protect.

The obsidian box holding the weapon laid beneath the roots of the tree, far below the place he called home. The shard, once used by Erebos to kill Theo's best friend, was inside and, like a siren's song, called to its master. The only magick Theo had left were simple spellworks from his culture. His waning energy just wasn't strong enough anymore.

Perhaps it was time to leave, to go back to his former life. But even as he considered it, he cringed at the thought. He had never been happy there and if he were to live elsewhere, he would be forced to live alone. The ladies he once knew wouldn't be content with moving so far away from the festive atmosphere of court. Once the king of a thriving culture, his self-imposed exile had changed him to a ruler of nothingness. No woman in her right mind would want him. He once again questioned his motivation to support Fate all those years ago.

The dark magick had taken so much away from all of them, and he grew weary of his part to play. Nevertheless, he remained steadfast. He was bound by his promise to Fate to keep the weapon hidden until nature found new stewards for the Power of Four. Once the new group harnessed the powers of the elements, he hoped they would send word that his penance was complete.

"Aperiam ianua." He waved his hands over the surface of the rune-covered tree. The glowing bark opened, as he had requested, showing a flight of stairs that led below the roots of the massive Dragon Blood tree. The command phrases were all he had left of his Elvish magick. He came from a long line of healers and empaths but worried the toxic energy would affect his immortality next. Gods help them all if that happened, he would be useless. Although Fate hadn't been clear on his role in the future, he had been around long enough to know she had plans for him. He just hoped he was still drawing breath when she put them into action.

Walking into the depths of his home, he wound around the spiral staircase that led to his living quarters. He didn't need firelight to see, since the glow from the magick was present inside as well as out. Every surface was covered with the symbols that had kept the magick contained inside the tree, but he was running out of empty spaces in which to carve them. He was at a loss as to what else he could possibly do.

He walked into the room he used as his library and threw another log on the fire. Confident the room would stay warm through the night, he walked along the wall of shelves that housed his immense collection of books. It was one of the few things he had thought to bring with him all those years ago. It turned out to be the best decision he had made, since the books had been his only company for well over seventy years.

He trailed his hand lovingly along the ancient spines. He was edgy and irritated that his musical reprieve had been cut short. Getting lost in a story was just the thing. He often used them as an escape. As he examined the titles on the leather-bound books, his mind wandered to another book once in his possession. He wondered if Fate still had the Elemental Journal or if Erebos had finally managed to claim it. With the current state of the tree he lived beneath, he dreaded the answer.

Theo selected a first edition of *Pride and Prejudice*, sat in his armchair, and opened Ms. Austen's story to page one. He had wondered years ago what all the fuss was about. It seemed every female he ran into had read and raved about Mr. Darcy. He had already been through most of the books on his shelves and was looking for something different. If it was a decent story, he didn't honestly care what he read.

He read aloud, as he always did. The sound of his own voice made him feel less alone. "It is a truth universally acknowledged, that a single man in possession of a good fortune, must be in want of a wife." He snorted. The opening line seemed ironic, especially with the paragraph that followed. It made him wonder if Ms. Austen had been part Fae.

He was familiar with the snares the pretties in court would attempt. Matchmakers had always assumed he was looking for the future Queen Helthon. That was the primary reason he had left the management of his kingdom to his advisors. His living in solitude started long before Fate dealt him his current hand of destiny. In the past, there were always ladies willing to grant him ease, especially at the lavish balls he threw each festival season. He would almost be willing to stomach one of those senseless affairs, just so he could feel like a man again.

He poured himself a scotch and knocked back the stinging liquid in one swallow. Visions of the women he once knew started flooding his mind and tightening his pants. It had been far too long between interludes, and he was getting worked up. He poured himself another drink and attempted to distract himself, which was getting harder and harder to do. Literally.

Reading the next few lines, he realized perhaps the story wouldn't be so bad after all, since the banter between the husband and wife was entertaining. Satisfied the story would be bearable, he sipped his scotch and settled in for a long night of reading. What the hell else did he have to do?

He wished he would have been able to at least bring a nixie with him. They were always up for a good time and never had any expectations beyond the pleasure of the moment. Pleasure. He wondered if he would ever know it again.

In another part of Wisteria, Fate was alone with her thoughts. She felt it in her bones but more so, the voices in her head verified it. The time had come. Her ability to speak in coherent sentences was back. It concerned her, since Theo had set the spell to tie her tongue in the first place. For the past several decades, she had only been able to speak in riddles or rhymes. Now that she was no longer forced to, it worried her. Perhaps something terrible happened to her dear friend.

Theo had done what was asked of him the day the magick was pulled from Erebos and the dark energy was released. Now, the final step in destiny's new plan needed a nudge. The Shadowman, Erebos, to those who knew him and Roy, to her sister, Zilla, had not given her a moment's peace in which to do it. He sensed something was happening, but since she hadn't been able to communicate in any other form but riddles, he grew weary of her responses. He didn't hover as much anymore, which worked to her benefit. But now that she could speak normally, he might demand new answers.

She had to be careful. The Shadowman held both her sisters hostage and used them to control her. The man he had once been loved Zilla, but that man's essence had long been pushed out of the body by another. Zilla dealt with the cruelty of the second entity, Roy, with only fleeting glimpses of Erebos in her interactions with him. It wasn't long until the Shadowman took over entirely. His essence hadn't made the memories, but he remembered them. He ruined any past tenderness with his wicked tongue. And the woman his host body once loved, was left to rot in a cell in the dungeon. Zilla had been through a lot, they all had, but Fate's treatment had been the least traumatic.

Fate's only solace was the knowledge that her sisters were together. Sevilla and Zilla were locked in a cell far beneath the stone floors of the caverns, where the Shadowman made his home. She wasn't entirely sure, but she thought perhaps Ryker, Sevilla's husband, was on the premises as well. She hadn't been able to confirm that, as there were some areas of the property she wasn't allowed to enter.

Fate hadn't talked to her sisters in weeks, and the only reason she knew they were still alive was the fact that she would know if they weren't. The souls of the deceased were the voices who whispered the secrets of the future in her mind. They were the eyes she saw through by the words they flashed in her mind. Her sisters would have certainly made themselves known to her if they had transitioned through that veil.

Her thoughts went to those who had already crossed. To her lover, Anton, the shifter who had passed much too soon and whose soul had never failed to return to her in one form or another throughout the centuries. The man they knew as Erebos had killed him as he attempted to drain Anton's essence and absorb his abilities. She wasn't sure if the Shadowman had influenced his actions, though it mattered little. Erebos was no longer allowed to surface in the body the Shadowman now controlled. Neither was Roy.

Although Anton had crossed, he was the only one she was unable to communicate with. Destined to return to her one day, in a form she couldn't control but only recognize, he waited in the void until destiny decided to reunite them. Such was the way with soul mates. She was always able to recognize him when he came back into her life, but he didn't always know her. There were times she needed to be patient. This was one of them.

Her pulse fluttered, and her cheeks warmed as she thought of him. Her soulmate had finally returned to her, but this time, he was human. She worried about his mortal shell so kept her distance. She wasn't willing to put him at risk, not until the danger had passed and the elements were able to keep the balance. So, she kept the secret to herself, locked up tight in her heart and mind. But the pull of his essence was hard to avoid.

There were times she had gotten close, just to feel the electric pull of his aura. Times when she had gotten closer still and spoke to him or snuck in a kiss. The Shadowman was suspicious but as far as she could tell, he didn't know the man's purpose. She was afraid that now, without Theo's spell tying her tongue in knots, the Shadowman would force the truth out of her. More than ever, she needed to keep her distance from everyone she loved.

Fate shifted in the cushioned armchair near the dying fire in her room. It was the one place where the Shadowman would leave her alone and for that, she was thankful. There was a long thin table in front of her, which she had dragged from the wall six steps back from the right of the fireplace. The height was perfect for her purpose, and she had spread the selected tarot cards in front of her in the order she had pulled them. Even though she couldn't see the images with her blind eyes, she could sense them by way of the voices.

As she held her hand over each one, the voices from beyond came to her and sent images to her mind to correspond with the cards. It was a slow process but since Fate had been blind from birth, it was the only way she was able to use the magical tools. She missed the days when her sister Sevilla did the readings, they were much more accurate when the three sisters were together.

The deck was old, the edges soft and the corners rounded with age. Sevilla's deck. There had been magical tools she had gone back and taken from each sister's home, and their favorite deck was the first thing she had packed.

She was hoping for a little more guidance than the voices were currently giving. She needed to understand what happened to Theo and if the final element was connected to his destiny. Earlier signs had showed she did, so she needed to make sure she found her way to him quickly. Especially since she feared Theo's Elvish magick was no longer able to keep the secret safe. It was only a matter of time until the Shadowman found the tree he had been looking for. The tree she had once accidently told him about.

She moved her hands over the three cards she had pulled to signify how she felt, what would happen, and how the future would impact the question she held in her mind. The voices in her head flashed images of a card with a moon and a path between two towers. The card, which represented dreams, was telling her to stay her course, confirming what she already knew to be true.

Visions of the second card flashed in her mind, showing six swords all pointed toward a common enemy. In the deck, the six of swords represented science, and she took that as an incredibly good sign. Theo was still alive. As she had hoped, he would have a major part to play when the elements came together.

The third card was a little more subjective. The images, which came to her, were of hot and cold, yin and yang. The alchemy card represented restraint or temperance, and could mean they would have trouble when the element of Earth entered the equation. This card warned that the energy they so desperately needed to balance, would be volatile at best.

According to the reading, the Elemental was on her way, and Theo had definite ties to her fate. It was fitting that the man who wielded the power of Earth last would be the one to mentor the woman who would embody it in the future. She was glad the reading confirmed he was still alive but worried the lack of the spell holding her tongue meant that his magick was all but drained. He might need healing, so it was even more imperative they find the final element quickly. Hopefully, she would instinctively know what to do.

A hesitant knock sounded on her door. It would have been more demanding had it been the Shadowman or one of his elemental golems. The last one, a fire golem, had all but burnt down the door.

"Come inside, I've nothing to hide," Fate called out. It was the best she could come up with in a pinch. She sat in place until the door closed, and a light tread came across the room to her chair. She scooped up the cards she had read and placed them back into the center of the tarot deck. "My solitude has come to an end. Is that you, Sansa, my friend?"

"Yes, ma'am," the young dryad answered. Fate was surprised she had heard her steps at all, since nymphs were notoriously light of foot. "Master Shadow has requested your presence for dinner. He said you have one hour to prepare yourself."

"I'll be ready," Fate answered calmly. "Remember, he is not to know anything about my ability to speak freely."

"I understand. I would never betray you, my lady. I swear by the roots of my tree."

"Thank you," Fate said with a smile. A dryad swearing by her tree was as close to a blood oath as one could get. Her secret was safe. "What kind of a mood is he in?"

"Foul, my lady."

"And what was the color I wore last that he went on about? You know the one he detested?"

"I believe it was yellow, my lady. He prefers somber colors and has everyone around him dress in black or gray."

"Sounds very drab, and since I come from a world of darkness and shade, I believe the presence of all colors should be celebrated. Please ready the yellow dress for me, Sansa."

"Right away." The young nymph's giggle tinkled in the room, warming Fate's heart. The Shadowman granting her a lady's maid had been the best thing that had ever happened to her. They had become close in the months Sansa had been helping her, and Fate had every plan to take her with her when she left. She would find her the perfect tree to connect to, since the Shadowman had done the unthinkable and burned Sansa's to the ground. Neither of them could leave without suffering his wrath, so in the meantime, upsetting him and feigning innocence was one of their favorite pastimes.

Sansa's voice washed over Fate. There was nothing more musical than a Dryad's joy.

"Let's leave your hair loose and in curls tonight, since he prefers it in a simple braid."

"Perfect," Fate laughed.

3

After getting the hikers back to the complex safely, Tara and Paytah clocked out and went their separate ways. They had both managed six hours overtime by the time Brent was admitted and lined up for surgery, so their manager told them he would get the next day's shift covered for them. Tara was appreciative of the extra time off, since she had an upcoming trip to pack for.

It was late when she got home, since she had stopped at the store on the way. It was way past the normal time when she would give Misty a bit of wet food for dinner. The fluffy Angora cat met her at the door, meowing as if she had been home for days without eating. Since Tara had only left at 8 a.m. that morning, she knew that was far from the case. Besides, she was pretty sure the neighbor boy, Peter, had been over earlier in the day, since there was an open bag of chips lying on her coffee table. He must have been gaming while keeping Misty company again. He took his pet-sitting duties seriously and knew he was welcome anytime he saw she wasn't there, especially on the days she worked late.

"Meow, rawr rawr." Misty sent Tara mental images of her cat dish filled with canned food.

"Give me a minute, Misty. You rubbing on my legs, while I'm trying to walk, isn't helpful."

"Mew."

"Don't get snippy with me," Tara laughed. "You have dry food if you're that hungry."

The cat gave her a look then turned away with a flick of her fluffy tail. A dejected "mrawr" was all she tossed back. Misty was in enough of a mood that she wasn't even speaking to Tara through their mental channel. That sometimes happened when she spent the afternoon with the neighbor boy.

Tara watched as she did the cat's equivalent to stomping up the hall-way, walking with purpose as her tail swished quickly from side to side. Right before she entered the second bedroom, she looked back pointedly to make sure Tara had been watching her.

"I see you. Give me a minute."

Misty turned her head to break eye contact and slipped silently into the room. More than likely she was going to hop up on the perch Tara set up in the window. She had placed a bird feeder outside the window last weekend. Next to eating, watching the birds was Misty's favorite thing to do.

Tara felt her phone vibrate in her purse and rushed to set down the groceries she had been juggling when she walked in. As she slid it out of her purse, she took a deep breath to squelch her disappointment. She wasn't sure who she had expected to be texting at this hour, but she wasn't honestly sure how she felt about this latest development. The hunky med-ic she had met and exchanged numbers with earlier had messaged her.

Hey, U want 2 get a drink later?

Tara checked the clock. It was past midnight. In her experience, the only dates that were considered dates were scheduled well before the witching hour.

Later as in when?

Tonight.

She was right, total booty call attempt. She was lonely but not desper-ate. Besides, it had started to snow.

Sorry too tired. Have a nice night.

She placed her phone on the counter and started emptying the bags from her late-night grocery run. There was no more buzzing from the phone. It seemed she had been right about it being a booty call, and tool-time Tyler had gotten the message. She wasn't interested in adding another ex-boyfriend to the list, best to nip it from the start.

A few years back, she would have jumped on the chance to twist the sheets with an amazing specimen like him. His smile had warmed her in places she hadn't thought much about since she had moved to South Dakota. But so much had happened since her days of insecurity and loneliness. In the last few years, she had come to terms with solitude and learned to love herself. Going back to school had a lot to do with her per-sonal growth, as did moving out of state. She was grounded here, much more than she was when she lived in Florida with Brooke.

The phone buzzed once more, and Tara picked it up with a roll of her eyes. She read the message, and a smile came to her face. Not Tyler, thankfully, it was her best friend Brooke. Strange. She had just been thinking of her.

You up? Too late to call?

Tara sent back a text, very much used to Brooke contacting her in the middle of the night. Back when Brooke's anxiety bothered her more, the calls were more frequent. Since Will came into her friend's life, the panic attacks happened less.

I'm up, and no. Give me 5.

K

Tara pulled a wineglass out of the cupboard and poured herself the last of the Pink Zinfandel from the bottle she had opened earlier in the week. She set the glass on the table near her couch and then went back to her room to slip into her pajamas. She was back on the couch, sipping her wine in less than four minutes. Brooke's call came in right on time.

"Hey girlie, I was just thinking of you!"

"Really?" Brooke remarked. "That's strange, you've been on my mind all day, and I thought I had better not wait until tomorrow to contact you. I was getting a weird vibe."

"It's always strange when you do that. I did have some stuff happen at work today that was a bit stressful. But in the end, it turned out fine. I just got home as a matter of fact."

"What happened?"

"Had a couple of hikers with an emergency. One of them had broken their leg and needed help down the hillside."

"That's awful. I hope they'll be okay."

"Yeah, I'm sure he'll be fine." Tara took a sip of her wine and settled her back against the couch. "Why are you up so late?"

"Just have so much to get ready for the shower. It's a bit draining. You still arriving at 9:40 a week from next Saturday then?"

"Yes, I hope that's still okay. It was better for me to work then leave right for the airport."

"That's brilliant, actually. I can pop out to get you after Will heads to work. He has two shows that night."

"I am excited to see the new illusions in his show. Is Trina still assisting him?"

"She is. Her baby girl is 16 months now. Hard to believe she's that old already."

"Well, you and Will have been together for that long, so it makes sense."

"I suppose," Brook mused. "I hope you don't mind, but I planned for tea with Will's parents the day after you arrive. They are anxious to see you again. And I think Will's mum Nancy wanted to talk to you about some ideas she had for the centerpieces."

"Sounds great. I'm excited to help. I can't believe your wedding is only a few months away now. Seems like just yesterday you and Will met."

"It does, doesn't it?"

Her voice sounded strained. Tara wasn't sure if it was because it was late or if there was something bothering her.

"How is James doing?"

"He's doing better. The therapy he received in Sedona really helped with his PTSD. He's made some friends and is thinking about moving to the States."

"I'm so glad. I know how worried you were about him."

"Yes, he gave us all a fright." Brooke quickly changed the subject. "So, how's Misty?"

"She's fine. Pretty pissed at me now though," Tara laughed.

"She's in a snit, huh? Why, what did you do now?"

"I was late getting home and missed giving her some wet food at dinnertime."

As if the cat knew she was being spoken about, she hopped up onto the couch and walked across Tara's legs, stomach, then chest to bring herself nose to nose with her owner. "You smell like tuna."

"Pardon me?" Brooke laughed.

"Not you. Misty. She must have found the wet stuff. God, it stinks."

"I can't wait to see you, Tara. It has been way too long between visits."

"It has but impossible between our schedules. Trying to get a day off here is like trying to move Mount Rushmore over three feet to the right."

"They aren't working you too hard, are they?"

"Naw," Tara said, taking another sip of wine. "I work at the more chill of the visitor sites. The Crazy Horse Memorial is way less busy. Besides, I love it. It is so peaceful out here, Brooke. I can see why my grandmother liked it so well."

"It's crazy to think how much our lives have changed in such a short period of time," Brooke said quietly.

"I'd have to agree," Tara answered. "Is everything okay, Brooke? Sounds like something's bothering you." Her tone made Tara think she was hiding something. Although who was she to judge? She had been hiding things from her as well.

"I'll be fine. I just have loads on my mind, and I miss my friend."

Brooke had a life now with Will, a life Tara knew little about and only visited on occasion. After the bridal shower and the wedding, she wasn't sure they would be seeing much of each other. She tried to keep up the pep in her voice that she didn't feel. "Well, I'll be there in about a week."

"Can't wait to see you, lovie."

"Me either," Tara answered. The strange things that had happened with her glowing fingers or healing co-workers by touch tickled her mind, but she kept her thoughts to herself. Her friend sounded anxious enough. "Get some rest tonight. I am sure part of it is that you haven't been sleeping well."

"You know me so well, my friend," She said with a laugh. "Sweet dreams."

"You too, Brooke. See you soon."

"Some friend I am," Tara murmured. "I can't even be honest about the things going on in my life." Misty was laying on Tara's stomach and scooched up higher on her chest. She bumped against Tara's chin and sent her images of comfort.

"I don't know, Misty. We just don't seem as close anymore." Saying it aloud had her throat tightening and her eyes watering.

"Meow."

"Yeah, I know. I just never imagined a life without my friend, and now it seems that will be exactly what I get."

Misty put her paws on either side of Tara's neck and licked the tears that slid down the side of her face. Tara rubbed her fur, thankful that all was forgiven for her earlier food mishap, since she needed the comfort right now. Her life had been a series of changes, and she wondered when things would settle down and she would find happiness. Even as much as she loved it in South Dakota, she still wasn't content. There was something else out there for her — she knew it — but what it was and when it would find its way to her, had yet to be seen.

"You'll be there for me though, won't you girl."

ALWAYS.

"Ah, so now you are talking to me," Tara laughed. "You're a good cat. I'm so glad Brooke couldn't take you with her. My life would have been much lonelier without you. Ready for bed?"

BED.

Misty sprung off Tara's chest and waited as she placed her empty wine glass in the sink and double-checked the locks on the door. She was drained and had no energy for a shower, so she would catch one in the morning. Her new haircut wasn't something she could let go without washing for more than a day anyway. She was excited to show the cut to Brooke; it was shorter than she had ever dared to go before.

She walked into her room and turned on her bedside lamp, quickly changing into her pajamas she left neatly folded at the end of the bed. She nabbed her book from her nightstand before sliding between the cool sheets. Misty curled up on the pillow beside her and watched with heavily lidded eyes. Tara opened the page to Chapter One and read aloud, as she often did. It made her feel less alone. Besides, Misty liked to hear the stories too.

"It is a truth universally acknowledged, that a single man in possession of a good fortune, must be in want of a wife."

She heard something that sounded like a snort. Had Misty sneezed? Looking down, she saw the cat curled up peacefully on the pillow next to her. She was sound asleep. Convinced she was hearing things, she settled back down into her pillow and continued to read. Within minutes, a masculine voice blended with hers, reading the exact words of Jane Austen that were on the pages of her book.

Tara paused her reading and pinched herself. Yup, she was still awake. The voice continued reading, first as if spanning a great distance but clearer with each phrase. His voice had a musical quality to it, soothing and peaceful. She wasn't afraid, even though she knew she should be. There was something familiar about the voice. Comforting. Then she realized she had heard it before. It was the voice that sang to her as she practiced her flute.

She looked around her room and tried to determine where the voice was coming from. Was she hallucinating? Perhaps she had burned too much of the smudge wand the other day? She didn't think so, but it was a theory. The voice didn't seem to bother Misty, so perhaps it was only one she could hear?

"Must be tired," she muttered. Deciding she was overdue for sleep, she slid the bookmark into place and set her book on her nightstand. With a click of her light, the room filled with inky darkness, but the voice continued to read. As strange as the entire thing was, she enjoyed being read to and found herself laughing aloud at the antics of the Bennett family. The reading would pause, as she chuckled, then continue where the story had left off.

With the lights off, she noticed a faint glow from her nightstand getting brighter by the moment. She picked up her grandmother's hand mirror and examined it. The glow was coming from the symbols carved in the frame. Now that she had it flipped over, it lit her room. Tara had believed the carvings had been her grandmother's way of keeping the evil spirits out of her image after her husband passed. Now, she wasn't so sure.

With the mirror lifted, the man's voice was louder. Curiosity outweighed any nervousness she had. Her mind registered that what was happening wasn't normal, but she was compelled to solve the mystery. Her grandmother's heritage wove spirituality and magick into their everyday lives, and Tara had been raised to be open to seeing it. More than most folks were.

She looked into the mirror, squinting her eyes to see beyond the reflection of her own face. There was something there, although it was hard to determine, since it wasn't moving. The outline of a chair, she thought, with the glow of a light behind it. As the voice became clearer so did the image. She could see him now, seated on a large chair in front of the light. He was holding a book open in front of him, presumably a copy of *Pride and Prejudice*, since that was what he was reading aloud from.

He shifted in his seat, pausing for a moment as he took a sip from a tumbler near him. As he set the drink back down, his gaze shifted upward, and he squinted. He leaned forward and cocked his head. His smooth voice was no longer reading but addressing her.

"Ah, there you are," he said softly.

He rose to his feet, and his image came closer to the surface of the hand mirror. She was stunned and tried to make sense of it, but she could hardly think straight. Before she could stop herself, an expletive came bursting from her lips.

"Holy shit!"

Ц

The man in the mirror paused his steps and tipped his head, clearly confused by what Tara had blatted out. There was something odd about his clothing as he stepped closer, but Tara could hardly concentrate. She was too busy calculating what exactly could be happening.

"I'm not sure what you mean, but am delighted by this turn of events." His voice was rich and most definitely the one she had heard singing along to her flute at work.

The symbols around the hand mirror glowed brighter, casting a golden light on his chiseled jawline. She was stunned, unbelieving that not only could he see her, but he was addressing her as well.

"I heard you reading earlier," he said conversationally. It was as if he had fully expected to meet her this strange way.

"Pride and Prejudice," she whispered into the mirror. The glow from the symbols started to dim, as did his image. His clothing was odd, like something you would see on the cover of a historical romance. The white linen shirt opened just enough to give her the impression of a well-built chest underneath.

"Please don't go," he said. She saw the tips of his fingers press to the glass, then his image disappeared. The mirror she held mere inches from her face showed only her hazel green eyes in the reflection. His medium-brown ones were no longer visible, and it occurred to her that if it was a dream, would she have been able to see color? Even though the entire incident had been surreal, she was hopeful it wasn't going to be the only time it happened. There was no fear in her heart, only exhilaration. Something important had just happened to her.

The glow from the mirror darkened, and the only sounds she could hear were the chirps of the night through her open window. She pinched herself again, confirming what she already knew. She was not dreaming. Clicking on the lamp, she opened her book and started to read where the voice had left off, but the magic was gone.

The next day at work, Tara couldn't stop thinking about the voice. He had somehow connected with her after she fell asleep. Her dreams had been filled with his calming tones. He went on to finish the first few chapters of *Pride and Prejudice* before she faded into a deeper sleep. In the morning, she woke refreshed and decided she could get used to being read to, especially by him. The lilt of his voice had comforted her like a weighted blanket.

As she went through the first few hours of her shift, she wondered if he was a figment of her imagination. It occurred to her that maybe the whole thing had been brought on by the recent conversation with Brooke. She had a similar situation her entire life, fearing an entity she nicknamed the "Shadowman" who came into her in her dreams. Tara's inquisitive mind couldn't help but consider the similarities between the two. Perhaps it was nothing more than her over-active imagination.

Later, while gathering her things for her break, she thought about her decision to leave her book at home. It had been relaxing being read to, but was she right in assuming if she waited to move forward in the chapter the spell would hold? Was it strange she hoped for a repeat of what had happened with her magical reader? She didn't care. Her plan was to read aloud from the book again after work to see if another connection could be made.

When Tara walked to her favorite spot to take her break, it was another mild winter day. The snow hadn't stuck to the ground from the storm the night before, and it felt as if spring was around the corner. The weather had been strange lately, not only in South Dakota, but also all over the world. Hurricanes were more destructive, tornados more frequent, and she had even noticed there was more seismic activity in the oceans. Mother Nature wasn't happy, and she was showing it. The indigenous community members in the area had been holding more ceremonies to pray for her forgiveness. Tara had even participated in a few with Mato.

She ate her packed lunch, a turkey and swiss sandwich and a bag of grapes, some of which she tossed to the chipmunk nearby that was interested in what she had brought. He was hungry. She could hear his jumping thoughts as he darted between the trees.

After finishing her meal, she pulled out her flute and worked on the tune she had started learning earlier in the week. She closed her eyes, allowing the airy notes to seep into her bones and float down the hillside. It wasn't long before she heard a voice singing along. It didn't sound like the chipmunk, their language was less fluid. The words sung were full of emotion and passion that she didn't always hear with the animals. The language was unknown to her, but she knew from the way it paused her breath that it was the man from the mirror.

She realized now she had heard the voice long before the strange encounter. Perhaps there was a magical channel that had been opened, and there were now a number of ways she could hear him. She continued to play, afraid of fracturing the moment. The words flowed, as the notes did, filling her heart with comfort and a sense of place. Strangely, she felt as if the words were for her alone.

The singing paused each time she lowered the flute from her lips. She looked at the carvings along the flute, carvings that had been placed long before the instrument had been gifted to her. She hadn't made the connection earlier, but there was no doubt in her mind that some of the symbols were the same as those carved into her grandmother's mirror. Were the symbols how it worked? Was the voice from another time or place?

There were things that couldn't be explained. Now she understood her grandmother's insistence that only those open to them could experience them. It made her wonder what had changed, why now? The mirror had been in her possession for some time. While she hadn't had the flute long, it hadn't done anything like this since Mato had given it to her. Perhaps it had something to do with the book. That couldn't be it though, as she had read it several times before.

As suddenly as the voice sounded, it quieted, and she was left once again with her tune. Strangely now, she didn't feel as alone. Convinced the voice wouldn't be returning until later, she packed up. She was anxious to finish her shift and go home. As she walked back, she hummed, even spoke, but there was no voice. It seemed it wasn't her constant companion and only came when the situation was right.

It made her think maybe it wasn't only that she did something on her side, but that he did something on his as well. There was something she needed to learn. A message she was meant to receive. She couldn't wait to get home and discover it.

Back at work, the afternoon hours dragged on, and she was having trouble focusing. Paytah was the first to notice.

"Is everything okay?"

Tara nodded her head. "I'm fine. Just have a lot on my mind is all."

"Getting ready for your trip to see your friend," Paytah said knowingly.

"A little of that," Tara laughed. "You know I hate flying."

"If we were meant to fly, we would have been born with wings."

"Agreed. I wasn't built for anything except keeping my feet on good old terra firma."

"It's a good thing you went into forestry then." Paytah smiled and handed Tara a stack of brochures. "Help me with the kiosk before you head out."

"Sure." Tara looked down at the brochures, reflecting information on the native tribes and events happening in the summer. While they had an extremely mild winter, Tara would be happy for the warmer weather. One of the brochures caught her eye, and she took a closer look.

The photograph was of a tribal member in full dress, demonstrating to tourists, who were looking on. What caught her eye, was the symbol embroidered on the sleeve. It matched those present on both her mirror and flute. It was simple, two triangles stacked point to point in the shape of an hourglass.

"Paytah, what does this symbol mean?"

Her friend looked over her shoulder where she was pointing and answered a-matter-of-factly. "As above, it is below."

"I'm sorry?"

"It represents the Universe and its connection to the Earth. Sort of like a mirror."

"Mirror?"

Paytah nodded. "Mhmm. The tribes saw the patterns in the sky change based on the time of year it was, so they made a connection. They learned whatever the stars showed, would be reflected on earth."

Something clicked in Tara's mind, like finding another piece of a puzzle. Folding one of the brochures and slipping it into her pants pocket, she slid the rest of the stack into the information kiosk. "Thank you,

Paytah."

"Sure," she said with a shrug. "I'm surprised your grandmother never told you that."

"She may have, I just don't remember. I was so young when I visited."

"Well, you are welcome to visit my grandmother anytime. She loves talking about this kind of stuff, and I've heard every story." She paused for effect. "A million times."

Tara laughed. "I may take you up on that."

"Anytime."

After work, Tara went straight home to do research on the symbol and its origins. She had been mistaken all those years ago. The symbol hadn't been put on the mirror as a safeguard, it was put on there to show the connection between both sides of the mirror. Quite possibly to foster one. She was sure of it.

Her grandmother's fascination with the mirror had been seen as mental illness. She had spent hours talking to her grandfather as if he were inside, long after he passed. Maybe it wasn't impossible she had seen him. There were theories about time, that days were layered, and with the right access, you could pass through them. Others yet that attempted to explain the limitless possibilities of the energy that surrounded the planet. Having her own experiment to work on thrilled her.

Tara believed they couldn't be the only life in the universe. It was far too vast. She wondered if the mirror was some sort of window into another dimension, although the possibilities were endless. Her mind was racing. She needed to understand exactly what she had in her possession and was extremely anxious to see if she could make it work on demand.

After taking care of a whiny Misty, Tara plopped down on her bed with her hand mirror and flute. She picked up her book from the nightstand and started to read aloud where the man had left off in her dreams. Her experiment would start with that.

As she read, she watched the mirror. After a few seconds, she saw it glow. It wasn't long before he had found the same place in the book she was reading from, and his voice was joining hers. She let him continue reading and picked up the mirror, anxious to see if he was in the glass. As the glow deepened, the picture cleared. She saw the same room as before, but the connection was more vivid.

He sat on a large cushioned chair, leather by the looks of it. Her grandfather had something similar in his office when she was little. The lamp nearby was small and only reflected light on his reading material. It didn't luminate the room, but it didn't need to. The room had a bright green glow from carvings covering every flat surface she could see. She put her thumb and pointer finger on the mirror and moved them apart, trying to make the image bigger, but it didn't work like a smartphone.

"Dumb," she muttered, drawing the attention of the handsome man in the chair. He rose from his seat and walked over, giving Tara a much better look at his face than the last time. His demeanor was authoritative, almost snobbish. He looked irritated.

"Excuse me?"

Tara realized how her last comment could have been taken. "Sorry. Not you. I was talking to myself."

"Do you often call yourself dumb?" He was trying hard to hide a smirk, and while it didn't reach his lips, there was no denying it was in his eyes.

"Among other things," she admitted with a laugh. "I'm Tara, by the way."

"Theothelm Helthon," he answered with a slight nod. If she wasn't mistaken, he had just acknowledged her with a bow. The historical romance vibe she had been picking up might not be far off. "My friends call me Theo."

"Theo it is."

Her response prompted a smile, and she was not prepared for its beauty. He was a gorgeous man, but not what she was used to. He didn't come off as someone looking to have a good time. His demeanor gave her the impression of a highly intelligent man who didn't have time for such foolishness. The word aristocratic came to her mind in a flash.

"Is Tara your proper name or merely what your friends call you?"

It was her turn to smile. He was perceptive. "My proper name, as you call it, is Tierra. Tierra Varela."

"Spanish?" His tone was interested and accepting. Strange, since she looked nothing like either of her parents or her grandparents. She raised her hand to her recently cropped and colored hair and absently rubbed it.

"Yes, my grandfather's side. My father was the one who insisted on naming me. My mother shortened it before I started kindergarten."

He cocked his head, a questioning look creasing his brow. She decided to clarify.

"You know, it would sound like I was named after a crown?"

He shook his head. "If I remember correctly, the name means Earth."

"How did you know…"

He turned his back to the mirror and walked toward a wall of books. After glancing over the spines, he selected one and returned to the mirror. He started flipping the pages and scanning the information. "I have notes here somewhere."

"You keep track of names and their meanings?" Tara started to wonder if she was doomed to always have strange men in her life.

He looked up from his book and addressed her. "There is a lot in a name. It can tell you not only where someone is from, but also the strength of their character."

"Okay, I'll buy into that."

"Buy into?"

Tara laughed. "Sorry. Agree with."

His eyes squinted for a moment, then he looked down to the book with a shrug. The movement wasn't as much discounting her, as it was acknowledging she was strange. She wasn't sure how she felt about that or him for that matter.

"Ah, here it is. Just as I thought. Tierra's meaning is earth."

"Interesting. What else is in that book?"

5

Tara was beyond distracted. Since the first night of their contact, she had connected with Theo daily, and was hooked. Real or not, he was by far the most interesting person she had ever met. Not only was he kind and unassuming, but brilliant to boot. She had mistaken his wisdom for snobbishness, learning quickly he did know pretty much everything. He was like a walking encyclopedia but never hesitated to check his facts.

After examining Tara's theory, they learned the connection had been made by something he had done on his end as well. While the mirror and flute both created the channel they spoke through, the book they were reading had been the key to unlocking the ability. It wasn't the first time she had read *Pride and Prejudice*, but it had been his. While the jury was still out on his opinion regarding one of her favorite books, he was at least keeping an open mind. She liked that about him.

Now that the communication door had been opened, so to speak, all bets were off. After examining her book cover to cover, she was somewhat surprised to find the Lakota symbol for Sun and Earth penciled in on the last page. His symbol was embossed on the cover. Another connection, which made universal sense.

At first, she had tried talking to him throughout the day at work, but the contact wasn't as reliable. They chose a time convenient for both and met in the mirror to chat after her shifts. They both preferred chatting with each other as the last thing they did before bed. They found it worked best when Tara was in a dream state. Theo's theory was that it was because her unconscious thoughts didn't put up barriers. She wasn't sure how she thought about that and had told him so. It was the first of their many debates.

She also loved to hear him laugh and tried her hardest to make him do so. He had a sense of humor like Brooke's, dry and somewhat sarcastic, but hilarious just the same. His delivery almost made it more so. Best of all, he wasn't bad to look at either.

It was the end of an all-day shift, and she wasn't due to meet Theo until later. She had brought her flute for the first time in days. It was typically left in her apartment, since he loved to hear her play and their connection was better at home. But she wanted to surprise him with a new tune she had been working on, and her spot on the mountainside was the best place to hear her notes. The tune was sporadic, as every few moments she was scribbling notes in her music journal.

FRIEND.

Tara jumped at the familiar voice in her head. The mountain lioness had found her, which didn't surprise her in the slightest. Their territories could be up to 10 square miles, and they were a little over a mile from where they first met.

Hello again. Where are you?

The large cat came up from behind her and rubbed her head along Tara's arm. If she wasn't mistaken, it was almost as if the feline was grinning. She had scared the shit out of her, to be honest.

You scared me.

SAD. Her rumbling purring stopped, and she backed herself up to a seated position beside her. She looked forlorn.

Tara felt terrible for bumming her out. She was obviously lonely and in need of some company.

You don't need to be sad. I'm sorry I'm so jumpy.

The mountain lion cocked its head, an examining gleam in its eyes reflecting a question. *JUMP?*

Tara laughed. *You're right. I'm not jumping, I'm sitting.*

She put her hand to her chest and patted. *I'm called Tara.*

TARA.

That's right. Tara held her hand in front of her and lightly touched the chest of the large cat. She didn't flinch, merely cocked her head and stared. The intelligence shimmering in her eyes took Tara's breath away. While she had always had the ability to communicate with animals to some extent, this was really something special. As she rubbed the animal's warm fur, she thanked whatever power had given her such an amazing gift.

TAKSI.

Tara paused at the unfamiliar word. Her mind thumbed through the memories of their conversations. She quickly realized the term was the cat's name. To be sure, she pointed back to herself and repeated her name then pointed to the mountain lion and repeated the word she was given. The large cat nodded her head forward and continued the forward momentum until she was head bumping Tara in the chest. Her hands came up around Taksi's neck, and she gave her a gentle scratch behind the ears.

Nice to meet you too, Taksi.

It didn't take long for the large cat to settle next to her, its long sleek body sprawled out with its massive head in her lap. Tara petted the top of Taksi's head until the rumbling purr started, and the cat's eyes closed in bliss. After a few minutes, Tara picked up her flute and played once more. When the notes sounded, Taksi hardly flinched. It seemed she was used to hearing Tara play.

The notes tumbled down the hillside and pooled at the base of the monument. She played from her heart, weaving her loneliness into a tune and imagining her arms reaching to a man she only knew by voice. If only he were real.

CHANGE.

Taksi's head raised from Tara's lap, just as she registered a green glow in the distance. When Tara stopped playing, the glow disappeared. While Taksi was attentive, she was not agitated. Tara took up the flute again and played her tune, and the glowing started back up. It seemed to be tied to her music and the longer she played, the brighter the light became.

Curious to know what it was, Tara stood, grabbed her bag, and started toward the area where she had seen the mysterious light. Taksi followed at a distance behind her, seemingly curious as well. Continuing down the hill, Tara played her flute once more until the glow started up again. It was coming from the space just below the flat surface, which would become Crazy Horse's pointing arm.

You don't need to follow.

FOLLOW.

Tara shrugged. Once she started the climb up the side of the monument, she was sure the bull-headed cat would turn back. Even though the tours were done for the day, the space was open, and there was a possibility that other people could be around. She hoped not, since she really shouldn't be climbing the side of a mountain, but her curiosity got the best of her.

"Seems like you and I have a lot in common," Tara mumbled. "Cat's curiosity and such."

Taksi glanced over before taking another sure-footed step. The path was rocky, but large platforms had been carved out into the mountain, which allowed for an easier climb. Taksi made her way up the hill just ahead of Tara and within a few minutes, they were at the base of the Crazy Horse Monument.

It seemed that Taksi instinctively knew where they were heading and paused every few steps to look back and ensure Tara was still following. The path she took looked to be stable, although it wasn't really what the staff typically used. Since it would be dark soon, Tara didn't want to take the time needed to get to the staff entrance, especially considering the space they were trying to get to. She decided to put her faith in the cat.

"You do know where we are going, right?" Tara grinned as Taksi turned her head to look back at her and blink.

HOLE.

"That's right, the hole." Tara laughed as Taksi turned and started up the hillside once more. If she didn't know better, she could have sworn the animal had shaken its head.

She decided to communicate telepathically, since employees weren't technically supposed to be on the hillside and voices carried in the dark. It had been a slow day, and most of the people were gone long before she had taken her flute to her spot and played. While her co-workers were used to her going there most evenings, there would come a point when she would be expected back. Her foot slipped on a steep spot, and she pulled out her flashlight to light her way.

Your feet are built for the climb, Taksi. Slow down.

The cat nodded and slowed its pace, taking a turn to the left and climbing in an area with more vegetation. The roots and low growing shrubs allowed Tara to climb with confidence. She clipped the flashlight to her belt in order to free her hands. Able to balance better, the extra light allowed her to take more accurate steps. Thankfully, the side they climbed wasn't easily visible from the museum. With Taksi's carefully placed paws, they made it to the ledge that led to the opening just below Crazy Horse's arm.

Taksi took the narrow ledge with ease, as surefooted as if she were walking on a flat surface. Tara wasn't as surefooted, since her hips were a little wider, especially with the things she carried on her tool belt. Her steps were slower, but she made it to the opening as Taksi took a seat and waited for her to make her next move.

The glow happened with the music. She took her flute from her belt and raised it to her mouth. *Here goes.*

Tara played the song she had been practicing, the one Theo's voice had joined in the past with his foreign tongue and baritone. She was disappointed she didn't hear him but thrilled that the glow had returned. Nervous energy quickened her pulse, but the calming effects of the area couldn't be denied. Something mystical was happening, and she couldn't help but wonder if there was something in the old Indian's cryptic message. As she played, Taksi rose to her feet and readied to move. Her being here was handy. What had Mato said about her spirit guide?

The glow within the circle brightened and the center opened, no longer showing her the other side of the hillside, but a wooded forest with tiny dots of the same glowing green flitting around their canopies. The dots moved in time with her music, swirling when the notes rose and swaying when she dropped their tone. The beautiful dance continued as Taksi stood and moved behind her. When Tara felt the nudge at the back of her legs, she knew what the mountain lion wanted.

We're really going to do this? Tara said mentally, then continued to play. She wondered if Taksi was losing her mind as she felt another nudge. *We could fall off the other side you know.*

CHANGE. MOVE.

Tara moved closer to the opening, unable to avoid the mountain cat's insistent nudges. The tune caused the light around the opening to glow brightly, like one of the glow wands she carried in her camping pack. Her mind tried to make sense of the vines that crawled from it, especially since they were on the side of a stony mountain. The vines curved out and swayed in time with the music she played.

As she looked through the hole, she was surprised she didn't see the other side of the mountain and the forest beyond. The trees seemed closer, as if they were on the same level as her, but that was impossible. Wasn't it? As she played, the glow stretched from the rim of the circular opening toward what should be the other side of the mountain. Tiny glows lit her path, almost lighting her way deeper into the opening. They stretched ahead and compelled her feet to move forward, especially since Taski was still bumping behind her.

As the glow went deeper into the forest and her tune rose to a crescendo, she took a deep breath and stepped inside, feeling the cool damp chill of the mossy forest. This was not the same place she had come from. The sounds were different. She saw a body lying on the ground. Someone was injured; perhaps that was why Tasksi was so insistent they enter the opening.

She hurried to the man and knelt beside him, placing her flute near his head. Her hand to his neck, she checked his pulse. It was thready at best. Thankfully, he was on his back, which would make it easier if she would have to perform CPR. His head was turned away from her, and it was hard to see his face, but there was something familiar about him. And was that cinnamon she smelled?

Tara removed her supply belt and placed it on the ground beside him, should she need her supplies. There wasn't much in it that would help him, but she didn't see any injuries when she did the once over. His chest rose much too slowly with the breaths that he took, and she decided on impulse to concentrate on his Aura. The colors surrounding him were fading. As she straightened his head to prepare for CPR, she gasped.

"Theo." She tried to keep the worry from her tone, as it was much harder to provide aid to someone you knew. Even more so if you cared for them. She swallowed her nerves and took a breath. She wouldn't be any help to him if she lost her focus.

His face was regal, much more so in person. His golden hair was thick and pooled around his head. He had a beard, which wasn't normally her thing, but it looked good on him, and he kept it groomed. She rubbed her hands to warm them then placed one on either cheek, resting them on the bristles. They weren't what she expected. They were soft under her palms.

She closed her eyes and concentrated on sending her energy to her fingertips. Warmth radiated up her spine and down her arms to her fingertips. For whatever reason, her energy was easier to control here. Stronger. She cracked open her eyes and looked down to her fingers, which were aglow with a white light. The florescent green light also pulsed, as if her energy was feeding it. She concentrated on pulling the bright green that surrounded them and redirecting it into the beautiful man she had only just started to learn about.

He started to stir as the bright green lights flickered and died from the moss around them. The light from her fingertips and his aura now surrounded his body in a vibrant red laced with gold. It was the most beautiful thing she had ever seen, and the effects of her energy were making a difference. His breathing was much easier, and he didn't look as pale.

The surrounding glow was all but gone and the next time she looked down into his face, his warm brown eyes were locked on hers. She stopped the pulses of energy and pulled her hands from his cheeks. His puzzled look wasn't as unnerving as the tip of his tongue wetting his lips. She gave herself more distance, allowing him the space to sit up. As he did, she glanced behind her. The familiar figure of the elder that had befriended her stood on the rocky side of the doorway. Where had he come from? Mato raised his hands palms up and bowed his head as if deep in meditation. The doorway started to close, much to her dismay. It took mere seconds for it to close completely.

"Shit," she whispered. She looked around, and while they were surrounded by trees, moss and ferns, it wasn't the same as the forest where she worked. The world they lived in was drier and sounds echoed. Their words and movements here bounced right back to her. The moisture in the air dampened her skin, and it felt as though they were in an aviary.

Her heart sunk. Were they stuck here? Why would Mato do that? Had he not seen her? Much as she had wanted to meet Theo, she hadn't really thought it all the way through. Somewhere in the back of her mind, she had continued the idea that it was all in her imagination.

"Tara?" The man's voice startled her out of her observations. She knew him, his rich lilt affected her the same way it had since she met him. She would know his voice anywhere.

"Theo," she whispered. It was sinking in that he was real and so was this place. Wherever she was. "How are you feeling?"

"Is it really you?" He was confused. Perhaps the fog in his mind still hadn't lifted. He turned his head to the side and spied her flute then looked back into her eyes with awareness.

She smiled at him. "Yes, it's me," she whispered softly. She leaned closer and kept her voice low to prevent the magical spell that brought her here from breaking.

He raised his hand to cup her cheek, and his simple touch made her heart flutter. He smiled softly, and his eyes seemed tired. "I tried to get to the music, but I was too weak."

His hand dropped to his side, and she placed hers over it. His fingers were cold. She needed to get him somewhere less exposed. Keeping him talking was key. "I can play later when we get you somewhere safe. Do you think you can walk?"

"I can try."

"Good. I'm so glad Taksi was insistent we come here."

He looked over to the mountain lion, who was resting just outside the clearing they centered. Looking back at Tara, he lowered his hand and smiled.

"I'm glad she insisted as well, since you probably just saved my life."

6

Theo couldn't stop staring at her. She was waifish, with delicate features like an elf, but judging by her ears, he guessed she was human. The elegant curves and dainty lobes were easily visible with the spiky cut of her hair. The color of her short style was pixie-like and reminded him of the darkened tips of a maple leaf in the fall. The pale silver streaks weren't an indication of her age, at least as far as he could tell. He noticed as the seconds went on, the gray faded.

The glow present in her hazel eyes, when he had first awoken, was gone. If he wasn't mistaken, she had been using powers earlier to heal him. It surprised him a human could wield so much energy, seemingly effortlessly, and it made him wonder if she had magical lineage. Perhaps she had a connection to magical beings she wasn't aware of. She had never mentioned it in their conversations, although much of what they had discussed had been about science and literature. He liked that about her.

All he knew was that he hadn't felt this good in years, and her worried expression excited him in a way it shouldn't. As an excuse to put his hand in hers, he accepted the help she offered when he rose. His legs were still shaky. She slipped her arm around his waist, and he had been right, she was tiny. Even though she hardly reached his shoulders while standing, she was strong. She braced his weight easily to keep him from falling. The drain from the toxic magick in his tree had finally caught up to him.

The mountain lion she had with her kept careful watch from the nearby boulder, and he couldn't recall the last time he had seen one so docile. Perhaps it was her familiar? A powerful witch lineage would make sense as well. There were some families that had lost touch with their descendants, perhaps she had ties she wasn't aware of?

More tingles came from her fingers where they touched his arm, and he wondered again about her magick. It came to her naturally, almost as if she didn't realize she was tapping into it.

"Thank you." He ran his hands along his pants before brushing a lock of hair from his eyes. He had long stopped cutting it but made a mental note that he might want to start.

"Your color looks much better," she responded. "You looked terrible when I first arrived."

"Thank you." He couldn't help but smile. He noted the pulse in her neck, fluttering like an anxious bird. His response embarrassed her, and he found he wanted to continue to find ways to bring that rosy color to her cheeks.

"I didn't mean..."

He surprised himself with the sound of his own laughter. "I know what you meant."

The beautiful flush again crossed her face but now, laced with a smile. His pulse quickened in response. Her beauty, along with the recall of their conversations, had him reacting in a way he thought he had long outgrown.

She glanced to the mountain lion, and it lumbered over and sat quietly at her side. Tara's hand dropped down to the top of its head, and she gave it a rub. It was her familiar, even if she didn't realize it yet. He could see tendrils of white and emerald magick flowing between the two of them.

Tara bent down and picked up her flute along with a bag she secured around her waist like a belt. She looked behind her then quickly glanced to his face and shrugged. "Looks like I might be stuck for the time being."

"How did you get here?"

"It's going to sound strange, but I think I opened a doorway somehow."

"A doorway?"

She turned and pointed. "Yes, just over there. It formed as I played my flute. But it's closed. I don't see the memorial anymore."

Looking to the area she indicated, he squinted to see any residual magic that had been left behind. He saw nothing but trees and moss. It couldn't be a portal. If she had that ability, she would be aware of it. "You could try playing your flute again."

"True," she said with a hesitant tone.

She looked down to the mountain lion, paused for a moment, then spoke aloud. "I'm not sure we can."

Theo was confused. "Not sure you can play?"

"Sorry, I was speaking…never mind."

The pretty flush was back in her cheeks. As she raised the flute, she turned her back to him. She played the tune he had grown to love, the one he had sung to each night using lyrics from his homeland. He watched expectantly, but the doorway she spoke of never opened. If she had indeed come by way of a portal, it was either one she had stumbled across or managed to create. The second of those options held implications that he would need to investigate further. His curiosity grew, but he remained silent.

Her shoulders slumped as she lowered the flute and then turned to face him. Was he mistaken, or was there more silver in her hair? Her eyes weren't as bright as before. While she didn't seem overly disappointed, he could feel the waves of exhaustion coming from her.

"I wasn't sure it would work."

"Perhaps now is not the right time. Maybe you need some rest."

She nodded and slid her flute beneath the strap of the bag around her waist. "I am pretty tired."

He took a step toward her and turned out his elbow. The mountain lion got to her feet and continued to watch them as Tara smiled and slipped her arm in his.

"I live nearby. We can get some rest there. It won't take us long."

"Thank you, Theo."

"Of course, my pleasure." As he walked alongside her, he relished the feel of her warmth beside him. He had gotten to know her well during their conversations, but nothing had prepared him for the feel of her energy. The constant pulses of relaxation soothed him like his meditation sessions.

As he led her up the path ending at the tree that he called home, he worried about the impression he might make. No one had ever been there, save himself. It was the first time in his life he had feelings of inadequacy and was shocked that the tiny woman walking beside him could be the cause. He could still feel the tingle of her power through the fabric of his shirt, however, the affects were more muted.

Her voice came to him on a sigh. "Have you started a new book?"

"I have a few selected but didn't want to start without you."

She looked up at him, a glorious smile beaming from her face. He was never so glad and frightened to have said the right thing at the right time. There was an urgent desire in his soul to please her that was tying him in knots. He really needed to get a hold of himself.

Smiling in return, he cleared the embarrassment from his throat and glanced back to the mountain lion that followed them.

"Does she have a name?"

"Taksi," she answered. The cat's ears perked up and her head tilted. When she realized she wasn't being called for, she continued walking.

"Danhnkshee? How is that spelled?"

"I had a bit of trouble with that. It's pronounced with a d but when I researched the spelling, it shows it as T, A, S, K, I. I believe it means 'younger sister' in Lakota."

"Lakota?"

"A Native American tribe from where I live."

"Which is?"

"South Dakota."

He thought for a moment. "Ah, United States?"

"That's right." She looked concerned. "Where are we, by the way?"

"Wisteria," he said.

"Which is where?"

"That will take a bit of explaining. We can talk about it in a minute. We're here."

"Here? Weren't we coming to your home?"

"That will need to be explained as well." He led her into the clearing, and his tree was centered before them. The rune symbols glowed brighter than the day before, and he wondered if it was safe to bring her inside. The drain on his power had taken decades, but he could already feel the tug on the energy she had filled him with. He decided the tree had served its purpose. He wouldn't be able to stay there, and he especially didn't want Tara near its toxic effects. It was time to move on.

She stopped walking, her arm sliding from his. "What is wrong with that tree?"

"Change of plans. We won't stay long, but there are some things I need to get here." He turned to her and put out his hand. "You can trust me."

Tara had no idea what he meant by his comment but was even more confused by the fact that there wasn't a house in sight. They were still in the forest, standing in a large circular clearing with a giant tree standing tall in its center. At least that is what she thought it was.

It looked like an enormous mushroom and had a thick wide trunk that went straight into a rounded canopy of long pine needles. She could hardly see the green at its tips, since the only thing visible from her viewpoint was the trunk that led to gnarly branches creating the dome.

The bark was riddled with intricate symbols that glowed, so much it lit the center of the woods like a night light. The light was a similar color to the doorway she had opened to come here but had veins of black working through it. Tara wondered if the tree would be able to survive the damage of the carvings, some of which looked like they had been there for some time. It looked to be hundreds of years old, but there was no doubt it was dying.

"Who did this?" She walked forward and placed her hand on the rough bark, running her hand along the symbols. The carvings had been made by hand, or so it seemed. What was left of the trees lifeforce pulsed beneath her fingers. "Carving in the bark hurts the tree. It isn't able to drink properly."

"It had to be done. There was something I had to keep from leaving."

She didn't like the sound of that. Pulling her hand back, she responded. "What do you mean?"

"Something I placed at its roots that needed to stay out of sight. But it seems the dark magick has found a way to escape."

"Is it dangerous?"

Theo thought about it for a moment. "I'm not sure it is immediately dangerous. But I'm not comfortable staying here either. Especially with you here."

"Theo, I'm not sure I'm…"

"The magick is dangerous to those who have abilities. It feeds on your power and makes you weak."

Tara put her hand back on the bark and traced the symbols. "So these markings are part of the magick?"

"Part of what has kept it contained," Theo answered. "But I have been here a long time, and the magick has now grown stronger than what is left of my abilities."

"Perhaps because the tree is weak," Tara whispered. She faced the tree and placed her palms on either side of the trunk, touching her forehead to the bark as well. As he took a step toward her, she pushed her energy forward.

The light she had come to expect surrounded her in a white and dark green aura and repelled the luminescent glow seeping from the symbols. Theo was close but allowed her space, as the bright green light backed away from her and pulled into the open wounds on the bark. The energy she was sharing with the tree wasn't something she was used to. It was starting to make her sick. She closed her eyes and willed her energy to push into the tree through the symbols. Then there was darkness.

Theo realized too late that the white streaks in her hair were more prominent. It wasn't until her legs collapsed from under her that he knew she had overdone it. He rushed forward, catching her before she fell. Taksi was pacing, keeping a watchful eye on him but allowing him to give her mistress aid.

As Tara's breathing settled, the streaks in her hair turned back to its vibrant color. He looked to the tree. The carvings, no longer glowing, were merely slices in the bark, and even a few of those had been scarred over. The tiny woman in his arms was more powerful than she knew, and he couldn't let her spend another minute anywhere near the weapon.

"Tara, are you okay?" He cradled her head in his lap, his hand gently caressing her cheek. As each strand of her hair changed back to its original reddish hue, the weight on his soul lightened a bit more. While the gray looked amazing too, he realized now it was a visible sign of her stress. The tree wasn't completely healed, but it was much happier. With her ability, she had somehow pulled the magick back to its core, and the symbols were now able to do what they were intended for.

"Tara?"

"I'm okay," she whispered. "Just need a minute."

Taksi nudged up against Tara's head and looked expectantly at Theo.

"I'll take care of her, girl."

The large cat took a step back and sat on its haunches. She would be making sure he did. When he looked down, Tara was looking up at him with a small smile on her face. The thought that she was exquisite crossed his mind, but he would never put that to voice. He had to concentrate on the next steps. Getting her to Fate was first and foremost.

"Can you sit up? I need to gather a few things."

"We aren't staying here?"

"Not on your life. Or mine, for that matter."

"Where then?"

"We'll start at Sevilla's."

"Why does that name sound familiar?"

"Not sure. She's a friend and one of the daughters of Destiny. It is her sister, Fate, I really need to find, so I am hoping she will know where she is."

"How long will it take to get there?"

"We will have to travel by foot, so it will take a couple days."

Tara's eyes widened. "A couple of days?" Theo wondered about the hesitation he heard in her voice.

"That's right. Is everything okay?"

She inhaled with her eyes closed then exhaled the centering breath. When she opened her eyes, a question wrinkled her brow, but she didn't voice it. Instead she nodded. "Everything is fine. I'm not sure I have much of a choice."

Theo was confused by her reaction, since they didn't match her words, but he shrugged it off. It had been some time since he had been around females, but the subtle nuances were starting to come back to him. He thought it best to keep moving, since the only way they would get any answers was to find Fate and her sisters.

7

Fate was dressed and downstairs for the dinner he had summoned her for, minutes before the allotted hour was up. She might have messed with the Shadowman in other ways, but she was never late when called for. His prior lesson had been harsh, and his power was growing by the day. She had her sisters to think of, so she no longer riled him in that way.

Although she'd been held prisoner there long enough to know her way around, Sansa guided her to the dining room. She had taken more time on Fate's hair than either of them had anticipated, and they needed to walk quickly to the dining hall. Fate was seated and enjoying her first sip of wine when the Shadowman entered the room.

He had a distinct essence. While she couldn't see his aura, she could certainly feel it. The unnerving feeling it gave her was something she was familiar with, since the voices in her head were always switching gears midstream when they described him. He was like a taut wire, pulled to the point that it burned. Goddess help her if he ever snapped. She went out of her way to ensure that didn't happen, but the calming techniques she learned years ago from Sevilla didn't always work.

"So, you are still alive," he spoke with a snap. He was in a mood. She would have to be careful with her tongue. "I was beginning to wonder since you've been in your room for no less than five days."

She pulled her shawl around her shoulders as if avoiding a chill, allowing her hands to shake a little. "It goes up and down without moving. What is it?"

"I'm not in the mood to decipher your cryptic messages, Fate. I'm not even sure why I bothered having you come down. And Sansa knows I hate that color — why on earth would she dress you in that?"

Fate bowed her head as if she were shamed but mostly, to hide the victorious smile that threatened to crack wide open. After slamming a glass on the wet bar, he made himself a drink, pouring a healthy portion, if Fate was hearing correctly. He was angry, and she hoped he was still unable to find the tree she had alluded to in the past. She had no doubt now the tree in her visions was where Theo hid their secret. The recent voices had all but confirmed it.

"Are you ready for the first course, my lord?" She couldn't be sure, but it sounded like Billy. She still had trouble telling him and his twin brother, Henry, apart. The Satyrs were new arrivals to the household and like all the creatures working under the Shadowman's command, they were forced to go against their nature. They had only drunk and made merry once since their arrival, and the mistake wouldn't be made again. The cost had been too high. They, too, had family they cared for.

"Bring it in," he answered gruffly. He made his way to the table, choosing to sit at the other end instead of to her right as he normally did. She was glad for the distance but curious as to why he chose it. Perhaps he wanted to observe her from afar? Thought that her powers of perception couldn't touch him at a distance? Whatever the reason, Fate was glad for the reprieve. She wouldn't be within striking distance if she said something that displeased him.

"I've grown weary of waiting. The clues you have given have gotten me nowhere." His voice sounded strained, as if he were furious but held himself in check. "If I didn't know better, I would say that your misdirection was intentional."

Fate opened her mouth to speak, but her denial was cut short.

"Hold your lying tongue. You need to think carefully about what you say to me from now on. Your sisters' lives are at stake."

Fate's intake of breath was noticed. The silence between them nearly suffocated her. She couldn't see his eyes, but she felt them. They were plucking through her soul and looking for answers. But she needed answers of her own.

"The elements aren't needed for the life you seek. The darkness you embrace will make you weak."

"You're wrong!" The dishes rattled with the force of his fist hitting the top of the table. "It will make me stronger, but I need the journal! The element's abilities grow with each passing day."

He had lost what was left of his patience. Perhaps he hadn't absorbed as much power from her sisters as he had originally intended. She thought the necklaces with the glowing jewels he made them all wear fed his power, but perhaps they only weakened them. In that case, where was the energy going? It was the voices that had originally warned her what the jewelry's purpose was. It was why she spent most of her days in her room, to be free of its draining effects.

"If the journal is your desire, it can be found with Earth, Air, Water and Fire."

"And that is exactly what you are going to do. You are going to take the journal from them. I know the key to the power is in there. I gathered enough of the material, but I need the symbols to create the magick."

"There are some magicks that should not last, and some secrets best left in the past."

"What do you know of the past? You and those voices you hear control the future."

Fate tried to think back to a time when she would have told him that, and she came up with nothing. Were his memories his own or blended with Erebos's as well? Nibbling at her dinner, she kept her thoughts to herself.

"You realize you say more in your silence than you do with your rhymes," he snorted. The clink of his silverware on his plate indicated he was eating as well. "When exactly did you start that by the way? You spoke normally enough to give Theo his mission after the explosion."

How did he remember that? The wine she was drinking lodged in her throat and caused her to cough. Her intake of breath was enough of a reaction, and this time, the interest in his voice was devious.

"You thought that memory spell you put on Erebos would affect me as well?" His chair rubbed against the stone floor as he pushed back from the table. Fate heard his footsteps cross back to the wet bar. He popped the stopper on the decanter and filled his glass with more scotch. "Interesting," he mumbled to himself.

Fate was still processing, trying to remember back to the fateful day the Shadowman was created. It had been the day Mt. Vesuvius had erupted last, the day her beloved Anton was killed by Erebos, and his other personality Roy had grown stronger. She and her sisters had successfully pulled the dark energy Erebos had been collecting from his body, but in doing so, they created something far worse. She didn't realize until now that the creature they helped form had been witness to the plans that she and Theo had made. She wondered how much of the conversation he had overheard.

"No riddles for me, Fate?" The Shadowman's question was laced with mirth. He was toying with her. He walked to her side of the table, directly behind her seat and paused.

She tensed, as she braced herself for his next move. He placed one hand on the back of the chair and leaned forward until his mouth was within inches of her ear. His breath warmed the side of her neck, and she could smell the oak of the scotch he had been sipping.

"My life began again that day, a clean slate as it were. But Erebos's thoughts merged with mine all the times I controlled his body. I know more about you and your sisters than I ever wanted to. Zilla, especially."

Fate tried not to react. He was much too observant. If he indeed had been a witness within Erebos's body, Zilla could have shared any number of things during her time in his bed. Her love for him had always been her weakness, and she had been desperate to re-connect his memories. She insisted their relationship hadn't been the same since Fate had removed them from his mind. Fate hoped for all their sakes that Zilla hadn't found a way to give those memories back. He might be aware of more than he revealed.

The Shadowman moved closer, his lips brushing against the curl of her ear. His voice came to her in the slightest of whispers, bringing tears to her eyes with their power.

"The memory you erased with that spell was only his. I was already brought back at that point. Although, admittedly, it did affect my ability to merge with him at first. But I got the hang of it, as Zilla can attest to. Roy provided a way in, to a great many things."

The tip of his tongue ran along the curve of her ear, and she held her flinch in check. What was his motivation? He lowered his head — his intake of breath, as he drew in her scent, made her skin crawl. There had never been anything sexual between them. It made her worry for her sister. Was she still alive?

"You two look so similar." His teeth grazed her shoulder, and tears pooled in her eyes. He was corrupting her memories of Anton, of every tender moment she had spent in his arms. Her neck had been her lover's favorite place to nibble.

His bite firmed, and Fate cried out. Tears spilled from her lashes and their warm tracks ran down her cheeks.

"So, the ice queen does feel."

Fate stilled as the Shadowman soothed his tongue over the bite. She didn't believe he had broken through, but the area stung. He was close enough that she could feel his smile against her tender skin. It would be the last time she wore anything without a high neck.

He stood and placed both hands on her shoulders, his thumbs circled her back as the tips of his fingers gripped firmly. She didn't dare move or say a word. The stories of the bruises Zilla had received by his hand had been shared with her. His voice was still low, but the threat behind it came through loud and clear.

"I know you gave Theo my blade and took the journal from him. What I don't know is what happened after. But you, my dear Fate, are going to tell me."

He didn't need to collect more darkness, she could feel its taint through his fingertips. She was right to hide those tools all those years ago. It had given the elements more time to come into their power. The women had yet to find Earth, but she wasn't sure she could delay the inevitable. The Shadowman was unstable, like the negative power he was gathering.

She and her sisters wouldn't be able to help this time, his use of the green substance made sure of that. It seemed he couldn't absorb the powers of others fully without the magick symbols, but he was able to weaken them. The last time she had been around her sisters, they had all but been unconscious.

He gave her shoulders a final squeeze then, thankfully, released them and moved back to his seat at the other end of the table. His silverware clinked against his china as if nothing had happened. His final comment to her assured her something had.

"Yes, you will tell me. If you don't, your sisters will be the first to suffer. And there are always other uses I might find for you."

The thought of that made her wince, just as she heard the hooves of one of the Satyr brothers come in with the second course.

"Perfect timing, Henry," Roy boomed jauntily. "I've worked up quite the appetite."

8

Tara waited on a boulder outside of Theo's home while he gathered some of his things. He had walked through a passage in the tree that had opened after muttering a cryptic phrase. Taksi sniffed around the perimeter and had found a hole the size of her head to investigate.

"I wouldn't mess with that if I were you," Tara warned. "We don't know what kind of creatures might pop out of it."

Taksi looked at her, sneezed, then slowly moved to investigate a fallen log on the other side of the pathway. She glanced over nonchalantly, as if to indicate that had been her plan all along. No matter the size, it seemed all cats had an attitude.

It wasn't lost on Tara just how bizarre her life had become in the last few months. What was strange was that she was so accepting of this new situation, that she wasn't thinking twice about meeting a man in real life she had spoken to through a magical mirror. That kind of stuff just didn't happen, did it? Her thoughts went back to Brooke and all the years she had been told she was living in a fantasy world. Had her therapist been wrong? Tara hadn't paid too much attention to the stories Brooke told, always trying to focus her sights on reality. The guilt of her response, insisting that Brooke had needed help back then, wasn't something that sat well with her. Especially now.

"I will have to come back for my library," Theo said. Tara glanced up just as he swiped his hand over the opening and sealed it. "I have far too many books to move in one go." He remained standing as if he were ready to leave.

"Theo, I need to know more about what is going on. I am a little overwhelmed. I don't know you very well, and this is a lot to take in."

57

He looked confused. He crossed his arms in irritation. "We have been talking for days."

"I realize that." She tried not to let her tone get away from her. "But the conversations weren't all that enlightening."

He was taken aback. Had she offended him?

"I felt the conversations were most adequate."

Yes, she had. Now, it was her turn to be offended. "Adequate? Really? If all you want to talk about is science, history and literature, then I suppose they were. But you never talked about this place, or yourself, and now that I'm here, I need answers."

"Our time was limited," he huffed. "The magick wasn't always reliable." He turned his back to her and started to walk away. There was nothing she hated more than a man dismissing her during a conversation.

She got up to follow. "So, we're done talking then?"

"No. Our conversation needs to occur as we travel."

"Why is that?"

He stopped and turned so abruptly she almost ran into him. He put up his hands to steady her, causing her to look up into his face. His expression was that of resigned patience. "Because it's not safe for us to stay here. We need to keep moving. You are my guest, and I need to see to your welfare."

Tara's irritation melted with the softening of his features and the fact that he had her best interests at heart. She decided to cut him some slack. "Okay, we can talk as we go. Did you need me to carry something? There is no reason you should have to carry both backpacks."

His smile was fleeting, and he shrugged a bag off his shoulder and into his hand. "Thank you."

"You're welcome." She hoisted the pack behind her and slid her arms into the straps in one fluid motion. Once settling it on her back, she looked up into his smiling face. "What?"

"Nothing," he answered with a shrug. Non-responsive responses were also something she couldn't stand. If you had something to say, then say it. He had a lot to learn about her, but she figured trying to educate him all in one day wasn't going to help anyone.

Adjusting the weight on his own back, he turned to leave, and she steadied herself against the anger of being dismissed yet again. He turned back to face her and took a step back to allow her a clear path. "We will need to head up this trail. Are you ready?"

Tara smiled. Small victories were her favorite. "Yes, I am. Lead the way."

They had walked for miles; Tara could tell by the burning in her legs and the rumbling in her stomach. They settled on a location near a stream to take a short break. Theo mentioned he didn't want to linger long, and he had a place in mind where they would rest for the night. As they walked, they hadn't seen any buildings or people. It made her wonder about the size of Theo's world, what sort of place he had in mind. She was too tired to worry about the strangeness of her situation and hoped wherever he was taking her at least had a bed. Considering one could wander in the wilderness in South Dakota for days, she wasn't holding her breath.

"This should be good," Theo said as he slipped off his pack.

"I think you gave me the heavier of the two," Tara joked. She slid her pack off as well and sat on the log beside it.

"Anything's possible," he quipped.

Tara shot him a smile. She wouldn't put it past him to do just that, with the intent of teaching her a lesson. He seemed like the type. He would learn quickly just how capable she was.

"You were saying that Sevilla's will take us until tomorrow afternoon to get to?"

"That's right. If I still had my powers, it would have been much quicker."

"How so?"

"I would create a portal and travel to a place just outside of her home-stead." He continued after he noticed the question in her face. "I've thought about it and from what you described earlier, I believe it is sim-ilar to what you opened when you came here."

"You can create those on demand?"

"I could, but not anymore."

"Why? What happened?"

He passed her some apple slices and dried meat, leaving a bowl of nuts on the bench between them. Taksi sat right next to him, gingerly taking the slices of meat he passed her between sentences. "I once har-nessed the power of Earth, the power that you seem to embody now."

"I have what?"

"The element of Earth. You must know there is something different

59

about you, something that perhaps has developed over time. Your ability to heal for instance."

Tara nodded. "Strange things have been happening, I will agree with you there. But the power of Earth?" Her tone was disbelieving, but her gut told her there was a truth in what he said. "What is that anyway?"

Theo rose with two cups and walked to a nearby stream as they chatted. "The power of earth is one of four elemental powers that must remain in constant balance for our world to survive." He bent down and scooped up some water before returning to her. "Earth is the most important of the elements in that it grounds the others."

"Thank you." Tara accepted the cup he offered and took a sip. "You think that I, what, tapped into this element?"

Theo nodded. "You have. Or at least I believe so. Although, I was never so powerful when I harnessed its magick. You, on the other hand, are practically glowing with it."

"Where I come from, that isn't looked on as a good thing. The whole glowing thing."

"I would imagine it wouldn't be. Your species, as a whole, is pretty closed-minded."

Tara practically spit out her water with a snort. While she should be offended, she couldn't help but agree with him. "You say 'my species' as if you aren't part of it."

"I'm not."

She looked at his face for the familiar cues that he was joking. He wasn't. "Okay, I'll play along. What exactly are you?"

"An Elf."

Tara snorted. "You are the tallest elf I've ever seen. What are you? Six foot, three?"

"About that. What did you expect?"

"I don't know. I guess something like what is on the side of a cookie package?"

"I have no idea what you are talking about, but I can assure you I am what I say I am. My people come in all shapes and sizes, much like yours."

"Okay, I'll buy in. How are you familiar with humans if you aren't from Earth?"

He shook his head with a sigh. "Like I said, closed-minded."

"What the hell is that supposed to mean?" Her anger started to bubble, making it hard to keep the frustration from her voice.

"There are more species than you realize that call Earth their home. Humans only choose to see a select few of them. There are many that travel between the dimensions to enjoy the best each land has to offer."

Tara watched his expressions for lies, but she only saw earnestness. He truly felt as if he was providing an educational moment, the excitement of it came off him in waves. He was an extremely smart man, there was no denying it, but she couldn't help but wonder if he was somewhat delusional as well. "So, this place we are in now?"

"Part of Earth."

"But a different dimension?"

"Precisely."

"And did you ever travel between dimensions?"

"More in the beginning. It's been a lot less in the last few centuries."

This conversation was taking a turn she wasn't prepared for, but his comment about humans being closed-minded niggled the back of her mind.

"So. You being an Elf and all, that would indicate you are a bit older than me."

Theo glanced up at her, a small smile tickling the corners of his lips. "I am. Is that going to be a problem? Can we still be friends?"

His tone baited her. Tara felt her sass rising. "Of course, it won't matter, I have friends from all walks of life. I'm open minded when it comes to that. Makes the world a more colorful place to live in, wouldn't you agree?"

Theo laughed and nodded. "I most definitely would." As he packed up their picnic, she readied her pack.

"Back to the element thing. Say I do have this power you say I do. What sorts of things should I be able to do?"

"Each being that embodies the power has different capabilities dependent on their species. When I had it, most of what I could do centered around healing, same as you."

"What makes you think I can heal people?"

"You healed me." His questioning look had her second-guessing her sanity. She supposed it was pretty simple when he said it that way.

"Touché. If you used to have the power, why don't you have it now?"

He lifted the pack she had been carrying onto his back and waited for her to lift the other. She had been right, hers had been heavier. They shared a look, and he swallowed a laugh. She sported a full-blown grin on her face as he nodded forward.

"I'll tell you as we walk."

They continued up the rustic path that had been cut through the undergrowth from centuries of travelers heading in the same direction. It reminded her of the nature paths she trekked during her internship through the National Park system. However, the air seemed sweeter here and the ferns lusher. She was surprised they hadn't crossed another soul, since she was so used to seeing other hikers. Taksi made herself scarce, circling back every so often from her perimeter checks.

"It's beautiful here."

Theo bristled with pride. "Thank you. I've called many places my home, but this is by far my favorite land to reside in."

"I can see why. It is quiet here. Easier to just be. If that makes sense."

"It makes complete sense."

"You said you would tell me about the power. I suppose I can't deny there is something strange happening to me. What makes you think that it has been given to me?"

"Well, I mentioned the healing, which of course I didn't know about until you got here. But the tune you played was also telling."

"How so?"

"It is an ancient song, one that is very special to my culture."

"It was something I made up."

Theo shook his head. "I assure you it wasn't. It is most definitely something that you channeled. I believe it's how we first connected. Well, that along with the book and symbols."

She pulled the flute from her waist and showed it to him. "I heard your voice a few times before we connected in the mirror. It wasn't until after I realized the flute has the same symbol on it as my mirror."

He pointed to the Lakota symbol. "This one here? That is the same symbol I've used my entire life. It's been around a long time and, for the most part, it means balance."

"My friend mentioned it symbolized a mirror for the universe. As above, it is below."

"She's right. As guardian of the Earth magick, that is your primary duty. To keep the balance. It is something that has been needed for quite some time."

"And how exactly does one pull that off?"

"That is what we are going to need to find out."

"And how is that going to happen?"

"We need to find the sisters of Destiny and get our next steps from them. Fate gave me instructions to keep something safe many years ago, but in recent days, my magick was no longer containing it."

"The symbols on the tree," Tara mused.

"Yes. They were meant to hold the toxic magick in, but it managed to find its way out over time. I knew when you came through that something had changed. I only hope that Fate has found the answers."

"Fate?"

Theo nodded. "Yes, one of the sisters of Destiny. She represents the future. Her sister, Sevilla, is past, and Zilla is present."

"Like the three fates in mythology."

"Loosely based and not nearly as old-looking. Unlike the way the hags are portrayed, these sisters try to avoid getting involved."

"But they don't always?"

"No, they don't always," Theo sighed. "Which is precisely why we are in the mess we're in. I just hope they've managed to find the other three elements. If Erebos is still around, we are going to have some real trouble."

"Who's Erebos?"

"Someone I hope you never have to meet."

He pointed through a clearing, and Tara noticed an ambient glow. There were buildings ahead, and she glanced around for Taksi, who was trailing behind them at a slower pace.

"Are we stopping for the night?'

"We can't make it all the way before dark. I believe it would be safer if we stay."

"Okay," she said. "Just a minute."

Taksi Find Tree. We sleep.

TAKSI HUNT.

"I suppose that works also," Tara muttered. *Will meet here. In sunlight.*

Taksi nodded as if she understood then faded back into the shadow of the woods. Convinced she would be safer in the woods than with them, Tara nodded to Theo.

"Okay, I'm ready."

9

With Taksi settled for the night, Tara and Theo walked on to the village. It was quaint, with simple wooden structures, colorful flower boxes, and paneled glass windows. It was the first sign of habitat Tara had seen since arriving, and she soaked it all in. Within minutes, she was in love with the town and the inhabitants.

There was music coming from nearby, and from the sounds of those singing along, the players were well received. The happy sound of the fiddle had her imagining those who were playing, up on their feet and joining in the revelry.

"Sounds like we are coming into a party," Theo groused. "I remember it being much quieter here."

"I like the music. I'm sure it will be quieter once we're inside," Tara reasoned.

He shot her a look. "The place where we're heading is precisely where the noise is coming from."

It was probably best they were staying for the night. Theo was grumpy. Perhaps he needed some sleep. "I'm sure it will be fine, Theo. Don't worry about me, I'm a heavy sleeper."

"I'm not."

Tara hid a grin by turning her head and ducking her chin. She was surprised he was so disgruntled, but then again, she got crabby when she was tired. With the weight of the packs, it felt as if they had been walking for days. It would be good to get off their feet.

Theo led the way, and they walked past some villagers, who stopped to welcome them. They each turned to face them and give a quick bow or curtsey with a curious stare. The younger villagers were nudged to follow suit, which they did without question. She watched Theo respond with a quick nod in each villager's direction. The villagers weren't acknowledging them both…only him.

He stopped in front of the building where the music was coming from. It was larger than the others and had balconies that jutted from the front and curved around the side. There were whispers from above them, and Tara saw a beautiful woman with a shimmering silver gown and blue hair whisper into the ear of the woman next to her and race inside. Her hair seemed a bit edgy for such a rustic environment.

"There isn't another village for miles, and it's far too dark to walk alone in the woods. I'm sorry, but we will have no choice but to stay here."

Tara was confused. He had seemed fine before he got here, but now he was acting as if he didn't want to stay. She didn't care how loud it was, she was ready to get off her feet.

"Don't worry, Theo. I've slept in some strange places. I'm pretty easy."

He gave her a side glance, which made her consider what she had just said. Her cheeks flared, and before she could give him a blathering back-pedal, he pulled open the door. He took a step back to clear the threshold, swiping his hand in the opening indicating she should enter first.

"After you."

The space they walked into reminded Tara of an old-time tavern, complete with a large stone fireplace to one side and a bar at the other. The cavernous room was lined with rows of rectangular wooden tables and benches. There were also smaller tables with chairs, but it seemed most of the people there were seated in large groups. She was prepared to be looked at with interest, but she wasn't prepared to have the entire room go silent at once. It was an uncomfortable feeling, being a stranger in a new place, but the silent staring took it to a whole new level.

The room was filled with people in all shapes and sizes, and like the woman on the balcony, many of them had colored hair. She even noted several animals and had a fleeting thought that perhaps it would have been okay to bring Taksi inside. A few birds flittering by her head had her changing her mind.

Theo marched up to the bartender, and Tara stayed back, observing the people in the room watching him pass. As he walked by them, some of them stood and almost all of them bowed their heads.

The man at the bar was beaming. "It's an honor, your high…"

Theo shook his head. "I'll need two rooms for the night please, Stuart."

Stuart looked to Tara then back to Theo. With apologetic eyes, he gave a nod to the onlookers, who proceeded to go about their business. Tara wasn't sure what to think of the entire scene. When the music started once more, she had to step closer to hear the conversation.

"I'm sorry, my lord, but the festival is in full swing. I only have the room at the top of the stairs available." The man looked uncomfortable, frantically wiping the top of the counter in front of Theo. "Perhaps I could request that someone move…"

"I won't hear of it. The room at the top of the stairs will suffice." Theo placed a tarnished gold coin on the bar. "We will be leaving early tomorrow, so I will settle the bill tonight."

"As you wish, my lord. I will send my daughter up with a pitcher."

"Thank you, Stuart. Say hello to Miriam."

"I will, my lord. She will be happy to hear you have finally returned."

Theo gave a nod and turned to face Tara. He didn't seem happy she had witnessed the exchange. His demeanor was gruff as he waved his hand in front of him to point toward the other side of the room.

"We are taking the stairs in the corner. Up three flights."

Tara nodded. While she was curious about the "my Lords" and the strange way people were acting, her questions could wait. Now was clearly not the time. She walked to the stairs and made quick work of climbing them, painfully aware he was right behind her.

The revelry from the lower level floated up to their location, and she hummed along to the tune that she had learned to play over the last few weeks. Clearly, he was right, she hadn't made the song up. She moved aside, and he opened the door, allowing her to step into the room before him. A glance to her left confirmed it was going to be a long night. There was only one bed, and it had been forever since she had someone in hers.

Theo dropped his pack near the wall just inside the doorway. "I will sleep on the floor," he said as he pulled a blanket from the end of the bed.

There was no way she was going to deal with his grumpy butt tomorrow after a terrible night's sleep. Tara pulled the blanket out of his hand and tossed it back on the bed. "Don't be ridiculous, there is plenty of room for both of us. Besides, you have some questions to answer, so it will be easier if I don't have to yell across the room to you."

Theo nodded as he rubbed his lower back. "Seems logical."

There was a knock at the door, and he opened it long enough to take a pitcher from the hands of a young girl with a white cap. Tara presumed it was the owner's daughter. He thanked her and closed the door quickly on her surprised face.

"The water is warm, and there are towels on the nightstand there if you would like to clean up. I'll step out for a moment to give you some privacy."

Tara had already removed her long sleeve shirt and hung it on the back of the door. "There won't be a need, I have thermals on." Her shoes and pants came off next, and she walked over to the pitcher to wet a cloth. She wiped her face and neck then undid the back of her bra, so she could slide the straps down each arm and loop around her hands. With everything unhooked, the bra came out of the front of her shirt and joined the other clothes she had on the floor. She pulled the shirt out and wiped underneath quickly before deeming herself clean enough for the night.

Theo was distracted by the scrap of red lace on the top of her pile of clothes. It looked as though he wasn't sure what to think about it. Sexy undies were the one luxury she afforded herself since she had to wear a uniform each day. When she had put it on this morning, she had also put on a matching thong, which he wouldn't be getting a look at. She was definitely wearing her long johns to bed.

After finishing, Tara stood with her hand on her hip and observed. Theo's weight shifted from foot to foot, and he didn't seem to know where to put his hands. He finally clasped them behind his back. His eyes took her in and lowered to the front of her silky undershirt, which was now conveniently clinging to her damp breasts. She crossed her arms in front of her prompting him to lower his eyes and clear his throat. She was slow to realize that the privacy he had offered was probably more for his sake than hers.

She hurried to the bed and sat down, looking through the pack she had with her. Never so happy to see a mint in her life, she popped one into her mouth and relished the snappy flavor that filled her mouth. Thankfully, she spied a few more for the journey tomorrow. She used her rollerball perfume, glad that she had tossed it in as an afterthought that morning.

By the time she looked up, Theo had his shirt removed and was wiping down with a clean cloth. He glanced back, and she lowered her eyes, attempting to afford him some privacy. But it wasn't as easy for her. He didn't have an undershirt, and he was built. Sculpted like a Greek statue was more like it. She didn't see an ounce of fat anywhere on his body, and his muscles danced beneath his skin as he moved.

She decided conversation would distract her from gawking. "What exactly was all that downstairs?"

"There is a festival going on right now."

"That is not what I meant, and you know it."

He turned and gave her a full-frontal view of his bare chest. He didn't have any chest hair, only a thin line of hair that went into the top of his trousers, which caught her by surprise. She and Brooke used to call them treasure trails, but it had been some time since she had seen one. Most men she knew took them off with waxing, but she had the definite impression that Theo was more old school.

The clearing of his throat drew her eyes up, and she bowed her head. Okay, so maybe she was wrong about distracting herself with conversation but to be fair, he didn't seem to mind her interest. He went right back to grooming and sat on a nearby chair to wipe his feet with the rag before joining her on the bed. Thankfully, he kept his pants on when he joined her. She wasn't entirely sure, but from what she could see with his loosened fly, he wore nothing underneath.

He propped the pillow behind him, leaned against the headboard, and crossed his legs above the covers. Even his feet were well built and muscular. Since when had she thought feet were sexy? She propped a pillow behind her as well but slid underneath. Besides their clothes, the covers would be the only barrier between them. Tara was quickly realizing it wouldn't be nearly enough. He had used the same water she had, yet he smelled amazing. The cinnamon smell was back, was it some sort of elvish magick? She could feel her body tingle in places it had no business tingling.

"Do you have any more mint leaves?"

Tara was confused at first. "Oh, you mean my mint? Yes, I have one here."

He looked at the small white candy she offered then back into her face. "This is what you have?"

"Yup." She stuck her tongue out to show him then promptly pulled it back in. "See?"

He took the mint, and before he could pop it into his mouth, she took it back. "You need to unwrap it. You really haven't had one of these?"

"No." His tone was snappish, but she hadn't meant to offend. She wasn't always sure how to read him.

"Here you go."

He slid the mint between his lips then nodded in delight. "These are tasty."

"Glad you like it." Tara placed her pack on the floor next to her then settled back into her pillow. "So, about what happened downstairs."

"I wasn't expecting a crowd."

"That was evident," Tara mumbled. Did she see amusement in his eyes? "They seemed shocked among other things."

"As was I, although it was no excuse for my rude behavior."

Tara wondered if that was his attempt at an apology. If so, he stunk at it. She had already decided it wasn't worth getting into. She could tell he had been caught off guard earlier.

"They recognized me, but I've been gone a long time."

"How long?"

"Over seventy-five years."

"That is a long time," she said with a nod. Going with the theory that he wasn't lying about his heritage, she supposed it wasn't a long period of time for him. It made her wonder just how long he had been around. "And you're some kind of royalty?"

Theo closed his eyes and sighed. "I am, but I don't expect special treatment because of it."

"You were acting strange. I thought it was because you were hiding something from me." If he was keeping a low profile, so people wouldn't fuss, Tara could respect that. He was full of surprises, and she found it didn't put her off as much as it interested her. "Are you a prince or something?"

Theo smiled. "Technically, the king, but it has been some time since I have been home."

Tara coughed and practically swallowed her mint. "King? Are you serious?"

"I'm always serious." Theo turned his head and looked her in the eye to make his point. "I would never lie to you."

She could hardly breathe. Never in her life had she had a man speak to her so directly. It wasn't so much what he said but how he made her feel when he said it. In the depths of her soul, she knew he spoke the truth. If she hadn't already figured that out about him during their conversations, she knew it now — Theo was an honorable man.

His unwavering gaze affected her pulse, so she lowered her eyes and asked her next question. "You haven't been home in over seventy-five years?"

"Technically, much longer."

"Longer?" Just how old was this guy? Her limited knowledge of elves was from works of fiction. She had no idea if what she read was based on any kind of truth. She thought about asking but decided it might be considered rude. "What kept you away?"

"For the most part, Fate did."

"Your friend?"

"That's right," he nodded. "She and her sisters had gifted the men in their lives with the power of the elements. They needed a fourth, and I was a family friend, so they granted me the honor of embodying earth. They also entrusted me with the journal that housed the secrets of the powers. It was important to Fate that it was given to another immortal."

"Immortal. As in live forever?" Well, there was her answer.

Theo nodded, his eyes squinting in confusion as if he didn't under-stand her question. She let the whole idea sink in and realized when she had packed her go-bag this morning, nothing could have prepared her for meeting him.

He continued with his explanation. "Anton was Lycan, and Ryker was Mage." Noting her puzzled expression, he explained. "That's pretty close to immortal but not the same, since they can't live as long without magick. And Erebos was human."

Theo's tone changed when he said his name, and Tara saw his hand tense as he fisted up some of the sheet on the bed.

"And the journal?"

"I studied it for years, and the magick made itself known to us over time. It wasn't until creatures started dying we realized something had gone wrong."

"What were they dying from?"

Theo shook his head. "There was nothing natural about the way they died. They were drained of their essence."

Tara didn't like the sound of that. "Like a vampire?"

"More like an incubus, but yes. Erebos had increased his power by somehow tapping into dark magick. The harpie queen, Cela, had figured out a way to funnel it using ancient symbols that directed the energy."

"Symbols like what you had on your tree?"

He shook his head. "No, although I suppose to most, they might look the same. The symbols weren't like anything I had ever seen before and weren't present in the journal."

"And you've been around a long time."

"Precisely. By the time we caught up to Erebos, he had already killed Cela and my friend, Anton. The weapon allowed him to absorb their powers."

"That's terrible. I'm so sorry for your loss, Theo."

"It was a long time ago, and I've seen loss much greater than this."

Tara supposed he was right. In his time, he had probably seen more than she could possibly imagine: The rise and fall of empires and the beginning and ends of world wars included. "What happened next?"

"We had planned to approach him, see if Zilla could talk any sense into him. She was his girlfriend and the most likely to be listened to, but something went wrong. I think the dark magick was too strong. When we tried to pull it with our combined powers, there was an explosion. When I woke, Ryker and Sevilla had been injured, and Fate was just stirring. She asked me to find Anton, but it was too late for him. The weapon used to kill him was near his body and by the time I returned to Fate to tell her, Zilla and Erebos had escaped."

"He's still alive?"

"As far as I know. I would presume so, since it seems the magick is still trying to worm its way to him."

"And that was what you were in charge of hiding?"

"It was, or at least the thing that gave him access to it. And to ensure Fate would never be able to give away its location, or the fact that I was still alive, I cast a spell on her to twist her words. From that point on, it pained her to speak in anything but riddles or rhymes."

"Wait. What? You have the power to do that?"

"I used to, but it was drained over time. Although I feel better now that we left the tree."

Her prone position was starting to catch up to her, and she caught herself yawning. "And how long ago did this happen?"

"It was during the time you know of as World War II."

She didn't know much about the war, but she knew it had been a long time ago. "And you've been alone in that tree ever since?"

"That's right."

Tara slid down and settled her head onto her pillow. Her eyelids were weights, and she just needed to close them for a minute. She pulled in a deep breath, and her next comment came out on a sigh.

"Sounds like a lonely existence, Theo of Wisteria."

She felt his weight shift, then the pressure of another blanket being placed on top of her. Too tired to move, she sighed again as she snuggled deeper into her pillow. The last comment she registered was slightly more than a whisper.

"It was, until I met you."

10

The next morning, Theo awoke to an arm draped over his chest and a tiny head resting in the crook of his shoulder. He could feel the warm puffs of breath from Tara's contented sigh on his bare skin and relished the feel of having a beautiful woman in his arms. It had been far too long, and he avoided moving, so he wouldn't wake her. He hadn't felt this good in decades.

The blankets that had been between them before sleep had somehow shifted, and Tara's body had gravitated toward his throughout the night. He didn't mind, but as she shifted and murmured in her dream state, her knee slid up onto his thigh. He stopped her leg just before it reached its destination — so much for not moving. He didn't know what would be worse, getting kneed in the jewels or having them knot up each time he drew in a breath of her.

He shifted slightly away from Tara's wayward knee, and she snuggled once more into his side. She was making it impossible for him to be a gentleman, and there was no controlling what his body was doing. He wondered about his reaction. How he had lived many years without the comfort of a woman and hadn't even given it a second thought. Yet, this woman came into his life, sharing his love of science and literature and smelling the way she did, and now, he could think of nothing more than how to keep her with him.

There was something special about her, something that made him take notice. He supposed it could be that she was meant to harness the power of Earth, and he was still deeply connected to it as well. It hadn't ever really gone away, not until the dark magick had seeped the last of it from his weary bones. But no woman, from any walk of life, had ever captured his attention like this. He felt so energized and alive. It was as if she had cast a spell on him. He had spent his lifetime focused on only his needs, and it was irritating and exciting that a wisp of a female was changing all that. He turned his head to get another look at her angelic face before he woke her. Something wasn't right. Realizing her hair and eyebrows were drained of all color sent him into action.

"Tara, wake up." He pulled his arm out from beneath her pale cheek and tried to keep the frantic tone out of his voice. "Tara, darling, you need to get up." Her hair was completely white, and her lips were blue. "What have I done?" He managed to pry her off and rested her head on one of the pillows, before layering every blanket he could find on top of her.

How could he have been that foolish? Of course, he felt great, she had been feeding power back to him all night. By all that was holy, if anything happened to her, he would never forgive himself. He struggled with wanting to touch her but knowing it would make matters worse. She had been practically laying on him, how could he have not realized how cold she was?

"So much pain," she muttered. "Must bring balance."

He knelt beside her, getting a better look at her face. Her lips were turning back to pink, and if he wasn't mistaken, there was some color returning to her hair. He caressed her cheek and was horrified to see energy start flowing from her skin to his. When her lips started turning blue again, he pulled his hand back. He had never been so helpless in his life.

He paced the room, trying to think of a way he could help her. "I don't have control of the elemental magick anymore. But perhaps, since she's healed me…"

Going back to her side, he dropped to his knees and hovered his hands over her sleeping form. He closed his eyes and visualized the golden glow of healing energy from his body, exiting his fingertips and connecting with her aura. It was working. He watched the glow around her brighten as he pushed his intent forward and shared the power that she had unknowingly fed him the night before.

Her color looked better, and her breathing was less labored. His heart fluttered, and he felt queasy, sweating from the strain he put his body through. He didn't care. Even though he wasn't used to wielding energy like this anymore, whatever she had shared with him last night was going back. Sevilla could heal him later if need be.

The glow around her continued, and the two colors of their energy blended quickly into the color he was familiar with when he looked at her. The color that her eyes now were as she looked up at him.

"Theo, what are you doing?"

"Thank the Goddess." He closed his eyes and broke the flow of energy he had been sharing. She looked much better. It wouldn't do them any good for him to weaken himself more than he already had.

"Why are you all sweaty?" She raised her hand toward him. "Are you running a fever?"

He pulled back, causing her to flinch. "Don't touch me."

"I'm confused. What has gotten into you?"

He stood up, taking a short moment to breathe through the equilibrium change, then walked to the chair and sat down. His legs were unsteady.

"Theo?"

"Give me a moment," he croaked.

She sat up in bed and pulled the covers tight to her chest. Defensive. He could feel her emotions floating to him like the seeds of a dandelion. She looked so fragile, but he could feel her strength. By the look of her hair, it was almost fully restored, but her worry came off her in waves. He had a compulsion to go to her, to take her in his arms. It took everything he had in him to fight the urge.

"Theo?"

"Don't worry, things will be fine. I just expended a lot of energy and need to sit for a moment."

She nodded as if she understood. He hoped she did. She had done precisely the same thing when they had first met. "What happened?"

He couldn't be sure, but something changed last night and now, they were connected in a way he couldn't explain. He looked up into her face, knowing full well he could never lie to her but at the same time, knowing he must. Or at least withhold some of the truth as he understood it.

"When I woke, you were pale and cold as if you were dead. Your hair had been stripped white, which is what I noticed it doing earlier, when you use your power."

"But I was sleeping."

"Yes, but we were…I mean you were…"

"Oh, for heaven's sake, Theo, spit it out. We are both adults."

He laughed at her tone, which for some unknown reason made her angrier. Ah yes, he could feel the heat of it now. "Calm down, it isn't what you think. Although I did wake to find you sprawled over me like a blanket."

The pretty pink color he was becoming so fond of, flared in her cheeks. He decided to explain before her mind traveled in the wrong direction. Her emotions were all over the place, and he wasn't sure he was strong enough to feel all that.

"Nothing untoward happened, however, I believe for some reason, you felt inclined to share your power with me during the night and may have overdone it a bit."

"Which is why my hair was white?"

"Precisely. And you were as cold as death."

She uncovered herself and stood up, walking straight to the mirror that hung on the wall. "Seems fine now." After a quick examination, she went to the pitcher and wet her hands, running them over her head and returning her hair to its dark spiky appearance. "You, however, don't look like you are feeling so hot."

"I gave the energy back to you. That was what I was doing when you woke. I may have overdone it a little, but I wasn't sure how weak you were."

Tara knelt down beside him but kept her hands to herself. It seemed the earlier warning was still on her mind. That suited him. He wasn't sure they should touch until she learned how to shield herself from unwanted draining. The Goddess help her if she ever ran into Erebos.

"What can I do to help you?"

He shook his head. "Nothing. I will feel better once we get outside." Her face reflected confusion, but her eyes something more. His reaction had done more than confuse her, it had hurt her. He didn't like the way it made him feel. "Let's pack up. We should be to Sevilla's by dark."

"Are we okay?"

The pain in her eyes was almost unbearable, what the Goddess was wrong with him? He hadn't felt another beings' emotions so keenly since he was a lad. It had to do with her power and the return of his. All the more reason to keep his hands off of her. His next statement didn't sit well with him, almost choking on the lie.

"There is nothing to worry about."

After each using the small room that housed an upgraded version of a chamber pot, they dressed quickly. The silence was uncomfortable. They were given a bag of freshly baked scones and some fruit by the kitchen staff before leaving. It was still early, and the dew on the grass glistened. They went back to the area where they promised to meet Taksi and only had to wait a few minutes until she joined them. She dropped a rabbit carcass at Tara's feet.

FOOD.

Tara appreciated the gesture, but there was no way. She pointed to the offering.

Taksi eat. She pulled an apple from the bag Theo held and bit into it. *Tara has apple.*

Taksi looked at Tara's food choice and then to Theo.

He caught on and pulled a scone from the bag and took a big bite. "Thank you Taksi, but we've had breakfast."

Taksi gave the equivalent of a feline shrug then scooped the carcass up in her jaws and slinked into the tree line. From what Tara could sense, she wasn't upset, just confused as to why they wouldn't want fresh meat. Tara sent her a visual hug.

Thank you.

"It was nice of her to offer," Theo said quietly. He lifted his backpack onto his shoulders and shifted it into place.

"It was," Tara laughed. "I will have to explain the whole cooking thing to her later. Are we off?"

"Yes, we have another long day ahead."

As they walked, Theo kept his distance. From what she had learned about Theo, he could be moody and slightly eccentric. His steps were less leisurely than they were the day before, but perhaps he hadn't gotten a good night's sleep. She guessed he still wasn't feeling well.

She couldn't remember anything from the night before, save the dream that she was a tree. He had mentioned the sharing of their energy, but she couldn't figure out why he was being so distant. Couldn't they still talk? Most people she shared her positive energy with were appreciative, but Theo was giving her the impression now he didn't want that. Which was strange because the first time she had done it, he had seemed grateful. He said she had saved his life.

His steps slowed, It looked like they were coming into a clearing. She was glad to think they might be stopping, since she needed a break. She spied a boulder and took a seat.

"We'll rest here but only for a moment. We need to keep moving."

Tara watched as Theo filled his canteen from a nearby stream. She hoped the water was clean, since she didn't have any water purification tablets to add to it. He sighed and shook his head. Was he irritated? She hoped he wasn't growing tired of her company already. Without his help, she wouldn't even know where to begin looking for a way home. When the word home popped into her mind, she thought of Misty again. She hoped she was okay.

Taksi had kept to herself most of the morning and preferred wandering off and checking in with them much more than walking along side of them. She was surprised not to see her on their break and hoped there wasn't anything she could run into that would get her in trouble. Speaking of trouble, how was she going to sort out missing her shifts at work? Even if she had a way of charging her phone, she doubted it would work from here.

She looked up. Theo was quietly observing her from the stream. Almost as if she had made her comments aloud, Theo responded to them.

"You worry too much." Theo walked to where she was sitting and handed her the canteen.

Her irritation flared, but she cooled it with a few sips of water. It was refreshing and clean but didn't do much to alter her mood. He was annoying her. She cooled an audible huff with another sip of water.

"I didn't say it to get you riled up, it was merely an observation."

"Didn't your Mother ever tell you that if you don't have a nice observation to share then keep it to yourself?"

"She may have told me something like that, although that was a long time ago." He had a smirk on his face, which she was glad to see, but it simultaneously angered her. At least he was done being anti-social.

"So, are you going to explain what happened back at the inn?"

"Are we back to that then?"

"Theo, we never left it. You've been distant since we left, and I am still clueless as to what exactly happened."

He sighed, clearly gathering his thoughts before he shared them. It made her sorry she brought up the observation comments. Since if he wasn't on his guard, he might have shared more.

"I don't know the why of it," he said with a pause. "But I do know that I can sense an energy that wasn't here before you arrived. For whatever reason, you seem to want to share it with me. However, this morning, you shared far more than was safe for you."

"I explained I wasn't aware of what I was doing."

"That is what makes it all the more dangerous for you," he said quietly. She calmed her thoughts, and then, she felt it. He was worried for her safety. She could feel threads of it coming at her now. It was like her emotional connection with the cats, but not nearly as strong. She had to really concentrate to sense it.

"I think it might be wise for me to show you a few techniques to block your energy from feeding those around you. The power of Earth can be replenishing and draining at the same time. You need to learn how to balance it."

"But I feel fine."

"That is because I gave back almost everything you gave me. But even now, you are sending me energy you can't afford. I think we should start with building walls around your energy, so you can channel it better. With guards up, you will be less likely to have something bad happen again."

"How do you make these guards? Is it something that I visualize?"

"It is," he sounded impressed. "Much like the power you shared with me when you first got here, but neither sharing nor taking."

"Neutral?"

"Precisely." He took her hands and pulled her from the boulder. It seemed like his earlier no touching policy had expired. She didn't mind, she liked the feel of his hands in hers. Crazy as it was, it gave her a sense of place. Grounded her.

"What do you need me to do?"

He slid off his shoes. "It's best if you have bare feet for this." She followed suit, untying and slipping off her hiking boots and tucking her thick socks into them. She rolled up her pant legs and pulled up her thermals for good measure.

When she was done, she stood up straight, and he took her hands in his again. There was a difference, he had been right. It was as if the ground was pulling her feet into it. "Place your feet shoulder-width apart and relax your shoulders."

She nodded and copied his stance, looking up into his expressive eyes and feeling their instant connection. It was like closing a circuit. The energy flowing up through his body and down through hers, back into the Earth, which fed them both. It reminded her of Mato's teachings, that all things on the planet were connected. Maybe Mato had prepared her for much more than she originally gave him credit for. She noticed though, for as many times as she had helped others with her energy, it never had felt like this. This connection was different.

"Can you feel it?" Theo whispered. His skin was glowing with a golden light, and his eyes were lit from within. She looked down to her arms and saw the white glow she was used to, surrounding her and swirling with dark green and gold where their hands joined.

"I can," she whispered back, afraid that anything louder would break the spell. Closing her eyes, she concentrated. She not only felt a connection to Theo, but incredibly, to everything around her. To the breeze as it touched her skin, to the firm ground and soft moss beneath her feet, even to the trees nearby that stretched their roots to meet hers. She had sent out roots as well, just like the tree she dreamed of the night before. They traveled beyond the nearby trees and under water sources, and images of a world she had yet to discover came back to her. Her dream of the tree had been more than a symbol for her. It was her path.

She connected to the birds in the trees, could see the world from their eyes as they flew above her. And she could sense Taksi nearby, stalking a rabbit in a field of flowers. Tara felt the rush of excitement in her blood. And there was Theo, steady as an Oak, giving her quiet strength to stand on her own but ready to lend his if needed. The connection to him now was by far the strongest, and she wondered if perhaps it was because their hands were joined. The emotions she sensed from him were much more than threads now, they were like a woven tapestry, connecting her to all their surroundings.

She opened her eyes and looked back into his. They reflected worry, but not enough to stop their connection. He smiled and gave her hands a gentle squeeze. "Now I need you to close your eyes again and visualize a cocoon between you and all you feel. It will all still be there, but you must stop the flow of energy to your surroundings."

Nodding to him, she closed her eyes once more and pulled back from all the things she had connected to in such a short time. It was harder than she thought. Everything attempted to keep the connection at the same time she tried to sever it. It was draining, and now she understood

Theo's worry. Even though he was concerned about her, he didn't break their bond. It was most important to him that she understand how to control her gifts. She sensed that now.

"You aren't trying to cut it, merely pulling the curtain on it for now."

"That is a much better visual, thank you."

"I could feel you struggling."

She smiled but kept her eyes closed. The cocoon would be much easier if she was only concentrating on one thing, so she put all of her energy into the man that stood before her. Every thought, every breath, every heartbeat was for him and him alone. The rest faded away, and soon, there was nothing but the sound of the sighs between them.

"You've pulled it in tight, now surround yourself with the intention of letting nothing in. Build a wall around yourself that is impenetrable on all sides."

Building a box around herself would disconnect her from Theo, and she didn't want the feeling to end so soon. She could sense his emotions now, pride, friendship, attraction coming off him in waves. It was addicting, knowing the heartfelt thoughts of another without any of the self-preserving walls that most hide behind. She was surprised that Theo was a swirling mass of confusion and fear, since he seemed to have it together.

"You are doing great," he said, but his voice sounded hoarse. She wasn't opening her eyes. She didn't want to break the spell. "Tara, the wall needs to shut me out as well."

She shook her head. That wasn't what she wanted. She was learning so much about the man she had come to trust. His voice came out of the fog of her mind. It was strained.

"Sorry. I have no choice."

Then nothing.

11

Tara was alone with her thoughts and sensations. He had shut her out. The place where she found herself was comforting, and the images in her mind shuffled and faded as she decided their importance. She allowed the image of Theo's beautiful face to linger in her mind, setting each line and curve to memory. Then fear crept in. Perhaps she was alone because something had happened to him.

She concentrated on the darkness, on a single point she could use to create an opening. Imagining her cocoon like a sleeping bag, she mentally pulled up on the darkness and let the radiance in. The daylight hurt her eyes momentarily, but he was still there, holding on to her hands and giving her strength. He looked tired but otherwise, unharmed.

"Are you all right?" His eyes were expressive, even more so after their recent connection. He was worried.

"I'm fine," she answered. "Feel amazing, as a matter of fact. You don't look so hot though." She was happy to hear his chuckle.

"I've been doing this a long time. I'll survive."

Feelings of warmth and admiration moved through their connection. She was compelled to break eye contact, the feeling was much too intense. She realized now she couldn't be mad for him breaking their connection earlier, since he did it for both their benefit.

"We need to break our circuit," he said softly. "Are you ready?"

"One moment," she said and pushed a healthy dose of healing his way. She realized now she had taken too much from him. "Okay, now."

He released one hand and then the other. "Take a deep breath and continue to visualize the grounding power between you and the earth. What you will want to do is send any excess power that you have back into the ground. We take only what we need."

She nodded and did as he asked. The connection was very much like what she had felt in the Black Hills with Mato, but stronger. This was, by far, the best meditation session she had ever had.

"Good," he said. "Pull your roots back when you feel you are ready."

Pulling them back was easy now that the connection between the two of them was muffled. It was still there, below the surface, but not nearly as powerful as it had been minutes before. Strangely, she didn't feel the connection to anything else around her, only him. She opened her eyes and took one last cleansing breath, feeling more centered than she had in her life.

She looked over to Theo, who was seated on the boulder, rubbing the top of Taksi's head. His color looked better. She was glad she thought to give him a shot of energy before breaking the connection.

Theo stood and slid his pack on then held the canteen out toward her. "You will want a sip of this before we go."

She took the canteen that was offered and drank from it, then lifted her own pack onto her shoulder. His emotions were easier to read now, and she wondered if that was why he was so anxious to get moving. There was attraction but also hesitation, and it made her wish that she could read his mind. At least when it came to his feelings. He seemed to keep them locked up behind the walls similar to the ones they just built.

"We still okay on time?"

He nodded. "We will cut it close but should be there before dark. You sure you feel up to the walk?"

"Don't worry about me. I feel great," she laughed. "Never felt better. That whole experience was incredible."

His smile warmed her heart. "It was, wasn't it?" He started up the path, with Taksi taking the lead.

FRIEND COME.

Right behind you, little sister.

"With practice you will be able to shield yourself with greater ease, eventually even as you sleep." She could still sense threads of his worry.

"I'll practice," she said quietly.

"I believe you will."

Their pace was brisk and left little time for conversation. They traveled in comfortable silence for most of the afternoon, which suited Tara just fine. Their earlier connection had been intense. It was blocked now, but not by her doing. Most likely Theo had something to do with that. Now that she knew why he did it, she wasn't nearly as mad. It was nice having someone look out for her for once.

She held a steady conversation with Taksi, who transmitted her observations from a mile ahead. Tara was glad Taksi was no longer going on about her lunch. Tara couldn't help but feel sorry for the rabbit, and the visuals were a bit gruesome.

TAKSI WAIT.

What do you see?

STONE HOUSE.

"Are we heading for a stone cottage?"

"That's right, how did you know?"

"I think Taksi may have found it."

"Ah. She should wait for us there. Can you communicate with her freely?"

"It seems to be getting easier, which is strange. But so many things are in this place, honestly."

Theo nodded. "I suppose it is always strange for outsiders when brought into a culture they aren't used to. The magick you are tapping into has a lot to do with your powers increasing."

"If normal people made their way here, would they receive powers as well?"

"What is normal?" The smile on his face was contagious. "In my world, nothing is normal."

"Actually, that goes for mine also. Good point," she laughed.

"To answer your question, even non-magical folk tend to get something. Even if it is only the ability to wield spells and make potions. You should tell Taksi to stay put and keep an eye on the house for us. I would be interested to know if there is anyone there."

That sounded like a good idea. It would be handy knowing what they were walking into. *Taksi see people?*

NO. TAKSI HIDE.

Good girl.

"She says she doesn't see anyone."

"Good. My guess is we are about a mile away, but it's strange I don't feel any wards."

"Wards?"

"Similar to what you and I just did with the walls but surrounding a place instead of a person."

"Like a forcefield?"

"I suppose, although not generated by energy alone. They are built first with intent, much like with any spell. Once we get there and I can reference the journal, I can show you more. It will be important that you learn as much as you can about your energy in the coming days."

She didn't like the sound of that. "Theo, what are you saying?"

He glanced over and shrugged. "I'm merely saying that I don't have any idea what we are walking into."

Taksi had been right, there wasn't anyone there from what Tara could see. The large cat waited patiently at the end of the path that led to the modest-sized home. Tara had the impression there hadn't been anyone there in some time. It was hard to tell, since the garden would be un-kempt this time of year anyway, but it seemed some of vegetables had been left to die on the vine. There were also brambles of a wild raspberry that had practically climbed over an entire window.

"There is something wrong," Theo whispered. "Sevilla never allows guests unannounced and always meets them on the path. Also, I've never seen her yard this much of a mess."

"Perhaps she's been ill," Tara offered.

"I hope not," Theo said. "Although that might explain the lack of wards around her property. We should head inside."

He unhinged the small wooden gate that broke up a low stone barrier around her yard. Taksi cautiously stepped into the yard, looking back at them to make sure they were following.

Taksi stay outside.

TAKSI COMES. PROTECT FRIEND.

Tara smiled at her feline friend and decided not to argue. Depending on what they were walking into, she and Theo could need the help.

Okay. Taksi follow.

Theo knocked on the solid wood door and waited a few seconds be-fore pounding again. He called out. "Sevilla? Are you home?"

There was no response, and Tara took a step over to peek in the win-dow. "I don't see anyone. I do see a fireplace, but no fire."

"She can't be here then," Theo answered. "There is a fire in the hearth whenever she is home. Since no one answered, I'm assuming no one else is here either."

He lifted the latch and stepped inside, looking from side to side before allowing Tara to step in. The air was stale, much like a cabin that had been closed over winter. Now that the sun was going down, it was much cooler. She understood now why fires were needed year-round in places like this. The stone didn't do much to keep the heat inside.

Rubbing her arms, she stood still as Theo looked around the house and called Sevilla's name. It was apparent he was familiar with the home, just as it was apparent someone had not been there for some time. It smelled musty.

As he looked upstairs, she walked around the kitchen, noticing that perhaps it wasn't as unkempt as she originally thought. The fruit bowl on the table was empty but without dust, and there was a jar candle that sat next to it. It was a seasonal scent, something she had just seen at the mall. It made her pause.

"Theo," she called out. "There's something you might want to take a look at."

The candle was not something that belonged. How on earth had it gotten here? More importantly, when had it been brought here? From Tara's estimation, it wasn't too long ago, since it was a holiday scent.

Theo's steps sounded down the stairs, and he joined her once more. "There isn't anyone upstairs, although it does look like someone has been staying here. The guest rooms have signs of a presence."

Tara pointed to the candle on the table. "Unless you have a mall nearby, I don't think this was purchased here."

He lifted it to take a better look and read the label. "It says made in the U.S.A."

"I'm familiar with the brand. I just bought the same candle not too long ago."

"I suppose Zilla could have given it to her." He placed the candle back down and faced her. "She likes to travel to your realm. It's where she met Erebos."

"Makes sense, I guess. Do you think Sevilla will be back? Did you want to wait?"

"I'm not sure we have much of a choice. Fate is generally impossible to find, and I don't dare go to Zilla's."

"Because of Erebos."

"Correct."

Taksi started to back away from the door with her hackles raised. A throaty growl vibrated from her throat and she bared her teeth with a hiss, finding a place to hide. The door flew open with a slam, and Theo pushed Tara behind him and faced the incoming threat.

"What are you doing here?" The man's voice echoed with power. "Who are you?"

Theo had his hands raised, and Tara could see the start of the golden glow that represented his magick. "Friends of Sevilla."

It was hard to see the man's face, as he was wearing a hooded cloak, but the magick he carried wasn't. Its brilliant blue glow traveled around his entire body in a matter of seconds. It surrounded him like a shield.

"You'll want to rethink that," he said, nodding toward Theo's hands. Tara was already pulling his arms down. She didn't think a fight would be in anyone's best interest. The man acted as though he wouldn't fight unless provoked. From the feel of his restrained power, they wouldn't have much of a chance if that happened.

"We aren't here to fight," she said. "We're just looking for Theo's friend and once we see her, we can be on our way."

"Theo? The elf king?"

Tara felt Theo's arm tense beneath her hand. This man was still a threat to him.

"Who are you? What have you done with Sevilla?"

The man lowered his hood and stepped inside. Taksi was still hissing from the other room but otherwise, not making a move. The man pushed his palm toward her, and the hissing stopped. Tara worried until she saw Taksi approach and rub up against his leg.

He scratched the top of her head while addressing Theo. "You're supposed to be dead. And I haven't done anything to Sevilla, I've been looking for her for weeks."

"What do you mean I'm supposed to be dead? You might want to start by giving us some answers."

"Let's talk." The man took another step inside and closed the door. He splayed his hands up in front of him and tipped his head. "I believe we are both searching for the same answers, so power down your hands and save your magick. In my estimation, you'll need it soon."

Theo did as he was asked but still kept Tara behind him. "Who are you?"

"An acquaintance of Sevilla's." The man shrugged off his cloak and hung it on a hook by the door. It gave Tara the impression he had done it a hundred times before. Perhaps more familiar with the space than an acquaintance would be. "My name is Kadar."

"I've known Sevilla a long time, and I've never met you."

The man smiled sadly. "Sometimes, even the dearest of friends can keep secrets from those they love. However, in your case, it's understandable. She and I met shortly after the last Vesuvius disaster."

"When we tried to stop Erebos," Theo whispered.

"Just so," Kadar confirmed.

12.

They sat at the large wooden table that centered the room, she and
Theo on one side, and Kadar on the other. Tara wondered what
type of spell he had cast on Taksi, since she seemed to be enam-
ored with him and much more interested in sitting by his side. They had
lit the candle to chase away some of the must, and the scent reminded
her of home.

"I suppose you should start from the beginning," Theo said. "How do
you know Sevilla?"

"We met some time ago. I'd say about 65 years, if one was counting."

"Long after we fought Erebos."

"That was what she had told me," Kadar confirmed. "She didn't remember much of what happened, only that there had been an explosion
and when she woke, she was here. I understand her sister Fate left shortly
after bringing her home."

"And has she been here lately?"

"Who, Fate?" Kadar shook his head. "I've never met her, although
some of the others have."

"Others?" Theo asked.

"The other elementals."

Tara tried to keep up but had no idea who either of them were talking
about. She supposed if Theo was convinced she harnessed Earth, that
they must be referring to Fire, Air and Water. All four were generally
called upon together from what she remembered of Mato's teachings.

"Good. They've been found. How many of them are here?"

"There are three. One lives here with her husband, and the other two
travel between the two worlds as needed. My understanding is they have
been trying to find the final element of Earth."

Theo glanced over at Tara then back to Kadar. "I think she's been found," he said. "I thought the sisters would know what to do."

"You have been gone for some time," Kadar said sadly. "During the last fight with the Shadowman, Sevilla and Zilla disappeared."

Another familiar name. The thoughts in Tara's mind started to form a link.

"And Fate?" Theo asked.

"I think she may be under the control of the Shadowman. I've seen them together but haven't been able to speak with her. She is never alone."

"Did you say the Shadowman?" Tara questioned.

"You've heard of him?"

"Wait. Who is the Shadowman?" Theo asked, turning his head and looking between them both. "And how would you know him?"

Tara shrugged. "A friend of mine had trouble with imaginary friends when she was a kid. It is what she called the one that scared her."

"This man is far from imaginary," Kadar said. He looked at Theo and explained. "The man Erebos, who you once knew, has evolved into something more. The Shadowman was the persona he chose to embrace as he came into power. I fear now that he is turning into something far worse. We're running out of time."

"Are you able to get word to the other elementals?"

Kadar nodded. "Sera is the one that lives here. I can get word to her, and she can summon the others."

"Without the sisters, I'm not sure what the next steps are, but I do know we will be much stronger as a group."

"Agreed." Kadar stood and gripped Theo's offered hand. "I should be back by the morning. In the meantime, make yourselves comfortable. You should know your way around."

"I remember," Theo said.

Kadar walked to the door and lifted his cloak from the hook. He slipped it over his shoulders and head with a snap. "I'm sorry to have met you under such terrible circumstances."

Tara's heart broke for him. The worry for Sevilla was coming off him in waves. She wasn't sure if Sevilla knew it, but it was clear Kadar was in love with her.

"See you soon," Theo said.

With a nod, Kadar left and latched the door behind him.

"He seems to be very worried about Sevilla," Tara said softly.

Theo nodded. "He does indeed." It didn't surprise him she had found someone of interest. Sevilla was a beautiful woman. However, it did surprise him her husband's name hadn't come up. He wondered if Kadar knew the entire truth. Frankly, considering this was the first he was hearing about a lot of things, Theo wondered what the truth even was.

"Do you think he can be trusted?"

"I do. You?"

Tara nodded. "I do. I didn't sense any artifice."

"Nor did I," Theo confirmed. "But I'm not sure I've ever met anyone like him before."

"Meaning?"

Theo thought better of sharing his concerns. Kadar had not only seemed mysterious, but he had been stifling a power that Theo hadn't seen since the day they fought Erebos. It made him hope that Kadar was truly on their side. He gave Tara a smile meant to soothe. "I meant nothing by it. It was obvious he has Sevilla's best interests at heart."

She nodded. "I felt that as well." Tara stifled a yawn. "Sorry, it's been a long day."

"It has," he said. "There are some things we should do before we settle down for the night. I thought it might be a good idea to show you how to create wards. We should put some in place around the house."

"Tell me what you need me to do."

"Follow me."

They went outside and once again stripped their shoes and socks off to better connect with the earth. The sun was low on the horizon and the cooler weather would soon warm. He had always loved spring.

"Building wards is like what I showed you earlier. But instead of it being an internal block from your energy, you create an external block against physical things. Once we put this in place, nothing will be able to enter unannounced."

"I like the sound of that," Tara nodded. "I'm looking forward to a restful night's sleep." She looked behind her and stared pointedly at Taksi. The cat sat back on her haunches and watched them with interest. Tara must have told her to stay put. She gave Theo a nod. "Okay, I'm ready."

He stepped behind her and faced her toward the outer wall

surrounding Sevilla's property. "It will probably be easiest for you if you face the area you are securing at first. It is important to have a good visual of where you are building your wall."

"So, I am going to leave my eyes open this time?"

"Yes," Theo confirmed. "You will be sending your intent forward then stepping sideways as we circle around the property. It will be easier if you can see where you are going. I will stay behind you and guide you."

Theo wrapped his arms around her slim waist and placed his palms on the underside of her forearms and bent them up. As he stepped closer, he felt her sudden intake of breath.

Her voice carried up to him. "What should I do now?"

He wrapped his fingers around her forearms. "Turn your arms, so your palms are face out."

She nodded and did as he asked.

"Now, same as we did before, you are going to imagine a wall of energy, but this time, between you and the tree line. Just on the other side of the stone wall will suffice. I can add some color to the energy, so you can see where it's going."

She took a breath then sent a stream of light from her fingers. He brightened it, so it was more visible, letting the power glow as they painted the energy against the field. As he asked, the wall formed just outside Sevilla's property and grew from the ground up. The dark green glow was soon joined by his gold light and swirled in a thick wall in front of them. He would have never been able to secure the house adequately on his own. Their combined power was impenetrable.

"You're doing great," he whispered. His chin was just above the top of her head, and the scent of peaches tickled his nose. With the energy flowing between them and the feel of her in his arms, it was hard to keep his mind focused. He needed to though, especially since she kept forgetting to cocoon herself from sharing her energy so freely.

"Now we are going to step to the left, and you are going to continue painting the energy around the perimeter. We can finish above us when we come back full circle."

"This is amazing, Theo," Tara said. He could hear the smile in her tone. What a gift it was that he was sharing this moment with her. The moment when she learned what she was meant to be and learned to control her power.

"Will the people we are expecting be able to get through?"

"After we create the ward, we can provide an opening for the elementals and Kadar. Watch your step."

Tara glanced down and continued to send the stream of energy from her hands without a hitch. Theo was amazed she had such a strong handle on her power this quickly. It would be good in the days to come, especially if Erebos was still alive. They continued around the back of the house, and he spied a leafless tree he didn't remember being there. It was black as coal and would be best to investigate in the light of day.

They finished around back and moved their way to the other side of the house. They were coming back up on the garden, almost to where they had started.

"So now we complete the circle, but here is where we leave an opening. This is where you close your eyes. You will want to do this bit with intent. Since we don't know any of the people you are allowing in by name, you will have to use their powers. Water, Fire and Air."

"And us?"

"We built the ward, so we can come and go as we please."

"What about Kadar?"

Theo wasn't sure about him but didn't really have much of a choice. He had a feeling with the power he had witnessed, he would be able to get through pretty much anything they put in place anyway.

"Yes, you can include him as well. He should come to mind easily since we just met."

Tara nodded as the light wove into the magick that had been placed earlier. The two blended and only because Theo was looking for them, could he see the openings they had left behind. She raised her hands above her and completed the portion above Sevilla's house. The dome was complete.

"I think we got everything," Tara said.

Theo gave her arms a gentle squeeze before allowing her to slip from his. The energy around them glowed like the Northern Lights. Theo nodded and took a step back. The warmth from having her in his arms was fading. "Full circle at last," Theo said. "Now, we dim the lights."

He raised his hands and pulled the light back into his hands, sending the excess energy back into the earth below his bare feet. He was feeling much better now, stronger. His ancient magick had come back to him like an old friend, only stronger. He knew Tara had everything to do with the way he was feeling, both magically and emotionally. He had a fleeting thought he mustn't mix the two.

"I can still feel it," Tara said softly. "Even though I can't see it. I forgot about Taksi — will she be able to go through?"

Theo nodded. "I took care of that. You can let her know it's safe. In the meantime, I suggest we go inside and try to get some rest. Once the others arrive, it will be harder to find quiet time. Grounding will be really important for you in the coming days."

They walked back toward the door, and Tara looked once again at Taksi. The mountain lion stood and rubbed up against Tara's leg before making her way up the path.

"She's out for the night. I let her know everything inside the stone wall is protected."

"Our perimeter is as secure as we can make it. I'll feel better knowing she is out there and can warn us if anything is coming."

"Me too," Tara said.

13

Fate waited in her room until Sansa came back to let her know that the Shadowman had left. It was determined he would be gone for some time, since he had taken Henry with him to carry supplies. Sansa had confirmed the trip with Billy, who was concerned about his brother's well-being. Henry hadn't been able to share too many details, only that there were some magical tools he would be required to carry for his master.

It wasn't until the warmth of the morning fire started to fade that Sansa returned. Fate heard the latch on the door close, and Sansa's quick steps as she approached where Fate was seated.

"Mistress, he is gone. I watched from the cave opening as they went into the woods. Billy has agreed to help us keep an eye out for their return, but Henry thought they might be gone at least overnight."

Fate nodded. "We must hurry. I don't want to put anyone in danger."

"Let's go then," Sansa said. Fate could feel her slender fingers wrap around her elbow. She used it as support to rise. "Billy's pants and shirt do fit you amazingly well. It's a good thing we got you dressed earlier," Sansa said. "It will save us some time."

"I appreciate the loan. It has been some time since I've worn anything but a dress, but I find them rather comfortable."

"The long skirts would have gotten in the way. We should be able to move much more quickly. Besides, his shirts smell like fresh air and pine needles. I don't mind wearing them at all, if I'm honest."

Sansa escorted Fate through the door and up the hallway. They had worn slippers, so their steps were muffled.

"You're sweet on him," Fate said with realization. "Does he know?"

"He does." Sansa's response was laced with a smile. "He brings me leafed twigs from a nearby oak tree. The bouquets remind me of home."

"Best to keep it to ourselves," Fate warned.

"We are discreet," Sansa whispered. "There is an opening we use that the Shadowman is unaware of. And we only go out for small bits of time."

They finished crossing the main gathering room and were now walking on the carpeted floors of the Shadowman's study. Fate hadn't been in the space for some time. She wasn't allowed. It reeked of despair, and she wondered what on earth he had been up to. She could smell the dank air now rising from the stairs. The stairs that would lead them down to her sisters.

She was glad Sansa was guiding her, it made the trip much quicker.

"Watch your step, Mistress." Sansa pulled tighter on Fate's arm and supported her as Fate found her footing. Once down the first step, she knew the pace and depth she would need for each. With Sansa guiding her, the steps were taken easily. "Once I get you down here, I will keep watch from the top of the stairs," she whispered.

"I can't thank you enough, Sansa."

"You don't have to thank me. I would do anything for you."

"You are a good and true friend."

"As are you," she responded as she gave Fate's arm a gentle squeeze.

The smells that had come to her in the study were stronger, now that they had come to the source. The distant drips of water hitting the pools below them echoed in the silence of the corridors. Fate swept her hand across the walls as they passed by, the stone was damp and had a smooth quality like glass. She wondered if it could be obsidian.

She and her sisters had been held hostage for weeks. Some of the staff had been here much longer. Fate was glad Sansa knew her way around, or she would have never found the holding cells on her own.

"We're here," Sansa whispered. "They are just there beyond these bars. They glow green like the necklace he forces you to wear."

"I can feel them draining me even without touching them," Fate said. "Where are my sisters?"

"Straight back and to the right," Sansa whispered. She raised Fate's hand and pushed a small metal object into it. "You can ring this when you are ready for me to get you. I will just be at the top of the stairs."

Fate nodded and heard Sansa's running steps go back the way they came. She slipped the call bell into her pants pocket.

"Sevilla? Zilla?" Her voice caught in her throat, not only for the fear that they were injured, but also with the worry that she hadn't been forgiven. For all the pain she had caused them both. She wouldn't blame them.

"Please let me know you are okay," Fate squeaked. "I don't have much time."

"Fate?" A voice croaked. "Is that you?"

Tears of relief ran warm tracks down her cheeks, and the breath she held came rushing from her lungs. "Sevilla?"

The voices were crowding her mind, sharing the various outcomes that this visit could cause, but she stifled them. She needed to talk to her sisters without interference. She knew that much for sure. Once she picked her path, the voices could help her once more.

She heard chains rattle, then the scrape of metal against stone as her sister slid closer. It didn't sound as if she had risen, merely shuffled across the floor as best she could. She was weak. It pained Fate that she had been treated as a guest, while her sisters suffered in abysmal surroundings.

The voice came from below, and Fate dropped to her knees to meet it.

"Can you be trusted?"

Fate reached through the bars, allowing the magick to drain some of the stores of energy she had been saving. The tears flowed more freely when Sevilla took her hand and gave it a gentle squeeze.

"I could always be trusted," Fate sobbed. "I didn't want to do it... There wasn't a choice."

Sevilla's grip was a little firmer, and Fate pushed all the energy she could into their connection. Fate heard her intake of breath and long sigh. She hoped the shot of energy helped.

"I see your tongue is no longer tied. What was that all about?"

"The riddles and rhymes were Theo's idea," Fate explained. "It was a safeguard, so I wouldn't be able to share his location if I were ever to find where he had gone. I put him in charge of protecting Erebos's shard."

"He's been hidden this entire time?"

"Yes," Fate said. "And his magick held my tongue until just recently."

"Perhaps something happened to him," Sevilla whispered.

"My thoughts precisely. And now, we have run out of time. I believe the Shadowman has left to find the weapon, the one that is the key to his power. Once he finds it, we will need all three of us, as well as the elements, to stop him."

"Zilla and I were taken before the final element was found."

"We must hope that the other three have been able to connect with her."

"If I know Brooke, she has made great progress on the journal and will have more answers by now."

"You have been a good mentor to her, Sevilla."

Sevilla sighed. The sound of her exhale squeezed Fate's heart. She knew what was coming next.

"I've had a lot of time to think since we last spoke."

Even though they didn't have time for it, Sevilla had to be given the chance to say her peace. Fate owed her that much.

"I've come to realize that Ryker was taken from me, not because of what he was, but for what he could give me. A child."

Fate's eyes watered anew. She nodded, confirming what her sister had already sorted for herself. She owed it to her to put it into words.

"Yes," Fate whispered. "It was a path that would not have ended well for any of us. I'm so sorry, Sevilla. It crushed me to hurt you both in that way, but I had no other choice. Has there been any word on him?"

"No." Sevilla whispered. "Only what I could piece together during Roy's visits with Zilla, which didn't happen often."

"There isn't anything of either he or Erebos left," Fate confirmed. "I believe we are out of time. The creature he has become has no remorse. We need to get you and Zilla far away from him. Who knows what he will do with us once he regains his key."

Fate heard a rustling of chains and the scratchy voice of her sister Zilla. "Did someone call my name?"

"Thank the Goddess, you are okay," Fate said. "We can talk about my part to play in this entire mess later. Right now, we need to work on getting you two out of here."

"Oh no," Zilla said. She was now at the bars next to Sevilla from the sound of her voice. "You aren't getting out of your explanation that easy. You are definitely coming with us."

Fate smiled. "I missed you too, Zilla."

"Who said anything about missing you?" Zilla's tone was tired but still laced with the sass Fate had come to know and love. "I just need to know how we fix my damn boyfriend. He's turned into a real ass."

Fate stifled a laugh, while Sevilla let out a chuckle. It felt good to be back with the other pieces of her soul.

"What? Well, he has."

"Be that as it may, the only thing we truly need to worry about is getting out of here before he returns. He is gone now, right Fate?"

"He is, but I don't know for how long. My friend is at the top of the stairs keeping a look out."

"This place makes me sick," Zilla whined. "How are we going to get past these bars when we are completely drained of our magick?"

"I would presume the Shadowman has the keys."

"I could ask Sansa to help me find them."

"In addition, there is a ring," Sevilla said. "A man's design with dragons embossed on the sides and a large sapphire stone in it."

"You mean the one I bought Erebos in the earth realm?"

"Precisely," Sevilla said.

"I saw you had it at your house and couldn't believe you had taken it from me. I took it back."

"I know you did, and while I can't explain now, the true owner has been looking for it ever since. My guess is that it is in something that masks the call of its magick. This entire place could if the walls are any indication."

"Obsidian?" Fate questioned.

"Exactly," Sevilla confirmed. "I believe it is how the Shadowman was able to hide a lot of what he was doing from us. The ring's call won't be heard until we get outside, but it will be helpful."

"The ring has magick?" Zilla sounded surprised.

"It does to those who know it's strength."

"Wish I would have known," Zilla mumbled.

"I'm glad you didn't," Sevilla answered. "The power the owner wields, added to your boyfriend's ambition, would have been a devastating combination."

"Yes, but it could have fixed him."

"Stop it, you two," Fate snapped. "We know what happened last time we tried to fix Erebos." Her comment met her with silence, each woman mulling their own thoughts. Fate proceeded. "We need to decide what we are going to do and then do it as a team. No deviations. Agreed?"

"Yes," Sevilla said.

"Agreed." Zilla's response was less decisive.

"Good." Fate placed her hands through the bars and gripped her sisters'. They formed a circle through the bars and shared the small amount of energy they had retained. Fate was in better shape, since she had been able to remove her necklace for days at a time.

"These bars are made of the same thing he has us wear, isn't it? The same stuff he used to kill with."

"I believe so," Sevilla responded. "It glows with the same energy, brighter as it is fed."

"It is possible he needs the key to channel the energy," Fate mused.

"If we can get to Brooke, we can have her reference the journal. Perhaps there is something in the older pages about it. Or if Theo is still alive..."

"I don't even want to think that he's not," Fate said firmly.

"Whatever this power is, it seems the walls keep it from escaping," Zilla added.

"If that were the case, it would make sense why my friend wasn't able to sense his ring."

"The ring bearer is male?" Zilla teased. Fate could sense a smile in her tone. "Why Sevilla, you are full of surprises."

Her sister ignored the comment and continued; they could argue once they were safe. "The ring would be where, Zilla?"

"Erebos kept it on his nightstand. Once Roy took over, it was worn less. Come to think of it, he had an Obsidian box that he kept it in."

"We'll start there," Fate said. "Pray to the Goddess, that it's here somewhere."

"It has to be," Sevilla said. "My friend would have caught up to it long before now, if he had left the premises wearing it."

Fate stood up and pulled the bell from her pants pocket. After ringing it, she heard her sisters rise as well. She slid the bell in her pocket and took their hands once more. She gave a gentle squeeze and took a deep breath. "I love you. I will look for keys as well as the ring. We will have to be prepared for any outcome."

"What do your voices tell you?" Sevilla said softly.

Fate shook her head. "I've decided there is only one voice I should listen to from now on. My own."

"The future is unknown to us," Zilla questioned.

"No, the future is what we will make of it."

Tiny steps walked toward her from the stairway. Sansa spoke to her in a hushed tone. "Are you ready, my lady?"

"I am. More than you know."

14

Tara looked around Sevilla's house while Theo attempted to find them something to eat. He had built a fire and placed a kettle to boil after finding a tin of tea Sevilla had in one of her cupboards. The fireplace opened to both the kitchen and the living area, where she stood to warm herself. The space was cozy, and the furniture well loved. The rocking chair near the hearth looked to be Sevilla's favorite space. It would be the first place Tara would want to sit as well.

While the house had originally looked abandoned, it was evident people had been present off and on. She had spied some jars of pickles and applesauce over Theo's shoulder earlier, which was the last thing she would think to see in such a rustic kitchen. It must have been something one of the other elements had brought back with them. She offered to help him, but he insisted on foraging alone.

His strong voice called from the kitchen. "Is the chessboard still there?"

"I think so." Tara answered. "There's something on a table by the fireplace, but I don't see a checkerboard pattern. Why? Do you play?"

"I do. I especially like playing with Sevilla's set. You need to do something special to set the pattern." Clanking came from the kitchen. It sounded as though he was setting the table.

Tara walked over to the chessboard, curious to know what he was speaking about. The board looked like a square of black marble, relatively unremarkable if she was honest. There were small drawers in the table, and she slid one open, looking at the tiny statues that lay in the velvet that lined it. Perhaps her hasty judgment wasn't warranted. The pieces were exquisite.

"These are amazing," she said as she lifted the larger robed piece out of its place. Glancing back down, she noted that the queen was also in robes. They looked like tiny Greek statues. "Are they Gods and Goddesses?"

Theo's voice startled her. She hadn't heard him enter the room. "They are. And you need to watch the one you have in your hand."

She looked down and could swear that she had seen the tiny man's head move. Tara looked up at Theo, who grinned and pointed to the piece. "He tends to flirt."

She almost dropped it after the tiny statue gave her a wink. Laying it back in the drawer, she slid it closed and looked up into Theo's smiling face.

"Let me guess — Zeus."

"At least he makes things interesting. I can show you how to work the board after dinner. I've managed to pull something together."

"Sounds perfect," Tara said. "I'm famished."

Theo turned to the side and held out his elbow, creating a space for Tara to place her hand. For such a formal gesture, Theo made it seem casual. It was as if everyone was escorted to the kitchen table. She found his elegant manners part and parcel of who he was. It was one of the things that interested her most about him. He was formal and conscientious but not in a way that made him seem arrogant.

He guided her to the table, and she had been right — it was beautifully set. He had even placed some of the dried lavender and rosebuds that were bundled along the hearth into a glass vase and had lit the jar candle. The added touch made her smile.

He stopped and pulled out her chair, having her sit facing the door. Then he took his seat across from her and gestured to the spread. "I did manage to find a few things."

Tara was amazed, she didn't think there was that much in the cupboards. He managed to take what they had left in their backpacks and add a few cans of things he had found available to create a wonderful Charcuterie display.

"This looks amazing, Theo."

"Help yourself. The almonds and dried fruits were a happy find."

"The wine was as well."

"I hope you like red. I thought it would go well with the meat and cheese. We have tea if you prefer."

"Wine is perfect, thank you." Tara clinked her glass to his then took a sip. "The people Kadar will be bringing — do you know any of them?"

Theo shook his head. "I don't believe so. I've been out of touch so long, I am not sure of anything. I just hope that Fate still has the elemental journal."

"How will that help?"

"It has not only my notes, but the notes of elements past. There is a great deal of knowledge in there about magick systems from a number of sources. I believe it will be of great help as we finish your training."

"Training? Not sure I like the sound of that. You make it seem as if there will be a battle."

Theo sipped his wine and contemplated his response. It made her feel as if he was holding something back. He took a deep breath and spoke softly.

"If the last time the elements were together is any indication, then the battle against evil will be the least of it. The earth has been sending warning signs to its inhabitants."

"Trouble is we aren't listening."

Theo nodded. "Exactly. The volatile weather is a harbinger of things to come. The humans never pay much attention to such things until it devastates a village."

"Even then, most only worry about the places they live in," Tara added. "And the interest wanes at the rearing of a new disaster. I've been watching the patterns too. If we don't start to make changes soon, I'm afraid there won't be a safe place for anyone to live."

"It has happened before," Theo said quietly. "And nature is cyclical, so it will happen again. The last time we got involved, Mt. Vesuvius sent a small warning. She is more active than most people think. I believe it last erupted during your World War II."

"And how were you involved in that?"

"That was when we attempted to draw the power from Erebos. He had become much too strong, and his ambition didn't serve the collective."

"What are you saying? That what you did here caused the volcano to erupt? That what is done here affects our planet?"

"What I'm saying is what everyone does affects everyone else. We are all connected. And nature is at the center, taking care of our needs. Trouble is, she isn't being taken care of anymore. We do our best here to prevent the worst of it."

"Like the mirror symbol," she said quietly.

Theo nodded. "As above, it is below."

Tara was having a hard time wrapping her head around the enormity of the topic. If she were truly meant to harness some great power, it made her wonder what she would be in for. What she would be expected to do in the coming days. It wasn't as simple as finding a magical doorway and meeting the most interesting man of her life. There were things happening all over the planet that were changing lives, devastating communities. Countries were killing each other for resources, and she wondered how one person would make a difference. If it was even worth trying.

Tara had gotten a second wind, and neither of them seemed tired after dinner, so they set up the chess pieces and started a game. Theo showed her how the board worked. With a wave of his hand, half the squares lit in a dull glow and created a checkerboard pattern. Once the pieces were set and another glass of wine was poured, they sat down to their game.

She was delighted to see that when a piece was captured, the figures acted out a scene and battled to the death. In Zeus's case, the nymph pawns didn't mind being taken by him and giggled and groped as they disappeared. Tara quickly learned they would end up back in the drawer, but she was better off not looking, depending on who was sent in there. The pieces had no shame.

About mid-way through the game, Tara stifled a yawn. The wine was catching up to her, and the fire was cozy.

"We can finish this game later," Theo said. He stood and put out his hand. "I can show you to your room."

She took his hand, and his strong fingers wrapped around hers. She had that sense of place again, of being grounded, as if she had come home. She couldn't help it. There was just something about him that seemed right.

"You're staying with me, right?" She tried to hide the worry in her tone. Staying alone in a strange place wasn't something she particularly wanted to do. Especially, with all their talk over their game of power-hungry sorcerers and energy-draining harpies. After learning about what Theo had been asked to hide and realizing it had now been left unguarded, she wasn't keen on ever being alone again.

"I wasn't planning on it," Theo answered as he led her up the stairs. "But if you want me to, I can."

Tara nodded. "I would prefer that."

Theo gave her hand a squeeze before opening the door at the end of the hallway and escorting her in. She poked around as he made a fire, and she was delighted to find as rustic as the house was, there was still indoor plumbing. The bathroom was small but serviceable. And the large wooden tub was something she had never seen before.

"This is an interesting tub," she called out. "Sides have to be about four feet high."

"It's an Ofuro, a Japanese Soaking Tub," Theo explained from the doorway. "It's amazing for stiff joints and aching muscles."

"Pretty much me every day," Tara laughed. "There's a shower here as well. I love this set-up."

"The idea is to wash in one and soak in the other. This is the guest room I used to use," Theo explained. "I was always most comfortable here. I guess maybe because of the amount of wood."

"It's beautiful. Like being in a spa. I would love a quick shower. Do you think it would be okay?"

"Absolutely," Theo said. "Towels are in that cupboard, or at least they were the last time I was here. I can see if I can find you something to change into, in the meantime. I'll clean up in one of the other rooms."

Theo gave her a quick nod then pulled the door closed behind him. It was the first time Tara had been alone in two days, and while she generally didn't mind the solitude, she was really beginning to enjoy Theo's company. Ever since his voice first wandered into her life, he had become the part of her daily routine that she most looked forward to.

She found the towels just where Theo had said they were and hoped he would have some luck finding something for her to wear. Her clothes weren't super dirty, but she had been trekking in them over the past couple of days. She pulled the inside zipper in her pack and tugged on the black lace she had stuffed in there after meeting the tattooed hunk at work. While Tyler had ended up being a dud, she was never so glad she had forgotten about the clean pair of panties she had packed.

The shower was heaven, the water poured down like the rain, and she was surprised once more that there were products from home dotted around the bathroom. She didn't need much with the new haircut, as a matter of fact, she generally used bar soap for everything. She had gotten in that habit after camping. Every once in a while, she enjoyed the girly shampoos, and she was thrilled to see one of her favorite scents in the shower stall. She dried off and wrapped the towel around her, smelling of peaches and cream and feeling much better. Her clothes were hung on the hook, as were her red panties that she had washed in the sink. Time to see if Theo had found her anything to wear.

She poked her head out into the room, but no Theo. She did spy a man's tee shirt with a pair of shorts on the bed and wondered who it was that was in the Army. Another sign this place touched the home that she was familiar with. Perhaps the myths and legends had a vein of truth in them, and the beings that were written about were creatures from a place like this. The power that allowed these two worlds to connect must be great indeed. She could see why they didn't want one person to wield it.

The shorts were too big, and the shirt hung on her to mid-thigh. Since they would be in bed anyway, she figured the shirt alone would do. She hoped that when the others got there, she would be able to borrow a few things, since she wasn't really looking forward to putting her stinky clothes back on. They were in worse shape than she thought now that she had showered.

She was standing by the fire when she heard a light knock on the door. "Come in," she called out and went back to gazing at the fire. She heard the door open, but no steps. Curious, she looked over her shoulder to see Theo partially through the threshold, dressed in flannel pajama bottoms and staring at her as if she had grown another head.

"What?" She questioned. "Is there something on me?" She turned and attempted to look at her own backside, before looking up at an unmoving Theo. His eyes were hooded, and she could tell from the way his chest paused that his breath had caught. He managed a head shake in response to her question. Had he seen something that scared him?

She crossed the room and met him where he stood. His hair was damp from the shower and slicked back, giving her a better view of his chiseled jawline and ears. Her hand raised of its own accord. Not wanting to be rude, and before it reached its destination, she looked into his eyes and asked permission. "May I?"

Theo nodded. His response was gravely. "Of course." He cleared his throat and tipped his head to the side, bringing it closer to her out-reached hand. Not scared, interested.

When Tara's fingers touched the outer edge, she heard a slight intake of breath and pulled her hand back in concern. "Does that hurt?"

He shook his head and guided her hand back to his ear. His hand cupped hers for a moment, and she hadn't realized how cold her fingers had been. "Doesn't hurt," he replied in a whisper. "Just sensitive."

She smoothed her fingers up toward the point on the top of his ear. The only difference between them that she could visibly see. "Sorry my hands are cold," she whispered.

After her examination, she lowered her hand, and Theo took both of hers in his. "That isn't quite what I meant about them being sensitive," he said. His eyes warmed her, and his voice twisted her stomach. "Let's get you by the fire."

Theo stepped into the room fully and closed the door. He led her to the couch by the fire, never once releasing her hand. Thoughts were racing through her head and other parts, if she were being honest with herself. She knew what her lady parts expected next. Trouble was, she wasn't sure Theo would be willing. The connection was definitely there, more so than it had been with any other man in her life. But he was hard to read.

He motioned for her to sit, which she did at one end of the couch, curling her legs up under her and leaning on the armrest. He glanced down, and she heard a quiet moan, causing her to pull her borrowed shirt down over her ass cheeks. He busied himself finding her a blanket and covering her legs.

"Thank you," she said with a grin. "I just couldn't do the shorts, they would have been too bulky."

He sat on the opposite end of the couch and spoke as he looked into the fire. "I don't mind."

It wasn't what he said but how he said it. He felt the connection too. She was as sure of it as she was of her own name. She was fascinated by this man, wanted to know so much more about him. The impending visit from the other elements, and the possibility that they would all have to fight a great evil, had her making her choice.

"Why are you sitting so far away?"

"It is what is proper," he said. "Is it not?" If she wasn't mistaken, the last bit sounded hopeful.

"Are you always this proper?" She couldn't help the smile in her voice. The dip in the octave was noticed.

Theo laughed, relief coming off him in waves. She could feel the tension leave his body, and anticipation took its place. "Not always."

He looked at her with the knowing stare of a man who would be having his dreams come true. His response, along with the firelight, had warmed her — enough that she let the blanket slide as she shifted her body toward him.

"I'm happy to hear that," she said with a laugh. "You have no idea what a relief that is."

As she slid closer, he raised his arm to drape around her. Her head fit perfectly against his shoulder, and she sighed into the embrace. His response vibrated against her cheek.

"I think I may have an inkling."

She laughed at the old-fashioned word. It was one of the things she liked the most about talking to him. "Now that's a word that doesn't get used every day."

He pulled her tighter. "It's a good word. One that pretty much sums it up." He looked down to her, and she turned her head to meet his gaze. It was his habit to look her in the eye when he said something important. "Are you sure about this?"

Tara tried not to let the excitement show in her response. "Of course." She was more than ready. "Are you?"

He smiled softly, his eyes creasing in the corners as they always did. His response was not much more than a whisper. "I've been ready since the first day we met. I just worry about your energy."

She was smiling as he lowered his lips to hers, and she tipped up her head to meet him. "Isn't what we are about to do about give and take?" His arm tightened, and she raised hers to his shoulder, gently pulling in as a physical sign of her desire. "I promise to be careful," she whispered. The kiss was exploratory, testing the boundaries of what they each expected from the moment.

Theo glanced up at her hair. Then a sigh of relief and a smile. Tara felt fine, but as promised, had pulled a partial curtain around her energy. It was time to turn up the intensity. All she knew was that she needed to be closer. Visions of hands, lips and tongues and what they would do in a matter of moments filled her mind. The emotions that were born from it fueled the fire. His guard was down, she felt his heart, and it was the place she wanted to be. The kiss would never be enough for her, tonight or any night. She was willing to risk a little white hair to take care of her current frustration.

She twisted her body and slid her leg over his lap. His arms came up around her and helped her shift, so she was dead center on his groin.

She could feel its length through the thin lace of her panties, and the kissing started anew. They were both wild with it, and as she moved over his length to feel him against her, it brought her a realization she hadn't thought of until that moment.

"Condoms." Her body slumped in defeat.

"What?" His arms loosened from around her waist. He looked pained, and her squirming wasn't helping matters.

"I have to look for something." What the hell was she thinking? She didn't have any with her or did she? She hopped off the lap of a surprised Theo and went to look through her fanny pack.

"Tara, I…"

"I think I might have one in here." She dug around in the contents, opening zippers in the hopes that she would find at least one. "By all that is holy, please let me have one in here."

Tara heard Theo stand up and walk toward her. She couldn't find one. How on earth was she going to face him? If he was anywhere near as worked up as she was, he was ready to explode.

His voice was soothing. "It's okay…"

It wasn't okay, she really wanted this. She found it hard to believe she could have an extra change of underwear but not a damn condom. It wasn't like they went stale. "I think I may have one. I mean, I don't usually carry them around. I mean I do, since a girl can never be too prepared…"

"Tara," he chuckled. "I think I have what you are looking for."

Tara stopped shuffling in the pack and looked over to him. He was tenting out the flannel pajama bottoms and holding a foil package in his hand. The look on his face was half humor, half worry. He was not in the physical state to put the brakes on now. Frankly, neither was she.

"Oh," Tara said. "Well, why didn't you say so?"

15

Theo stood holding a tiny foil packet, hoping it was the key to Tara's kingdom. He had never desired a woman so strongly in his life. The thought he could be close to spending the night with her based on whether he had made the right guess was more than he could bear.

He had spied the condoms earlier in his search for something to wear. Zilla had been the one that had mentioned them years ago, and while they never had the sort of relationship that would warrant one, she was happy to chat about her sexual escapades. Since she spent a lot of time with humans, she was used to his endless fascination with them.

He had taken a few out of curiosity more than anything else, since he had never used one. It was sheer luck that had him tucking them into the pocket of his borrowed flannel pants. "I thought this might be something… I read about these…"

Relief swept over Tara's face, and her shoulders relaxed as she stepped toward him. It was precisely what she had been looking for, and the waves of her passion were starting anew. He should warn her not to share so much, but her energy was addicting — he could feel every one of her emotions. It was like reading the pages in a book, albeit it was like reading a book that tightened his balls and staff. He tended to stay away from those.

"Where did you find that?"

"It was in the blue room up the hall. It's where I found these." He indicated down to the pajama pants, and their heads looked down in unison. When he looked up, she was still staring at his predicament.

She pointed to his erection. "Did you find that in there as well?" She looked up at him with a wicked grin and walked a step closer. She smelled of peaches and sunshine.

"No. This has been making an appearance off and on since the day you walked into my life," he said honestly. He was happy to see his comment made her glow.

She took one last step, bumping into his erection and sliding her arm up around his neck. "Well, I guess we need to do something about that."

"Indeed, we do." He pulled back slightly and held up the small foil package. "However, if this has a part to play in what we are doing next, I will need some tutelage."

She tipped her head and a confused look swept over her face. "You've never used a condom?"

He shook his head. "It wasn't something... what I mean to say is..."

"Just spit it out, Theo," Tara said with a grin.

"While I am familiar with the concept of what these do, I have never had need for one. My partners generally had no need for such things and if they did, they took care of it."

"I see," Tara said. He wasn't sure he liked the tone. There was something she didn't like about his last comment, but he couldn't tell what. Knowing Tara, he would find out soon enough. If he knew nothing else by now, he knew she spoke her mind.

"I guess it wouldn't be fair for me to ask how many partners, considering how long you have lived," she mumbled. "So, how about this? When was the last time you did this?"

"Stood and had a discussion with a woman about my past lovers while sporting a powerful erection?"

She laughed aloud, and the sound of it filled his heart with joy. It startled him to feel her hand wrap around his penis through the flannel, but she had his attention.

"No. When was the last time you used this?" Between the low tone of her voice and the smooth pressure she was applying to his staff, he was ready to explode. He knew what she was asking.

"A few hundred years," he groaned. She slid her hand up and down his staff and moved closer.

"That's a long time," she said. "We'll need to do something about that also." She raised her left hand, palm up. "Hand me the package."

He dropped the foil package in her hand and immediately regretted the decision. The warmth from her hand disappeared, as she walked over to the bed and sat down. He stood there watching her, unsure of what she wanted him to do. In all his years, he had never had such insecurities with his prowess. But with her, it was different. With her, he wanted to be sure he was everything she needed.

He let out a sigh of relief when she crooked her finger and wiggled it, indicating he should move toward her. She spread her legs and pulled him to the edge of the bed between them. His erection jumped in response, but thankfully, her head was down, working on opening the foil package, so she missed it. She put the opened package on the nightstand then slid her legs up on the bed, so he could join her. As soon as he hit the bed, she straddled him, and the kisses started once more.

Against his nature, he allowed her to take the lead. It didn't matter what history he was coming to her with, she had her own set of needs and desires, and he would be happy to spend a lifetime learning each and every one. The change he was embracing was surprising but liberating. When the kisses paused, he looked up into her beaming face and practically heard the lock on his heart open with a click. He was hers.

She pulled the tee shirt from her body in one swift motion then sat back and waited for his response. His pulse stuttered, and his eyes widened to take her in. Her creamy breasts pebbled in anticipation, and he knew it was the next place his lips needed to be. The next steps weren't going to happen with him lying on his back and his pants on. He pulled her down to him, kissing her with the fever he felt inside, and rolling over until she was beneath him. She squeaked in delight, and her hands made busy work of tugging at his flannel pants.

"Part two requires these to be taken off," she said between kisses. She managed to get them down below his hips, and he kicked them off the rest of the way. As he came back up her body, he allowed himself to pay homage to her beautiful breasts. She arched at his attention, bucking up against his erection and causing him to pray to the Gods that he would be able to last.

He felt her hands on either side of his head, thumbs grazing the shell of his ears and working their way up to the point. He shook his head gently and moved up her body to her face. "You can touch those during part four."

Curiosity sparkled in her eyes and realization laced her tone. "Well then, we better get the other steps moving."

He raised up on his knees as she twisted her body to grab the package from the nightstand. Slipping the rounded latex from the package, she touched it to the head of his penis and rolled the excess back slowly. The sensation was not unpleasant, and he took great pleasure in having her hands on his body in such a way. She swept the black lace she was wearing off in one swift motion. With a wicked gleam in her eyes, she crooked her finger at him. "Time for part three."

He willingly complied, kissing the other parts of her that had been crying for attention as he worked his way up. He started at her core, at the perfection that she had finally unwrapped for him. It was his for the taking. He spread her legs wider and smiled at her gasp as his tongue tasted her for the first time. Her bucking slowed his progress, but he finally prevailed, pulling a small scream from her as her first orgasm racked her body.

He could feel the moment when she let go. Her fears cast to the wind in abandon. For some reason, it brought a lump to his throat. It was an incredible moment, to be able to experience how he made her feel. In moments, she was tugging on his arms and pulling him up toward her. He didn't need to be told, he could feel her passion and curiosity. Her willingness to open her heart to him. He would have to have a talk with her about building her emotional guards, but so far, her hair remained dark. He relished in the connection.

She cupped his cheeks and looked into his eyes. They were wet, had she been crying? "Tara?"

"I'm fine," she laughed. "Kiss me, Theo."

The joy bubbled over and wrapped around them. He kissed her as if his life depended on it, which in reality, he felt it very well could. He kissed her in the hopes that every confusing thought and hesitation in his mind would work itself out before being transmitted to her. He knew she connected to his emotions too, and he knew he would need to get his feelings straightened out if he wanted her in his life. He kissed her with the truth that she would be the last woman that he would ever love. There was no doubt about that in his mind.

Her hands were back on his ears, naturally caressing the very place that drove him wild. She knew without him telling her, smiling in delight between their kisses and wiggling her hips in invitation.

His voice was deep. He was beyond ready. He covered her neck and shoulders in kisses, murmuring between. "Ready for part four?"

"Yes. Oh, Theo, hurry."

He didn't hesitate. He slid into her and relished the feel of it. The sensation was unique and as he thrusted, he found the tiny lines on the condom gave her great pleasure. They were kissing again, and her hands were on his ears, rubbing the points frantically as her body prepared for another release. He waited as long as he could and thanked the universe when he felt the pulse of her second orgasm. Her hands remained on his ears as she bucked, and it shot a spark of lust to his groin he could no longer hold back. He lost himself as the years of pent up frustration left his body at last.

When he opened his eyes and finally looked down, Tara was looking up at him with a sated smile. He was still semi-hard and relishing the feel of her warmth. He lowered down to his elbows and kissed her gently. It was a kiss from a man, who had lost his heart to a woman who knew she had captured it — long before he had realized it himself. It made him wonder when she had first known.

He leaned up and pressed his lips to her forehead before lowering to the tip of her nose and then her rose petal lips. Three kisses representing mind, breath, and voice in his culture. Something he had always known but had never done with another soul. He would tell her later that it signified that she would always be in his thoughts, he would love her until his last breath, and that he would never forget to voice his affection for her.

"I need to know something," she whispered. He was busy nuzzling her neck and responded against it.

"Anything."

She hesitated, which caused him to rise up and look into her face. There were tears welling in her eyes, and he had been right. She had been crying. He lifted a hand to caress her cheek, wiping a stray tear with the pad of his thumb.

Her voice was wobbly, her emotions scattered. "I just wondered if perhaps the energy in this place influenced how... I mean, I've never felt anything that intensely before... I just wasn't sure..."

Theo slipped his finger over her lips to quiet her. "Shhh now. I won't have you thinking that magick had anything to do with our connection. It goes way deeper than that for me."

She closed her eyes and breathed deep in a sigh of relief. "It was so powerful. I didn't want to be the only one — "

"Who was feeling the connection?"

"Exactly." She lowered her eyes to hide her embarrassment. He waited until she looked back up before he spoke. He needed her to understand and believe his truth.

"We most definitely have a connection. And I am acknowledging it here and now. It goes deeper than the magick we are surrounded by, and I am a willing participant in seeing where it leads us."

She pulled him down to her and wrapped her arms around his neck, holding him close enough for him to feel the sobs that she had attempted to hide. He wasn't worried, they were tears of joy. He could feel her happiness as it covered him in waves.

"Thank you, Theo. You said just the right thing."

"Easy to do when it's the truth."

"When you put it like that, it seems so simple."

He leaned back slightly, so he could look at her. "If people were honest about their feelings from the start, things would be much less complicated. Don't you agree?"

"I do," she said. "Leave it to you to sum it up so eloquently. I am so glad I met you, Theo."

"And I, you," he replied. He gave her one last kiss and slid to her side. She turned from him and snuggled her way back to him. Her contented sigh came to him, as his arms gathered her body to his. "Now, let's get some sleep. I have the feeling tomorrow is going to be a busy day."

She leaned over the side of the bed and pulled her shirt from the floor, slipping it on with a tug. She settled her head into her pillow, lacing her fingers with his and pulling it tight to her chest. Her emotions roiled once more: first insecurity, then worry, and lastly fear. He pulled her tight against his frame, spooning against her and sharing his stability. It helped her settle and soon, he heard the soft snores of her deep sleep. Tara shared her feelings with him even in sleep and remembering the morning at the Inn, he pried his arm out of her embrace and slid a few inches away from her. She had been right, sex had been give and take and hadn't been a strain on her system, but what they did in their sleep still couldn't be controlled.

He slid a pillow up behind her before taking his place on the other side of it. They couldn't remain in each other's arms. It would have to be good enough for her that they were in the same bed. First thing in the morning, they would continue her training. She needed to learn how to turn the blocks to her empath abilities off and on at will, first and foremost. For tonight, he would put guards up for them both. It seemed his honesty would have limits, at least until he could be sure she fully understood what she was capable of.

Now that he knew she would be part of his life, he needed to hold her and know that she was safe in his arms. Until she learned to control her powers though, neither of them were safe.

16

Theo was dressed and moving before Tara awoke, which irritated her. She had hoped, with the fantastic sex they had the night before, that she was due for a repeat that morning. It was apparent Theo had other plans. She followed his sexy gait as he added wood to the fire and stoked it.

"Are you always this active in the mornings?"

He stood and looked at her with delight. "Ah, you are awake! Excellent."

"Why? Did you have something you needed me for?" She couldn't help the hopeful tone in her voice.

He nodded then turned and stoked the fire. "I have a lot to show you today."

"You could come over here and show me."

He glanced at her over his shoulder, his expression confused. He shook his head and stood up. "I think it would be best to go outside for our session."

She perked up. "Outside could be fun."

Again, he tipped his head, this time taking a few steps forward toward the bed where she sat propped up. "Why do I get the feeling you and I are speaking of two entirely separate things?"

With her balloon sufficiently deflated, Tara swept the covers from her legs and hopped off the bed. She searched the sheets for her black lace cheekies, which were wedged at the foot of the bed. She straightened and looked back at him, prepared to give him a snappish reply. The look on his face stopped her short, and she quickly realized the Army shirt she had pulled on in the night wasn't quite long enough to cover her ass as she bent forward.

"You sure we aren't talking about the same things?" She had sass in her tone, she couldn't help it. It had been a long time since she had the attention of an attractive man, and she had never been one to hold back on pursuing mutual interests.

His eyes rose to hers quickly, as if he was caught doing something he shouldn't, then he cleared his throat. "Why, what is it that you are talking about?"

She strolled past him, holding the cheekies in one hand and pulling the tee shirt off with the other. A glance over her shoulder confirmed he was watching. "I suppose you will have to come into the shower to find out."

His feet were already moving him to follow, even with his denial. "But I've already taken one."

A wicked grin and a shrug of her shoulder presented the comment she shot over her shoulder. "Yes, but I haven't."

She walked into the bathroom, ever so glad she heard his hurried steps behind her. Ah yes, finally. Now they were on the same page.

Theo managed to find a few more pieces of clothing while she was finishing up in the shower, so Tara could at least wear a clean shirt. It reminded her of something Brooke would wear, a tied-dyed pattern with green and blue, that would have matched the streaks in her long blonde hair. The thought occurred to her there was a definite chance she would be missing the bridal shower in California that was planned. There was no telling how long Tara would be stuck in Wisteria.

When they finally made it outside, Taksi was there to greet them. It made her think about Misty again. If Brooke's cat had been pissed the other night over a delay in dinner, she would be super miffed now. Thankfully, the neighbor boy had a key and would be by to keep her company. It made her feel bad though, and she wondered, if she ever did manage to get home, if Taksi and Misty would get along.

Theo led her to the back, where she got a better look at the black tree they had seen before. She walked up to it and placed her hand on the surface. It was jet black and smooth like glass, even though the shape reminded her of lava shooting up out of a volcano.

"That wasn't here last time," Theo said.

"Last time for you was a while ago though, right?"

"1944, by your calendar," he answered. He draped his arm around her and leaned sideways to kiss the top of her head. He was definitely more affectionate than he had been before. She preferred him that way. The shower had done the trick, either that or her promise to not let her guards down.

"That was a while ago. Wonder what caused it?"

"My guess is a burst of molten lava from the ground that was cooled suddenly. It is most definitely black obsidian but how it was created is a mystery."

"Perhaps one of the others will know," Tara suggested.

"Speaking of that, we should get started before they arrive."

"Okay, what is it you need me to do?"

Theo pointed to the space in front of him. "I'll have you stand here and face me. Like we did the other day."

Tara complied, removing her socks and shoes as they had done before. She was going to need to invest in some comfortable slip on shoes if they were going to keep this up. She tucked her socks into her boots then tossed them a few feet from where they stood, so they wouldn't trip over them. Taksi proceeded to give them a thorough sniff.

They joined hands, and his thumb caressed her knuckles. It was soothing and different than holding hands had been before. The simple connection felt more intimate to her now.

"There are a couple of things you will need to practice on your own," Theo said. "The most important is for you to get better at blocking your energy stores."

"The cocoon thing you showed me the other day?"

Theo nodded. "Precisely. Our connection during sex doesn't seem to be an issue, but I do worry that you will overdo it at other points in the day and share too much of yourself with me."

"That shouldn't be a bad thing in a relationship."

"In our case, it can be dangerous until you are able to shield yourself. Especially while we sleep, it can be toxic for you to be drained to the point where you can't wake up. Depending on my situation, I might not be able to reverse it. I can't ever let what happened at the inn happen again, and frankly, it is getting harder for me to keep my distance from you."

The serious tone of his words had her swallowing any sassy rebuttal she could have come up with. But she was happy with his confirmation of their intimacy. "I'll practice, I promise."

"Good." Theo nodded then spaced his feet shoulder-width apart. He continued speaking as he prepared his stance. "The magick that controls the Earth element is passive. Your use of it will be more about putting up defenses and promoting healing. However, if the fight comes to you, you will need to do things that are more offensive in nature."

She straightened her stance and looked into his eyes. It was important for him to know she was taking him seriously. The time for play had ended in their shower. "I'm ready."

"When we practiced in the woods, you connected to your surroundings, is that right?"

"Yes. I could feel the trees and even Taksi at one point." Taksi stopped rolling on the ground and looked over, most likely because her name had been called. Tara's shoe fell out of her paws and down onto the ground beside her.

Taksi don't chew.

TARA SMELL. NO CHEW.

The large feline got to her feet and sniffed toward the discarded boot. She strutted off, flicking her tail much like Misty would when she was scolded for something. Tara had the feeling that the two of them would get along just fine.

"Sorry, I had to say something to her real quick. I'm ready."

"Much like before, you will close your eyes and connect to your surroundings. When you are ready, nod your head, and I can guide you through the next step. It will be best for you to keep your eyes closed, so you can visualize what I am saying to you. Eventually, you will be able to do the same with your eyes open."

Tara nodded and closed her eyes. She widened her stance and stood straight, breathing in deeply and tuning her senses into her surroundings. She was immediately connected with Sevilla's yard, and she understood the benefit to having her eyes closed. With one of her senses gone, the others were stronger. She wondered if the ability to channel all senses down to a single one was something she would be able to do. It would be something to discuss later.

She put herself out there, visualizing roots growing from her feet and pushing deep into the earth. The tree behind them was definitely obsidian, and she felt its fiery pulse through the fingers she sent out in all directions. The stone was powerful but didn't interfere with her magick. If anything, it made her feel better.

"Good," Theo said softly. "Now, I need you to focus on the trees within Sevilla's property and request they help you. I want you to visualize a wall of twisting vines and get the trees to comply with your request."

Tara sent her intent to the root systems of the trees. She wasn't exactly sure what Theo was expecting and struggled a little before settling on a design. She kept the image in her mind and no sooner had she said please, she heard the rumble of the tree's response.

She was tempted to open her eyes but kept them closed tight. She heard the ground cracking, and rocks and dirt shifting as it made way for the roots pushing their way from the ground.

"Excellent," Theo said as he gave her hands a gentle squeeze. "You are doing amazing, Tara. Although, it doesn't look exactly like a wall."

She smiled at his confused tone and kept her eyes tightly shut. "I was shooting for an arch."

"Ah, well I think you succeeded. Want to take a look?"

She opened her eyes and looked to the place where she asked the roots to go. They were still forming the arch shaped sculpture she had requested, coming out of two areas in the ground about six feet apart and winding their way down toward the other side. The arch looked like one of the pictures Brooke had sent her when they were talking about wedding ideas. The roots reminded Tara of curly willow.

"It's beautiful! Can the roots go back?"

"They will do anything you ask of them. I find trees are the most helpful of all the natural materials. I used them before in battle to wrap around my enemies. Stone is a little harder to manipulate."

"I would imagine so." Tara took a breath, then sent her intent toward the squirming roots and imagined the space as it was before. She watched, amazed, as the roots unwound themselves from each other and sank back into the loosened dirt. Soon, there were only two small areas of disrupted earth and gravel.

Theo pulled her into a hug. "Fantastic job! You're amazing."

She pulled back and looked up into his excited face. His enthusiasm was contagious, and she couldn't help the grin that split her face.

"You caught on and did that with your eyes open. That happened much quicker than I thought it would."

MAN COMES.
Where is Taksi?
WOODS TRAVELED.

"Taksi said there is a man coming. She's at the front of the house." She hurried to grab her shoes and started to walk toward the front.

"Only those we planned for will be allowed to get through the wards." He pointed to the shoes Tara held in her hands. "You should put those on just in case we need to move quickly."

Tara sat on the bench near the front door, while Theo sat on the ground next to her. They made quick work of pulling their boots on, and as they were finishing the lacing, they spied Kadar come out of the tree line and into the clearing.

He stopped just outside the perimeter of the stone fence and raised his hands to his sides with his hands splayed. Moving them as if he were running them against glass, he nodded his head. At first, Tara thought perhaps their barrier was going to stop him, but then he walked through it as though it was made of the air they were breathing.

"Impressive," he shouted out as he waved. "Sera and Logan are behind me."

"Who are Sera and Logan again?" Tara whispered to Theo, who shrugged his shoulders.

"Not sure, guess we'll find out."

She and Theo walked halfway to the stone fence to await their guests. Tara saw movement from the tree line behind Kadar then saw Taksi bolting toward him as if she were going to pounce on him. She ran past, skirting around the two of them before darting to the back yard.

WOLF. HIDE.

"Taksi said there was a wolf coming," Tara whispered to Theo.

"It won't be able to get through even if it ventures this far," he replied. He kept his eyes on their approaching guest, who walked up the pathway with purpose.

"Sera contacted the others," Kadar said as he approached. "She and Logan are bringing supplies. We'll have a houseful for dinner."

"Will they all be staying here?" Tara had noticed four rooms at the top of the stairs, but it didn't look like there was more than one on the lower level.

"We can sort that out when they get here. In the meantime, I'll head in and start the fire," Kadar offered.

Theo nodded his agreement. After Kadar entered the house, Tara looked back out into the tree line. She still didn't see any sign of the wolf that Taksi had mentioned, but she did see a couple walking toward them.

The man had long dark hair and the start of a beard. Was that a kilt he was wearing? The white sleeved shirt was left untucked, and his black boots looked utilitarian in nature. He was carrying two large bags, both hoisted over his left shoulder, so he could hold hands with the woman walking beside him on his right.

The woman was in jeans and a flannel shirt, one that belonged to the enormous man walking next to her by the look of it. It came to her knees and was belted at her waist. Her hair was a lion's mane, black, curly and poofing out like it had a life of its own. It wasn't until she was closer that Tara realized there were bright red streaks in it. She didn't wear makeup, but in Tara's opinion, she didn't need to.

"You must be Tara and Theo," the woman said, extending her hand. "I'm Sera Blackwood."

17

Tara took Sera's hand in hers and was instantly warmed by the connection. The woman's brilliant smile sparkled in her eyes, like she was privy to a delicious secret. Tara immediately liked her. She took a step back for Theo to introduce himself.

"Nice to meet you," she and Theo both said.

Sera pointed to the man standing next to her. He too had a way about him. The couple's energy was extremely compelling. "This is my husband, Logan."

Tara waved, and Theo gave him a nod after shaking his hand. "The name Blackwood sounds familiar. Any relation to the Lopez clan?"

Logan shook his head. "Nay. Not the Blackwoods, we come from a different pack. But Sera's roots extend to that clan through her grandmother. Are ya friends with the family?" The Scottish accent connected the kilt in Tara's mind.

"I was," Theo said with a sad smile. "My friend passed some time ago, before your time."

Logan tipped his head. The comment had confused him.

"Sorry for your loss," Sera said sincerely.

"Thank you. He was a loyal friend," Theo responded.

"Aye, the family is loyal, but they have their share of troubles. The alpha is a right pain in the arse."

"Logan!" Sera's head snapped sideways, and her eyes squinted at her husband. Tara watched in awe as the towering man before her took her hand in his and kissed it gently.

"Sorry, my love. You know I am right."

She shook her head. "I do, but we…never mind. Tara, where should we put these?" Sera was pointing to the bags Logan still had over his shoulder, and he was still looking at her forlornly. Tara felt sorry for him. He looked like a lost puppy.

"I can help you with those if you'd like, Logan," Theo offered.

"Nay, I have them. Just lead the way."

Once inside the kitchen, the women put the supplies into the cupboards. At Sera's suggestion, they opened a bottle of wine and pulled down ten glasses. Not all of them were wine glasses, some of them were jelly jars, but Tara was sure anyone who wanted a drink wouldn't care. Sera cut up some cheese and sausage, while Tara passed filled glasses to the men. Kadar stepped into the living area, as the others sat around the large wooden table centered in the room.

It seemed Logan had been forgiven for his outburst, since Sera was sitting close enough to him to exchange whispers and secret glances. Tara had never seen a couple so in love, and it caused her to cover Theo's hand in her own.

"The others should be here any minute," Sera explained. "I got a hold of Amie, and she was going to call the others." She looked at Tara pointedly and explained. "Amie is Air, her husband is — "

"A pain in the arse," Logan interjected. His comment caused Sera to glare and pull her hand from his.

"You really need to stop with that already. He is here to stay, so you just need to get over yourself."

Tara felt Sera's emotions; she was irritated, but not angry. If anything, she was used to dealing with Logan's attitude. It seemed Logan might have an opinion about most things, but when it came to his wife, she had the final say.

"Anyway, as I was saying. Amie's husband, Aleck, is an air marshal, and she's a pilot. She was going to get a hold of Brooke and the others after her flight."

Tara's ears perked up at the name. "Brooke?" The name was too much of a coincidence. Wasn't it?

Sera nodded. "Yeah, she's the element..."

There was a swift knock then the door opened, and a clean-shaven man with his hair cut close to his head stepped in. He gave Sera a curt nod then continued to scan the room before stepping aside to let the woman in behind him. Tara heard a throaty rumble then looked to Sera, who had given Logan's arm a slap.

"I came as soon as I could," the woman in the doorway said. "The airport had delays."

The woman slipped off her coat and put it on the hook near Sera's. It seemed everyone was familiar with Sevilla's house and where she kept things. Unlike Sera, this woman was tall and lean, and her golden-red hair was all natural, or at least looked to be from what Tara could see. It was swept up in a serviceable bun, and now that her coat was removed, Tara recognized the uniform.

"I'm Amie Petridis, Element of Air," the woman said with a friendly grin. "This is my boyfriend, Aleck Eyres."

He walked to Theo and shook his hand then gave Tara a two-fingered wave. As he turned, she could have sworn she saw him flip off a sulking Logan before greeting Sera. The move was subtle, but the testosterone filling the room was anything but. Tara didn't need to be an empath to know that there was something between the two.

"I'm Tara, and this is Theo. We have some wine poured if you would like some," Tara offered.

"None for me, thanks," Amie replied. "Tara, you will have to fill us in on your story when the others get here. We all have one, don't we, honey?"

"Every time we come here," Aleck grumbled. He wasn't happy they were here, which stemmed more from his concern about his girlfriend and less because he didn't like the company. At least, that was what Tara was picking up on.

"It was definitely strange coming here," Tara admitted. "I'm looking forward to hearing everyone else's story. I'm guessing, Amie, since you are the Element of Air, and Sera here seems to be giving me Fire vibes, that the missing element is Water."

Sera smiled. "I give off Fire vibes you say?"

"That's because me love is flaming hot," Logan said proudly. His comment warranted him a kiss and a nuzzle, which prompted a shake of Aleck's head and an eye roll.

"They're newlyweds," Amie said by way of explanation.

It wouldn't have mattered if they had been married for three decades, Tara got the impression they would have still acted the same.

"Do the men have powers as well?" Tara was curious, especially about Logan since there seemed to be something strange about him.

"I suppose anti-power is my power. Magick doesn't seem to affect me," Aleck explained.

"That can come in handy," Kadar said. Tara had almost forgotten he was in the house. He had been on the other side of the fireplace during the greetings.

"Indeed," Theo added. "And you, Logan?"

"Just a Lycan, tho' that's powerful enough."

"Lycan? As in werewolf?" Tara was confused at first, but the pieces fell quickly into place. Taksi had caught a whiff of his essence, not a wolf's.

"Aye," Logan said cautiously. "Will that be a problem, Lassie?"

Tara shook her head. "Of course not, I've just never met... I mean, I didn't realize..."

Sera laughed. "Don't worry about it, Tara. There will be a lot of firsts for you. We've all been through some shit."

"What about you, Theo?" Amie asked. "Do you have any abilities?"

"A few," Theo confessed. "Most of them were taken from me years ago."

"He's an old family friend of Sevilla and her sisters," Kadar explained.

"Considering how long the three sisters of Destiny have been alive, that makes ya pretty old," Logan stated. Sera shot him a look, and he shrugged. "What? I'm just statin' a fact, my heart."

"Let's just say I've been around longer than some of the trees outside."

"That's a long damn time," Aleck muttered.

"You have no idea," Theo said, which prompted a laugh from the group. It seemed that the ice was sufficiently broken.

Tara looked around the table, at the group that had been brought together under similar circumstances to her own but, she assumed, in their own unique ways. It made her curious about their stories and curious about the last woman that would complete their group.

Just then, the door opened, and a petite woman bounced inside. Tara would recognize the blue and green streaks in her blonde locks anywhere. As she hung her coat and addressed the group in a crisp British accent, Tara's earlier suspicions were confirmed.

"Sorry, I'm late. James insisted on coming, so I sent Will to gather him while I headed...Tara?"

The entire room looked Tara's way, and she waved and gave a sheepish smile. "Hey there."

Tara stood and skirted around the table as Brooke dropped her bag and welcomed her in an enormous hug.

"Tara? I don't understand," Brooke gasped. "What on Earth are you doing here, Lovie?"

"Exactly," Tara laughed. "I guess I'm Earth?" Tara stood smiling as her best friend absorbed the enormity of what she was saying. She looked to the others who shrugged, which made sense to Tara, since she had yet to prove her abilities. She was excited to see what the others could do.

"Why couldn't I see that," Brooke said, shaking her head. "I didn't understand how the pages could be showing the element of Earth as found already. It must have been because you were one of the first."

She wasn't making any sense, and Tara's eyes followed her friend pacing and speaking animatedly to herself. It was how she worked things out, so Tara waited patiently until the thoughts came to her.

Brooke paused in mid-stride then turned to Tara with a thought. "When you found me in the bookstore after I had blacked out."

"You mean that day I found you on the scattered pile of books?" Tara looked to the others, they were all interested in hearing what Brooke had to say. As if this was part of the puzzle they were all meant to solve. Tara remembered that day. She had never been so scared in her life, and she thought Brooke had been attacked. She had stayed for hours after helping her set the store back to rights.

"That's it," Brooke said as she hugged her friend once more. "That was the day you helped me with the Shadowman."

"He was there that day? This guy is real?"

"He's real all right," Aleck grumbled. "And when I see him next, I am going to beat the shit out of him."

"Not before I do," Logan added.

"Apparently, he's been waiting for my fists since 1944," Theo interjected. The other two men nodded and considered his comment, but before they had a chance to declare him the winner, they heard from Kadar.

"At least you haven't lived in servitude to him," he said softly.

Every head in the room snapped around to look at him. The women wore expressions of pity, the men's jaws tight. Tara wasn't sure what was going on, but it seemed Brooke's childhood fear, the man that had tormented her dreams, was real, and he had more enemies than she would wish on anyone.

Theo, Logan, and Aleck exchanged glances then looked at Kadar and replied in unison. "You win."

"Who has the elemental journal?" Theo had risen from the table and walked over to where Tara was standing. The warmth of his hand on her shoulder helped settle her. She had been feeling a little overwhelmed.

"I have it," Brooke answered as she dug around in the large canvas bag she had on her shoulder. "It came to me at the bookstore, which is when I met Will, and the Shadowman got really aggressive."

"The trip you made with Will, all the time you spent together, was because of that?" Tara said, finally connecting the dots in her mind.

"My portal was in Maui," Brooke confirmed. "This book was the key to finding it."

"Mine was a flute," Tara said. "It opened a doorway where I work."

"At the Crazy Horse monument? I can't believe it," Brooke gasped. "Had you never left Florida, you may have never found that place."

"We are all connected in ways you can't even imagine," Kadar exclaimed. "The universe is a mysterious place. But once you understand the webs that our paths create, the easier it is to solve those mysteries."

Theo pointed to the book in Brooke's hands. "That journal can help. I had made a lot of progress in it when I was its caregiver."

"I thought it would only show its pages to the elements, to the keeper of the book," Brooke said. "How is it that you had it in your possession?"

"I was the last element of Earth," Theo said. "I was the one that..."

"I must go," Kadar yelled out before disappearing in a plume of bright blue smoke. The jelly jar he had been holding dropped to the floor and scattered what was left of the contents.

Each member of the group looked at each other for confirmation of what had just happened. It seemed to Tara that they were all just as surprised as she was.

"I'd expect something like that from Will," Sera cracked. "What the hell is he?"

"I haven't figured that out yet," Theo answered with a shrug.

"He smells of a great power, but I cannae determine the source," Logan added.

"I believe he's genuinely here to help," Theo said. "We need to hear from the sisters of Destiny to get more of the story."

Brooke leaned over and gave Tara one more hug, whispering in her ear. "It is so good to have you here. We have so much to catch up on."

Tara whispered back. "Sounds like it."

Brooke put down the bag and walked over to the bottle of wine, pouring herself a glass. "I'm not sure about you all, but I could use one of these. Anyone need to be topped off?"

18

ater in the kitchen, they were well into dinner, and Kadar still hadn't returned. No one seemed too worried about it, but Tara was curious why he had left so suddenly. Even though he came across as unassuming, he harnessed some pretty powerful energy. Tara had felt the pulse of it when he disappeared, and in that moment, they had been connected. If she didn't know better, she would think he was tied to a natural element somehow. She didn't get the same vibe as she did from Theo — his connection to the trees was apparent. This felt different. Almost like Kadar's connection was to a rock or crystal.

The energy that had come in and out of her life for the past few months had entered her life full force. She was picking up on things she had never been able to before. Perhaps it took meeting Theo to have her really focus on her ability and hone her skill. Mato would have liked him.

Theo had been withdrawn through dinner, mulling over some of the clues he had seen in the journal Brooke brought with her. He had been surprised the pages were blank when he held it, so he looked over Brooke's shoulders as she turned the pages. It seemed the book only answered to her, and Tara felt bad for him, as he struggled with his role in the past versus what he was expected to do now.

"Are you okay?" Tara whispered as the conversation bounced between guests. "You're quiet."

He raised her hand from where they were joined in his lap and kissed her knuckles before lowering it back. His response came with a small smile. "Just thinking. It's been a lot to take in."

"For me, as well," Tara agreed.

"How did you two meet?" Brooke had been watching the exchange, and Tara realized there was a lot that she hadn't shared with her friend in the past several weeks. How could she possibly be upset that Brooke hadn't shared this part of her life with her, when she was guilty of the exact same thing?

She was relieved when Theo responded to the question. "Through *Pride and Prejudice*," Theo answered with a shrug. "For whatever reason, we were reading the book at the same time, and it opened a connection."

"What were ya reading that for?" Logan clearly didn't agree with Theo's book choice. "Isn't that a romance?"

Sera nudged him again. It seemed he was used to it.

"I had run out of things to read, if I'm honest," Theo laughed. "Even though it's considered classic literature now, it wouldn't be my first choice."

Tara gave him a nudge with her elbow. It seemed that Sera's habits were rubbing off on her. "I thought you said you liked it."

He smiled, his next comment low and intended only for her. "I liked the connection with you, the material not as much." He cleared his throat, and Tara felt his embarrassment. He wasn't used to public displays of affection, and she felt bad she had put him in that situation. She squeezed his hand in response and watched as a wide grin split Brooke's face.

Tara gave a quick shake of her head, and Brooke busied herself with another sip from her wineglass. Their old ways of communicating without words were back as if no time had passed. Brooke got the hint. There would be plenty of time later for them to catch up on Tara's new relationship.

"Let's just say we knew each other for a little while before I traveled here," Tara said.

"Fair enough," Brooke said with a grin. She would change the subject for now, but Tara knew from her smirk that they would be coming back later to the topic. "Sera, how are Mila and Annabelle?"

"They're doing great. Mila is my abuela, and Annabelle is our daughter," she explained to Tara.

Her comment prompted a kiss on the cheek from Logan. Uncontained happiness poured from him in waves. If they were newlyweds, Tara assumed the daughter was from a past relationship. It seemed it didn't matter from the love on their faces.

"Mila Lopez?" Theo's expression implied he made the connection he had asked about earlier. "She's your grandmother?"

Sera nodded. "That was her maiden name. My grandfather was

human, his name was Delgado."

Theo nodded. "She was Anton's niece. I remember her story."

"I wasn't raised knowing this part of my heritage," Sera said warily. "My father wanted me raised as human, and it wasn't until I met Logan that I connected the dots. It was a lot to take in at the time, but I wouldn't trade being a wife and mother now for the world."

The comment prompted a neck nuzzle from Logan.

"Annabelle is a doll," Brooke said. "I'm glad they are doing better." She looked at Tara and noted her squint. "There was an attack at Logan's village, and she was badly injured."

"Oh no," Tara exclaimed. "That's horrible!"

"She's much better now. We just finished the last of the repairs to the structures," Logan said. "Another thing to thank that bastard for."

"A lot has happened since I found this journal," Brooke said. "I think we should wait until everyone is here to fill you in."

"When are Will and James going to get here?" Aleck asked.

"Will had to go to Sedona first and pick James up from there, but you are right — they should have been here by now."

"Your brother, James, has been here?"

Brooke nodded. "Only just. Now I can't keep him away. Anytime he gets wind of us traveling here, he begs us to bring him."

Tara wondered if it had anything to do with the fact that James had never believed that the Shadowman was real and kept Brooke going to therapists her entire life. She knew how he felt. She was guilty about not believing her as well.

"I'll be excited to see him again. It's been a long time." Tara heard a voice calling from the distance. Then a rumbling growl and hiss. "Did you hear that?"

Everyone stopped speaking, and the voice called again. It sounded as if it was coming from the front yard.

"Brooke, you in there? We could use a little help."

"That's Will," she said. Tara got up and followed her to the door, and when they opened it, Brooke gasped. "Where did that come from?"

The two men were standing on the other side of the forcefield, clearly unable to get through. Even if they could, their steps would be slowed by the feline mass lying in the center of the path staring at them.

"That's Taksi," Tara explained. "She's with me. She's harmless."

"She doesn't look harmless," Brooke laughed nervously. "Is there something preventing them from coming in?"

Theo joined them in the door. "Yes, Tara and I reinforced the wards. They would have needed one of you with them. We can open them up to include them. It will just take a moment."

As they made their way into the front yard, Logan and Sera followed them out the door. Taksi's head raised as if she had caught the scent of something then turned her head to look behind her. She jumped to her feet and hissed at Logan then bolted to the back yard.

Tara looked back at him, and he commented with a shrug. "Cats dinnae care much for me."

"It's the wolf thing," Sera winked.

Tara smiled and wondered if she would ever get used to this cast of characters. The whole thing was surreal. If she hadn't seen so many strange things with Mato and her grandmother, she doubted she would have been as accepting of it all. She followed Theo down the path and out to the perimeter where Will and James were standing.

"What are you doing here?" Will was confused.

"Nice to see you, Tara," James said. "Seems like we are just in time for the party."

"You are," Tara laughed. "And we can talk about why I'm here in a minute."

Theo took her hand then put the other up toward the invisible shield. Tara did the same and concentrated on opening a slice in the shield in front of the men. When Theo added some color to their magic, it made the opening visible, and they walked through. Theo closed it before turning to introduce himself.

"I'm Theo," he said, shaking Will's hand and nodding to James. "Now that we're all here, we can compare notes."

"Have they found Sevilla yet?"

Theo shook his head in response to Will's question. "Not yet. But hopefully what I have to tell you will help shine some light on our situation."

Inside, the group sat back down around the kitchen table. It seemed to be the place where they spent most of their time when they gathered. The kitchen was the largest room in the house, so it made sense with so many people.

Extra chairs were pulled into the kitchen from the adjacent room, and another bottle of wine had been opened and poured. Neither Amie, nor James were drinking, so Brooke made a pot of tea for them instead. It was getting dark, and Tara had already heard from Taksi, who was going on the prowl for the night. It was probably best until Logan and Sera went home. Like Aleck, Taksi had an issue with Logan.

"A group of men, myself included, used to harness the power you are now wielding," Theo started. "The elements were divided between Elf, Lycan, Mage and Human. As I mentioned before, I held the power of Earth, while my friend Anton was Fire, and Sevilla's husband, Ryker, was Air."

"Anton Lopez?" Logan asked, with a question in his tone. "The pack you spoke of earlier."

Theo nodded. "That's right. He was a good man."

"Aye, I heard he was," Logan agreed quietly.

"Ryker was the one who held me captive," Amie interjected. "We didn't find out until later that he was Sevilla's husband. The fortress where he kept me was flattened to the ground."

"Cela's old domain," Theo explained. "She was the Queen of the Harpies. It was the place where we had banished him."

That caught Brooke's attention. "Wait a minute, you left Sevilla's husband there and then what, told her he died? I came here all my life, and there was never a man in Sevilla's life. She was always alone."

"Perhaps there was a man, but you just never saw him," Sera suggested. With the emotion Tara had felt from Kadar earlier, she thought she was on the right track. Brooke's expression let Tara know she didn't appreciate the comment.

"What happened all those years back, Theo? Sevilla didn't give us much to go on. Hell, I didn't even know she had sisters until recently," Brooke said.

"There were deaths," Theo answered. "Creatures being killed and drained of their magick. Before we could stop it, Erebos killed Cela, as well. Anton had already been taken by the time we faced him, and Ryker had been knocked unconscious and thought to be dead. It was left to the sisters and I to pull the energy from him."

"Erebos," Brooke whispered. "He was the element of water, wasn't he?"

Theo nodded. "He was. With the addition of the dark magick he had been taking, he became much too strong. An explosion occurred as we were drawing it from him, and I watched as a toxic power rose from the space. Fate was the one I found first, and she told me to take Ryker upstairs, which was where I found Anton. She confirmed later she had already known he had died."

"Erebos killed the element of Fire?" Sera was stunned. "No offense, Brooke, but Fire's energy is pretty volatile. You mean to tell me he was able to overtake him with Water?"

"None taken," Brooke said, with a shake of her head. "And that isn't the point, Sera. The fact of the matter is that they all worked together to balance this energy, and it only took one of them going off on their own to shift that balance. At one point, they all considered each other friends. Much like the four of us." She looked to Theo for confirmation, which he gave with a nod.

Tara's heart was breaking for him, the pain coming from him was getting hard to absorb. He had been more than friends with the Lycan who had died, he had considered him a brother. She could feel that now. Finally facing what he had been through was bringing his pain to the surface. She gave his hand a gentle squeeze and watched as he quickly wiped his face with the other.

The room was silent when he cleared his throat to continue. "We were friends, just as all of you are. You are right, Brooke. Erebos was human and always felt as if he had something to prove. At least, that was the impression he gave. We were never close. Since he and Ryker spent more time together through the sisters, they were better friends."

"What about Fate?" James acted as if the question had popped from his mouth without his permission. "What I mean to say is, did she have a husband?"

"For all intents and purposes, Anton was her husband. They were in a committed relationship. She and I were heartbroken when he died, but we both knew we had a job to do. The power released was something neither of us had encountered before."

Confusion and curiosity were swirling from James like smoke from a fire. What Tara found strange was that he knew Fate at all. Hadn't he only just started coming to Wisteria? If the women all didn't know where the sisters were, how would they have met?

The questions from her brother didn't faze Brooke. She got the conversation back on track. "What happened after the explosion, Theo?"

"I went to Fate for guidance, since she can see the future. She shared her vision, and it was clear that if Ryker survived, he needed to be banished. We agreed that Sevilla mustn't be told he was alive in that case."

"She thought he had died," Brooke whispered.

"Until we came along," Amie added. "She was surprised with the knowledge. From my impression, Zilla was as well."

"Zilla and Erebos were gone by the time I had secured Ryker upstairs."

Brooke stood up and started to pace. Her hands were shaking, and her voice cracked. "Why would she let him go? Was she completely mad?"

Will shot up and went to her. "Calm down, babe," he soothed. His hand went to her shoulder, which she shrugged off with a side-step.

"I will not calm down. That man tormented me my entire childhood. He made it so I was ostracized from society because I talked to imaginary people. People that were real, by the way, but no one ever believed me."

Tara glanced to James, who lowered his head. The guilt she felt from him almost surpassed her own.

The tears started then, and she allowed Will to take her into his arms. "We will sort this out, Brooke. We'll find the answers."

Sera and Amie both stood and walked to Brooke, giving her hugs and words of encouragement. Tara joined them, and Brooke cried anew as she wrapped her arms around her. "We'll figure this out," Tara whispered. "Theo can help. He knows the history from this place better than anyone."

Brooke nodded as she gathered herself. Everyone returned to their seats, which was when she noted the men had all stood up. Each of them had taken a different place in the room, some pacing, some leaning, but they were all clearly tired of sitting. The restless energy was snapping at her muscles, and folks were getting edgy.

"When the explosion occurred, something happened with the energy that Erebos had been gathering. It seemed to have split off. When I mentioned it to Fate, that was when she sent me upstairs with Ryker. After we separated, Fate was left to tell Sevilla about Ryker."

"She knows the truth now, "Brooke muttered. "And it broke her heart all over again."

Tara felt Theo's regret, along with everyone else's energy in the room. Her right leg was bouncing, and she acknowledged the excess energy that she was having a hard time channeling. The leg bouncing was something she had done her whole life to focus. It didn't seem to be helping much in this case.

"Fate has never led us astray. If she tells me I must do something, I know that I must. Her purpose is tied to universal balance. She will do everything in her power to ensure that it remains so."

"If Ryker survived, why is it that he didn't come looking for Sevilla?"

"I had erased his memory," Theo answered.

"The Shadowman fucked with my head in the same way," Will interjected. "Is that something you do as a matter of habit around here?" He wasn't happy.

Theo shook his head. He didn't take Will's tone personally. "No. It is an ancient magick and only used in extreme cases. It seems the Shadowman, as you call him, has tapped into it somehow. Even with the precautions that Fate and I took."

"What is it that you were asked to do?" Aleck asked. His mind was tactical in nature, so him remaining quiet and taking it all in had made complete sense to her. It amazed her just how quickly she was picking up on everyone's personalities through their feelings. It was as if she had known them all along.

"There was a weapon he used to kill his victims. A knife of sorts, crafted from a glowing stone, with symbols that weren't familiar. I believe it was how he channeled the energy from the creatures he killed. The obsidian box I found it in blanketed the magick but didn't completely shield it. Fate tasked me with hiding it."

"Where is the weapon now?" Aleck paced. He was a man of action and anxious to get things moving. Unlike Amie, he wasn't comfortable talking about magick.

"I had taken it to the most remote place I could think of and hid it at the base of a tree. My magick kept it hidden there, although the toxic energy kept trying to escape. I was able to contain it until recently. When Tara arrived, I knew things had changed, and it was no longer safe to stay there. I knew Fate would know what to do next."

"You left a dangerous weapon behind?" Aleck's voice was incredulous. "That bastard is out there, what if he finds it?"

"You're missing the point," Theo said calmly. "I wasn't meant to keep the weapon from him indefinitely. I was tasked with buying us some time while the new elementals were found. Keeping the Shadowman away from his weapon would have been impossible."

A flash of blue smoke in the room behind the fireplace stopped their conversation. Aleck stepped over to shield Amie, who sat behind him, and Will and James had crowded around Brooke. Tara and Theo stood, as did Sera with Logan behind her.

Tara heard shuffling from the room, as if there was more than one object that had appeared there. Kadar's strong voice rang out to her. "Tara, I need your help."

19

Fate left the dungeon with a sense of purpose. She knew they were all running out of time, and their window of opportunity was closing. Knowing what she needed to look for helped her. Not being able to see didn't.

The irony that the universe chose her to lead others in an escape wasn't lost on her. However, knowing that one must always be grateful, she focused on the positive and thanked the powers for the aid of her friends. She clung to Sansa's arm as the dryad nimbly guided her up the stairs from the cells where her sisters were held.

"Where to next, Mistress?"

Fate's response was breathy, as she tried to keep up with Sansa's rapid steps. "The Shadowman's bedchamber." Sansa's grip on her arm tightened, but her steps never faltered.

"What are we looking for?" Her voice trembled. Fate understood how she felt, as she was nervous too. If he returned, the outcome would be devastating.

"We need to find the keys that release the locks on their cell. Without those, we won't be going anywhere."

"Maybe Billy will know better where they are and what they look like. We can go through the kitchen and get him before taking the servant's stairs to the bedroom suites."

"I'm placing my trust in you, my friend."

They crossed through the study. Fate recognized the scent from earlier, and their footsteps were muffled against the carpets. The voices in her head sent foreboding visions that she was doing her best to ignore. They would soon adjust to her new path, but until they did, their warnings were unnerving.

Their steps tapped on a new surface, an area of the domain Fate didn't recognize with her limited senses. She sensed they were in a hallway by the way the sounds bounced back to her. "Thank you, Sansa. I will be forever in your debt."

"You don't need to thank me, and you owe us nothing. Billy and I will be leaving with you. We've already packed our bags." Sansa's grip pulled Fate closer to her body. "Watch your step, some of the stones are loose."

They couldn't afford any injuries, so Fate didn't mind being pulled about. They were in a hurry after all. The sound of their footsteps went from echoing quickly, to a fading pop. Fate could tell by the way Sansa's grip loosened that they were in a larger space.

"Billy," Sansa whispered.

"The Shadowman hasn't returned." Billy's hooves clicked on the stone floor as he moved toward them. Sansa dropped her hand from Fate's arm. A sigh of relief was shared, then the quick snap of a hurried kiss came to Fate's ears.

"Are we leaving now?"

"Not yet." Sansa's hand went to Fate's arm once more, and they started moving across the room. His steps followed.

Fate responded to Billy's question. "We must find the keys to the cell where my sisters are being held."

"We are on our way to the Shadowman's bedchamber," Sansa added.

"I believe I may know what you are looking for. I'll lead."

They entered another stairwell, even narrower than the one that led from the dungeons. Billy led the way and had taken Fate's hand, pulling her behind him. Sansa's hands were steady on Fate's hips behind her.

"How on earth did you ever walk these stairs with room trays? This stairwell feels impossibly cramped."

"It is, Mistress," Billy answered. "We have all gotten pretty good at balancing the trays above our heads."

"I'm sorry for all the times I took dinner in my room," Fate said.

"Don't you fret about it," Sansa said.

"It's just up here. Watch your step."

Billy let go of Fate's hand, and Sansa took her arm once more. They were no longer climbing and were able to spread out more. Sansa's steps slowed to a stop, and Fate heard the click of the door latch as Billy opened the door. There was a slight pause before he whispered to them.

"There is no one here. I lost track of the other two servants, but they mentioned taking advantage of the Shadowman being gone. I would assume we have a few minutes alone here. I will look for the keys." Billy's footfalls walked away from them.

"Sansa, we need to find an obsidian box. Zilla mentioned it might be on his nightstand?"

"I think I see it. This way." Sansa's hand gripped the underside of Fate's arm and gently pulled her forward. Fate then heard the scrape of stone upon stone as the lid was slipped aside. "There are several pieces of jewelry in here."

Fate stepped forward, feeling the pulse of the magick that called to her. She found the box and ran her hands along the smooth edges, getting a clear picture in her mind sent by her voices. Their messages had adjusted to her decision to leave. The visions were jumbled with multiple outcomes, but the ring was key to them all. She splayed her hands over the open box and felt a pulse on her palm. The voices whispered its location. As she gripped the cool metal, a small pulse of energy tickled her fingers. Lifting it from the box, she heard a small gasp from Sansa.

"The detail on the dragons is incredible."

"And the color of the stone?" Fate knew she had the right ring by how it felt, but she wanted to be sure.

"Blue. The biggest sapphire I've ever seen."

"Perfect. Let's hope it helps," Fate replied. She slipped it into her pocket next to the bell as the click of Billy's steps and the jangle of keys moved toward them.

"Did you find what you were looking for?"

"I believe so."

"I have the keys. Let's go."

They took the same way back, since it was much quicker to access the dungeons from the kitchen. Sansa's steps slowed as they crossed the center of the large room.

"Time is of the essence. We'll be quicker if you stay back."

"I understand," Fate said. "I'll wait here. Hurry."

Their steps faded, and Fate shuffled slowly with hands spread until she reached a large oak table. She pulled the bench beneath it out far enough to sit. She was glad for the few minutes of reprieve. She needed to decide what to do about Ryker.

He was there. The voices had confirmed it when she spoke to her sisters. His destiny was the one thing she had not been completely honest about in the past. She had a choice to make that would have bearing on all their futures. As she concentrated on the impressions of him she had received in the years she had known him, her question came to mind. She was wise enough to fear the answer.

"Do we take him with us?" The response to her whispered question was only heard in her mind. Every possible outcome of the action she proposed flashed like pulses of lightning. Each outcome ended in disaster — all but one. In less than a minute, she had made her choice. A choice that would haunt her for the rest of her days.

She crossed her arms and laid her head down on them. The deep breath she took did little to dispel the weight coming down on her shoulders. The decision went against everything she felt in her heart. Everything she had wanted for her sister. The encumbered steps of the satyr cemented her decision. It was too late to turn back now. Fate stood as Zilla pulled her into an embrace.

"Sevilla's too weak to walk. She keeps going on about that damn ring."

Fate reached into her pocket as Billy's weighted steps came toward her. Sansa's hurried steps and the creak of wooden doors gave Fate the impression she was gathering things for the journey. She joined the group and dropped two sacks at their feet.

"I gathered your tools, mistress." Sansa pushed a fabric pouch into Fate's hands, allowing her to feel the outline of Sevilla's tarot cards. There were other items as well. It brought tears to her eyes that Sansa had been so thoughtful.

"I don't know how to thank you, Sansa."

"I knew you would at least want these things. I know how much they mean to you." Fate gave her a hug, then slipped the bell from her pocket into the pouch.

"I'll carry it for you until we get outside." Sansa let out a small huff as she lifted the bags. "I have our things, Billy. I'm ready."

"The ring," Sevilla croaked. Her hand was limp as it grasped onto Fate's arm. Fate held up the ring, and her sister, Zilla, stood quietly at her side. The fingers that removed it from her hand were as cold as ice. "Thank the Goddess," Sevilla whispered. "Now we can go."

"Is she going to be okay?" Fate's impression was that their time was limited. Sevilla sounded terrible.

"She can't walk, but I can carry her," Billy answered. He was already moving. "But we need to leave now. Sansa, you lead. Zilla, you take Fate's arm, and I will follow with Sevilla."

"This way," Sansa said. "It's just through here."

Zilla's firm grip slipped in around Fate's elbow, and they followed the sounds of Sansa's footsteps. Fate's choice to leave Ryker behind swirled sourly in her stomach, and bile burned her throat. While she knew it was the only decision she could make, she wasn't at peace with it. She hoped that leaving him here wasn't tied to Sevilla's weakness.

"Are you ill? You look as pale as Villy."

"I'll be fine," Fate responded, with a forced smile. "I'm just tired is all. I'm more worried about Sevilla. Her fingers were like ice."

"He used us each for different things," Zilla replied. Her voice was strained. "He allowed me to keep a little more of my energy as a matter of habit. Sevilla wasn't as lucky."

"He's drained her dangerously low. I just hope once we are out of here that we are able to rebalance her."

"Me too. Perhaps the ring will be of help."

They had taken a couple of turns, and in doing so, the surface they were walking on had changed. The energy surrounding them was different here, more palatable. She could feel the wisps of nature's call touching them from ahead. The subtle breezes were already helping replace her energy.

"There are steps here that lead up to an opening," Zilla whispered. "They are uneven so be careful."

"Once we get outside, there is a small path to the right," Billy said breathlessly. His steps were slower with the weight of his load.

"This way," Sansa said.

Zilla led Fate to the right as the cool night breeze touched Fate's face for the first time in weeks. She didn't know how much she had missed being outside until that very moment. "There is a step here, and we will be in a clearing."

"Sansa, be sure you take us into the tree line. I don't want to be seen by the couple that left earlier."

"This way, everyone."

"I don't recognize this place," Fate said. She thought she had been in every corner of Wisteria but couldn't pinpoint the energy surrounding them.

"Those that lived here deserted it long ago. It is an unoccupied part of the land now," Sansa said.

Fate slowed her steps at Sevilla's murmur and turned with her hands out. "Billy, put her down. Let me see if I can help her." He placed Sevilla at Fate's feet then walked a few steps to join Sansa. She heard the murmur of their conversation as she tended to her sister. When she kneeled and reached out to her chest, her palms landed on Sevilla's fisted hands. They were still ice-cold, and her breath was uneven.

Fate had lost track of Zilla's location until she gasped. "A blue light. I've never seen it do that."

"Help me with her," Fate urged. Zilla settled across from her on the other side of Sevilla. Fate placed one hand on Sevilla's head and the other on her hands, feeling the brush of Zilla's fingertips as she did the same. "Only share what you are able."

"It won't be much," Zilla said.

Fate nodded and took a centering breath. Before they were able to close their minds and concentrate on their task, an echoing crack split the night. The pulse of energy was so great, Fate felt it deep in her chest. The power was unknown to her, as was the voice that sounded from it.

"What happened to her?" The man's rumbling voice wasn't angry, it held concern. It seemed he was friend, not foe. At least for now.

He kneeled at Sevilla's head between the two of them. He smelled of myrrh and cedar, and his hands were callused as he brushed theirs aside. His power raised the hairs on her arm as it pulsed over her. She had once been caught in a lightning storm with Anton, and the pulses that quivered in her belly were very much like what she felt that night.

Fate heard Zilla shift, and her voice sounded as if she had stood. "Your eyes glow like the ring," Zilla said accusingly. "What are you?"

"You know what I am," the man stated flatly.

"I thought I did," Zilla said. "But the man I knew was servant, not master."

"Perhaps I've always been a little of both," he murmured.

"Mistress, we need to leave this place. The Shadowman could return any moment," Sansa warned.

"Sir, can you help us," Fate asked. She didn't care who he was or how Zilla knew him, her only concern was getting Sevilla home.

He paused, as if struggling with the question. "It's complicated."

"Well, uncomplicate it, Kadar," Zilla said with a huff.

Fate sensed he was hesitant to speak freely in front of her. Zilla wasn't the easiest person to trust, so she understood it. "Zilla, get my bag from Sansa. She and Billy should leave now."

Sevilla's hands loosened as she murmured incoherent phrases that Fate tried to translate. "Kadar, is it? Please tell me what I need to do."

He shifted his body toward Sevilla's ear, his words barely audible. "Say the word, my love."

Fate felt the ring push into her palm and with a thready breath, Sevilla gave her a message. "Wish."

Zilla's footsteps returned, and the man sat still at Sevilla's side. Fate was still confused as to what his hesitation was, but as the voices in her head started to show her flashes of a failed escape, she could no longer wait. A few more flashes, and she understood the ring's power and Kadar's connection to it.

"I have your bag, Fate. What have we decided to — "

"I wish the four of us back to Sevilla's."

Before Fate had the chance to take a breath, the atmosphere around her changed. Her next breath drew in the comforting scents of sage and dried lavender. The soft wool of Sevilla's rugs comforted her fingertips. There was movement from the kitchen she heard through the fireplace. It gave her bearing. They had made it home and according to the voices in her mind, without much time to spare. She pushed a small prayer to the Universe that Sansa and Billy would be safe.

Fate pulled the ring from her finger and closed it in her palm. She didn't fully understand the power, or the man tied to it, but she understood one thing. No one should have access to the ring until Sevilla awoke. She held out her hand and Kadar took the ring from her with a whispered "thank you." Zilla knelt beside her, and they both reached out to lay hands on the still body of their sister. Zilla was uncharacteristically quiet.

Kadar's strong voice called out. "Tara, I need your help."

It was then Fate felt it, the tug and pull of all four energies searching for harmony. Relief filled her soul. The final element, Earth, had been found.

20

Tara rushed into the sitting room and saw Kadar and three women grouped on the floor. The one in the corset styled top was dirty and bruised but seemed otherwise unharmed. The other, a woman with long white hair and clouded eyes, handed something to Kadar, then stood in place. She was dressed in ill-fitting men's clothing. Although the three were practically identical, it was the woman he kneeled beside who worried him the most.

"What's wrong with her?" Tara asked.

"I don't know," Kadar answered. "Most likely exhaustion."

"Take that necklace off," the dark-haired woman said. "That isn't helping."

The others had stood and were crowding in the doorway behind Tara. Tara removed the necklace, noting that the two other women did the same.

"I'll take those, Zilla," Theo said. He stepped into the room and took the necklaces that were offered to him. The woman with the white hair started to sob, and he gathered her in his arms. Her relief swamped Tara, as did Theo's. The emotions were overwhelming her.

"It's been a long time, Theo. Nice to see you," Zilla said.

"You all need to get out of here," Tara snapped. "I can't concentrate."

"Come on everyone," Theo said. Feet shuffled from the room and murmurs sounded, but thankfully, she was finally separated from the flood of emotions hitting her. She blocked all the whispered conversations happening in the adjacent room and focused on her task.

"Is this Sevilla?" Tara looked up into Kadar's worried eyes and waited for his confirmation. He gave a quick nod and cleared his throat.

"She was unconscious when I arrived. She won't come to," he explained.

There was a pulse of energy coming from his hand. She watched as he slid a man's sapphire ring on Sevilla's left ring finger. It had the same energy she had felt from him before. She didn't have the impression that it was interfering with her health like the glowing necklace had been. She hoped Theo would be okay holding those. They were extremely toxic.

Tara lay one hand on Sevilla's forehead and the other on her heart. She closed her eyes and focused on her breaths, which hitched and stuttered to start. After a few deep breaths, Sevilla's breaths matched her own.

She pushed as much healing energy as she could spare toward Sevilla and noted her stores were desperately low. Kadar had brought her back just in time. She wouldn't have lasted the night.

The light from her energy filled the room, she saw it through her closed eyelids. She felt Sevilla's spirit touch hers, the touch was apologetic and light. Proper, if she had to give it a tag. The woman was conscious now and worried that Tara was giving her too much energy, but at the same time, she was in desperate need of it and knew it.

"Tara, your hair," Brooke whispered from behind her.

"I'm fine," she answered back and continued to concentrate on her task. Sevilla started to stir, and Tara pushed one last pulse of energy toward her before pulling back her hands. Theo was behind her and helped her to rise. She hadn't heard him come back.

"Let's go," he said crossly. Was he mad at her?

"I need to stay," Tara argued, but her legs were wobbly, and she couldn't focus. Her vision blurred as he led her from the room.

"We are going outside," he said, although it didn't sound like he was talking to her. Why was his voice muffled?

"I'll get...door, do...help?" she heard a man question. Perhaps Aleck? Will? It wasn't James or Logan, since there was no accent.

Her sight was dimming, and sparkles of light danced across her view. Tara was swept off her feet and was floating against Theo's chest. She was being carried. His strong arms cocooned her, and she relaxed against him, drawing in his spicy scent she had come to love. She settled into it and breathed deep. Then accepted the darkness.

She woke at the base of the obsidian tree in Theo's lap. His arms were draped around her, and he had her sitting directly on the cold ground. She hoped the thing poking into her ass was a root from the tree behind them. Not that she would have minded if it were him, but the entire household was standing around them and staring.

"Hey there," Tara whispered. Her voice was weak. The power she had given to Sevilla must have drained her stores. The fog from her mind was lifting slowly.

She felt the release of breath behind her. Theo's relief relaxed his arms, and his head dipped forward into the crook of her neck.

"Thank the Gods," he whispered. "I should have known better, keeping you in there so long."

Tara was confused by his comment at first but then realized what he was saying. There had been a lot of energy flying around the room, and it had been draining. She probably hadn't been in the best shape to heal anyone.

"Her hair is changing back," Sera commented.

"Coloring is better as well," Will said. "You gave us quite the scare."

"Sorry," Tara said softly. "I only wanted to help. How's Sevilla?"

"She's good," Brooke said as she kneeled down and pulled her into a hug. "Kadar and the two sisters are taking care of her inside."

"Good."

"I think it might be best if you give us a few more minutes alone," Theo said to the group. They nodded their agreement and made their way into the house. Brooke was the last to leave. She stopped and turned to look at Tara, her eyes glistening with unshed tears.

"You scared me," Brooke said quietly. "What was worse was that I couldn't help. All this power at my fingertips, and I couldn't help you." She looked at Theo and smiled. "Thank you for taking care of her. I don't know what I would do if anything happened to her."

"Nothing will happen to her as long as I take breath," Theo answered. His response lightened her anxious heart and relaxed her immediately. His honest tone had a way of doing that. You knew immediately that you could trust him. Tara thought it had a lot to do with his matter-of-fact presentation. If he said it, it must be so.

With everyone in the house, Taksi finally came forward and laid down beside her. She wiggled then placed her large head in Tara's lap. Tara's hand absently stroked her head, and a rumbling purr came from Taksi's chest.

SCARED.

Don't be scared.

TARA SICK.

I'm okay.

"She's been keeping watch over you the whole time," Theo said. "She stayed mainly in the tree line."

"How long was I out?" Tara was feeling much better; the toxicity had been pulled out of her by the tree she sat beneath.

"Almost an hour."

"I can tell," Tara laughed. "My ass is killing me."

Theo chuckled. He pulled her up by her arms and shifted beneath her, lowering her to his lap. "Better?" His low voice in her ear made her feel all sorts of things. Better was certainly one of the words she would use.

"Much," Tara said, snuggling into his warmth. "By the way, that was quite the promise you gave Brooke."

"What do you mean?"

"Well, you said nothing would happen to me as long as you live."

"I meant it." His lips found their way to her neck, and she tipped her head to allow him access. Oh yes, she was definitely feeling better.

"Well, considering your lifespan so far, I would say I'm in good shape."

"You are definitely in good shape."

"Theo," she gasped. "Was that an innuendo? From you?"

His chuckle warmed her. "What if it was?"

"I like it," Tara laughed. She turned her head and looked up at him. The worry he had been transmitting to her was gone. Deep in his eyes, there was something else, something that had yet to be named between them both.

He lowered his head and kissed her. They would put a name to it later. As far as she was concerned, they had plenty of time.

Before heading inside, Theo made sure that Tara's legs were stable and that she could walk on her own. He also had her take a few minutes to connect to her surroundings and meditate. Much as she would rather be in his arms, she had to admit the few minutes outside breathing in the crisp night air had really helped.

He explained that part of her earlier trouble was because she hadn't effectively put her guards up during the conversations. Considering their connection, and after she had drained herself with Sevilla, he put guards up of his own, so she wouldn't be harmed any further. Until she learned to control her power, they would need to take precautions.

During her meditation, Tara put up mental walls alongside Theo's, so there would be no further drain on her growing energy stores. She felt better, but she knew she still had a ways to go. When they entered the room, the first one to greet her was Brooke.

"You look so much better," she gushed.

"Thanks," Tara smiled. "I feel better. The tree outside really seemed to help. It's like it pulled all the bad stuff from me."

"One of the qualities of Obsidian," Zilla said from the other room. Tara spied her then, sitting alone near the fireplace with a glass of wine. She looked around the kitchen. All of the elemental couples were there, but James was missing, as were Fate, Sevilla and Kadar.

"Guess my mishap a few months back came in handy," Sera mumbled.

"How are the others?" Tara was curious to know if her healing had helped.

"Sevilla and Kadar are resting. And James and Fate went for a walk. She seemed upset and wanted to go outside. He offered to go with her."

"That was nice of him," Tara said.

"Indeed." The comment was mumbled in the other room. It seemed as though she was the only one that heard Zilla. The men had their heads bowed deep in conversation, and Sera and Amie were tidying the dishes.

"He said he could use the fresh air also," Brooke explained. "A lot has happened in such a short time. It was a bit overwhelming."

"You've got that right," Tara smiled. "It's been a crazy few days for me as well."

"I bet. I just still can't believe that it was you all along, but now it seems so obvious. I saw in the journal that Earth has the ability to connect to animals. If you connecting to Misty wasn't a sign, your mountain lion friend certainly would be."

"Yeah, she sort of followed me into the doorway that led here," Tara laughed. "She's pretty young, and for whatever reason, she's decided she likes me."

Theo came up to Tara. "We were just figuring out sleeping arrangements," he explained. "Amie and Aleck will head back with Sera and Logan, and the rest of us will stay here. They can come back in the morning, so we can start comparing notes. I think it would be best for you if we had less distraction here."

Brooke nodded. "We can be a little overwhelming when we are all together, that is for sure. Why don't you two head up. I can finish up down here and let everyone out."

They said their goodnights, and Theo quickly led her up the stairs and back into the room they had stayed in the night before. When he closed the door, she let out a sigh of relief. She hadn't realized until then just how much she liked her alone time with Theo.

"Thank you for looking out for me."

"If I'm honest, it was self-serving on my part. I'm not used to being around so many people anymore. Not since court anyway."

"I like my solitude as well," Tara said. "I think I'm going to catch a shower." She looked up into his face, but he was deep in thought. "You want to join me?"

He shook his head, looking apologetic but as if he wouldn't budge from his decision. There was something going on in that mind of his, and Tara wasn't sure she was going to like it.

"I think it would be best if we didn't."

His tone dropped the floor out from her stomach. "Didn't what?" She tried to relay a confidence she wasn't feeling. Her mind was jumping to conclusions, trying to figure out why she always seemed to pick men who were emotionally unavailable. "What do you mean?" She had hoped Theo was going to be different. Had she misread the signs...again?

"You need rest, and I have some things I need to do. I thought, perhaps, I would see you settled in then say goodnight."

Tara's heart sunk, but she swallowed her pride. "Okay, sure," she said with a shrug. "I get it." She gave him a small smile that she didn't feel and turned to make her way into the bathroom.

"Tara?"

The tone more than anything had her turning around. The look on his face caused her heart to flutter and race.

"Yes, Theo?"

Would this be the moment? The moment they would put words to what they had started? He was holding something back, Tara was as sure of it, as she was in her own heart. She could practically see the decision of what he would say next click on his face.

"Goodnight."

She took a deep breath and attempted to squelch her disappointment. He was right, she was tired. Perhaps it was best they separate now before she said something waspish. "Goodnight, Theo."

It wasn't until she had left him in the room behind her and closed the bathroom door that the word that had popped into her head came from her lips.

"Coward."

A single word that defined the next logical step in the progression of their relationship, and the brakes he had effectively put on it. She had never met anyone like him, but the pain of his distance was familiar to her. There had been others in her past that held back as well. Others that she had shared her heart with, only to have it shattered when they pulled away from her. She learned her lesson. There was no way she would be the one to bring up the "L" word first.

For once in her life, the man would be the one to say it first. Trouble was, for as honest as Theo was, she wasn't sure he was completely honest about his own feelings.

Yes, the word summed up the situation nicely...for each of them. They were both cowards.

21

The Shadowman had finally found it. The tree to which Fate had inferred to months ago. He was drawn to it, like a moth to a flame, feeling the power seeping from it grow stronger with each step he took toward it. As they approached it, his manservant, Henry, timidly stood by as the Shadowman ran his hand over the carved symbols on the bark. Not quite the symbols he was looking for but so very close.

"Henry, unpack the shovel and get to work. It is here, at the base of the tree. I can feel it."

"My Lord, this tree is decades old, and the roots are wide. I don't have any idea where to start, and even if I did, it would take me weeks to up-root a tree this size."

"I'll find you help," he snapped. "Start digging."

He left the servant at the base of the tree, struggling to find loose soil and a place to start. The ground was firmly packed with hardened earth and gnarly roots. The glowing green symbols were even there, carved into the top of the visible roots that popped from the earth. Theo had been busy.

He walked to the edge of the clearing to the row of trees that stood in silent defense. Their opinion of him fluctuated between distaste and fear — the second emotion more prominent, as he raised his hands in front of him, and they started to glow with the power now fueling him.

Yes, he could feel them. While the power Theo once held was something he would have to wait to obtain, there were remnants of it that had been left behind. Pushed into the symbols he mistakenly thought would keep his secret safe, strands of his ancient Earth magick were now blended with the energy calling to its master. He could sense the trees, and they had a right to fear him.

He chose a sturdy Elm first, assessing the lifeforce within its bark. Standing before it, he lay his palms on the bark and closed his eyes to concentrate.

The communication was slow at first, since Ents were notoriously hard to wake. Once they were moving though, they were as strong as the tree they were made from. He worried the small portion of the power he controlled wouldn't be enough to bend these beings to his will, but he let the worry slide from his mind. The Ents were convenient, but if they didn't work out, he could always burn them to the ground and find another set of creatures to help him.

The Shadowman connected to the spirit of the tree, then gave his commands, much like he had done in the past with other found objects he had manipulated. The skeletons in the desert were by far his most ingenious army yet, surpassing even the golems he created to destroy Logan's village. He was getting better at making them, and what he would obtain beneath the glowing tree would make him unstoppable.

The sleepy Ent defied him at first, but it didn't take long for the magick that had been coming back to him slowly over time to take hold. Soon the Ent had no other recourse but to follow his master's commands. The creature drew its roots from the ground and twisted the masses together to create limbs. Soon, it made its way to the tree where he had left Henry digging.

"Marvelous," he mumbled. "Perhaps just a few more."

Once the Ents joined Henry, the work went quicker. It was a struggle to override their compassion in order for them to destroy a fellow tree. But with the powers he drained from the sisters and the negative powers that he tapped into, he prevailed. That energy grew stronger each time one of the elements came home.

Henry called him over. They had dug deep enough for the glow to be blinding. It pulsed from the hole, and Henry had taken a step back from it. "I think we found something, my Lord."

The tree that once stood proudly over the space had all but been toppled over. The carved symbols remained, but they no longer glowed with the bright green glow of the magick he had come to collect.

The Shadowman pointed to the hole. "You are looking for a black stone box, carved from obsidian. There is nothing to fear."

The satyr nodded, not quite believing the lie that the Shadowman told, but having no other choice. He was weak that way, always worried about what would be done to his brother or to the rest of their family that had been left behind. Their love was what made them weak. The Shadowman used every bit of it to his advantage when it came to creatures he controlled.

Henry was digging with his hands, pushing the loosened dirt from the area where the glow was the brightest. The Ents lowered the tree to its side and now stood waiting for their next order.

"I found it," Henry said. He lifted the box and placed it on the edge of the hole before climbing out and standing near the Shadowman. Henry bent down and lifted the box up, holding it in front of him, so his master could get a better look at it. "It's beautiful," Henry said humbly.

"It's what's inside that interests me," he said as he lifted the lid. Relief flowed through his body, as he gazed down on the key to his power — the final remaining piece of the material, adorned with the symbols Cela had used but never fully understood. He smiled as he lifted it from the box, feeling the pulse of the surrounding magick strengthen him. It made him wonder why Theo had left so much of his ancient power behind.

As Henry looked on, the Shadowman turned the shard of glowing green stone over, twisting it back and forth to ensure that all of the symbols were visible. He would need Ryker to copy them, line for line, in order for the magick to be duplicated. Thankfully, they had found another way to access the stores of material. Using the ground and cave dwellers, they dug toward Cela's old fortress and tapped into the source far beneath the flattened rubble that was once her home. Some powerful energy was released the day he used Ryker to fight the Element of Air.

"That was what we came for?" Henry seemed confused.

The weapon wasn't much to look at, in that much he would agree, but it served its purpose. "It is what we came for," he said with a smile.

Henry's eyes widened, and he dropped the box, grabbing at the shard that the Shadowman had jammed firmly in his gut. He watched as the realization crossed the satyr's bearded face. The realization that he was going to die at the hands of his master.

Henry couldn't speak. Instead, he choked on the blood pooling in his mouth. It had all come back to the Shadowman, like an old habit that was impossible to break. The thrill of the kill had been more Cela's thing, but the power he absorbed, now that was something that got him hard. He would almost be tempted to do something about it. Perhaps he would pay a visit to Zilla when he got back with his prize. As the satyr gasped and sputtered, the few magical abilities he had at his disposal transferred to the Shadowman by way of the shard. It didn't take long, as saytrs didn't have much more than charisma and long life to steal.

The Shadowman yanked his shard from Henry's body and turned to walk away before he hit the ground. "Follow me," he commanded the Ents, who had watched the grisly display in silence. Everything that they had come with was left behind. He had everything he needed. For now.

22

Theo could sense Tara's disappointment coming to him all the way from her shower to where he stood outside. If he wasn't connected to her emotions, the word she muttered would have been clue enough. Coward. Perhaps he was, but he knew he was doing what was best. No matter how much he wanted to keep her in his arms for the night, he knew he had to fight the urge. She wasn't safe with continued exposure to him. Much as he hated it, it would be best if he kept his distance until she was able to better shield her energy.

He trudged across the yard, followed by Taksi, who seemed happy with his company. "At least you're speaking to me," he grumbled. He paced for a moment, not quite sure of what he could do, but knowing that he needed to stay away. He looked at the mountain lion, who sat patiently staring, as if waiting on his decision.

"You want to go for a walk?" He watched in awe as Taksi stood and started in the direction of the woods. Even though he couldn't communicate with her, it seemed she understood him just fine. He was glad. The walk wouldn't be nearly as lonely. He knew where they needed to go and hoped some of the older portals he and the sisters used were still intact. Now that his powers were returning, he thought he could use them.

Why he hadn't thought to try them until now was a mystery. He stopped himself. Perhaps not such a mystery. Tara had been in his every waking thought since they met. Had he not been so distracted, he probably would have at least attempted to find and use them sooner. He made a mental note to show Tara how to create them as well.

"There's something I should check on," Theo said aloud. "You ready for a hike?" Taksi bobbed her head, then sneezed, and he took it as a yes. "All right, follow me."

He was able to locate a few older portals, which took them within a few miles of their destination. The same wards were on them that the sisters had set decades before. They had allowed their group access but masked their view from other magical creatures that might stumble upon them. Sevilla had demanded the wards after the pixie incident. Chuckling to himself as the memory tickled his brain, he wondered if she ever figured out the whole story.

Taksi didn't find issue with going through the portal, if anything, she was intuitively leading him back to where he was heading. He was thankful she had joined him. Her sense of smell would warn of any enemies long before they arrived at their destination. He wasn't sure what they would be walking into, but as they got closer to the tree where the magick lay, his feelings of dread grew stronger.

The mountain lion walked a few paces in front of him, and every few steps, she would stop and look back, ensuring that he still followed her. He wondered at Tara's use of a familiar and decided that he would have liked one all those years alone. It would have made his task bearable.

The mountain lion's pace halted, and she stood still as a statue in the path that led to the tree. Tiny waves of fur rose and crested along her spine. She took a few tentative steps backwards.

"What is it?" Theo whispered to Taksi while stretching his senses wide and attempting to pick up on what was upsetting her. He felt it now. There was something wrong. "I feel it too. We will be cautious."

Taksi stepped with intent then looked back at Theo and hissed, melting into the tree line on their left. Theo decided her plan had merit and went to the right. They would come around the tree at both sides and make sure it was safe before their final approach.

He was glad he decided to come without Tara. The energy coming toward him was foul and, in her weakened state, would have affected her greatly. Especially, after healing Sevilla. The toxic feel was familiar, it had left a lasting impression on him all those years ago. The Shadowman was here, or at least had been. The latter was his hope.

As he moved closer, he lightened his steps, darting between the larger of the trees and masking his approach behind them. The hum from the area was gone, as was the tree's. Something was different. While the imprint of its existence was still strong, it seemed the energy source had been moved. He knew long before he saw the destruction that the Shadowman had the magical shard.

The moon shone through the opening in the clearing, and what he saw almost dropped him to his knees. The massive tree he had created to guard Fate's secret was uprooted and thrown on its side. He looked around. There were no signs of movement, so he stepped further into the clearing. That was when he saw the body.

Wondering the entire time if it was a trap, he fought through his hesitancy and went to check for a sign of life. It was his nature. He had been born into a culture of healers, learned the arts at an incredibly young age, and the passive magick was something he connected to even now. He hoped that his teachings would come back to him like an old friend.

He knew long before he knelt beside the Saytr that he was dead. The body had turned to ash, similar to the bodies Erebos and Cela had drained all those years ago. There was no denying that he had been there. The obsidian box that had held the shard was tipped among the tree roots. The tree was dead as well, and Theo felt a pang of guilt for that, even though he knew it would have died whether or not Erebos had yanked it from the ground.

The satyr was young, unknown to him, especially considering his forced solitude in the past several decades. There was no need to bury the body. Once the wind picked up, there would be nothing left of it. The weapon still worked. And worse, evil was once again in possession of it.

Taksi approached him, and he took that as reassurance that Erebos, or the Shadowman as others called him, had indeed left. Theo decided it would be better to think of him that way as well. He couldn't wrap his mind around a man he had known doing such atrocities.

He wondered about the power he now seemed to harness, the power Theo and the sisters of Destiny had taken away from the creature all those years ago. Or at least that is what he and Fate thought at the time. It was evident that the Shadowman's abilities had grown, he was now able to manipulate creatures. There was no other explanation for what Theo was seeing. Only the Ents could uproot a tree this size, and they would never willingly attack a fellow creature.

Theo remembered back to the time he knew him, when Erebos bemoaned the fact that he was human. Back then, he had been concerned with being Zilla's equal, but that didn't seem to be the creature's motivation now. The power that he tapped into had seduced him and had him believing that draining the power of others would give him what he wanted. It seemed for all their efforts no change had been made. How were they to have known something much worse would be born from that day?

He moved to the fallen tree and knelt down beside it, resting his hand on the bark and thanking it for its service. Taksi bolted into the tree line, and Theo looked behind him. He heard it then, the slow shuffling pace of something making its way to the clearing. Picking up the box, he rose to his feet. He had the fleeting thought that he should get a bag from his house then realized, to his dismay, the access was gone. The place he had called home could only be accessed if the tree were still alive.

"You weren't here." The Ent's voice was deep and gravelly. Even though the tone was not accusing, Theo couldn't help but take it that way.

"I'm sorry," he said. "It couldn't be helped."

"Balance has come," the creature said slowly.

Theo was confused by his comment until he realized the trees must have been speaking amongst themselves about Tara. "I hope so," he said. He was more hopeful now that he had gotten to know her. "All of the elements are accounted for, and the sisters have returned. We will get the answers we need."

"Draw the negative." The Ent was closer now. Theo saw the facial features protruding from its bark. The trees only showed them when talking to non-tree folk. Otherwise, they communicated through their roots.

Theo thought about what he could be implying then nodded. "I agree, but we tried pulling it from him before. We only made matters worse."

"Funnel the negative," the Ent said. "Then ground it."

The comment was curious, but Theo found Ents, for the most part, were an intuitive culture. Their longevity allowed them to witness generations of change and gather their thoughts over long periods. They were creatures of few words, but the words were always worth hearing. It made him wonder if he had done himself any favors by cutting off communication entirely from the outside world. At the time, he had worried the word would somehow get out about his location, but he saw now the trees were as they always had been. Loyal to the cause. They would have kept his secrets.

Taksi stepped back into the clearing and settled down in a bed of moss. She didn't come close but seemed to be at ease with Theo talking to the Ent. He took her relaxed state as an indication that she knew he would be here a while. Ents were notoriously slow communicators. She had the right idea. Theo had some questions, so he sat on the ground, leaning up on the tree he called home for so long. He placed the obsidian box next to him, running his fingers across the top and touching the carvings that were there. He wondered about them, as much as he wondered about the entity who had put them there.

He prepared for a long conversation. "What can you tell me about the Shadowman?"

Tara woke the next morning alone in her bed. She had started out that way, but part of her had been hopeful that she wouldn't stay that way. She wasn't sure why. Theo hadn't given her the impression that he would be changing his mind, but she was a romantic at heart.

Pulling back the tears that threatened to fall, she sniffed her disappointment. There was no reason to cry, or at least there wasn't yet. But it wouldn't hurt to prepare for the inevitable. If her past relationships were any indication, she knew the friend-zone talk was coming next. This would especially be true since the circumstances forced Theo to spend time with her. Had they lived back home, chances are he would have just ghosted her like a lot of them did.

If Theo had decided that they wouldn't be a thing, she would need to make sure that she didn't invest in their friendship. She wasn't getting hurt again.

A knock sounded on the door, and she struggled to keep the hopeful tone from her voice.

"Come in."

The door opened slightly, and Brooke peeked her head through the crack.

"You alone?"

Tara couldn't help but snort. "Aren't I always?"

Brooke moved the rest of the way into the room and shut the door behind her. "I thought you and Theo were a thing." She sat on the bed and watched Tara as she paced.

"Frankly, I did too," Tara answered. "I don't know, Brooke. Maybe it's for the best. So much has happened in the last few days. I'm so confused."

"I understand completely," Brooke said. "Trust me, no one is more familiar with the games this place plays on your mind than I am."

Guilt rose from the pit of Tara's stomach and soured her throat. She didn't sense any anger from Brooke, even though she had every right to be. Her brother, and even Tara herself, had a part to play in Brooke's self-image.

"I'm so sorry I didn't believe you," Tara whispered. "Had I known..."

"How could you have?" Brooke shook her head and walked to where Tara was pacing. "How could anyone have?" She held Tara's shoulders, so her next comment wouldn't be ignored. "Tara, the only one that has any blame in this situation is the Shadowman."

The tears pooled once more. Tara couldn't help it. She was relieved by her friend's acceptance but horrified that she hadn't been there for her. "I just realize that so much of what you went through could have been avoided. I wish I could have been a better friend."

Brooke smiled, her eyes lit from within by strength and understanding. "You were a great friend," Brooke soothed. "And frankly, got me through some of the most desperate times of my life. I would have never given Will a second chance if it hadn't been for you."

"That was mostly Trina's doing. Although, I suppose I was good at keeping a steady flow of wine going during your misunderstanding."

"Exactly. Which is precisely what I will do for you."

"Meaning?"

"Meaning that I will keep a steady flow of wine going, while you both sort things out. He is totally into you, Tara. Not to mention that social lubricant helps during our training sessions. We found it's best not to be too tense, especially Sera. You saw the black stone tree in the back yard."

"That was her?" Tara started to wonder if perhaps they had the wrong girl. All she could do was talk to cats and heal people.

"It was," Brooke laughed. "She was learning to control her powers and really missed Logan. They were having issues at the time."

"Well, they both seemed to have gotten over whatever it was," Tara said. "They couldn't be more into each other if they were one person."

Brooke laughed and gave Tara a quick hug. "They definitely don't have trouble with PDA."

"Well, I don't either — within reason. But it seems Theo might."

"I didn't get that impression," Brooke said as she perched back on the bed. "It seems to me that he's quite taken with you."

"Really?" Tara shook her head. She wasn't sure she was seeing the same thing Brooke was. "I don't know, Brooke, he's so hard to read."

"Honestly, I believe quite the opposite. He is extremely forthcoming."

"That is what I'm worried about. When he left last night, he said he thought perhaps we shouldn't."

"Meaning what?"

"How the hell am I supposed to know?" Tara's irritation was starting to rise again. "I know what I want, he's the one that's hot and cold."

"I think it is more that he is a proper gentleman, and you don't quite know what to do with one of those."

Tara laughed. "Well, you have me there. I have dated some real creeps."

"We both have. I think you need a distraction," Brooke suggested. "Come on, Lovie, get dressed, and we'll join the others downstairs. Theo will come around. I have a really good feeling about him."

"I hope you're right," Tara mumbled. "Who knows what I could end up doing in Sevilla's back yard if I stay mad at him."

"I'm actually excited to see what you are capable of," Brooke said. "If what I've been reading in the book is a mere percentage, we should be in for some fun."

"Not sure about that, but I'm right behind you."

Brooke paused on her way out the door and looked back. Her face was glowing with love and happiness. "I'm glad you're here, Tara."

"I am too."

Brooke nodded and shut the door behind her, leaving Tara alone in her room to prepare herself for a new day. Perhaps her friend knew what she was talking about. After all, she knew the Shadowman was real, long before anyone else did, as her insight allowed her to see things more clearly. Things ended up muddled in Tara's mind when the emotions from the outside world blended with her own. Maybe it wouldn't be a bad idea to listen to a voice other than her own for once.

She decided things with Theo couldn't be forced. That, unlike her previous relationships, she would allow the time he needed to make his decision. It wasn't as if she had plans to leave anytime soon. Brooke needed her, and she was going to stay and help as long as it took. She finished dressing and went downstairs where the others were gathered. It was time to figure out just what she had been sent there for. Her relationship issues with Theo would have to wait.

There was a bustle of activity in the kitchen by the time Tara went downstairs. Brooke was helping Sevilla prepare breakfast, while Kadar got the fire going. There was no sign of Theo, but the other men were absent as well, so she considered that they might be together.

"Need me to do anything?" Sevilla was overdoing it, and Tara could feel her energy waning. She heard murmuring from the den and saw Sevilla's other two sisters having a private conversation. She couldn't tell from outside appearances, but she had the distinct impression Kadar was listening in on what they had to say.

"Could you hand this to Kadar?" Brooke gave Tara a large iron kettle filled with water. "It needs to go on for the tea."

"Got it." Tara walked up to Kadar and startled him into action. He stood quickly and took the kettle from her hands, sliding it on a hook in the mantle that held the kettle over the flames. She could pick up a few words here and there; she had probably assumed right, Kadar was listening in. Her ears perked up when she heard Theo's name.

Brooke's question drew her attention. "Tara, could you help me with these eggs?"

"Of course," Tara said. She glanced up at Kadar, and he gave a wink, sharing a knowing moment with her before she joined Brooke by the stove.

"Let me get the bread out of the oven," Sevilla said. She creaked the heavy door open and pulled out the two loaves that barely fit inside. Tara was amazed that she was able to cook anything at all in the cast iron giant. It looked like something that belonged in a museum.

"Hello, Tara," she said with a nod. After placing the loaves on the table to cool, she walked back and gave Tara a hug. "I want to thank you for what you did for me," she said softly.

"You're welcome, Sevilla," Tara said, taking a step back. "I'm just glad I could help."

"It's appreciated more than you could know," Kadar said from behind Tara. She glanced back in time to witness an exchange between him and Sevilla. There were no words, but Tara had the distinct impression that she had walked in on a private conversation. She decided to concentrate on the eggs, since they were the only thing in the room that didn't have feelings.

"What did you need me to do with these?"

"I think they just need to be stirred for now," Brooke said. "Sevilla's stove takes a bit of getting used to."

"I can imagine," Tara said. She lifted the wooden spoon and stirred eggs in the pan, which were already starting to cook. "I should be able to handle this."

"Are you sure?"

Tara's head snapped to the side, and she looked into Brooke's smiling face. Leave it to her to bring up her lack of cooking skills. She used to be in denial of it, but now she had fully embraced it.

"I can handle cooking eggs."

"Not from what I can remember," Brooke grinned.

Tara laughed. "You are the worst! Go finish cutting the fruit."

There was a knock, and Sevilla opened the door to let Theo inside. He was carrying a load of wood, which he stacked by the fireplace. Tara did a mental check for injuries. Finding none, she turned her attention back to the eggs.

"You are looking much better, Sevilla." His voice was raspy, as if he had stayed up all night talking. Where had he gone? And more importantly, who had he been with?

"Thanks to Tara," she responded. "The others should be here shortly. Make yourself at home."

Tara heard Theo's hesitant footsteps as he approached her. She could feel him hovering behind her, looking over her shoulder to see what she was cooking.

"Good Morning, Tara." It didn't matter if her mind told her to keep her distance, her body had entirely other thoughts. His voice did funny things to her. She tried not to let her reaction show in her reply.

"Oh, hello, Theo."

He leaned in closer. He smelled of pine needles and mint. The mint didn't seem so farfetched, since she knew Sevilla had herbs close to the house that hadn't been killed off by frost. But the pine needles, were something else. Had he slept outside? His warm breath tickled her ear as did his whiskers that had lengthened over the last couple of days. She locked her neck in place, fighting against the urge to tip her head and give him access.

He spoke softly into her ear. "You're burning them."

"What?" she said, snapping her head around and glaring at him. She looked at the eggs in the pan, and sure enough, they were smoking. Grabbing the nearest kitchen towel, she took hold of the handle and marched toward the door. "If you hadn't distracted me, I would have been fine."

He came up from behind and stepped in front of her to open the door.

She blew past him, the scent of smoldering eggs wafting behind her. Sera and Logan were making their way up the walk as he replied. Amie and Aleck were a few steps behind them.

"You're acting as if this is my fault."

She made her way around the back of the house and stomped to the nearby creek. He was still behind her, step for step. Flipping the pan released most of the eggs, but there was a blackened crust at the bottom.

"It is your fault," Tara argued. "If you had just left me alone, we wouldn't be in this predicament."

She squatted down, picked up a rock, and started scraping the pan. The aggressive nature of the rocks peeling the burnt eggs almost drowned out his response.

"I'm confused. Are we speaking of the eggs or something different?"

She left the pan on the ground as she stood to make her point. "You know, for someone so smart you sure are clueless at times."

"Is that a yes or no on the eggs?"

"For heaven's sake," Tara shouted. "This isn't about the eggs!"

"Clearly," he said dryly. "What I am trying to determine is why you are upset with me when I wasn't even around this morning."

Tara looked at him pointedly, pursing her lips. She couldn't help the sarcastic look on her face. Folding her arms in front of her, she continued to stare at him in the hopes that the light bulb would go off. Did she really have to spell it out for him?

His lips pulled up in a smirk, which he hid quickly beneath his hand. He rubbed his facial hair as if that was what he had intended to do all along. That he was trying not to laugh at her was even more infuriating than the fact that he couldn't make up his mind if he was into her or not.

"I think I understand," he said softly. He lifted his hands and spread out his arms. Did he honestly expect her to go to him?

She shook her head. Her arms were still crossed as he took the few steps it took to bring her into his embrace. "I don't think you do," she said with a pout.

His arms wrapped around her, and she stood stiffly as he settled into the embrace. She breathed in deeply, and her face gravitated toward his chest. She could hear his heartbeat, and her arms loosened of their own accord and wrapped around his waist. She melted into him, blocking out every emotion she was picking up from the others and focusing only on his strength. There were no friendship worries, no burnt eggs, only Theo and his calming presence.

Theo kissed the top of her head then laid his cheek there, pulling her tighter as she settled into the hug. "You needed grounding," he said quietly. "You really need to learn how to block the other energies. You can't keep absorbing everyone's excess."

Her response was muffled in his chest. A chest she would be happy to be pressed against the rest of the day. "I know, but it's all so new. I am having a hard time connecting all of the dots."

"It seems my effort last night to keep you from draining your energy stores had the opposite effect."

"I find I'm much more relaxed when you're around."

"Well, since we're being honest, I'm more relaxed when I'm around also. I just worry about the strain on you at night when I am not awake to block its effects."

"That is why you stayed away last night? Because of what happened at the Inn and again with Sevilla?"

"Precisely."

"It wasn't about you not wanting to be around me?"

"No. If anything, it's the opposite. I want to be around you all the time."

Tara tipped her head up and smiled at his honesty. Finally, what he said was matching the emotions he had already shared with her. He raised his hands to cup her face, dipping his head down to kiss her softly. The reverence by which he did so almost brought her to tears.

"I will speak to Sevilla. There must be something we can use that will block your abilities. A stone or a crystal."

"Thank you, Theo."

"If I'm honest, I would rather stop trying to fight against it. I just hope she has something, since it's getting harder to keep my distance." He gave her another kiss then walked over to the discarded pan and picked it up by the handle. "Shall we try this again?"

"All right, wise guy," Tara laughed. Her heart was light, and her cheeks flushed from his earlier admission. "But this time, you can do the cooking, and I will do the distracting."

"I might quite like that," he said with a grin.

By the time they got back into the kitchen and finished another batch of eggs, Will and James had arrived. With everyone present and accounted for, they sat down to a hearty breakfast and planned their day. It was agreed that Brooke, Amie, and Sera would take Tara outside and show her some techniques that they used to tap into the higher levels of their powers.

Tara's healing and ability to speak to animals were only the beginning. If what Theo had seen in the Elemental Journal all those years ago was correct, she would end up with abilities that even he had never been able to harness. She would need to tap into them quickly. It wouldn't be long before the Shadowman made his move, according to the Ent.

With the expected spike in her energy and her inability to balance her own emotions, he needed to find something that could help him channel her energy. There was no way he would be leaving her side from now on.

"Theo, what do you think? Should we reinforce the wards now that we are all here?" Sevilla waited for his response, but he had a feeling he had missed part of the question. Tara wasn't the only distracted one.

"That would be a good idea," he answered. "The women's combined energy could act like a deterrent. We don't want any unwanted visitors."

"Perhaps a few of us could patrol the perimeter outside of the barrier," Aleck suggested. "That could give us advance warning of an enemy's arrival."

"Good idea," Logan nodded. "Zilla will patrol the outskirts with me." He pointed to Will, who was sitting beside James. "Ya can stay closer to Sevilla's with Aleck."

"The Mountain Lion could be helpful," Zilla said. "She came with you, right Tara?"

"She did. I can let her know what we need, but I'm not sure she will be much help with you Logan."

"I dinnae need help," Logan said with a grin. "She can walk with Zilla, since they're both cats."

Tara had no idea what he was implying but let the comment go. There were too many conversations to keep track of with so many people present. She felt Theo's hand slide over hers and give a gentle squeeze. She felt instantly better and slipped her hand into his.

"Sevilla, I was hoping you had something that Tara could carry to buffer her from being drained so dangerously. Or taking on too much."

"Say no more," she said as she rose. "I have just the thing, Theo. I'll be right back."

The third sister, Fate, spoke for the first time since her arrival. She was the spitting image of her other two sisters, save the white hair and eyes. "I will remain inside with Kadar and Sevilla," she said, more to James, who was sitting beside her than to the rest of the group. "It will give us an opportunity to catch up."

James looked slightly worried then murmured a response after meeting Tara's glance. He wanted to protect Fate; Tara could feel it from across the table. But something was holding him back from voicing his concerns. Tara thought there was still an unresolved issue between them. At least, that was the impression she had. Fate was harder to read than James was, which she found interesting.

Sevilla returned with a bracelet, made with black shiny stones, which looked like the tree behind her house. At closer look, Tara noted there were smaller lavender stones in between each larger black one. It looked like something you would find at a New Age store but had chain links holding it together instead of elastic.

"Here, put this on," she said as she wrapped it around Tara's wrist and did the clasp. "This should help you tune most of what is coming to you out."

"It's beautiful," Tara said. "What is it made of?"

"Black Tourmaline," Sevilla answered. "And the lavender stones are amethyst. They will help with healing."

"It's beautiful." Tara felt the effects almost immediately. "I'll be sure to take good care of it."

"It's a gift."

"Thank you, Sevilla," Theo said with a nod.

"Yes, thank you," Tara added.

"It's my pleasure," Sevilla said with a smile. "Now, what is on the agenda for the day?"

24

As had been discussed, the four women went outside after helping Sevilla clean up. The men had already decided on their plans and went out to start their rounds. Tara was curious about Logan and wondered which form he would choose to make his watch in. She didn't get the chance to watch him change into "wolf mode" as Sera called it, which was somewhat disappointing.

Zilla walked out to Tara in the yard. She was also preparing to make her rounds, although Tara thought the corset, black leather pants, and heeled boots weren't the most appropriate thing to wear for a stroll in the woods.

"I'd like to meet your familiar," she said to Tara. "I'm ready to head out, much too stuffy in there." She nodded back to the house then shifted her corset up and checked her nails.

"Familiar?"

Zilla looked at her as if she were dense. "Yes, darling. Your giant kitty cat."

Her impatience rattled Tara. The woman's confidence made her insecure. "Oh, okay. Give me a moment." Tara closed her eyes, mainly so she could block out Zilla's body language.

Taksi, come. Even though she knew she wouldn't understand the word, she added it anyway. *Please.*

She watched the tree line, the place where Theo said he had left her when he returned. He had explained that she kept him company the night before, and Tara wasn't sure how she felt about that. On one hand, she was glad her feline friend kept watch over Theo, but on the other, she was jealous of the alone time they had.

"She's beautiful," Sera exclaimed.

Tara glanced back and followed to where Sera was pointing. Taksi was coming out of the wood from the other direction. It seemed that she had already been doing patrols. Tara wouldn't put it past her to avoid all the places Logan was checking.

Taksi strolled past the ladies, raising her head and acknowledging the oohs and ahhs, but walking straight to Zilla. She circled around her, sniffing the air then coming around where Tara stood and flopped right on her back. She stretched and batted at Zilla's boots as if there were a cat toy dangling from them. Not that Tara was an expert on mountain lions, but she had never seen anything like it in her life.

"Well, there's a good kitty," Zilla said as she bent down to scratch behind Taksi's ears. "Aren't you a lovely?" Rumbling sounded from Taksi's chest as she wiggled closer to Zilla's hands.

"She seems to like you," Tara said.

Zilla stood up, and Taksi pulled herself up and sat beside her. It made Tara feel as though Zilla had been chosen over her in some strange way.

"It's a cat thing," Zilla shrugged.

Tara had no idea what that meant until Zilla shrank down, clothes and all, and morphed into a small black cat. Tara glanced back to Brooke, looking for confirmation that she wasn't seeing things. Brooke gave her a lopsided smile and nod. Amie and Sera were chatting and ignoring the scene, as if Zilla made the change every day.

The cat was tiny in comparison to Taksi, but it was clear who the alpha female was in their friendship. Tara watched stunned, as the black cat gave her a wink then strutted down the path, followed closely by her new best friend. There was no denying the cat was Zilla, not only did it have her brilliant emerald eyes, but there was no mistaking the strut.

"There's something you don't see every day," Tara exclaimed.

"You do at my house," Sera laughed. "You'll get used to it."

Brooke took her arm and led her to the back of the house. "There are a few things I am still getting used to as well. Best to keep an open mind."

"I'll try," Tara promised. "What do you need me to do?"

"I think for starters, you should tell us what you can do so far," Amie suggested.

"Okay. Well, you've seen me heal. That was something I had started doing back home. Small stuff, like headaches and such. It's only gotten stronger since I've arrived here."

"We all went through similar situations," Brooke explained. "For whatever reason, mine came to me a little earlier than Amie's and Sera's. I'm not sure why but may have something to do with what was happening here."

"Fate and Theo seem to be the key to it all," Sera said. "Perhaps we will get some answers now."

"Not sure how much Theo knows, honestly. He spent the last 75 years alone, living in a tree."

"Doesn't sound fun," Sera said.

"Sounds like what they did to Ryker," Amie suggested. "They seem to have a thing with banishment."

"Maybe we can find some answers later in the journal to explain that," Brooke said. "Once you two started tapping into your energy more often, the book filled in."

"I remember," Amie said.

"Okay, new girl. Show us what you've got." Sera swept her arm sideways as if she were clearing a path. Tara stepped further into the back near the obsidian tree.

"We found this is the best place to practice," Brooke explained. "The stone absorbs our excess energy and allows us to practice longer. You have your bracelet?"

Tara nodded and held her arm up to show her.

"Brilliant. That should help."

"It already has," Tara said. Between wearing it and standing near the stone tree, she could hardly feel the ladies' emotions at all.

"You also mentioned communicating with animals. Have you tried manipulating your surroundings?"

Tara looked at Brooke in question, creasing her brow.

"You know, like moving rocks and such," Sera said. She pushed her arm forward, and a ball of fire shot from her fingertips. Brooke pulled her arms up, and a gush of water from the stream doused it. "Show off," Sera smirked.

"Look who's talking," Amie laughed. "My abilities center more around me turning into actual Air. Although, I can also manipulate it to the extent that I can move or uproot things."

"Don't let her kid you," Sera said. "She is a full-on tornado if she sets her mind to it."

Amie smiled. "Nothing compared to what these ladies can do."

Tara's feelings of inadequacy snuck in as the women looked expectantly at her to chime in. "I have been known to help plants grow."

Sera and Amie shared a look with Brooke, then Sera patted Tara on the shoulder. "Not exactly offense material, but maybe we can work with it," Sera said. "Let's see what you've got, Earth girl."

Inside the house, Fate, Sevilla, and Kadar had settled down in the den with some wine. It was one of Fate's favorites, a buttery Chardonnay that made her taste buds sing. She hadn't had any since the last time she was with Zilla, since the Shadowman had always preferred reds.

As she sipped her wine, she contemplated just how much of the future to reveal. The voices had shown her a few paths, but it was the one that included Sevilla's friend, Kadar, that interested her the most. Fate had the impression that they had been friends much longer than anyone realized.

Sevilla's voice broke the silence. From her tone, Fate could tell she was nervous. "I presume you have questions about my relationship with Kadar?"

Fate nodded slowly. Her questions stemmed deeper than that, but it was a good place to start. "When did you two meet?"

Kadar cleared his throat and responded. "About 10 years after the Earth's second world war."

"That was some time ago," Fate said quietly. Over 65 years, how had she not sensed that?

"We weren't speaking," Sevilla explained. "You had left me here thinking that Zilla had been the one that caused Ryker's death. It wasn't until recently that I learned that wasn't the case."

Tears formed in Fate's eyes, but she refused to let them fall. Now wasn't the time.

"When Brooke came into my life, we felt it would be best if she thought I lived alone. She was so young. Kadar helped me by keeping watch over her in the Earth realm."

"I also worked for Erebos," Kadar added. "I earned his trust and when Roy took over and the Shadowman's power grew, I reported back to Sevilla when I was able to get away. He had no shortage of errands he sent me on."

"Did you know Zilla?"

"I did," he answered. "Erebos had a love/hate relationship with her in the early days. He was fighting her allure years before Roy showed up. After which, she was there a lot more."

Fate nodded her head, taking it all in. Kadar's ability to keep secrets didn't sit well with her. It made her wonder if Sevilla truly knew who, or what, he was. How he was able to mask the overwhelming power he held at bay was a mystery to her. His knowledge was vast. How had Zilla not seen it?

"And did you know Ryker?" Fate waited for the answer that she already knew. The answer that would bring more heartache to her sister.

"He couldn't possibly," Sevilla started, then shifted in her seat. "Kadar?"

Fate couldn't see his expression, but from Sevilla's reaction, she knew it was one of guilt. A crack echoed in the room, the sound of a palm on skin, then the rub of the chair legs on the floor as Sevilla stood. "Get out," she sobbed.

"Sevilla…" he pleaded. "Let me explain."

"Years, Kadar. You have had years to explain," she insisted. "I trusted you with my thoughts. My mind. Please leave now." Her sobs echoed in the room.

"As you wish," he said softly, and as he walked slowly from the room, Fate finally realized what he was. She felt sorry for him, he clearly cared for Sevilla but was also true to his nature. The D'Jinn were known to be powerful but extremely manipulative.

Sevilla dropped down next to Fate. She placed her hand gently on Sevilla's head as she cried into the lap she had ready for her. It would be some time, long after the tears had slowed and the sobs turned to hiccups, before Sevilla would say another word.

"We must reinforce the wards."

"You know we cannot," Fate said softly. "He moves in and out of all dimensions. Our magick is useless against him."

"You know what he is then?"

"I do. I also know that you gave your heart to him."

"I did," Sevilla said quietly. Fate could feel her lip quivering on her leg. "Things are so complicated now. I didn't know when I met him that Ryker was still alive. Now, I don't know how I will ever face my husband. I no longer know my place in all of this."

Fate laid her hands on Sevilla's shoulders, calming their shake. "It seems that none of us do," Fate agreed. "But I do know that we need to stick together if we are going to get through this. The Shadowman won't stop until he gathers every bit of power here in Wisteria. And when he's done, he will set his sights on new worlds."

"The sapphire ring we spoke of earlier can never go back into the Shadowman's possession. He cannot know the power Kadar wields."

"Access through Kadar would be devastating. Zilla can't know of its power either."

Sevilla sighed and rested her head once more in Fate's lap. She soothed her sister's long hair from her face, giving her a few more minutes to pull herself together before the others returned. She didn't have the heart to tell Sevilla that the Universe wasn't finished with her and Kadar yet. It wasn't in her nature to share such things, but it made her wonder if by not sharing what she knew, if that got them where they were in the first place.

Just as it had been in the past, she knew only time would tell.

25

After the training session, Tara needed some extra grounding, so she remained outside near the obsidian tree. Everyone else had gone inside to have an early dinner, except for Logan and Will, who were taking their shift of guard duty. Brooke wasn't entirely comfortable with the decision, although it surprised Tara to learn that his magical ability was real, not just sleight of hand. Tara was impressed, especially since she had seen him do some incredible stuff. Brooke had explained that Will had some dormant powers that came to life when they traveled to Wisteria the first time.

She had her eyes closed and her head back against the tree when she heard Mato's voice. It startled her, but it didn't surprise her he had come.

"You've embraced your power." She opened her eyes to see his form floating in front of her. The trees in the distance could be seen through him, like seeing images through the smoke of a fire. With all that she had seen and the belief system he instilled in her, she wasn't surprised by that either.

"It was much easier with your teachings. I can't thank you enough."

He nodded slowly, allowing a small secretive smile to light his eyes. It was always that way with him. As if he was always responding to much more than you had asked.

"I did what was asked of me. What was expected."

A part of her already knew the answer to her question, but she asked it anyway. "Expected by whom?" She held her breath as his kind smile calmed her expectant heart.

"Your grandmother and all who came before her. We have been waiting for the one who brings balance, the flute bearer. The doorway opening to your song was a sign, as was the arrival of your spirit guide."

"Taksi," Tara whispered.

"Little Sister," Mato said. "She has waited a long time for you and will finish what I started. It is time for me to go home."

Tara had a sinking feeling he didn't mean his house. Her question caught in her throat. "What do you mean?"

His bowed his head, and his soothing aura covered her like a blanket. "You know what I mean, Wakanyeja." She smiled at the term of endearment, the meaning "little sacred one" now gave her pause. She always thought he was being evasive in his responses, but perhaps she had only ever heard what she was ready for.

As much as she didn't want to say goodbye, she knew it was time. "I will miss you," she said quietly.

"And I you, but I am ready for the next world. The challenge before you will be faced with your new family. Remember to keep the balance."

Tara watched as his image faded, raising her hand to meet his. There was no regret, contentment flowed between them.

"Your work friends were worried. I told them you had left for your journey sooner than expected."

She was grateful he had told her. It was one less worry for her mind. "Thank you, Mato."

He faded from view as his final words were said. "As above, it is below. Within your being, let the energy flow."

After Mato disappeared, she stayed outside for a few more minutes. As peaceful of a goodbye as it was, she was still misty over it. She meditated on their relationship and Mato's teachings, and quickly found her center. Once she did, she felt she was ready to face the others.

It was a good thing she had taken the time to ground, since she entered a house awash with broken trust and heartache. Sevilla and Fate were quiet, and Tara wondered if it had to do with Kadar leaving. She had seen him walk into the woods earlier. Tara had assumed he was doing his assigned duties, but it had to be something more.

Theo and Brooke were oblivious to the mood and had their heads bent over the Elemental Journal. They were examining the pages as Sera chopped vegetables. It warmed her heart to see the two most important people in her life getting along so well.

"It shows here that in addition to manipulating roots and stone, there is a way for the Earth element to create golems," Theo said.

"Like what the Shadowman does?" Sera said.

Theo looked up at her, confusion, and then shock crossed his face. "He's able to create golems? How can that be?" He looked back down at the book and pointed to the page he and Brooke had just been reading. "It says that energy is harnessed by Earth. I wasn't even able to do that with ease."

"He seems to have a blend of powers," Aleck added. "He is able to control lightning and fire as well."

"That just doesn't make sense," Theo mused. "Has he had this ability all along?"

"Not at first," Zilla said. "They came to him slowly. I tried to distract him as best I could. His ambition soon out-weighed his libido."

"TMI," Amie muttered.

Zilla shot her a sad smile then made her way into the den.

"Excuse me." Amie stood and followed her. Tara was glad. Amie had some unresolved issues with the seductress that needed to be worked out. It had nothing to do with Aleck, as Tara had first presumed. Broken trust seemed to permeate more than one relationship in the room.

"If the power grew over time, maybe the Shadowman did the same," Tara said. She thought of Mato's final message to her. "I can't help but think of the mirror the Lakota speak of. What is above, is below. Circle of life and all that."

Brooke nodded and started to pace the room. "Let's examine that," she said. "If while we were gathering energy, he did as well, where does that leave us? And how was he able to tap into it?"

"It was available all along," Fate said quietly. "He and Cela just managed to find a way to gather it. When we pulled it from him, I'm not sure it dispersed to the four corners like it should have."

"I think you're right," Theo said. "At least as far as the toxic energy went. Perhaps that is what he has been tapping into all along."

"And the ladies have been gathering the positive side of that?" Sevilla looked as if a lightbulb had gone off in her mind. "If that's the case, there is just as much of an imbalance as last time."

"It was a mess last time," Zilla said as she walked in from the den. Amie followed behind her. Tara noted they both looked much more relaxed.

"Part of that had to do with the fact that you guarded Erebos at the last minute."

"Yes, but you were going to kill him," Zilla said to Fate. "It wasn't all me, by the way. Ryker also sent buffering energy."

Tara took in a deep breath and placed her hand over the bracelet on her wrist. The movement was noticed by Theo.

"That's enough." His no-nonsense tone stopped the bickering. Tensions were running high. She decided to stay as long as she could then would go outside to chat with Taksi. A walk would do her some good. She could tell by Theo's expression he was looking out for her.

"I believe the thought Tara had earlier was good," he said. "If we think of the energy as a mirror, with everything on both sides needing the other to survive, it's possible that we're looking at this the wrong way."

"What do you mean?" Tara placed her hand on his arm and instantly felt better.

"I mean perhaps we weren't meant to destroy the negative energy that Erebos had gathered. Maybe we were supposed to absorb it."

Tara thought about Mato and the conversations they would have for hours on the delicate balance between ambition and obsession, between guidance and control. It all boiled down to how you looked at things, and how each person lived with their choices. "What are you saying? That the power would have needed to be split four ways?"

"Yes, and when we tried it before, Anton was already dead," Fate said softly. James's arm slid closer to her side, and Tara presumed he had slid his hand over hers. He was giving his support, but he looked uncomfortable with the topic.

"Precisely. And like it shows here, each of us would have been responsible for balancing their own energy. There was no way we could have succeeded without all four of us."

"We have all four elements now," Theo said.

"No fucking way!" Aleck stood and pounded his fist on the table. His chair tipped back and crashed to the floor, silencing the room. "Amie isn't doing it."

"I'll be okay, Aleck." Amie rose to her feet and pulled him into an embrace. He hid his face in her neck and murmured things only she could hear. She rubbed his back until he was finished, and her soft response was the only thing Tara heard from the entire conversation. "We'll be okay. I need to do my part, so we can all be safe."

He nodded at her, and she gave him a gentle kiss before settling back down in her seat. He stood beside her for a moment then looked at each one of the people sitting around the table before landing his eyes on Theo. His jaw was tense as he spoke. "You'd better know what you are doing. One hair on her head gets hurt and you'll wish you never met me." He stormed out of the house, leaving the door wide open as he made his exit.

Amie looked as though she was torn between standing her ground and racing out the door after him. She looked relieved when James offered to go talk to him. Zilla righted Aleck's discarded seat and murmured in Amie's ear. It prompted a smile and a shake of Amie's head, after which she thanked her quietly.

"He's worried about the babies," Fate said quietly.

There was a gasp, then everyone at the table turned to look at Amie. Even Brooke seemed surprised, which was odd, since she and Amie seemed close. Amie's cheeks flamed, and she struggled to put her thoughts into words. She took a deep breath then confirmed Fate's comment.

"He is worried about the babies," Amie said. "All three of them."

"Triplets?" Sevilla's question wasn't to Amie but to her sister, Fate. Fate nodded slowly but remained silent.

"That's right," Amie said. "We knew about the pregnancy but didn't know specifics until recently."

"Why didn't you say anything?" Sera was up on her feet and joining Brooke as they took turns hugging her. "I knew something was up. I can't believe I didn't put two and two together."

"Well, you were getting married to Logan, and things have been so crazy lately."

"It's brilliant, really," Brooke said. "I'm so happy for you, Amie."

Tara made her way outside as the rest of the group made their congratulations. The past few hours had been a bit much, and she needed to regroup. She snuck out without anyone noticing and went to find Taksi.

26

The power had been coming back to the Shadowman in small bits over time, but now that he found the key, it was as if he was a conduit. He was tapping into energy all around him. He was confident that once he was able to drain the powers the women held, he would be free of the burdensome life forces he kept bottled in his study. Erebos, the man who started it all, who brought the pieces of his soul back together and allowed him another chance at existence, would soon be no more.

He had evolved, first allowing the weak human to believe he was the one in control. The Shadowman whispered in Erebos' mind, forming paths into his psyche that his power-hungry soul would follow. It didn't take long for the energy known as "Roy" to take hold. He had been stronger than Erebos, more willing to make the necessary sacrifices.

But the Shadowman realized quickly that Roy was harder to control. He was only interested in carnal delights so spent more time fucking than he did concentrating on the future. He too served his purpose and had been reduced to a sparkling liquid in a bottle. Roy's essence was dark with bits of light, Erebos' bright with black veining. Opposites in the bottles as they were in life. When he was able to live without his current corporeal shell, the Shadowman would crush the vials under his heel and be free of them both.

"Billy," he called through the echoing halls of the place he had called home for an eternity. "I need you to come with me now."

The Shadowman had left the Ent outside. The lumbering creature would quite possibly come in handy, so he instructed him to find a place nearby to root. The others, he had left behind. He had been in a hurry so picked the youngest of the trees to bring back, as it was much easier to manipulate than a more established one would have been. The Shadow-man hardly gave the creature another thought. He was more interested in checking on his army.

"Billy," he called again. Where was he? The satyr wasn't normally this unresponsive. Perhaps the time had come for him to find another man-servant, especially since he had killed this one's brother, and he would most likely be upset about it.

The Shadowman made it all the way to his study, and there was still no sign of the satyr. "Disappointing," he muttered, lifting the lid on his black obsidian box centered on his desk. He had recreated it years ago after his other one had been hidden away from him. Looking at the shard, he ran his fingers over the engravings that Cela had unlocked the secrets to. "I finally found you."

Dipping it in a nearby pitcher, he watched as the water turned pink with Henry's blood. He had a flash of regret as he watched it swirl, think-ing to himself that it was hard to find good help. He wiped it clean with his sleeve before placing it in his stone box.

"Billy!"

After a half hour, and with no luck finding the saytr, the Shadowman was forced to proceed without him. He would deal with his lack of atten-tion later. Finding new help would be first on his agenda but only after checking on his project. Slipping his hand into his box, he grasped the engraved shard and carried it to the stairs. He walked down to the lower level and turned opposite of the holding cells to make his way into his workshop. Perhaps after he met with Ryker, he would visit the cell on the end. His excitement would need some release, and Zilla was always hungry for his attention.

The opening to the lower cavern was just as he had left it. He waved his hands over the smooth surface of the obsidian until the glowing green symbols he carved centuries ago formed in the stone. He shuffled the images into the combination that would grant him entry. This place had been a lucky find, but each time he was left without a suitable shell to house his memory, he was forced to start anew.

It had taken him centuries and a variety of hosts to get this far. With each body, the holes in his memory took longer to piece together, but he always managed to make his way back to the place where his past was waiting. His stories were carved in these walls, meticulously created by each form he came back in. He knew from these carvings the next phase of his evolution was near, but he was losing patience.

His journey was becoming tiresome, considering how many times the witches had stopped him, or the bodies he chose gave out on him. Erebos had been the easiest to manipulate, but he was human, and mortals never lasted long. The Shadowman wasn't interested in finding another body to dwell in. He wanted his own form back. He needed to unlock the secrets the Elements had pulled from him so long ago.

He knew the key to his immortality was in the journal as were the spells to heal those that most called dead. Miracles were what they were known as to humans, and at one point, Erebos saw a few scribblings in the Journal over the Elf King's shoulder and put it to memory. The Shadowman used the knowledge, as well as the green substance, to slow the aging process down in Erebos's body, but it wasn't enough.

The Shadowman wanted immortality, and he wanted to be free of the bonds that tied him to a body. The life he was forced to borrow had lost its luster. Not only did he need the elemental powers but also the book that held their secrets. He wanted his life back — the one that had been taken from him so long ago.

A bright green glow lit his path up a narrow hall and down several flights of stairs. He learned from the carvings that his home had been built before the pyramids in the Earth realm were constructed. He had found veins of the material in other sites, even mined it along the way, but this was the one place he always came back to. The place he called home.

The final hallway had pockets carved on each side where the workers rested, and he was happy to note they were all working. There were all types of creatures here, all under the command of Ryker in his absence. As he turned the corner, the empty hall opened into a cavernous room, and what he saw delighted him.

Glowing green statues stood awaiting their command. Rows and rows of them standing in silence as the craftsmen chipped out their features. They were rustic, no more features than were necessary for them to be effective once animated. That was the only reason Ryker was still alive. He was foolish enough to believe the witch would be spared when the time came. Like so many that came before him, the Shadowman used his weakness against him.

He stood nearby, watching the workers as they chiseled the next block. The smaller pieces were picked up and placed in baskets, to be used for things such as knives or arrowheads. Unlike the chains that held his other captives, the chains around Ryker's ankle were made from plain iron. The Shadowman felt it was necessary for him to have his full strength. All other creatures were secured with chains made from the material which provided a constant stream of energy he was able to tap from at will.

"They have made great progress," the Shadowman said. Ryker acknowledged him with a nod then gazed out at the creations that stood waiting.

"They have," he said with a sigh. His shoulders slumped in defeat, and the Shadowman knew the cause. He didn't concern himself with Ryker's moods. There were far too many things that still needed to get done.

"I have found the key," the Shadowman said proudly. He lifted it in front of him and looked again at the symbols. They had been created for another purpose entirely, and he remembered it was Hecate that wove magick into the language. When she added intent, the symbols were infused forevermore with a power he longed to harness.

Ryker sighed. "And the journal?"

"I don't have it yet," he admitted. "But you can have the workers start carving these into the statues."

"I told you the journal would ensure we would be able to control the golems. Without it, I can't be sure that the magick will work."

"I will worry about the magick. Your only responsibility is to keep this safe and keep the workers carving."

"Yes, my lord."

He placed the shard in Ryker's outstretched hand and hesitated as the Mage wrapped his fingers around it. He had a momentary thought that perhaps he shouldn't leave it in his hands, but it wisped away like smoke from a fire. There was no need to worry. The Shadowman had control over Ryker through his wife, Sevilla. He wasn't going anywhere.

Ryker shuffled over to the first glowing statue and called the nearest worker over to him. The Shadowman left the room just as Ryker was giving his instruction. The shard was firm in his grip as if his life depended on it. The irony was, he was right in many ways.

The final stage of his project was now in play. The time had come to force the truth from Fate. He needed that journal.

27

Dinner had long finished, and Theo was concerned about Tara. She had left during some heated discussion, and the effects showed in her tense gait through the door. He had wanted to give her time alone in order to repower her drained stores, but she had been gone too long.

Most of the couples had already made their way to bed. Logan and Zilla had returned from their patrols with Taksi, who remained outside. Aleck, James, and Will went out to take their place on the rounds. Even though Tara was most likely catching up with Taksi, it was cold, and she hadn't taken a jacket.

He went outside and looked for her, his eyes adjusting in the dark. He found her near the Obsidian tree, curled up with Taksi. She looked up as he approached, her eyes were lit from within like reflections in a pool. The glow of energy present let him know she was feeling better.

"I needed to ground," Tara explained. "Emotions were high, and I'm not good with being around that many people."

"The conversation was a bit volatile. There are a lot of past issues that remain unresolved. With your friends and mine."

"Human nature, I suppose," she shrugged.

"Pretty much every living creature's nature," he added.

"True," she laughed, moving over to allow him to sit next to her. He shifted her to his lap and felt the cool touch of her bottom on his thighs.

"You're half frozen," he complained. "You really shouldn't have stayed out here that long."

"I was just catching up with Taksi," she sighed. The feline rubbed her head in Tara's lap, forcing an ear scratch. "Just a few more minutes, then we can go in. Besides, I'm starting to warm up quite nicely now."

"To the detriment of my legs," Theo said. "Although I have to admit, I do like you close like this."

"I like it too."

Theo's arms wrapped loosely around her, and Taksi paused for one more scratch before wandering off and leaving them alone. He presumed she was going to see what the men were up to, since he had seen Will earlier at the edge of the property. Theo was surprised by his ability; the human was a natural born Mage. The way he manipulated energy was impressive, and the spheres of electricity lit the night like will-o'-the-wisps from his part of Wisteria. He thought of the beauty of his kingdom and found himself wondering if Tara would love it as much as he did. For the first time in ages, he longed for home.

He shifted, and she slipped off his lap, standing up and holding her hand out for his. She pulled him up and slid into his arms as he stood. The kiss warmed him to the point where he almost didn't feel the cold, but when her fingers touched his face, he led her inside.

The house was quiet, and the fire was dying. He tossed one more log on to provide embers the next morning. He pulled the kettle from the hook and motioned with his head toward the stairs. "You head up. I will be right behind you."

Tara nodded and slowly walked up the stairs. She looked tired, and a good night's sleep would help them both. Theo took the kettle to the counter and pulled some mugs from the cupboard, along with some of Sevilla's lavender tea. He poured cups for them both, adding honey, lemon, and a shot from what was left of Logan's bottle before joining Tara.

He walked into the room with the mugs and noted that a fire had already been started in their room. It helped with the chill, and Tara was already curled up on the small couch that sat in front of it. She took the cup he handed her gratefully.

"What did I miss after I left?" Tara asked. "Anything good?"

"Not too terribly much," Theo admitted. "Although Brooke and I did get a few more answers from the journal." He sat next to her on the couch, and she slid nearer, resting her head on his arm.

"I don't feel as if I'm going to be much help," Tara said quietly.

"I disagree," Theo soothed. "In fact, you are going to be the most help of all the elements. Without your ability, there are those that would die.

I've seen it happen first-hand."

"I suppose."

He kissed the top of her head, conveniently resting in the crook of his arm. He could stay that way forever. "One thing I know for sure is that for this to work, all four of you will be needed. Which brings me to the next thing I need to tell you. It's about the other night."

"We already talked about that, Theo."

"Not about you being angry with me. The part about what I found while I was out. I ended up going back to the tree."

"You went back there? Without me?"

"Taksi went with me," he offered. "So, I wasn't completely alone."

"I suppose that makes me feel better," Tara said with a shrug. She sipped on her tea, and her shudder made Theo chuckle.

"What did you add to this?"

"I believe it's a shot of Logan's scotch," Theo said. "I couldn't find any whiskey."

She took another sip. "First one was a surprise. The second not so bad. I think it's helping."

"I thought it might," he said. He sipped his tea, and the effects were soothing. Sevilla's tea had a calming quality even without the addition of Logan's spirits.

"Thank you for taking such good care of me, Theo. I really do appreciate it."

"You're welcome."

Tara took another sip of tea then leaned forward to place the cup on the floor. She sat back and closed her eyes, sinking back into his chest and warming him.

"What is it that you wanted to tell me? About the other night?"

He hesitated. He almost didn't want her to know just in case she insisted on going there. But for her safety, and the safety of the others, he thought she should know.

"When Taksi and I made it back to the tree, it had been pushed over on its side. Torn up from its roots."

"How can that be? Oh, Theo, I am so sorry. Your home."

"There was nothing there I couldn't live without. But the thing that I had guarded for all those years has been taken. The trees confirmed it."

"Who caused it?"

"It was Erebos, or at least what used to be Erebos. I'm not convinced there's any of him left from what the others are saying."

Tara nodded against his shoulder. "I gathered that from the few things I picked up from the girls too. They were filling me in on what they had each gone through with him. How do you suppose he was able to uproot it like that?"

"He somehow managed to control the Ents. Caused them to kill one of their own kind."

"The Ents? Those are real? Like J.R.R. Tolkien real?"

Theo looked down into her upturned face and smiled at her. Her awe-filled voice made him laugh.

"He was a good man, and most of what he wrote was based on fact," he said. "He and I would have long conversations about my homeland. You would love it there, by the way. One day, I'll show you."

"I would love that but mind blown on the fact that you even knew him. I can't even think about that right now, way too tired." Tara covered a yawn. "A topic for another day."

"Fair enough."

"So, the Ents told you that it was Erebos?"

"Yes. They watched him as he killed the satyr that he left there and drained his magick. The creature was killed the same way he and Cela used to all those years ago. It is why we hid the weapon."

"That is what he has now?"

"I'm afraid so."

"We need to tell the others." Tara prepared to stand, and Theo laid his hand on her arm to keep her seated.

"There's no sense in waking the house. Whatever he has planned will take him some time to prepare for. I think the best thing for everyone is to get a good night's sleep. We can let the others know in the morning."

"I suppose you're right," Tara said. "You're staying, right? You aren't leaving me alone tonight?"

"No, Tara," he said softly. "I won't be leaving you alone any night in the future if I can help it."

Tara shifted by his side and looked up at him. The expression on her face was soft and adoring. He hadn't been able to help the comment, any more than he could stop his heart from loving her.

"Well, that's nice to hear," she said with a sigh.

"It's the truth," he whispered. He raised his hand and ran his finger along the curve of her ear. She closed her eyes and tipped into his touch, sighing as he caressed her. He had once thought she might be Fae, but if she was, he saw no visible signs of it.

"You have a thing for ears," she said with a smile. Opening her eyes, she looked directly at him. If he were a lesser man, it would have caught his soul.

"It's one of the more sensitive parts of the body." His comment prompted her to stand and move into his lap, facing him. Her hands went on either side of his head and grazed his ears. He closed his eyes in ecstasy and could hardly hear her next comment over the pounding of his heart.

"Let's test that theory."

Their lovemaking was intimate in a way that no longer scared him, at least it seemed that way to Tara. He had spent hours afterwards telling stories of his homeland and describing a world she very much wanted to see. He promised to take her there, and her heart squeezed at the thought he was considering a future with her. She tried not to worry about what kind of a future a human could have with someone who had seen generations of her kind born, live, and die. She decided to take it a day at a time, much as she would any relationship and make the best of the time they had together.

They had both slept as if there were not another soul in the world that was designing to end it. Even though Theo had built a physical and mental barrier between them, she had spent half the night snuggled up against his back. She had moved before he woke, careful to replace the pillows she had tossed to the end of the bed as they slept.

She wasn't concerned anymore; for whatever reason the bracelet seemed to help. That, and her being more aware of the signs her body gave her. When her heartbeat fluttered, and bile rose in her throat, that was a sign she needed to walk away. She found the stone tree out back was the best place for her to be and wondered if she could speak to Sevilla about fashioning a necklace out of a small piece.

By the time they had gotten downstairs, the men were returning from their rounds. Will looked exhausted, more so than the other men. She had a feeling it had less to do with the amount of time he had been up, and more to do with the energy he had expended. Brooke had already poured him some tea and was fussing over him like a mother hen.

"You need to drink that. And where is your stone?"

"I left it at home," he sighed. He could hardly keep his eyes open.

"Sevilla?"

"I have more hematite, just give me a moment." Sevilla left the room in search of a stone. Tara looked questioningly to Theo, who explained.

"Similar to what we do outside, it helps with grounding. Tonight, we should build a fire, so he doesn't have to provide the light."

"That's a good idea," Sera said. "I may have some flashlights as well back home. I can look when I go check on Annabelle. Any requests?"

"Would you mind if I went with you?" Tara said. "I could use some things to wear."

"Of course," Sera said. "Looks like we are about the same size. I'm sure we can find something. Give me a few minutes, and then we can go."

Tara glanced up to Theo, who had a slight frown on his face. She wasn't sure why he would be upset, since she would be perfectly safe with Sera. Besides, she really needed some clothes if she was going to be here much longer. The pants she had on were practically walking themselves.

Taking a biscuit from the table, she slathered butter and honey on it and ate it standing.

"There's coffee on the table if you need it," Amie offered. "Cream and sugar are on the counter."

"Thanks." Tara filled her mug and sipped with a sigh. "This is incredible. Is this a French press?"

"It is," Sevilla said. "Have had that one for years. My understanding is they're making a comeback in your world. Make yourselves at home, I'll be in the den with Zilla and Fate."

"I'll join you," Theo said, brushing a quick kiss on Tara's cheek before following Sevilla. It seemed to be he was already over his earlier worry.

Sera was standing by the door and gave Tara a nod. "You ready?"

"I am," she said as she finished her coffee.

"You can leave the mug," Brooke said. "Amie and I will do some research on the Journal while you guys are gone, then we can practice when you get back."

"What are we practicing today?" Tara was curious. She wasn't sure there was much more she would be able to do.

"We thought we would see if you could actually turn into your element," Sera said. "You know, like Brooke can turn to water and Amie air."

"Are you telling me you can turn into fire?" Tara's eyes were wide as she stared at a grinning Sera.

"Not yet, but I'm working on it," she laughed.

"So, what, I get to turn into dirt?"

The women all laughed. "I guess that is what we are going to find out," Brooke said.

Tara couldn't convince Taksi to join her, and when Sera explained they were going back to the village where Logan's pack was, Tara decided it was probably best. If one wolf bothered her, an entire village of them would send her over the edge.

They walked outside the perimeter, and Logan moved silently out of the woods to greet Sera. His presence didn't surprise her, it was almost as if he was expected. Tara caught him out of the corner of her eye and jumped. He had moved on them almost as silently as Taksi could.

"Ya checking on the wee one?" Logan pulled Sera into his arms and nuzzled her neck.

Sera pushed him away with a half-hearted admonishment. "Logan, please. We need to go, so we can get back quickly."

"Aye, my heart. Give Annabelle and Mila my love."

She kissed him on his bristly cheek, and he gave her a wink. "I will. We won't be long."

They walked through the barrier that she and Theo had designed, and Tara could feel the difference immediately. It was as though someone had opened a door and allowed a breeze inside.

"We won't have to walk too far," Sera explained. "I have a place I can create a portal not too far from here. It will take us just outside the village."

"The one I came through activated on its own. You are able to create one?"

"Yes. Although it is my understanding that the portals opened because we were ready to connect to them. You know, the whole element thing. I have to admit, Logan dragged me backward through mine."

"That had to be terrifying!" Tara exclaimed. She was relieved when Sera shook her head and laughed.

"He pissed me off more than anything, the big brute."

"You seem very much in love."

"We are. I have never met anyone so devoted to his family. And he's hotter than hot, so there's that," she winked. "Here we are."

Tara paused as Sera stood with her legs spread apart and her head bowed. She was calling her energy to her, Tara felt the heat of it push by her as the tiny woman drew it in. Her hands were out to either side, palms up to receive it, then she circled them both up above her head in a clap. In one smooth movement, she brought both hands down chest level then pushed out in front of her. A flame lined circle formed in front of her then grew larger as she swirled her hands. In a matter of seconds, they were looking through a doorway to another part of the woods.

"Incredible," Tara whispered.

"It's definitely the only way to travel," Sera said. "Come on. I'll introduce you to my daughter and abuela."

28

Tara and Sera arrived back at the cottage with more supplies. They had been a little longer than the hour they had planned on, since Sera decided a quick trip to her apartment was in order. She was still living between both worlds and hadn't moved all her belongings to Logan's. The arrangement suited the couple, since Logan was fascinated with Sedona and its vibrant culture.

Sera was right, her clothing did fit Tara, and they even had time to shop for a few things, so Sera took her to the mall. Tara could understand why Logan was so enthralled with the area, the colored rock formations alone were incredible. Sera mentioned when they had the situation under control back in Wisteria, she would be happy to host a girl's weekend and show everyone around.

Theo was pacing the front path when they arrived and walked to meet them, taking the handles of the pull-cart and hefting it behind him as he moved into the yard. Neither she, nor Sera, said a word about the fact that they had been pulling it fine the entire way from Logan's. The look on his face stopped the laugh she and Sera had been sharing. Her new friend gave her a wink.

"Going to find Logan. Good luck, sweetie."

"Looks like I'm going to need it," Tara muttered under her breath. Sera's laugh faded as she walked away to find the man that had been her pain-in-the-ass but turned love-of-her-life. The conversation had been great that afternoon; Tara already felt closer to the sassy ex-fireman, who had made her home in Wisteria with the man she loved. The thought occurred to her that her situation might very well end up the same, although looking at Theo's face, she wasn't sure.

He was already yanking things out of the cart, and when he pulled out the pink striped bags that held her lingerie, she took them from him.

"I can take those," she said with a flush. Why was she embarrassed? If she was honest, all the items were purchased with him in mind.

"You were longer than I expected," he said gruffly.

"We had some things to pick up that required a trip to Sera's apartment. We stayed only as long as we needed to."

"It's not safe to travel to the Earth realm with all that is happening."

"We were fine. It was a quick trip."

He huffed, and she realized that had been a dumb statement. She knew how quickly things could go south.

"What's in the pink bags?"

"Nothing you are going to see at the moment," Tara said. "You're grumpy."

She pulled the small duffel from the wagon and stormed up the walk to the front door with her bags. Irritated that he wasn't glad to see her, she struggled opening the door to Sevilla's. The first face she saw was Brooke's, who raced over to help her with her bags. Before closing the door behind her, Brooke squealed in delight.

"Oh! What did you buy from Vickie's?"

Tara spent a few moments upstairs unpacking. The few things she brought back from Sedona would get her through her stay, however long that might be. Brooke gushed over Tara's finds, which Sera had generously paid for.

"I love this bronze set, Lovie. This is going to look sharp on you."

"That's my favorite," Tara said.

"When things calm down here, we can get you back home to get things settled. Once you know how to make a portal, you will be able to travel back and forth like we do."

"I was looking forward to coming out to California. What is going on with the planning, by the way?"

"I popped back home for a few minutes earlier. I called Will's mom. You had a change in schedule and couldn't make it this coming weekend. She was disappointed but understood. She doesn't suspect anything out of the ordinary, since you were just coming for a few days this time around."

"Yeah, good thing the flight was so cheap. I'm a little worried about making the shower in a few weeks with all that you have going on here. How have you been keeping it all together?"

Brooke's laugh filled the room, then tears filled her eyes. "I have no idea." She looked up at Tara and shook her head. "I am utterly at a loss about my entire life. Things with Will are fine, he hasn't had much that has changed. But I've moved, changed jobs, found out my imaginary foster mother was real, and that I harnessed the power of water in my fingertips. Not to mention, I can't get my hair to turn back to blonde no matter what I try, and I'm worried how it will look in our wedding pictures."

Tara sat on the bed beside Brooke and put her arm around her. The meltdown wasn't nearly as bad as the few she had witnessed during their friendship, but she knew she was on the hairy edge of losing it entirely. She knew how Brooke felt.

"I think your hair looks terrific," Tara said, pulling her friend into a side hug. "As for all the other stuff, I can only imagine how hard it was to navigate all of that without a sounding board. But I'm here for you now."

"Thanks, Tara," Brooke said. "And, yes, Will is great but venting to him isn't nearly the same as doing it with you."

"We now have the added bonus that I will know what the hell you are talking about."

"I think that was the hardest thing for me," Brooke admitted. "That I had all of these things happening, and I couldn't share the truth with you. Made me feel like rubbish."

"You aren't rubbish. And I get it. I had things I didn't share with you either. I figured you already had too much on your plate, and besides, I felt it was stuff that was too crazy to share. Now I realize you would have been the perfect person to share it with."

"No more secrets, then?"

"No more secrets," Tara agreed.

"Brilliant. On that note, what's going on with Theo? I assume the new knickers have something to do with him."

Tara hesitated then took a deep sigh. "Let me tell you about Theo."

After her vent session with Brooke, Tara felt as if a load was lifted from her body. It was amazing to her how freeing it was when she finally shared what had been happening with her over the past several months.

With Brooke's help, they were able to make sense of all the signs her power had been showing as it trickled to her at Crazy Horse.

Brooke was especially interested in Mato's teachings, and the significance of him giving Tara the flute that had opened the portal. The journal had been Brooke's key, lighting the stone of the Molokini crater and granting her and Will access. For Sera, it had been the tattoo she had gotten to soothe her Abuela's mind and meant to provide protection when she fought fires in Sedona. Amie was the only one that had been gifted with her key, a small golden feather given to her in friendship. The trouble was, the friend was Zilla, and she was known to twist the truth.

They discussed Mato's motivation, which Tara doubted there was any, and the way he gifted the flute to her. There was no sense of deceit or influence, at least from what Tara could remember. Mato was one of the most spiritual and unassuming people she had ever met in her life. She had been meant to have the flute through divine intervention, not through the fact that Mato was influencing her arrival here. Brooke didn't look convinced.

Tara was glad Brooke had filled her in on everyone's background, it helped her understand the underlying tensions and friendships. It was strange though, when Tara asked about James and Fate, Brooke had no idea what she was referring to. She decided to drop it, realizing perhaps James hadn't fully made his move. She didn't want to ruin his chances because she put his sister on the trail.

By the time they had gone downstairs, Theo had unpacked the food items, which the women had put away. Sevilla let them know that he had taken the wagon with the rest of the supplies to the men, and they were setting up stations around the perimeter. At least if they were going to keep watch 24/7, they would be more comfortable. The nights tended to get cold.

She followed Brooke, Amie, and Sera outside, and they started where they had left off the day before. Attempting to unlock the right combinations of thoughts and actions to connect Tara to her element. Amie had been the first to alter her actual physical state, so she was the one giving the lessons.

"I found that if I draw from what I understand about how things work, I am able to manipulate the energy." Tara's blank stare had her continuing. "Engines, for instance. I was familiar with the way a turbine worked and imagined the way the air flowed through it, and the force it would cause. Then I connected those imaginings to my will, and the power did the rest."

"But you did have some trouble at first getting out of that state," Brooke added.

Tara couldn't help her voice from squeaking. "So, I could be stuck in whatever form comes to me?"

"We would talk you through it, but it might help if Theo was out here. For some reason, it seems that the men in our lives counterbalance our energy. Allow us to ground. Aleck was the one I hung onto when I rematerialized."

"Not sure we are at that level of relationship quite yet," Tara muttered.

The three women exchanged small smiles then looked back to Tara as if to say yeah-right-sure. Sera was the one that spoke up first.

"Whether or not you have admitted it to yourselves or each other, you are at that level. It's pretty obvious in the way he looks at you."

Tara's inner runway model flicked her hair and gave a small snap before striking a pose. "Thanks guys," Tara said shyly. Whether or not things worked out with Theo, she was glad she had come here. Getting to know these women made it all worth it.

"Perhaps there is a way she can come back without him for now, especially with all four of us together," Brooke suggested.

"Sounds good to me. What do I need to do?"

Amie spread her legs shoulder-width apart and put her hands to her sides. Tara followed suit, in fact, they all did. "Make sure you don't lock your knees," Amie suggested. "We don't need you passing out."

"Got it," Tara said.

"Now, you will need to visualize your desires. Is that something you are familiar with?"

Tara thought about what she had been visualizing lately but figured that wasn't quite what they were shooting for. With Theo's attitude, he might never reap the rewards of her dirty mind either. She got her head out of the gutter and nodded. "My grandmother explained how to do that years ago. More recently, I had a Native American friend who was helping me channel my energy."

"Perfect," Amie said. "Then close your eyes, and we'll start there."

Theo sat watching the women from the tree line. Perhaps not the women as a group, more the one in particular. As upset as he was with Tara, he couldn't stay away. Especially, because she was tying into her energy and sending root systems out to things around her, drawing them back into center. He couldn't resist the delicate pull of her energy against his. Touching him in places no woman ever had, or ever would again.

The three women made excellent mentors, and each had a handle on the power that had been gifted to them. As much as he wanted to be part of Tara's training on the elemental magick, he knew she was in much better hands with her friends. His knowledge of the power had stopped long ago, and he wanted to be sure she was educated with anything that had changed. The feelings of inadequacy weren't lost on him.

Taksi rubbed up against his thigh and nudged under his hand, forcing him to rub her head. Just like her mistress, Taksi had no trouble conveying what she wanted. Theo was beginning to question the logic in his failed attempts at keeping his hands to himself. Tara clearly enjoyed his company, and he couldn't deny the attraction.

He just worried at the end of all his musings, that destiny had another plan for her. If that were the case, their relationship could end long before it ever had a chance to start. He saw what it did to Sevilla and Ryker, and he wanted to save Tara from that heartache. Honestly, he didn't look forward to picking up the pieces after losing her love, if that is what it came to. Especially since, unlike her, he would have to live with his choice for eternity.

"Taksi, I think it's time to talk to Fate." He gave her a scratch behind the ears, which she leaned into with delight — if the rumbling emanating from her was any indication. "You watch over your mistress."

She looked at him with gentle awareness then rubbed against his legs once more before heading off into the woods. He felt better knowing she was keeping an eye on Tara from the perimeter.

As he walked into the house in search of Fate, he thought about the questions he would ask, about the information he needed to have. It seemed strange to have been alive for centuries but to feel as though he had missed so much in only 75 years. He was used to being a part of the process, now he felt more like an outsider.

He didn't like the helpless feeling and hoped some of the answers Fate would provide would help bring him back into the fold. He needed answers, and quickly, if he was going to be of any help to the woman he had fallen in love with. There was too much at stake.

29

Theo found Fate inside playing chess with James. He had learned James was Brooke's brother and was friends with Aleck, but he was curious as to what other connection he had to Wisteria. He seemed to be at ease around the others, and more so, he was clearly infatuated with Fate. She felt the same, if the look on her face was any indication.

"Theo, this is James. I don't believe you've properly met," Fate said softly.

James took the hand Theo offered and shook it firmly, meeting his gaze. His face was open and engaging, and his smile pulled up his eyes in mischief. It was as if he had learned a great secret that he was anxious to share. He met Theo's gaze directly, but with an openness that reminded him of a friendship lost long ago. He didn't understand why he would think that but knew he liked him instantly.

"It's nice to meet you officially," Theo said honestly. He looked down at the chess board, not surprised to see who was winning. "Looks like your game is at an end."

James laughed. The sound of it brought a beaming smile to Fate's face. "Quickest game ever, we only just started. It's been some time since I've played chess, and these pieces seemed to have their own agenda in mind."

"Well to be fair, it is a challenge to play any type of strategy game with someone who can see the future," Theo said with a grin.

"I don't ever use my powers in these games," Fate exclaimed. "You know the voices are way more hindrance than help anyway. Besides, I can't help it if I've had longer to practice than most of my challengers. Or the fact that the pieces would much rather be in the drawer doing what they do."

James looked blankly between them, as if he didn't quite understand the entirety of her statement, then glanced to Theo with a grin. "It seems to be common knowledge what they do in there."

"I didn't mean to get you riled," Theo offered with a smirk. "And yes, James, there have been times we had to stop playing in the middle of the game just to allow the pieces to pull themselves back together."

"I can imagine," James laughed. He looked at the board once more then shook his head in disbelief. "Theo's right, this game is over in about three moves."

"Two," Fate and Theo said simultaneously. They all laughed, and James stood up.

"Well on that note and, to salvage what's left of my dignity, I'll go stretch my legs. You need anything while I'm up, my love?"

Fate shook her head, her clouded eyes shining like silver beads in the sunshine. James bent over the table and placed a kiss on her cheek, pausing near her ear and whispering something only she could hear. The interaction was natural, and the chemistry between them couldn't be denied. As brief as the movement was, it told Theo all he needed to know. Fate had fallen in love once more. As much as the thought of it should pain him, he found that he was happy for her.

"Nice to meet you, mate." James nodded at Theo and made his exit, leaving the two of them in the house alone. With the women practicing, the men making their rounds, and Sevilla and Zilla gathering herbs and crystals, their conversation would remain private. He took the chair James had vacated, across from Fate, and rearranged the pieces to start the game anew. Fate waved her hands over hers, and they all slid back into their starting positions.

"I had always wanted to learn that trick," Theo said. "They seem to like you better."

"It has nothing to do with that," Fate laughed. "They just know the quicker they line up, the quicker I will let them get back to their party." Once the pieces were in place, she made her first move.

"I like him. He seems good for you."

"I knew you would," she answered softly. "How could you not?"

It took Theo a moment to connect what she was saying to the emotions that he had received from the couple. There had been feelings of friendship, trust, loyalty, and love. And beneath it all, a humor that, when shared, could lighten anyone's load. Could it be? Theo looked up into Fate's shining face, and she confirmed his thought with a nod.

"Anton," he whispered. "I wondered why he seemed so familiar to me."

"James doesn't know," Fate answered. "I wasn't able to tell him before with the spell you put on me. And there hasn't been an appropriate time lately with all that has happened."

"Anton was always good at riddles. It was part of the reason I chose that spell."

"Well, James is incredibly bad at them," Fate laughed. "It made for a challenging, first few meetings. I was never so thankful when my tongue was finally untied. Although, now I fear what comes next."

"I do too," Theo admitted. "Considering he's human, I would imagine that you only just met."

Fate nodded. "My sisters knew him before I did. He's been coming since Sera tapped into her power. She met him in Sedona where she used to live."

He moved his first piece. "Pawn to King's fourth." He sat back and allowed her to contemplate her next move. He knew he could continue the conversation as they always had. "Seems to me he has a lot of ties to you through this particular group that has been chosen to protect the Elements."

"That didn't go unnoticed," Fate said as she touched one of the pawns momentarily then pulled her hand back. The piece moved on its own accord. "As I'm sure you remember, I wasn't able to speak with Anton once he crossed. But, one of the last things he said to me was that he would do what he could from the other side. I think he somehow had a part to play in connecting everyone here."

Theo reached across the board and lay his hand on top of Fate's. Her clouded eyes shined with tears that no longer held sorrow. "Knowing Anton, as I did, I believe that is absolutely the case," Theo said. "He would do anything within his power to help you."

"I believe that too," Fate said. "Let's just hope that he was able to make enough of a difference before he was brought to life again in James. I couldn't bear to lose him again so quickly."

Tara had been practicing for what seemed like hours. Sevilla and Zilla had come back with a basket full of herbs to dry and crystals to clean, and she was still no closer to tapping into her element. Tara took a small piece of the obsidian tree that had broken off during training and asked if something could be fashioned out of it that she could wear. When she explained she felt it would help her with grounding, the two sisters took the crystal and argued about the best setting to put it in as they went inside.

Theo had been inside, and alone with Fate, for the better part of the day. She had seen James leave, and while he didn't look upset, it was clear that he felt uncomfortable. She felt waves of inadequacy from him, although the love he felt kept them at bay. It was like a third-wheel kind of vibe, which she completely understood. She had been familiar with that feeling ever since Will had come into Brooke's life.

Although Theo and the sisters were old friends, perhaps James hadn't been told. Tara felt bad for him. He clearly had designs on Fate but was still unsure about his place in the scheme of things. After he hadn't come back for some time, she assumed he had sought out Aleck and Will. There was no way she was getting involved in Brooke's brother's love life. She had enough trouble of her own.

Brooke and Amie were the only ones able to change their physical form, but Sera had been practicing, and she was close. She was able to turn her entire arm into flames, and it was only a matter of time before it engulfed her entire body. It was a good thing that a fire-fighter was the one that tapped into the flaming element. There was no way Tara would have been as calm with half her body on fire. She would take Earth over the other elements any day, although it too had its fair share of issues.

She had been practicing all afternoon, and much to Amie's dismay, they were no closer now to her morphing into her element than they had been that morning. Amie was patient, even though the change had come naturally to her. Tara was finding that the hardest part with the visualization was the fact that she kept seeing writhing roots in her mind that reminded her of snakes. Not that she had a problem with them in nature, but she didn't feel much like turning into something that was a cross between a tree branch and Medusa. The fear of what she would become held her back, and the knowledge that she might not be able to turn back at all stopped her in her tracks.

"You really need to relax," Amie suggested with a sigh. She had the ladies carry over the bench from the front of Sevilla's house and sat on it close enough to lean her back against the side of the house. She kept adjusting her posture and rubbing her back. "The element needs to be able to flow naturally. Think movement. You know, like water, the breeze…"

"Snakes," Tara blurted.

"Not quite what I was going for," Amie said.

"It is literally the only thing that comes to mind," Tara sighed. "I know I am being ridiculous, but it freaks me out that I am going to get stuck in some weird cross between a human and a reptile. I'm having a hard time relaxing."

"I know what helps me relax," Sera purred with a grin. The batting of her eyes was the frosting on the innuendo cake.

"We all know what helps you relax, Sera," Brooke joked. "To be fair though, she's right. You do tend to feel pretty relaxed after."

"You guys! That is not an option right now," Tara blurted.

"What's not an option?" Theo's voice startled her. She had been too preoccupied to sense him behind her.

Tara looked back at him then snapped her head to glare at her friends, giving them all the don't-you-even-think-about-it look that they were each innocently ignoring.

She turned to face him and shrugged. "Nothing. Just hit a wall with the training."

"Maybe I can help," Theo offered.

"Oh, you can help all right," Sera said. Tara heard an oof and turned to witness her rubbing her ribcage, and Brooke's bent elbow pulling away from it.

"Maybe we should take a break," Amie suggested. "My back is killing me. And besides, the guys will be back soon, and we should probably help Sevilla inside."

"Brilliant idea," Brooke beamed, pulling Amie up off the bench and grabbing Sera's hand. She was practically dragging them into the house as she called out to Tara. "Come inside when you are ready. We can work on some journal stuff."

She was never so happy to hear the snick of a door. It was embarrassing enough dealing with Theo at the start of a new relationship. She would be completely horrified if he found out that their sexual escapades had been the brunt of the women's giggling.

"Is everything all right?" he questioned. "You seem tense."

She couldn't help but flush at his question, considering what she and the girls had been talking about. He placed his hands on her shoulders and started rubbing. His fingers moved rhythmically and relaxed her instantly. She closed her eyes against his ministrations. "That's helping," she said quietly.

His fingers continued to work their magic, and her excitement rose at the thought of his hands being on her body. She blocked everything around them out and concentrated on him. Theo and his magical fingers.

"Your muscles are tight. You need to relax." He slid his hands up the sides of her neck. Making light circles on her throat and caressing behind her ears. The touch had turned into something more than a massage. She dared not open her eyes, hardly taking a breath as she waited for him to make his next move. She didn't need to wait long. "Tara," he whispered.

Before she had a chance to respond, his lips were on hers. In the middle of the afternoon, in the center of the yard, Theo was kissing her. She didn't understand the change in his otherwise cool demeanor, but she liked it. Her arms wrapped around his waist, and she pulled him closer, their bodies close enough that she could feel his wild heart.

His hands had slid down to her thighs then behind to cup her and pull her in tight. She felt his urgency, hard and long against her, and she fought the urge to jump up and wrap her legs around him. She was so engrossed in Theo and the way he was making her feel, she hadn't heard the door open. She didn't know they weren't alone until they heard a throat clear.

"Like I said," Sera laughed.

Theo's lips left hers, and Tara shot a glare over his shoulder into a grinning face.

She turned to go back inside, calling over her shoulder. "Brooke sent me out to get you guys. She thinks she found something."

30

The Shadowman paced the floor in his study, stepping around the items that were littered beneath his feet from his earlier bout of rage. How could he have been so stupid. He should have locked her up with her sisters. Now, he was left without an oracle, and the one person that had kept Ryker working for him without complaint. Zilla being gone was also an inconvenience, although he had been craving her body less as time went on.

That damn dryad Sasha had helped them, it had to have been her. If he hadn't already destroyed her tree, he would have gone out and chopped it down himself. That was when his anger was a white-hot rage, when he had stormed through the halls to Fate's bedroom and found it empty. His anger was less toxic now, it was more of a brooding simmer.

Fate and her sisters disappearing was a hindrance. But it wasn't anything that could stop him at this point, if he kept Ryker from knowing the truth. He couldn't know that his wife had been safely removed from the premises, nor that the Shadowman had no idea of their whereabouts. So far, the Mage was unaware, of that he was sure. He had just left the room where Ryker was putting the final touches on his army, and as he made his inspection, his confidence grew. When the time came, he would be ready for them, and he would drain every last bit of their powers for his own.

He had just poured himself a scotch to calm his nerves when he heard a familiar voice behind him.

"I'll take one while you're at it." He fought against the flinch his body naturally made. One more sign of weakness he was looking forward to eliminating when the time came. This was the only man that had ever been able to startle him. He had always hated that about him.

"Rather presumptuous coming from a man who once called me Master."

The Shadowman turned to look into the dark face of his visitor, curious as to how he came and went without a sound. His unassuming nature was a carefully crafted cloak he wrapped around himself, much like the hooded cape he wore to hide his features.

"You and I both know it was merely something to call you. I never put any meaning behind the title."

He felt his rage rising again, but he didn't allow it. Erebos, and even Ryker, may have both been too distracted to see it, but the man in this room had power. He had yet to find out its extent.

The Shadowman turned to hide his displeasure in the guise of pouring the creature a scotch. It was obvious he had something he needed to get off his chest, and the Shadowman was currently lacking company. It would be nice to have a conversation with someone who didn't speak in riddles.

He walked the glass to his guest, pasting a companionable smile on his face. If nothing else, he was curious as to the visit. It was also an opportunity to solve the riddle of what the creature truly was. "What can I do for you, Kadar?"

Kadar held his glass up, and the Shadowman clinked his against it, watching him closely as they took their swallows of the fiery scotch. His eyes betrayed nothing, much like the times he worked for Erebos and then for Roy, they were brooding but pleasant. The Shadowman knew that behind their depths, there were secrets to unlock. He was interested to learn what had brought him here.

"It's more about what I can do for you," he said finally.

Interesting. He hadn't been expecting that. "Go on."

31

Tara and the other elementals sat around the table with Theo. The three sisters were in the den, polishing crystals and bundling herbs they had foraged for earlier. They listened in from the other room as Theo helped Brooke navigate the secrets of the Elemental Journal, as was apparent by their random interjections.

They mostly clarified what had happened in the past, and Tara was learning a lot about the bond that the sisters shared with Theo. They were much more than friends, they were family. The occasional bickering was a tell-tale sign.

Brooke had the journal in front of her and flipped the pages as Theo looked on. The writing seemed to react better that way. He seemed to recognize most of the information inside, but there were some pages that had been added as each of the women came into their powers. He spent much more time reading those.

"When did this symbol show up?" he asked, pointing to the hourglass shape he and Tara were familiar with.

"Honestly, that's new," Brooke said. "Probably right before Tara arrived. The book reflects new things as each of the elements are found. We just assumed this was a symbol related to Earth."

"It symbolizes balance," Tara said. "A mirror, so to speak. The top part is the universe, while the bottom represents earth."

"As above, it is below," Fate murmured. Tara glanced over, but the woman was quietly binding the herbs she had been given. It was as if she had said nothing at all. The other sisters had their head bowed over their tasks as well. Perhaps Tara had been hearing things.

"Maybe Theo was right the other night," Amie said. "Maybe we are meant to absorb the negativity and re-balance it somehow."

Tara was thankful the men were outside. She wasn't sure Aleck would want to hear what they were discussing. She looked at Amie and felt resolve, but also fear, coming from her. While she worried about the effects that the magick had on her unborn children, she also was in for whatever the group decided.

She thought about her ability to heal and how that could counterbalance any toxic effects. "It could mean that Earth is the one meant to absorb it," Tara suggested.

Theo's head whipped around, and he stared at her, his eyebrows quizzed and his jaw set. He too was a mixed bag of emotions. He shook his head. "That can't be it. You couldn't possibly be expected to harness it all."

"There is a new page forming here," Brooke said.

Theo looked back down to where she was pointing, but his worry still caused Tara's stomach to roil. He hadn't been happy with the direction she was taking the conversation. He was calm and cool on the surface, but she felt the riptide beneath.

"It looks more likely that we were right the first time," Theo said. "The mirror symbol is surrounded by the symbols of the four elements."

"There are some other symbols here as well, Brooke. Here, forming on the edge," Tara said as she pointed. The symbols darkened at the outer edges of the page, and the swirls and squiggles, while they seemed random, looked as though they could be a language. "They remind me of what you carved on your tree, Theo."

"Not the same, but it is a language I have seen before."

"I have been doing a ton of research, but this isn't anything I've come across to date. Could it be an ancient form of hieroglyphic?"

"Could be," Theo said. "But I think it may be older than that. I've seen something similar before in this book and then on the weapon that I was charged with hiding. Whatever it is, it's ancient."

Sevilla had come into the kitchen to hang the bundles they had completed and wandered toward the table. "Let me see." She looked at the page, and her face paled. What she saw frightened her, Tara sensed it. What she couldn't tell was why.

Tara looked down at the page again, the symbols had completely filled in the outer edge of the page in a thick border. Strangely, she felt as though she had seen the symbols before as well, and she stared as she tried to put the pieces of the puzzle together.

Conversations in the room continued, but they were muffled. The symbols darkened on the page then started to move. It was subtle at first, but then the pictures on the page wiggled and squirmed like snakes in a pit. She looked around the table, it was apparent from their continued conversation that no one else had noticed the movement. Sevilla, however, was back in the den whispering to her sisters along with Theo.

When she looked back at the page, the movement had stopped. "What is it with me and snakes?" Tara mumbled.

Brooke shot her a quizzical look. "Not sure what you mean."

"Never mind," Tara shrugged. "I'm sure I just need to rest. It's been a draining morning."

Sevilla and Theo came back into the room and glanced down on the book once more before addressing the women. "We believe these symbols might be something you are meant to understand but never use. A language from a darker form of magick."

Brooke thought about it for a moment then nodded her head. "That makes sense." She stood up, so she could move about the room. It was how she did her best problem-solving. "If our goal is to balance both energies, we might need to use spells from both sides to do so."

"We thought the same thing," Theo said. "In the meantime, we need to see if any of these pages have unlocked to show you specifics about your energies. It will be important that you understand how to completely control your element, and block outside energies, before anyone attempts to balance anything."

"It's best to be prepared for anything," Fate said as Zilla moved her from the den into the kitchen. "These energies are volatile, as you have witnessed in your home world. What happens here affects your world much more than you realize."

"What sort of effects?" Tara asked with a squeak.

"Tidal waves, earthquakes, tsunamis, even widespread fires have been the result of the turmoil that has gone on here with Erebos and his predecessors. Larger battles in our realm generally cause something more devastating. The eruption of Mt. Vesuvius is an example."

"Hasn't it erupted more than once? Which time?" Brooke asked.

"All of them," Fate replied.

Tara let the enormity of Fate's reply sink in. The city of Pompeii had been wiped out in days. She was familiar with the volcano from her classes in college and knew it had erupted several times since that fateful day.

The last of which was during World War II.

"So, the last time it happened? In 1944?"

"We tried to control the outcome with devastating effects." Fate quietly left the room, and Tara attempted to squelch the emotions coming from the three sisters in the other room. There was heartache and loss, mistrust and pain, but most of all, there was conflict. Tara didn't hold out much hope that the sisters would be reliable allies. They had a lot of their own baggage they were sifting through.

The room was silent, each person taking a moment to let the conversation sink in. Tara decided it was a good time to excuse herself and lie down.

After a glance in the mirror, once back in her room, she could see why everyone agreed she should rest. The white in her hair was prominent, as were the thoughts and emotions that had prompted them. There had been so many things brought up, which were now swirling around in her head and causing her heart to race. She had a sinking feeling she wasn't built for this and wondered how the other women remained so confident with all that they had been through. It was ridiculous really. She was supposed to have healing abilities, but she couldn't keep herself from feeling ill.

She lit a candle she brought up from the kitchen and lowered herself into the steaming water in the tub. A long soak was just the thing she needed. As she relaxed against the side of the tub with her eyes closed, the bedroom door opened then shut. Theo's familiar steps stopped outside the bathroom door. After a slight knock, she called out. "Come in."

"I feel terrible disturbing you, but I think we should talk."

She opened her eyes and took in his concerned face. For a split second, she worried he wanted to talk about their relationship, but after lowering her blocks and touching his emotions, she realized it was something more.

"I have spoken at length with the sisters. They, in turn, have used the tools at their disposal to determine the path we should take for the best possible outcome."

"Theo, you're scaring me. I'm not sure I can trust their judgment after what I sensed down there."

"They've been through a lot," he confirmed. "But they have come through worse." He slid the chair from the vanity to the side of the tub and sat down. She reached a wet hand over the side, which he took in his own. "If I'm honest, I'm a bit scared myself. It would be much easier for me if I was the one wielding the Earth energy."

"I didn't ask for this. And if I had my choice, I would give it all back to you, believe me."

He smiled at the comment and gave her hand a squeeze. "I do believe the powers were gifted to the right people. My comments are merely from a selfish standpoint. I don't want to see you get hurt."

"Trust me, I don't want that either. And what is it that you've discussed that has you so freaked out?"

"The sisters and I have thought about your earlier hypothesis. We agree. You are the funnel."

"Funnel, as in, Lakota symbol funnel."

"The last time we tried to draw the negative energy from Erebos, not only were we missing some of the elements, but we also didn't realize that, once removed, the power had to be directed back into each of the energies. The toxic cloud we pulled from him wasn't grounded back into the source, so it floated out into the open. Even though we took precautions with him, I believe he eventually found a way to tap back into it."

Tara wasn't sure she liked the sound of that. "What kind of precautions?"

Theo took a breath and held it as he caressed her hand with his thumb. He was unsure, she could tell by the friction caused by his rubbing. "Fate erased his memory and forced Zilla to live in exile with him in the Earth realm."

"She erased his memory? She can do that?" Tara could hardly reconcile that kind of power with the unassuming woman downstairs.

He nodded. "Her power is the strongest of the three sisters, but they each have their strengths. There are spells I can cast as well that come close, but my magick isn't nearly as old as theirs."

"Not to be rude, but what exactly are they?"

"It's a fair question," he shrugged. "They are the three goddesses of Destiny. Sevilla represents past, Zilla the present, and Fate the future. They have wielded their powers as long as I've known them, although Fate did share once there had been others who harnessed the powers before them."

"The duties weren't always theirs?"

"No. Much like the duties of the elements, they are passed on after a time. Because she can see the future, it is usually up to Fate to decide the best path to follow."

"And she was the one that decided Erebos and Zilla should be banished after his mind was wiped clean?"

"That's right. She also had to keep Sevilla from knowing her husband Ryker was alive. I was able to use some Elvish magick to keep him from leaving the fortress but refused to tamper with his memories. But I did lead him to believe Sevilla was gone."

"And what was Sevilla told? That he was dead?"

"I'm not sure. Fate took care of that."

"She sure did," Tara exclaimed. "I am honestly surprised that the three of them are still talking. Talk about dysfunctional."

"No matter what each of them has done in the past, they are bound to their purpose. They each know that, so it is much easier to forgive someone when they are doing what they were designed for."

"And have you forgiven her? Fate, I mean."

He tipped his head and thought about her question. Now that it had been posed, she sensed he was conflicted about it. Seventy-five years was a long time for anyone to live alone, although it could be argued that it was a shorter span for someone immortal.

"I was displeased when she put me in charge of lying to Ryker and hiding the weapon Erebos had used. He and Cela had been fashioning weapons out of the glowing green stone, which was harder than any iron I had ever come in contact with. There were too many of them to take with me, and the one piece I was charged with hiding made me ill. At this point, other than meeting you, I'm not sure what it was all for. He managed to get it anyway."

"Yes, but he got it after the four elements were found," Tara said. "I would imagine that it all worked out the way the universe designed it. Or perhaps how Fate did."

"That is what I hope. But from the information I have gathered from each sister, it seems the only thing we managed to do is to give the dark magick seventy-five years to fester and grow inside of Erebos. It took some time, but the power finally managed to take over his body. He is no longer the Erebos that any of us knew. He has evolved into something much more powerful."

"And if you were unable to defeat this power all those years ago, what makes you think we can do it now?"

"Because, as much as I have had issue with the things Fate demanded of me, I have faith in her abilities. Everything she has predicted has come to pass. Even the seemingly random occurrences have purpose. She has seen our future and has determined that you have a key part to play moving forward."

"I'm not sure I'm ready for all that. I can't even keep myself from draining my energy stores dry."

"I think I found something in the Elemental Journal that will help us. I will help you in any way I can."

"Because Fate asked you to?"

"Because I want to," he said honestly. "You asked if I had forgiven Fate, and up until I met you, my answer would have been no. But now I know that everything I have been through has led me to this moment, and I would have never met you had things turned out differently. So yes, I forgive her, because the path she put me on led me to you."

He pulled her hand to his lips and kissed it gently, his eyes never leaving her face. Tara warmed under his attention. They were finally at a place where she felt comfortable with where they were heading.

"I forgive her too," Tara said with a smile. "For all the things we haven't done yet that I'm sure we aren't going to like. I think she has some plans for us."

"A truer statement has never been made," he said with a grin. "Now, that water is probably getting cold, I should step out."

"Or you could hold my towel," Tara said with a grin as she stood in the tub.

His eyes drank her in, and she relished the feel. There was no denying his feelings, especially since she had caught him off guard, and he hadn't taken his usual precaution with them. Much like his eyes, his emotions were flowing over her and warming her from the inside out. Passion, loyalty, devotion. Lust.

He cleared his throat and spied the towel hanging on the back of the door. He held it out for her then helped her step down from the tub. "Was there anything else you needed?" His voice was husky and hopeful.

"As a matter of fact, there is."

32

B y the time Tara and Theo made it downstairs, the meal was prepared, and most of the men had made it back from their rounds.
The fish that Logan had caught in Sevilla's stream was a welcome
addition to the menu, and she was glad that he was engaging Sera, as
she wasn't sure she was up for more of her knowing looks and innuendo.
While Sera had been right about what had been needed for her to relax,
she didn't want to advertise what she and Theo had been doing while she
was supposed to be napping.

James and Fate had already eaten and were taking a walk. Theo mentioned doing the same after they were done, so he could test Tara's abilities with some of the spells he thought would be helpful in the coming
days. He wanted her to be prepared for anything, since they didn't have a
clear idea of what the Shadowman was up to.

Fate was no help. She wasn't able to determine future events for energy, only beings. Because she could no longer see what he was up to, they
determined the entities, known as Erebos and Roy, were no longer part
of the Shadowman's essence. He had evolved, and it was unclear what he
was made of, or what was holding him together.

Dinner was quick, and conversation was light. After helping Sevilla
clear the table, most of the couples paired off for some alone time. It
seemed as though she and Theo weren't the only ones that wanted to "relax." Amie and Aleck said their goodnights and left with Sera and Logan
to check on his village. It would be up to James and Will to keep watch,
which was why they were spending time with their significant others
now. Zilla was already out with Taksi, who had reported in that there was
nothing of concern in the areas she had visited.

Theo had Tara's arm as he looped her around the other side of Sevilla's house. She was able to get a better look at the garden and saw someone had been out working on it. It was in much better shape than it had been when they first arrived.

"There's a table and chairs down by the stream, I thought that we could sit there and go over a few things," Theo said.

"Sounds good. Did you want me to go back and get a candle? It's pretty dark."

"I think we will be okay. Here, take my hand."

He led her to the table and sat down next to her. "The wooden surface should be a good place to practice."

"What are we practicing again?"

"Writing symbols in my language, which can then be infused with intent. It is the basis of a spell."

"Won't I need something to write with?"

Theo shook his head. "No. We can carve into the wood with our minds, and then I can wipe it clean when we are done."

"Like a chalkboard?"

"Precisely. Once you have this down, you should have a pretty easy time creating portals on demand."

He held his right hand out over the table and indicated she should follow suit. "I will create a symbol, and I want you to try to copy it as best you can. It will require visualization, much like what you have been going over the past several days."

"Okay, I'm ready."

Theo hovered his hand over the table at about three inches and kept it in place as the symbol formed beneath it. The symbol glowed gold and lit his face with an ambient glow. She now understood why he wasn't worried about bringing a light source, the light lit the area like the moon on a clear night. Once he was done, he pulled his hand back and allowed her a better view of the shape.

It was an inverted triangle, with a line through the lower third. She had seen the symbol in Brooke's journal earlier. She vaguely remembered seeing it sooner than that. "This looks familiar."

"The symbol for Earth," he answered. "I thought we could start out with simpler figures before moving to some more ornate ones. What you will want to do is imagine the energy from your hands, merging into the wood using the same outline as my figure. The reaction will cause it to glow."

Tara nodded, holding her hand above the table as Theo had. She took one more look at the figure then closed her eyes to concentrate. She imagined the triangle coming out of her palm and pushing its way into the woodgrain of the table. It wasn't as easy as Theo made it look.

"Try it by working with the wood itself," he suggested. "Asking the wood to receive the symbol might be easier."

As soon as she switched her mindset, the process was much smoother. Her intent slid over the woodgrain, much like a pen over paper. When she opened her eyes, she was delighted to see an exact duplicate of the symbol Theo had crafted.

"Excellent," he said. "You are a quick study."

"Thanks. Coming at it from the table up was much simpler."

"Ready to learn some more?"

"Absolutely."

By the time they were ready for bed, they had scribbled over every flat surface of the table and benches. Theo had shown her symbols that guarded against negative energy, which he felt would help her the most in the coming days. He explained that drawing those symbols and then infusing them with intent bound them to the magick that they were fed by. There were some creatures that could unlock symbols created by others, but for the most part, areas that reflected the ancient magick were left alone.

He explained that Dwarves often used symbol magick to mislead those looking for their treasures. They would have false doorways leading to dead ends and put layer upon layer of magick to slow the invaders down. He had also seen similar symbols in the fortress where the harpy Queen, Cela, had lived. Before he had left, he used the trick he learned from the Braidbeards to layer a few doors of his own over hers. It would have taken too long for him to relocate the room full of weapons. There hadn't been enough time.

Theo had always worried that his precautions hadn't been enough and was glad to hear the fortress had been flattened when Amie had come into power. It would make finding the room full of material much harder.

Before leading Tara into the house, Theo erased the symbols and returned the table to its original state. With the glow from the symbols gone, it took her eyes a moment to adjust to the dark. He took her arm and led her inside, quietly shutting the door behind them, since the rest of the house was asleep.

"Do you think Sevilla has any books?" Tara whispered. "I'm not sure I'm quite ready to sleep yet."

"I brought some with me," Theo whispered back. "You can look through them and decide if any of them suit."

He followed her up the stairs to their room, and once inside, she continued their conversation. "I had hoped you would read to me. I miss that."

Theo smiled. "I would like that." He went to his backpack and pulled out a small stack of books, which he placed on the bed, before going to the fireplace to stoke the fire.

She readied for bed quickly then looked through the selection he had brought from his home in the tree. Among them was the copy of *Pride and Prejudice* he had used when they had read together, and her decision was made.

He stripped out of his clothes, pulling on the flannels she had purchased on the shopping trip she had taken with Sera. There was nothing sexier than a man wearing flannel pants riding low on his hips. She admired the way the green plaid looked on him.

He slid into bed next to her and looked at her curiously. "Didn't we already read this one?"

She laughed. "We did, but I thought perhaps it would read differently if I was in your arms."

"I see," he said, putting his arm around her shoulders and allowing her to settle into his chest. "Well, since our selection is limited, I will grant your request." He kissed the top of her head, opened the book, and started to read. "It is a truth universally acknowledged, that a single man in possession of a good fortune, must be in want of a wife."

"I was right, it reads better," Tara sighed. Before he was done reading the first chapter, she was fast asleep.

SOMETHING COMES.

Taksi's voice startled Tara awake. Theo was laying on the other side of a wall of pillows he had placed between them.

What do you see?

She had already slipped out of bed and was tugging her pants on before she received an answer.

GLOWING ROCKS.

Glowing Rocks? She tried to think like Taksi, what would she call a glowing rock? She didn't think she would call large men rocks, and she dismissed the thought that she confused an Ent for what she was seeing. The rock reference was something she understood, and the glowing she could also get behind with everything she had seen since meeting Theo. The "something comes" statement was what confused her.

She finished dressing and went to Theo's side of the bed, shaking him awake. "Theo, get up. Taksi saw something."

Theo sat up and wiped the sleep from his eyes. Noticing she was already dressed, he got out of bed and started to do the same.

"What did she say?"

"She said glowing rocks were coming, which makes no sense whatsoever."

"Unless they are golems," Theo said. "I think it might be wise to wake the others."

Tara nodded. "I can do that while you finish getting dressed." She grabbed her hiking boots and socks and slipped out into the hallway. She had completely lost track of who was in the house and who was on watch, so she decided to knock on all the doors.

She went to Brooke's room first and knocked on the door. Just as Will pulled the door open, there was a crash that shook the house.

"What the hell was that?"

Brooke's face peeked around his shoulder. "What's going on, Tara?"

"I'm not sure, but Taksi sent a warning. Theo sent me to wake everyone."

"We'll get dressed."

"Is James here?"

Brooke nodded. "He's at the end of the hall. I wouldn't be surprised after that noise if he was already dressed."

As if to confirm Brooke's comment, James came out of his room like a shot tugging on a shirt. He walked up to Tara and gave a nod to his sister and her fiancé through the door. "What do you need me to do?"

Theo joined them in the hallway and gave him instructions. "Wake the sisters. We will need to find a way to get word to the others. Tara, come with me."

"We're right behind you," Brooke said.

Theo took her hand and led her down the stairs, leaving James to knock on the other doors upstairs. Sevilla was already bustling in the kitchen, filling buckets and gathering items such as dried herbs and linens. Tara had no sooner registered some of the piles on the table when the door flew open, and Zilla came barging in.

"We're going to need everyone. They are as far as the eye can see." She was panting, as if she had run for miles without stopping.

"What are?" Tara asked, unsure she wanted to know the answer.

"Golems," she said as she caught her breath. "They are still way out, but they are moving this way. And there are hundreds of them."

Brooke and Will had come down the stairs with James and Fate and started to help Sevilla bundle the supplies for easy transport. Brooke spoke to Zilla as she divided everything between several baskets. "We managed golems before. We will need the others though, depending on what they are made from."

Theo shared a look with Zilla, and Tara had the impression they were about to be told something that was a game changer.

"They are made from the glowing green rock that drains our magick."

"As we fight them, they could make us weaker? That's unfortunate," Will said.

"We will need everyone here," Theo said. "Zilla, is there any way you can get word to Logan and Sera?"

"I can. Perhaps we can call upon some allies as well. I'll see what I can do."

"Thank you," Theo said. "In the meantime, Tara and I will reinforce the shields surrounding the house."

Zilla nodded then opened the door as she started to change. Tara was surprised to see the wings form on her back, as she had been expecting a cat. By the time Zilla had crossed the threshold, she was fully converted to a griffin. She spread her wings, and in a matter of seconds, had flown from the yard.

Theo caught her questioning look. "She can morph into any feline, she just prefers the black cat. It's a witch thing."

"I see," Tara said, even though she really didn't. There was so much to unpack in this place.

Fate started to move toward the door with James and called back to her sister. "Sevilla, are you coming?"

"In a moment. I have a few more things to do." Her voice was thin, and her hands shook. Tara didn't know her well, but Sevilla seemed to be out of it. She was still gathering things and mumbling.

Fate paused for a moment then spoke to James. "I'll stay here with Sevilla. You should go with your sister and Will."

"I would feel better if you remained in my sights," he murmured into her ear. She cupped his face with her hands and kissed him softly, calming him with her gentle touch. "I will be right behind you, I promise."

"Okay. Be careful." James went through the door, and there was another crash, which sounded much closer. Tara looked behind her once more to Sevilla, who stood with a pained look on her face. She was shaking her head and mumbling, almost as if she was speaking to someone. Tara looked up to Brooke, who mouthed the words, "Fate's got her."

Will and Brooke left next, followed by Tara and Theo. They left Fate and Sevilla behind, making preparations to Tara that seemed to be a waste of time. She shut the door behind them and walked out into the yard. The night sky was clear, and the moon was full. The light would make it harder to hide.

GLOWING ROCKS COME.

Warn us when they get close.

WARN FRIEND. HIDE. SAFE.

Thank you Taksi. You stay safe too.

It seemed the moonlight wouldn't be the only light they would be surrounded by. She looked into the tree line to gauge their distance and saw a green glow. They were close.

She looked at Brooke and Will expectantly. "Okay, so what's the plan?"

33

The Shadowman watched as row upon row of his creatures moved toward their destination. He had made final adjustments based on Kadar's offer and a few of his own, since he didn't trust most of what the man said. He still didn't know what he was, but what he did know was that he upheld his promise and had brought him the Elemental Journal.

The pages had been blank, and the book had been useless. The Shadowman was tempted to destroy it, but Kadar suggested that perhaps once the power was transferred to him, the pages would show themselves. In the meantime, Kadar explained he was able to read the ancient language that was on the Shadowman's weapon. He had no other choice but to trust the man who once was his servant, and true to his word, he unlocked the secrets to the symbols and brought his creatures to life. Not even Ryker had had any luck doing that.

Ryker hadn't been completely useless. He had managed to duplicate the passage on each one of the golems, painstakingly ensuring each copy was identical to the last. He would still be of use. His love for his wife was a great asset. The material he had been working with over the past several months had been slowly draining him, and he was all but a shell of the man he once was. He couldn't think on his own, but that was exactly what the Shadowman needed from him anyway. He needed a puppet-master for his army.

He and Kadar had a gentleman's agreement of sorts. His worth had yet to be proven, but he explained he had the trust of the three women and the elements they mentored. That was also valuable to the Shadowman. Not only was Kadar familiar with the lay of the land, but he would also be able to gain access to the others in a way that he couldn't.

At the end of it all, Kadar couldn't be trusted, but the Shadowman had no choice. Fate had escaped with her sisters, and he needed someone with some understanding of how their elemental magick worked. Golems were unpredictable, they needed a heavy hand to control them. What Kadar ultimately promised was a diversion.

"I will travel ahead and give them the message we agreed on," Kadar said. "The shield they have in place is weakest at the northern most point."

"Once I get Ryker in place, I will expect your return."

"Do you have what I asked for?" Kadar's eyes flashed brilliant blue for a brief second then were dark, like the night surrounding him.

"Here." The Shadowman held up the vials he had hung on a chain around his neck. The dull light of the two essences barely gave off a glow. When the light finally faded, it would be worthless, but for some reason, Kadar was intent on having it. "Once I have transferred the power of the elements, they are yours."

"Excellent," Kadar said. "Then let's finish what you started, and we can all get on with our lives." He glanced to Ryker, who stood quietly at the Shadowman's side, staring blankly into space.

The Shadowman looked between them and shrugged. "Everyone, except Ryker, of course." He gauged Kadar's reaction, looking for the slightest bit of remorse for the part he would play. He didn't need to wait long.

"Obviously." The sarcasm laced his single word, and he turned on his heel and left. Soon he was in the tree line, and in an instant, he was gone. The Shadowman worried for a brief pause that he had just made a deal with a power he didn't understand then reconciled himself with the decision. He had something Kadar wanted, and as long as he kept it safe, the Shadowman felt he would keep his promise.

He tucked the chained vials beneath his shirt and felt the warmth of it pulsing on his chest. When the time came, he would turn it over, but only after he had gotten what he came for and the last bit of life was drained out of what was left of Erebos.

"Come, Ryker, let's get you in place."

Inside Sevilla's kitchen, Fate waited patiently for her sister to pull herself together. She had never witnessed Sevilla so scattered. Her sister was talking to herself, and Fate couldn't make any sense out of the pieces she was hearing. She was talking to someone, but everyone else was outside.

"Are we alone?" It was the first coherent sentence she heard Sevilla utter, and it seemed to be directed at her.

"We are," Fate confirmed. "The others are outside, and Zilla has left to gather Sera and Amie."

"Good," she said decisively. "It will be less complicated that way. Considering you see the future, I'm sure his visit won't surprise you."

"Kadar's?"

"Yes."

"I can leave if you need some privacy," Fate offered, realizing after she said it how ridiculous it sounded. She had seen most of what had transpired in the last few days, decades ago. The trouble was, Destiny could change in a breath, and there were still so many alternate paths that could be followed.

"There's no sense. He knows you're here."

Fate could hear her rummaging around in her bedroom. Heard the tinkle of chains and crystals as she searched for something. "Where is it?" She was muttering. "I left it tucked in the lining."

"What are you looking for?"

"The sapphire ring, the one we brought back from the Shadowman's keep."

Fate's heart sunk. The voices were whispering to her that something had changed, the unpredictable nature of the Universe was in play. There wasn't anything she could do about it, since the decision wasn't either of theirs to control. But she knew what she had to do next. It was time for the truth.

"Sevilla, you can't save them both."

She heard a gasp, then sniffling. Fate walked into Sevilla's bedroom and put her arm around her. "The ring is gone, in the hands of someone who will also have a choice to make."

"I made a promise to him," she sobbed. "How will I face him?"

Fate realized, with a sinking heart, that her question was equally about Ryker as Kadar. She didn't envy the choice her sister would have to make and hoped when the time came, it would be taken from her hands. This last dance with Destiny had drained them all.

"I don't know, but we shall do it together."

Sevilla's arms came around her, and Fate held her tight. She wished she could transfer what was left of her strength to her, but she would need it for what was to come. There was a whooshing sound in the kitchen, then bootsteps sounded across the floor. Fate gave her sister one last hug then spoke to Kadar as she exited the room.

"She's been through a lot."

"I know," Kadar said. His voice was laced with sadness. Fate couldn't sense deceit, but there was no way to know if he was hiding anything with his nature. The D'Jinn were tricksters, and Sevilla putting her trust in one all these years wasn't something she had foreseen. They traveled on a whole other level of energy and were impossible to detect unless they chose to show themselves.

"I'll give you a moment."

Fate moved away from the bedroom and stopped near the fire. Sevilla had lavender and rosehips brewing, and the scent was soothing. It reminded her of the day she brought her home all those years ago. The day she had lied to her and told her Ryker was dead. Sevilla had been through a lot, but Fate had created the most chaos in her sister's life.

Their private conversation didn't last long, and she soon heard two sets of footsteps coming out into the kitchen. Kadar was the first to speak.

"He comes with an army fashioned out of magick green stone. The material has qualities that absorb energy, which has been enhanced by symbols, that will allow for the transference of that energy."

"Similar to what he did all those years ago with Cela," Fate said.

"It sounds like it," Sevilla said.

"I'm not familiar with the material, but I can tell you that its draining quality is hard to diminish. They will be hard to destroy entirely."

"And by the time you finished fighting it, it could have drained all of your powers," Fate said.

"Precisely," he confirmed. "I had hoped that I would be able to help, but that power is not in my hands. Or, it seems, Sevilla's."

"The ring," Fate whispered. "It is what you are tied to."

"Yes."

"We must find it," Sevilla whispered. "We are all out of options."

"I must go," Kadar announced. "They draw near, and you must warn the others of what they are dealing with."

"Thank you, Kadar," Fate said.

"Never thank a D'Jinn until you've received your wish," he said quietly. Fate had never heard that, but she supposed it was true. Sort of in line with "be careful what you wish for." There was a moment of silence, then fabric upon fabric, lips upon lips, then a comment from Sevilla that Fate wasn't sure she was supposed to overhear.

"Keep your promise."

Another pop of energy, and he was gone. Sevilla cleared her throat then took Fate's arm and moved her to the door. "We have to warn the others."

Fate couldn't help the question that crossed her lips. "Can you trust him?"

Sevilla paused and sighed. The weight of the world released in the slight sound. "Once, I would have said yes without hesitation. Now, I'm not so sure. Either way, I don't think I have a choice," she finally said. "I don't think any of us do."

As they opened the door, there was a rending split of wood, then a rustling thud as the tree crashed to the ground. Fate heard yelling, she believed it was Aleck. He was giving instructions as he ran across the yard. It seemed that Zilla hadn't let them down and did get word to them. Logan's voice yelled back, but she didn't hear the women.

"Sevilla, tell me what you see."

"Nothing yet, but the men are pulling everyone back into the perimeter. It looks as though the women are helping Theo reinforce the barrier."

"That will be the best job for us as well," Fate said. "Take me to Theo."

33

Tara tried to stay focused, but with everyone running around in panic, it wasn't easy. Theo had added an extra barrier around her to help with the emotions, but she worried it would be too much of a drain for him. He had already expended a ton of energy reinforcing the wards. She was relieved to see Fate and Sevilla running up to join his efforts.

Sevilla had pointed Fate facing the outer yard, and once her feet were firmly planted, she started weaving her magick into theirs. Sevilla had the barrier lit, and they were filling in the gaps in the magick, weaving the colors of light like a tapestry. Sevilla was on one side of Fate, and Tara on the other. Theo had already moved down to create another part of the forcefield.

"He's going too quickly," Fate said. "There will be gaps."

"I was filling in behind him," Tara explained. "They are too close to worry about perfection, and they approach from all sides."

Fate nodded. The explanation made sense. "We will reinforce as long as possible. You and the others must stand at the four corners of the circle."

Tara looked at Sevilla and couldn't help the frustration in her voice. Now was not the time for riddles. "I don't know what she is talking about."

"The four compass points. The front of the house faces west, that is where Brooke will need to be. East is Air, so Amie will need to be in the back. Fire is South, which is opposite of where we are. Your point is here or North."

Tara looked behind her, the obsidian tree shining like black glass in the moonlight. No wonder she had felt such an affinity to it.

"If we are outside the barrier and need help?"

"The barrier should hold enough to allow you to regroup. You should be able to fight from behind it, but your magick won't be as effective," Fate explained.

"You haven't had as much time to practice with your magick," Sevilla said. "We will try to stay with you as much as we can. Try to save your stores as much as possible, your power will be needed most at the end."

"Sevilla, go get the other women in place. I will stay here with Tara."

Sevilla gave her sister a quick hug then left to do her bidding. She caught up with Brooke first, who was given instruction, then ran off toward the back yard. Sevilla ran to the opposite side of the house.

"Why is it that Sevilla said my power will be needed at the end?"

"Was Theo able to talk to you about our theory?"

"The funnel?"

"Yes. When the time comes, you will need to use your ability to pull all the toxic energy in then distribute it evenly to the others."

"I don't understand most of what you are saying," Tara said. "And I'm not sure I can do what you think. But I'm willing to try."

"Then we can ask no more of you."

Tara held her breath as the glow brightened, and when the first golem broke through the tree line, she marveled at its beauty. It was moving slowly, lumbering toward the barrier at a snail's pace. If she looked through her mind's eye and colored the magick around her, she could see the golem wasn't as helpless as it seemed. There was no magick coming from it — all the magick was being drawn to it, like a moth to the light. For all the effort they had put into the barrier, it was being pulled away one tendril at a time.

"The first golem is through, and I see one coming behind it. It seems to have an effect on the barrier."

"The magick will be drained as we build," Fate explained. "The best we can do is continue to reinforce it as you and the others fight them."

"How are we possibly going to fight them?" Tara cried. "They are made from stone!"

Fate looked at her calmly, as if she hadn't just heard an outburst from her nervous lips. She continued her work, weaving her light and pulling the threads of the barrier together. "It is made from material under your command. Find its weakness, every creature has one. If nothing else, the trees are at your disposal."

Tara glanced behind her, there was a bright green glow surrounding the area. The light seemed more concentrated on the south side of the house. Theo had made it around the entire yard and was stepping toward them from the other direction. He called out to Tara. "There are more of them on the other side."

She heard yelling, first from the men then from the women. She couldn't tell what was being said with the distance, but she heard their magick as it hit its target. Tara looked back at the lone golem, which stopped just outside the barrier and raised its hands. It wouldn't be long before it was through.

Tara raised her hands and closed her eyes, concentrating on the trees behind the stony creature. She blocked out the sounds around her, focusing on her breathing and connecting with the oaks and maples beyond the yard. She pushed her intent through her palms and out into the woods. The earth responded, cracking open to allow the roots to burst forth. Tara opened her eyes, just in time to witness several of them wrapping themselves around the golem's legs and pulling back. The structure of the golem didn't allow it to bend or brace itself, and it fell face first into the grass before being covered in the vines she had called forth.

It had fallen but was still glowing, causing a drain on the barrier that surrounded the house. She hadn't stopped it completely.

"I don't know how to stop the magick from weakening the barrier," she yelled to Theo. He was finally beside her and raised his hands toward the pile of glowing stone. Two more golems were coming at them from the tree line.

"If you can knock them down, I can keep the material from draining the barrier entirely." There was a rending split behind them, and she heard Aleck yell to James, something about a breach.

"What about the others?'

"The others know what to do; Sevilla has given them instructions. The most important thing for you to do is stay focused and try to take out as many of his pieces as possible. Like chess."

"Except unlike the pieces that want to have sex all the time, these want to kill us."

"Good point."

She pulled the roots back from the broken golem and directed them to the latest threats. Since they were moving, she would use their forward momentum against them. Just as she had tripped them, there were three more behind. "They keep coming."

"Maybe it's time to call on the Ents."

"Can we do that?"

"It's worth a try," Theo said. They might be able to hold them off deeper in the woods and give us an idea of what the Shadowman is up to. You should be able to connect to them, just like you connect to the trees."

"I'll try."

Tara sent her thoughts out with the intent of connecting to her element but connected with Taksi instead. She would be able to use the cat's night vision to her benefit.

Taski safe?

TAKSI HIDES.

Where are you?

SEE YOU.

Tara presumed that meant she was straight out from where she stood. There were more golems coming out of the tree line as they spoke. She continued to add more and more roots to the ever-growing mass in front of her. The yard beyond the barrier was littered with glowing green rubble. The golems were stopped, but the stone was still weakening the barrier.

She thought about how Taksi might think of an Ent then posed her question.

Taksi see Tree Man?

WITH THEO.

She called over to Theo, who was helping Fate seal above them. "Was Taksi with you when you spoke to the ents?"

"Yes, why?"

"I'll tell you in a minute."

Yes, Taksi. Just like with Theo.

TREE MAN.

That's right. Do you see any now?

NEAR STREAM.

The stream was to her left, closer to where Brooke was if her directions were accurate.

Taksi, stay hidden. Tara didn't want the mountain lion hurt. It would be one less thing for her to worry about if she could keep her out of the battle.

TAKSI HIDES.

With the knowledge her feline friend was as safe as was possible, she pulled up more roots and pulled down the final two golems that had cleared the forest. She could tell by the glow she had a few minutes to check on Brooke.

As she ran toward Brooke's area, she was in awe of the sheer power and magnificence of her friend's ability. She had seen it in action earlier, but never in this capacity. A freezing force from her fingertips stopped the golems in their tracks, and Will's lightning strike blasted the stone creatures apart. She didn't want to distract them so remained just outside of their vision. She closed her eyes and reached out to the spirit of the trees.

"We need help," she transmitted. "The barriers must be held."

There were no less than three Ents who returned her call.

We shall come to you.

With the Ents on their way, she gave one last look to her friend then ran back to her place. Several golems worked their way along the path, and one had almost gotten through the barrier. Theo frantically tried to reinforce it as she took her place.

"Are they coming?" He was tired, she saw it in his face.

"They are," Tara confirmed. "They will use me as a beacon."

"Good. We'll need all the help we can get."

Tara left Theo and continued to fight the golems with the roots as best she could. With the Ents on the way, she hoped that they would be able to create a barrier between the house and the forest. The sounds coming from the other sides of the house not only included the crash of fighting, but also howls and caws. Perhaps the others had called in reinforcements as well. When she saw a large wolf run past her and into the woods, she had her answer.

Fate moved toward her, the exhaustion clear in the way she held her shoulders. This was as much of a drain on her as it was for Tara. Sevilla came up as well, and they talked as they worked.

"The waves are much heavier on the other side of the house. So far, the women are fighting them off, but we can't keep this up indefinitely."

"Has anyone been able to secure reinforcements?" Fate asked.

"I saw a wolf run past me and into the woods," Tara answered.

Sevilla nodded. "A few of Logan's pack have come to his aid. He is using them as scouts more than anything. We need to find the Shadowman. If he is stopped, the golems will stop advancing."

"Once we find out where he is, we need to start moving Tara closer to his direction. The transfer won't be as effective within our wards," Fate said.

Tara wasn't fond of the word transfer, as if she would be used like some universal conduit to move energy, but at the end of the day, that was what they were expecting. "Where is Theo?"

"He is reinforcing the wards near Amie," Sevilla explained. "Because Aleck and James are not affected by the glow of the stone, they were able to circle around and attack them from behind. Amie found if she lifted them with a wind funnel and allow them to fall, it stops them from moving. The men are breaking them apart as a precaution."

"And where is Kadar?"

Fate's question surprised Tara, and she watched Sevilla's face for the answers. She would find them in her demeanor, much more than in the words she would say.

"He said to look to the north."

She gave Tara a weak smile, barely held up by the hope that he wouldn't disappoint her again. There were waves of heartbreak and reading her energy was exhausting. Her emotions were a jumbled mess. It was clear that Sevilla was unsure of her path and place, which was the complete opposite of her sister Fate, who calmly faced everything that came her way.

Theo ran up to their group, sweaty and stressed, but Tara had never seen such a welcome sight. She felt as though she was being led toward decisions that she didn't truly understand and didn't like the way it made her feel. Being near him at least grounded her.

"We need to find the source of their control," he announced. "We can't keep this up forever. The others are getting tired, and their magick is now being effected by the stone that surrounds your property."

"I feel the effects as well," Fate confirmed. "Have the scouts reported back? Have they seen anything?"

"They have reported that they have seen two men not too far from the edge of the northern barrier. It seems they both were directing golems from their location."

"Then that is where we must go," Fate said. "Where is Zilla?"

"I haven't seen her," Sevilla said. "I thought she was with Sera and Logan."

"I didn't see her over there," Theo said. "But depending on the shape she is holding, I may have missed her."

"It may be better if we do this without her," Sevilla suggested.

The Ents had finally arrived and planted themselves in a row just outside the wards. Once rooted, their branches were lowered and woven together, forming a wooden fence. Tara was thrilled to see that the golems were not able to make their way through and opted to go around. Since there were no less than a dozen Ents that ended up answering her call, they would be forced to enter from either the East or West.

"You did great," Theo whispered proudly. "That should secure this end of things while we move forward. Keep your energy walls up, you are going to need them."

She took his hand, and Sevilla slipped her arm through Fate's.

"Tara, once we get closer, have the Ents make an opening for us. We won't need long."

"Got it."

35

Theo and Tara led the way with Taksi, with Sevilla and Fate a few steps behind. Tara was clearing the path ahead of them, and Theo was impressed by just how much Tara had managed to learn in such a short time. She had amazing control over her element, and the creatures that were part of it listened to her without question. With a flick of her wrist, she created an opening in the root mass, and they were through in a flash.

The golems were plentiful but slow. He had questioned the Shadowman's use of them, since they weren't effective fighters. They were cumbersome and sluggish. But he realized it wasn't the destructive power of the golem that was the danger, but the material that they were made from. Even after they were destroyed, they were a threat to all within their radius. He was familiar with the material. He had studied it all those years ago when Erebos first used it.

They evaded the golems easily and ran into the tree line to get their bearings. It was Fate who spoke first.

"We need to find their master. He will be surrounded by the magick he wields."

"He may also have other creatures surrounding him," Theo added. "The dark energy draws to itself, and once under its spell, most would die to protect it."

Tara's eyes grew wide at the realization of what he had said. They had just left the protection of the barrier, only to have opened themselves up to more than just golems to fight. "Are you sure we should be going without the others?"

Fate replied. "We will get word back to them when the time comes. It is more important that we get you in place first."

Tara took Theo's hand and wove her fingers in between his. It was as if she was trying to merge into his body through the contact. He squeezed her hand and gave her a quick kiss. "You've got this."

She looked up at him with a crooked smile. "I'm not sure I want it," she whispered.

"I won't let anything happen to you," Theo soothed.

She wasn't convinced, but the comment quieted her. Theo looked to Fate, who nodded serenely. Sevilla looked like she was about to jump out of her skin. He didn't have a good feeling about where they were heading but knew what he wanted wasn't even part of the equation.

"The energy feels most concentrated straight ahead," Tara said.

"I agree," Fate said quietly. "We need to get close enough for you to see who is with him but stay far enough away that we remain hidden for as long as possible."

"Sevilla, you take hold of Fate and follow us. Quietly."

Theo kept hold of Tara's hand, slowly transferring as much energy as he could spare into her body through the contact point. It seemed to be helping, her anxiety wasn't coming at him with as much force. He pulled her along, stepping on the areas where the most moss was present and avoiding as many sticks as possible. He wanted to be sure their approach was not heard. The noises from the battle were muffled. It was much quieter in this area of the woods.

The green glow was concentrated in the clearing in front of them, so he slowed down their pace, circled around, and found a large stone to duck behind. He stood up slowly and looked over the top, spying two figures standing within feet of each other. One was hooded, the other looked like Erebos. They were both motioning their arms, with swirls of dark green and black energy coming from their fingertips. They were close, but the men had their backs to them.

He motioned to Sevilla then to Fate then pointed to the ground. In the next movement, he pointed between Tara and himself then further into the woods. Sevilla nodded and whispered to Fate. He leaned over and spoke to Tara. "I want to get on the other side of them."

She nodded and squeezed his hand. He looked ahead in the dim lighting and found their path. He pulled Tara further into the woods, leaving the two sisters behind to prepare for their part to play. He moved Tara between the trees, careful to pause behind the larger trunks to shield their approach. He was relieved the men were alone, having found a quiet place to control their puppets. So far, there was no sign of sentries like he had first feared. It was a bold sign of confidence, one that Theo hoped would work in their favor.

He and Tara got as close as they dared then tucked behind a giant redwood. Unsure of when he would have another chance to do so, he pulled Tara into his arms and kissed her with every ounce of passion he felt for her. She melted into his embrace and kissed him back, filling his soul with a warm peace, despite the chaos around them. For an instant, it was just the two of them, with the glow of their newfound feelings warming them.

She slowed the kiss then tucked her head under his chin, snuggling into his chest. His arms tightened around her, allowing the grounding sensation to flow between them as they fed each other's energy. Knowing things could change for them in an instant and without knowing what the Universe had in store for them, he decided to speak his truth.

He pressed his lips to her forehead. "You are always in my thoughts." Then kissed the tip of her nose. "I will love you until my last breath." Her eyes shimmered with tears as he kissed her lips gently. "And from this day on, I won't ever forget to tell you how much you mean to me."

Relief radiated from her as she reached up and cupped his face with her hands and whispered. "That is the most beautiful thing I've ever heard. I love you too." He lowered his head and kissed her once more, allowing himself one more moment of peace before going into the fray. "Now, let's stop these bastards, so we can get to more important things."

A woman's voice sounded, sultry and low, like a siren's song. There was no denying it was Zilla, and Theo glanced around the side of the tree to get a better visual. He was right, it was her. The men stood with their backs to them, and she approached from the other side with her hands raised.

"What are you doing here, Zilla?" The Shadowman addressed her with raised hands, the power snapping between his fingers, but he didn't push it toward her.

"I come as a friend," she said meaningfully. "I want to help you."

Tara tugged at Theo's sleeve. When he looked down at her she whispered fiercely. "What is she doing here?"

Theo shook his head. "I don't know," he whispered back. "I'm not sure Fate expected this. We need to be ready for anything."

Tara nodded then peeked around the other side of the tree trunk, so she could see what Theo could.

The man in the hood, next to the Shadowman, circled his arms then pushed another pulse of toxic light forward. If Theo's assumptions were correct, he had just sent another wave of golems toward Sevilla's house.

"I don't need your help," the Shadowman snapped. Theo sensed he was intrigued though, which was apparent by the way he lowered his hands and dimmed his magick.

"You might not need my help, but you know you want it," she purred as she approached him. She was holding something up that glowed with a bright blue light. "This is something that can bring you your every desire."

"What I desire is my immortality back."

"This shall give it to you, my love." Sevilla stepped closer but was still feet away from his location. "With this ring, you will wield a power greater than the elements combined."

"Show me," he commanded.

He heard a woman yell, then saw Sevilla run to the edge of the clearing. "Zilla, don't," she cried.

Zilla looked back to her, shook her head, but it was too late. The Shadowman sent a bolt of lightning toward her, knocking Sevilla to the ground, and she was no longer moving. Theo couldn't tell if she was still alive. The cloaked man took a step forward, as if to help her, but the Shadowman shot a smaller bolt toward him like a warning. The man stopped and started his movements once more.

Theo glanced over next to him and realized Tara had moved. She was heading further into the woods, following Taksi and making her way around to the other side of the clearing.

He had no other choice but to follow her. Zilla was still negotiating with the Shadowman, so thankfully, he wasn't paying attention to what was happening behind him. He wasn't sure what Tara was thinking, he only knew that he needed to stay by her side. He ran between the trees as Zilla took the glowing light and slipped it on her finger. It gave Theo the impression it was a ring.

There was a great blue flash, and as the smoke cleared, Theo saw that Kadar was standing next to Zilla.

"What is your wish, Mistress?"

⧖

Tara was tired of feeling helpless, and when Taksi called out to her, she guided her to her location. They had discussed a safe way for them to travel, to get closer to Sevilla. She hoped that she was still okay and would be able to at least drag her to safety.

There was a flash of blue light, and Kadar appeared. When he addressed Zilla, Tara understood what Kadar truly was. The ring Zilla wore glowed with the same blue brilliance that showed in his eyes. The two were connected. Sevilla had tried to stop Zilla. It all made sense. Kadar was a slave to the ring, and she was trying to save him from being abused.

"My wish is for you to explain to the Shadowman what you truly are and have been all along."

The Shadowman looked intently between the two as Tara made her way around the other side of the clearing with Taksi. Sevilla was lying just a few feet away. Tara didn't think she could get any closer without being seen, so she quieted her mind and attempted remote healing. Eyes closed, she tried to block out the conversation, but it was hard.

Kadar paused for a moment, clearly fighting against what he was being asked to do.

"Well?" The Shadowman was growing more irritated, and as he raised his hands toward Zilla, Kadar finally spoke.

"I am D'Jinn. A Jinni from a parallel realm. I respond to the call of the one who controls the ring."

"So, if Zilla gives the ring to me?"

"I would be bound to call you Master. Again."

"And the power you have access to?"

"Endless. Unbound. Timeless."

"Excellent," the Shadowman purred as he took a step forward. "What is it you want, Zilla?"

"I will give you the ring, if you release the hold you have on Erebos, Roy, and Ryker."

Tara kept her eyes closed as the Shadowman contemplated his options. It was the perfect time to channel her healing powers toward Sevilla's unconscious form. She cracked her eyes open just as Theo reached her and saw that it was working. Sevilla was starting to stir.

"And this power is greater than the powers of the elements?" He questioned Kadar, who answered him honestly.

"You will be part of a universal energy that is stronger than any magick you have available to you here."

The Shadowman reached his hand under his shirt and pulled out a chain hanging around his neck. There were two glass vials dangling from it that glowed green. He pulled the chain up over his head and held the necklace in front of him with one hand, while holding out the other palm up.

"This is what is left of Erebos and his darker half, Roy. Now, give me the ring."

Sevilla raised her head, her eyes wide. She rose to her feet as Zilla took a step forward and tore the chain holding Erebos' essence from the Shadowman's hand. The next thing Tara saw was a bright blue light being tossed backward from Zilla's hand to land in her sister's.

The Shadowman howled in rage as Zilla ran back to join her sister. Sevilla screamed as the man in the hooded cloak stiffened then looked down to his own chest where a bright green stake was protruding. The man raised his head and the hood fell away, causing Sevilla to call her husband's name.

"Ryker!"

His final words to her were cryptic, hardly heard over the gurgling of his lungs as they filled with blood. "Release Erebos."

Sevilla wailed, and Ryker's form turned to dust within seconds. The light surrounding the Shadowman became brighter, almost as bright as the golems he had created. He spread his arms wide, the bleeding shard in one hand and lightening forming in the other. Before he could send a pulse toward the sisters, Sevilla had slipped on the ring, and Kadar was at her side.

"I wish for the Shadowman's energy to be anchored to his current shell."

Kadar nodded, and a pulse of energy circled out from him and surrounded the Shadowman. The Shadowman lifted his hands and shot out a bolt of lightning, only to have it return to him. His frustrated scream shook the trees.

Theo waved to Tara and indicated they should get closer to Sevilla. She agreed. The time had come. As they moved toward her, the Shadowman had started to walk to them, light snapping and crackling from his closed fists. He was hesitant; Tara wasn't sure why but was glad. Tara called to the trees, who all sent their roots to the center of the clearing and wrapped around the Shadowman's legs. Before he was able to send any magick from his hands, the roots bound them as well.

"Now, Zilla," Fate cried.

Tara called to the roots to squeeze, and Zilla went to him and opened the vials. The fading lights wafted up and wiggled their way through the air and into the Shadowman's nose. He was forced to breathe it in, even as he shook his head to avoid it.

"Come back to me, Erebos," she said as she took a few steps back until she was well outside of spitting distance. "You need to merge and fight your way back to me." The roots held him tight, and the Shadowman growled in frustration at not being able to use any of the power he had absorbed.

"I wish for you to bring the rest of our group here unharmed," Sevilla said.

Kadar's face reflected resignation. He was not fighting against his nature, but he didn't like the fact that the woman he loved held power over him. Tara could sense it. He nodded and closed his eyes. There was a flash of light, and then a group of people stood there, confused as to how they arrived. Tara ran up to Brooke and gave her a hug, pulling her hand and indicating to the others that they should follow.

"The golems have stopped," Brooke said.

The pain in Sevilla's heart was almost too hard to bear. Ryker dying was the reason the golems weren't advancing. Tara blocked her heartache. She had to.

"The four of you should stand around him in the four compass corners with your partners behind you. When the power releases from him, it will remain near him," Fate said as she walked up to her sisters. "You must hurry, there isn't much time."

Zilla wrung her hands and kept whispering for Erebos to come back to her. Tara noticed a slight difference in the Shadowman, he seemed to be thrashing around a lot less and was breathing deeper. He wasn't as pale, his coloring was much better. Soon, Tara saw a dark green and black smoke coming out of the Shadowman's nose and mouth.

The women all stood in place, the men behind them with their hands on their shoulders. Tara touched on everyone's feelings. They were scared but resolved. Unsure but had faith in their friends. More than anything, Tara felt love, and she knew with that, they could withstand just about anything.

She stood facing the Shadowman and watched as his eyes cleared, and the toxic energy stopped pouring from his body. He looked confused, as if he didn't understand how he had gotten to this place. He looked into Tara's eyes and mouthed the words, "Thank you." His eyes rolled back up in his head, then his head flopped to the side.

Over their heads was a dark green mass with black strings woven through it. It pulsed and oozed, hovering above them and sending arms out to touch the heads of the people surrounding Erebos. It was trying to find another host, but Sevilla had taken care of that with her first wish.

Tara closed her eyes and took a deep breath, raising her hands to the sky and preparing to pull the energy down into her body. Once centered, she opened her eyes and gazed at the night sky. Every star was out in a universal display, and she had never seen anything more breathtaking. She reached out with her essence and connected to the cosmos in the same way she was taught to connect to the Earth.

She saw them then, the swirling lights in the distance coming toward her and forming a picture. The familiar shapes were mostly of people, but there were also animals and mystical creatures. Most she didn't recognize, but there were a few she did. Her grandmother was next to Mato, and they were both smiling serenely. Their voices whispered in her mind.

"As above it is below."

Their presence strengthened her. She closed her eyes and imagined she was the funnel. Her mind pictured the swirling mass of dark energy that had just been pulled from the Shadowman, being drawn into her with the deepest of breaths. Theo's hands were warm on her shoulders, and he spoke words of encouragement in her ears. She felt his energy surging into her, building walls between her energy stores and the toxic power that would be coming in.

With a deep breath, she pulled the cloud in and channeled it into a separate room in her mind. A special room she had built to store it, covered in symbols infused with her intent. She would keep it there until she was given instruction, and she knew now she had the strength to withstand the energy's effects. She had the help of her friends and the guidance of those who had gone before her. Most importantly, she had embraced her own power and knew what she was capable of.

As the toxic mass slid past her energy stores, it sent its tendrils out to attach to other areas. She didn't allow it and pushed the energy through a point in her mind that became smaller and smaller until it finally ended in the place she had designed to keep it.

"I have it," Tara said, struggling to keep the bile down as she spoke. The energy was rancid, and though she had it locked away, its toxic effects still pulsed at the wall of the barrier she had built. There were wisps of pain and fear sliding under the crack of her mental door, reminiscent of the snakes she had imagined before. She felt movement under her skin, primarily under her scalp, and she knew the power was worming its way out.

"We need to join hands." She held her hands out. There were long narrow lumps forming just below the surface of her skin, wiggling and winding their way down toward her fingertips. For a moment, she feared no one would complete the circle, that she would be left to fight the toxic energy on her own, but then she felt her hands filled with Brooke's and Amie's. Sera stood across from her, directly behind Erebos, with her hands joined to theirs. Their arms were circling around where he was bound.

Her next statement was hardly recognizable, it sounded as though she had swallowed gravel. "This must go to the place you prepared for it. The ones we built together."

The women nodded and widened their stances. The men each tightened their grips on their shoulders, and Tara made sure to maintain eye contact with each one of them. They made a promise to stand by the decision, although she could tell none of them had quite known what to expect. She had worried about Aleck the most, but he seemed the least upset out of all of them and even gave her a quick nod of encouragement.

Her skin bulged and swirled now, there were more tendrils of the power that had leaked from the place she kept it. "Make sure the walls are strong," she rasped.

The women each closed their eyes and concentrated on reinforcing their rooms like she had showed them during their sessions. Tara closed her own as well, allowing herself to only feel the warmth of Theo's hands on her shoulders and the touch of his emotions in her mind. He was pushing energy toward her, but the strength of it wasn't as pure anymore. She opened her eyes, and the women were all looking at her expectantly.

"Are you going to share some of that shit or what?" Sera's comment broke the tension.

"I'm ready when you are," Tara growled. Her skin bubbled and roiled, and she was close to passing out. She hoped once the magick was balanced between them, that the effects would be easier to handle. She had never felt so sick in her life.

"Ready," Amie said. Aleck gave Tara a thumbs up then kissed the back of Amie's head. James was standing behind him with Fate and her two sisters.

Sera had turned her head back to give Logan a kiss then nodded at Tara. "Let's do this."

She finally let her eyes rest on her best friend Brooke and the man she had chosen to live her life with. A life Tara was truly hoping wouldn't change now with the addition of this new burden. A burden she wasn't sure her anxious friend would be able to handle. Brooke looked scared out of her mind, but her jaw was set. She nodded with resolve and gave Tara's hand a squeeze. "Let's end this," she said firmly.

Tara nodded and closed her eyes. At first, she felt only the toxic energy, and it seemed that her magick was all but gone. But she dug deeper, and at the roots of her soul was where she found it, the last bit of resolve she had inside her. Theo's presence was steady, but there was another magick she didn't recognize. It was coming from the outside in. When she questioned it in her mind, it was Fate's voice that she heard speaking to her.

"We can't do this for you, but we can share our strength."

Their energy helped, the movement under Tara's skin subsiding. She traveled to the room where she had temporarily stored the magick and stood in front of the door for a pause. She reached out and felt the connection from the others; Amie, Sera, and Brooke were all present and ready for the next step. Tara took a deep breath and opened the door.

36

Theo felt the toxic effects the moment Tara opened her mental door to the negativity. It wormed its way through their connection, so he was forced to pull his energy back from her. She shook from her efforts. Her hair had long since turned white, and her skin was nearly translucent from the strain.

The symbols he had taught her raised up on her skin like blisters, circling and swirling in a language only he knew. To the others, it would appear the toxic magick was taking its toll, but he knew better. She fought its effects with the magick of his culture, and he hoped her efforts to balance it wouldn't have irreversible effects on her health.

He looked up to Kadar, whose face showed no emotion. He was waiting for his final command, and he made no move to help or offer support. The three witches, however, provided an energy shield around them all, which had a calming effect on the men, himself included.

Theo kept his hands in place on Tara's shoulders, as much as he wanted to break her free of the circle and pull her away from her purpose. He didn't know how this magick would change her, how it would change any of them really, and he was glad he had shared what was in his heart earlier in the night. It may have been his only chance to do so.

The movement beneath Tara's skin quickened, as if the symbols were being chased by the evil. The blisters puffed and lowered, down the sides of her chest and arms, to the place where her hands linked with her friends. Their joined hands glowed with the color of their individual magicks. Dark green for Tara, Aqua for Brooke, Amie's was Lavender, while Sera's was a fiery orange. Theo watched the colors start to blend and merge with one another, as the braided energy was shared around their circle.

Once the energies were woven, it pulsed with the power of four, an unbreakable bond that they would carry until death. Theo and the men had never completed the process, and perhaps that was why they had failed to keep the power safe. The women were brave to share so much of themselves with each other. To open themselves with faith and trust.

Theo looked over to Erebos. His head hung low, and his shoulders slumped in defeat beneath the roots that held him. Theo felt shame. Shame that he had let his friends down all those years ago, and regret that he hadn't been more of a friend to the man who most needed it. They had all let each other down, but he doubted any of these women would do the same.

"I believe in you, my love," Theo whispered and felt it with every fiber of his being. What these women were doing was going to work. It had to. The movement under Tara's skin slowed, and he kept his eyes on their joined hands and waited. Tara's shoulders tensed, then she let out a groan. Theo felt her shoulders relaxing now and continued to hold his breath. "Stay with me."

Another whimper then a shudder. Between the bands of brightly colored magick shared between them, Tara released the putrid energy. The transfer had begun.

The foul green and black light wove its way around the circle, and he watched as the women each strained against their nature to repel it. Their concentration was complete, each of them pulled deep inside themselves to sort out their individual energies. The darkness spread around both sides, through each of the women then back to Tara. The circle was complete, only time would tell if the women would be able to balance the energy.

He nodded to the other men, each helpless to do anything but lend their support. He knew how they felt. It wasn't something he had an easy time doing either. Tara's shoulders relaxed beneath his palms. she was getting some relief, as the toxic energy was shared. The raised symbols on her arms were disappearing.

The witches' energy covered them. They had built a barrier to contain the energy, allowing none of it to escape. There were creatures answering its call from all four elements, sitting quietly outside of the circle behind the mistress each answered to. He turned his head to see Taksi seated behind him, surrounded by Ents and members of the fae community. The harpies had arrived and perched in the trees behind Amie, and the Lycans stood behind Sera and her Alpha. Even the water sprites and merpeople had taken their landform to support their element. The magick had drawn them all, just as it connected them.

The colors were fully braided now, and the strained expressions on the women's faces let him know that the transfer was complete. How the energy affected each of them had yet to be seen. Tara wobbled in place as they slowly released hands. As soon as the women had disconnected the chain, they were turned into the arms of the men they loved. Tara's legs gave out from under her, and Theo barely had time to catch her before she hit the ground.

Brooke pulled away from Will and kneeled next to Tara. "What can we do?" She was in no shape to worry about her friend, she was shaking herself. Like the others, she still needed grounding. "Is there something we can get?"

"Some of the obsidian tree might help," Theo said helplessly. He had no idea what kind of shape Sevilla's house was in or if the tree was still standing.

"We will help," one of the harpies squawked. "Tell us where to go."

"I'll show you," Zilla offered then morphed into her griffin form and lifted to the sky. The treetops swayed as at least a dozen harpies followed her through the night sky. He glanced over and saw Fate speaking to Erebos, the roots still holding him tight as she spoke. He nodded, his eyes were glazed and swollen.

Theo glanced at Sevilla, who was being comforted by Kadar. He seemed less disconnected and shared in her sorrow as she walked to the pile of ash that was once her husband. Theo pulled back the tears of guilt that threatened to fall for the part he had played in keeping the couple apart. He channeled his sorrow and locked it away for a time when he would be able to examine it. For now, he needed to concentrate on Tara and her friends. All four were needed to maintain balance, and all four had to live.

So much loss, so much change. For reasons beyond the fact that she was needed to maintain balance, he prayed to the God and Goddess that she pulled through. He wasn't sure how he would be able to live his life without her, and even though her humanity would one day take her from him, he wanted to spend every minute until then with her by his side.

The three women seemed to be doing much better with their portion of the power. It made him worry that Tara had kept more than her share.

Amie was seated on a log nearby with Aleck beside her. Her hand was on her slightly rounded belly. Their heads were bowed in conversation, and Theo felt the worry on their minds.

The harpies were back in a flutter of wings and left the obsidian branches in a pile nearby. Brooke, Sera, and Amie got to work, taking the pieces and creating a circle around Tara. Theo snugged the pieces up as close as he could, and when he noted her breathing was labored, he placed them on her chest as well.

The sisters went in between each of the women and prompted them to join hands, creating a circle around him and Tara. The women closed their eyes, and the sisters started whispering the healing prayers of the immortals. They were prayers the priestesses and healers had passed down for thousands of years, the same prayers the Oracles and their supporters had been given at the temples that were no longer relevant in Tara's world. Perhaps no longer relevant, but the words were still powerful, nonetheless.

The creatures moved in one by one, creating their own circle of protection behind the women. They bowed their heads in reverence for the words they didn't understand, but the worth they recognized.

Theo sat at Tara's head with his palms on her cheeks, and his lips pressed to her forehead. With his eyes closed, he put every ounce of energy he had left into her sleeping form. He felt earth's energy around him, tried to tap into as much of it as he could, as he pushed his healing power through his connection with her. When he had run his stores dry and last pulse was spent, she stirred.

"Stop, Theo," she croaked. "You go too far."

"Thank the goddess," he heard Fate whisper. "Tara, you can release Erebos now. It's safe."

Tara nodded, and the roots pulled back as Zilla raced to his side. It was one less thing she had to expend her energy on, and Theo was glad to see it was already helping.

Erebos looked weak, still drained from the internal battle Theo knew he had fought. Had he not been able to merge with Roy and expel the Shadowman from their shared body, they would have had a different ending altogether. Zilla wrapped her arms around him, and he buried his face in her neck. She soothed his back as his shoulders shook. "Forgive me, Kitty," he murmured. Theo felt the depth of his sorrow and at the same time, a deep peace. He was whole at last.

They all had their parts in the fight against evil, Erebos included. Kadar and Sevilla joined them, and words were exchanged. Erebos broke down once more, and Sevilla embraced him, her own tears running freely. Erebos had been close to Ryker, brothers in a different time, and his anguish was bottomless as he begged her forgiveness. It would serve him well that Sevilla represented all things past but didn't live in it.

Theo took it all in, the emotions from everyone swirling around him and Tara like a vortex. He didn't have anything left to shield them with. He took a piece of the obsidian and slid it into his pocket, hoping it would neutralize the effects the emotional energy was having on him. So far, it seemed to be working for Tara.

Brooke kneeled beside her friend, with Amie and Sera standing watch. "You scared me," she announced. "I wasn't sure you were going to make it."

"How are you feeling?" Tara asked. "How are Amie and Sera?"

"We're good," Amie answered. "Everyone's okay, we will just need some rest."

"I'm concerned about the glowing rock around Sevilla's," Sera said. "It won't be a safe place to go."

One of the harpies came up to Amie and bowed. "Mistress, allow us to help. We know where we can take the pieces where they won't be found."

"Thank you. And you can call me Amie."

"Very well," the harpie smiled. "I am Aello. Sister to Celaeno. And it will be my honor to serve you." She bowed once more then went back to her group to give instruction. Soon, they were lifting off again in the direction of Sevilla's cottage.

"James and I can go back to supervise, since it doesn't have effects on us," Aleck said decisively. James nodded in agreement, and Logan chimed in.

"My fellow lycans can help ya as well. I ken where the stones are being taken and can get you through the portals."

Aleck nodded, and it was discussed that the sisters would join them with Erebos momentarily. They followed the harpies' path back to Sevilla's, leaving Theo and the elements alone with Erebos and the witches. Kadar had separated himself from the group but kept watch from a log nearby.

Tara stood up with Theo's support, as the sisters came forward and addressed them. It was Fate who spoke first.

"Those who are here now, along with their partners, are the only ones meant for this next message. And you must all promise us, and each other, that not another word of this will be spoken until the time comes." She raised her hand toward Kadar. "This means you as well, Kadar."

He stood and hesitantly walked over. Theo wasn't sure what was going to be shared, but he knew Fate well enough to know it would change all of their lives. Sevilla reached over quietly and took Kadar's hand. He seemed pleased, as if the gesture was a welcome sign of unity to him.

"And you, Erebos."

Fate waited as each one of the people surrounding her agreed to her terms. She took a deep breath and began. "To every beginning, there must come an end. To every pain, a soothing balm. And for every instance of malice against us, there must be forgiveness. Only then can the energy truly be balanced."

Theo looked at Erebos, his head bowed in remorse. He wondered just how much of what he had done was still imprinted in his mind. Even if he received forgiveness, he wondered how he would ever forgive himself.

Kadar was a different story. Theo still wasn't sure what part he had to play in Ryker's death, but it seemed that he too was feeling guilt. It wasn't up to Theo to sort it out. It would be Sevilla's choice to stand by him or not, and from their linked hands, her choice seemed clear.

He thought about his part to play, and the forgiveness he needed to obtain, and realized they all had things to overcome. Perhaps it was as simple as that. Maybe the energy was soothed with forgiveness and balanced with hope and love. Trust would move them forward. He could see that now.

Fate lowered her head, and the tension rose, everyone quietly listening for what she had to say. "As we move forward on this path, there are some things you should know. Things I am finally allowed to share with the rest of you. There will be three that follow to take our place."

"Whose place?" Amie whispered as she placed her hands over her stomach and took a step back. The women weren't sure what was upsetting her but instinctively took a step toward her to soothe her.

"My sisters and me. The three daughters of destiny."

"Holy shit," Sera whispered as she caught Amie's fainting body.

Theo's intake of breath caught Fate's awareness, and she smiled fondly at him. She leaned down and whispered in a voice only he could hear. "It isn't as bad as it seems."

37

Tara sat up, then moved to Amie's side. Sera had settled her on the ground and supported Amie's head on her lap. Brooke picked up a small clump of moss, and Tara saw a light blue light surrounding her hands before she rang out some water then placed it on Amie's forehead. Tara laid her hands on Amie's chest and pushed forward calming thoughts.

Her breathing was deeper, and she was able to catch a breath. "I'm feeling better," Amie whispered. She placed her hands on her stomach as if she were shielding something precious. In a way, Tara supposed, she was.

"You should lie here for just a moment," Tara suggested.

"Here's some ice," Brooke offered. "I figured it was easier than trying to find a glass."

Amie laughed. "The ice chip thing will be something that you will be good at when the time comes."

Fate and the sisters had moved closer, leaving the men who were present to watch from a few steps away. Erebos had his head bowed low as Theo spoke to him. Tara couldn't hear what he was saying but saw Erebos nod in agreement several times. It was obvious Kadar was listening in, even though he tried to pretend he wasn't interested. She wondered what other secrets he was aware of by quietly observing others.

"I believe I understand what you were implying," Amie said to Fate. "And that my children will have a part in all this."

Fate nodded. "They will, and ultimately, they will have a choice."

Amie's eyes teared up. "I'm not sure any of us have had many choices since this whole thing began. Sometimes, I feel as if it has all been laid out for us."

"We know how you feel," Zilla said.

"We do," Sevilla added. "And we too were given a choice. By the time we were ready to accept it, we saw all the reasons why it was the right path."

Amie sat up, and Sera helped her to her feet. "I will need some time to absorb this. And to figure out how I'm going to tell Aleck."

"I'll help you in any way I can, my friend," Zilla said. The two women embraced before Zilla made her way back to Erebos.

"We will be here for you all," Sevilla said. "Anything you need, we will help." She walked toward Kadar, who rose from the stump he was seated on and approached her. He opened and closed his hands, as if he wanted to reach out and touch her but was stopping himself. Like Erebos, Kadar stood with his head bowed and nodded.

Tara was much too drained to pick up on who was feeling what anymore. It was as if everyone was a swirling mass of emotions that had no hope of settling. Fate was right, forgiveness would be needed for all of them to move forward. For as strained as things had gotten between the couple, it seemed that Kadar was forgiven now. Tara watched as Sevilla pointed into the woods, and Kadar put out his elbow for her hand. The darkness surrounded them, and the last thing Tara saw of them was the small blue light from her ring fading into the night.

Fate called out to Zilla. "We will see you both in the morning. We have much to discuss."

Erebos looked frightened and took the hand Zilla offered. He grasped it like a lifeline. "Very well," she said. She turned and snapped her fingers, opening a portal that was within feet of where Theo was standing. She slid her arm around Erebos and laid her head on his shoulder. Tara felt the relief coming from them both, and as they slipped through the doorway, Tara saw him lean over and kiss the top of Zilla's head. The opening closed with a blink, and they were gone.

"We could all use some rest," Fate said. "But Sevilla's home is off limits until the others get the site cleared up.

"We could go back to my village," Sera offered. "I just need to let Logan know where we are going."

"I can take care of that," Theo said. "Tara, can you lead Fate? I will go back and check on the progress and get a few things. I can meet you at Sera and Logan's."

"Okay," Tara said. A bed and a good night's sleep sounded amazing.

"Thank you, Theo." As he leaned down, she put her arms around his neck and slid into his strong embrace. "Are you feeling okay?"

Tara nodded. "So far, just a little queasy," she answered.

"I'll try to bring something back to settle you." His deep voice tickled her ear. "I won't be long."

"You better not be," she whispered back. His attentions were making her feel better already.

The kiss was quick but intimate, and a smile warmed his eyes. As he walked away, his step was light. Long after he had disappeared from sight, she could still hear his rich baritone, singing the song she now thought of as his. Her life was going to change, and she couldn't help but wonder if perhaps Brooke had been right — maybe Mato had something to do with it after all. She looked up into the night sky just in time to see her answer in the form of a shooting star.

Tara smiled then took Fate's arm. "Are you ready?"

Fate nodded. "The question should be, are you?"

Tara laughed at her insight. Fate saw more than she ever led on. For once, Tara was ready with an answer. "I believe I am."

"Come on guys," Sera called. "We have a bit of a hike to the portal."

"We're right behind you," Brooke said as she got on the other side of Fate and took her other arm to help Tara lead her forward. Amie had already started walking with Sera. Brooke whispered. "Is everything going to be all right?" The worry in her friend's tone couldn't be hidden, and Tara tried to tamp down the feelings that came to her. She was still weak and couldn't take on any more emotions.

Fate's response seemed to soothe her. "Everything is just as it should be. As above, it is below, all around us, energy flows."

It didn't take long for the women to make it to Sera's village, and Amie offered for Fate to come back to the cabin where she and Aleck had been staying. Tara didn't blame her. She was sure that there were more questions that needed to be asked. So far, she and the other women were doing fine with balancing the good and bad energy.

Sera took her and Brooke to her Aunt's house, and her abuela, Mila, directed Brooke to the spare room. Tara could see a lot of bright pink and several stuffed animals from the doorway, as Brooke was getting Annabelle's bed for the night.

"You can show Tara to the guest cabin," Mila said.

Tara hugged Brooke and said her goodnights. They were all drained and couldn't get to their beds quick enough. Sera walked her outside and along the path to the back of the house. There was a rustic cabin toward the back of the property that, at first glance, looked like a shed.

"It's small, but the bed is comfortable," Sera explained. She pointed to the outhouse alongside it. "Only toilet we have here. There's a flashlight inside." She opened the door to the house and waved her hand toward the back wall. A fire instantly lit in the fireplace. "There are some candles on the hearth if you need more light. I'll let Theo know where you are."

"Thanks, Sera." She gave her a quick hug. "This is perfect. I'll see you in the morning."

Tara gave her a wave from the doorway then turned to face the quaint room. She spied a lantern, which she lit from the fire and placed on a small table inside the bedroom. It wasn't far from the main room, and it would take a while before the chill was gone, but there were a lot of blankets available. She unfolded them and stacked them high. She slipped off her clothes and placed the folded pile on the dresser before slipping in between the cool sheets. She shivered until her body heat adjusted, falling asleep to the crackling of the fire.

After getting Sevilla's place cleaned up, Theo went into the small cabin Sera directed him to and removed his shoes and coat. There was a light coming from the adjoining room, and while he felt it was warming nicely, he put another log on the fire for the night. He paused in the doorway to the bedroom, smiling at the tuft of white hair he saw poking from a mound of blankets.

He undressed and dimmed the lantern she had left for him. She moved of her own accord as he slid into bed behind her. His arm went around her, and he drew her to him, no longer afraid she would be hurt. He had a necklace that matched Tara's, fashioned from the Obsidian tree. It had survived the battle, with only a few of its branches littering the yard. She and Kadar had arrived at the house right before he left with Logan for his village.

The harpies and lycans had done a good job of cleaning up the glowing stone; there was hardly any sign of it by the time he left. The toxic effects were all but gone, and even though it didn't seem that any creature had made it inside her home, Sevilla spent some time smudging all the rooms.

Kadar had been building a fire when Theo left. He seemed more relaxed, as if a weight had been lifted from his shoulders. Sevilla was more settled as well, and Theo made his excuses, promising he would be back in the morning. As he left, he noticed the Elemental Journal centered on the table, thinking it was strange that Brooke had left it behind. As tempted as he was to retrieve it, he left it there.

He drew in a deep breath and filled his lungs with Tara's scent. She was as relaxing as the sage and lavender that Sevilla had burned in her home. Tara sighed against him and settled deeper into the thick mattress. He closed his eyes and faded into a contented sleep. Their worries would be put aside until the morning.

Theo let Tara sleep in the next morning and went along to find Sera and gather something for breakfast. She was outside with a young lycan, who was all laughter and smiles. Amie was seated beside her, and he hesitated as to not interrupt the private conversation. Sera waved him over.

"Good Morning, Theo," she said as she bent to lift a nearby basket. "My abuela put a few things together for you and Tara."

"Thank you," Theo nodded as he took the basket. He glanced over at Amie, who was being much more reserved than normal. "How are you two feeling this morning?"

"I've never felt better," Sera said. "I almost have too much energy. I'll be joining Logan for a run later."

"I am pretty pooped," Amie laughed. "Pretty much goes with the territory though, no major changes so far. I think Brooke has a bit of a headache she's trying to shake but, otherwise, she's good too."

"How's Tara doing? Is she still out of it?" Sera asked.

Theo nodded his head. "I left while she was still asleep. She needed the rest."

"Is her hair still white?"

Theo responded to Amie's question with a quick nod. It prompted a worried look on both of their faces, which he diverted by thanking Sera for the basket before heading back.

Tara was still where he had left her, bundled unmoving under the covers. He placed the basket on the small table then went to the fire in the hearth and stoked it. It was much warmer in the house now that the sun was up but knew that from the way Tara's hands and feet felt, that she would have a hard time warming up.

He went into the room and frowned at the white spikes of hair poking from the top of the comforter. This was the longest it had ever taken to turn back, and he wondered if it ever would. He thought she was beautiful either way but worried about the effects of the dark energy on her. The other women seemed to be fine, why wasn't she?

He slid off his shoes and tucked himself up behind her. Even fully clothed with blankets between them, she affected him in a way that no woman ever had. It was much more than the magick that bound them. He craved to see the contented smile as he read to her, to hear the playful frustration in her tone when he teased, and to feel her melt beneath him as their bodies joined. She was all he could think of, and his chest ached with the realization that she might not be the same.

He pulled the blanket back and examined her skin, which still showed traces of the symbols that she had manifested. The script was slightly darker in some places than others and was hardly visible unless you were looking closely. Like her hair, the changes hadn't reverted entirely back to normal, and that concerned him.

As he pulled the blanket down, he saw her arms were covered with the inscriptions as well. There seemed to be more of them than before, and he wondered if she was having a hard time keeping some of the darkness, she had taken in, locked away. Most of the symbols he recognized, but there were many he didn't.

He ran his finger along her cheek. Much as she needed to rest, he knew he needed to wake her. He would feel better once he could look into her eyes, once he knew that it was still Tara that looked out through them. She shifted under his insistent tickling and brought her hand up to bat at his. He smiled at her irritation.

"Stop it," she whined. "Don't you have something better to do?"

"Bothering you is by far my favorite pastime," he grinned into her squinting eyes. He was glad to see they were clear and the same beautiful hazel color he had come to know. Nothing glowing or red, or even rimmed with gold, was a good sign. The messages on her skin were something entirely different.

"I'm thinking we would both be better off if you find another hobby," she laughed, and the sound of it made his heart soar. She sat up in bed, and other than her white hair and marked skin, she seemed to be back to her normal self. She put her arm behind her and scratched her shoulder blade then ran her hands through her hair to "fluff it" as she referred to it. Her stomach growled, and he smiled even wider.

"It seems that it is fortunate that I brought us back breakfast." He slid off the bed and walked into the kitchen, lifting the napkin from the basket. "Mila made us some scones and biscuits, and this looks like a jar of raspberry — "

"Theo."

It was her tone that stopped him mid-sentence, her expression had him crossing the room immediately. She was standing in the doorway shaking, not because she was in her undergarments, but because she was frightened. The quiver of her lip confirmed it.

"Theo, what is wrong with me?" She fell into his arms and started to sob. "What is all over my body?"

He pulled back and cupped her face, wanting his words to calm her but knowing he didn't have the answers she would expect. "I believe it's your body's way of containing the dark energy. Once you are stronger and can build better shields, I believe you will no longer need them."

The sniffles subsided, and she wiped her tears with a nod. Then she reached her arm up and scratched her upper shoulder, before leaning back against the doorframe and scratching her back along the corner. "I hope you're right," she said as she rubbed her back from side to side along the corner. "I think maybe I got bit by something. It's driving me mad."

"Let me look," Theo said, spinning her around in place. He didn't say anything right away, and she looked over her shoulder at him with agitation.

"Well? What is it?"

"I'm..." he cleared his throat, not believing his own eyes. "It's just that..."

"Oh, for heaven's sake, Theo. Spit it out."

"I think they're wings."

"Come again?" She spun on her heels to face him and attempted to look behind her. "Did you say wings?"

She looked up into his face, and he tried not to let the shock he felt

275

register. He had been right all along. She was part Fae. Otherwise, he doubted this type of transformation would have taken place. The symbols made a little more sense now as they swirled and changed like the ocean tide.

"Tara, you need to calm down."

"Calm down? Calm down you say?" Her voice was shrill, and her eyes wild. "That is easy for you to say, you don't have wings sprouting from your... aahhh!"

She fell to the floor, and he watched helplessly as she writhed on her hands and knees, and dark purple wings split the pale skin on her back. He had heard from others who had gone through the transition that the first time was the worst. Once the wings broke through, there wasn't as much subsequent pain.

He knelt in front of her and pulled her up, so she was facing him. He placed his hands on her ears and caressed them, already feeling the changes they were going through as well. "Tara, I need you to look into my eyes and focus only on my words."

"The pain," she groaned as her face scrunched in agony.

"I promise it won't be much longer." He couldn't know if it was a lie he just told, but he would do anything to stop the tears streaming down her face. Her ears were nearly transformed, and he did the only thing he could. He started to sing.

The words from his culture calmed her as they always had and caused the symbols on her skin to slow their rapid movement. The wings on her back unfurled and fluttered behind her, dark and strong, with silver veining to match her hair. He knew the answer then to his earlier question. Her hair wouldn't be changing back.

He continued to sing as she allowed herself to be calmed by his words and his fingers. Her wings fluttered, and he saw the strength in them, knowing she would be able to fly if she chose. He prayed she would be able to draw them in, as most of her kind could, so that she didn't have to ever feel that the choice was made for her where she would have to live.

With his words, the symbols had all but left her body, only one remained on her upper left arm, the symbol representing balance that had brought them together such a short time ago. The funnel symbol, representing the universe and Earth, was dark purple, like her wings, and streaks of the same color dotted its way throughout her spiked white hair. Her transformation was complete, and he had never seen anyone more utterly beautiful.

He lowered his hands and stared in awe. Her face no longer showed pain, but tears were streaming down her cheeks. She put her face in her hands and started to sob.

"What happened to me? What have I become?"

"A fairy," Theo said quietly. "At least, that is what I believe."

"Will I turn back?"

Theo's heart squeezed at her innocent question. "No, my darling, I don't think so."

"I'm seriously stuck like this?"

"I believe that you will eventually be able to retract and extend your wings on demand. But yes, I believe the transformation is complete."

She stared at him unbelieving, her hands on her hips and her chest heaving. He wasn't sure what she had wanted to hear, but it was obvious from her reaction that hadn't been it. "And you have nothing to say about it?"

He wasn't sure what he was expected to say, so he told her the truth. "I think you are magnificent with wings or no. With red hair or white. I decided not long ago that I would ask you to be my queen, even if I would have to mourn your human death and spend the rest of my eternal existence alone. I wouldn't be telling you the truth if I said that I wasn't happy with the turn of events."

Tara's wings fluttered in delight, the silver veins sparkled in the firelight. She stepped toward him and took his hands into hers, weaving her tiny fingers between his. "You sure about this? It's a big adjustment for us both."

"An adjustment I am most ready for. You are the woman I've been waiting for. I know that now." He kissed her softly, feeling the sharp points of her teeth nip his lip. She would have more adjustments, but he would need to ease her into them. He wasn't worried; now they had plenty of time.

EPILOGUE

6 months later...

Theo had been right. Tara had been able to retract her wings, something she learned how to do, right before Brooke's wedding. It took place on a beautiful day, and the timing couldn't have been more appropriate, for rebirth and hope, than the day of the spring equinox. Tara was amazed just how great the guys cleaned up. Even Theo allowed her to rent a tux for him, which she insisted he looked fantastic in. Much as he hated formal affairs, he had to admit afterward that the wedding was fun.

She hadn't been the only one that had gone through changes. Shortly after she sprouted her wings and announced she was part fairy, Sera had morphed into a phoenix during a full moon run with Logan. It seemed that her dormant Lycan blood had finally taken hold. Logan was over the moon with pride, and she and Tara would often go on flights together. She had gotten close to the feisty fireball, which was good, considering she would be staying in Wisteria as well.

Brooke and Will visited often but stayed primarily in California to help with the family firm. Will's father had all but retired, and Will had taken in a few partners to help with the workload. Brooke helped run the office from their home, which they purchased to be close to his parents. Since Brooke had lost hers at such a young age, she was happy to go all in with a relationship with his.

Amie and Aleck were also in California, and when the time came, they called Brooke to come help with the triplets, who came into the world as quietly and patiently as their mom. Aleck had been told what destiny had in store for them, and he took the news pretty well, considering.

Sevilla remained at the cottage. The only change was that Kadar was openly staying there. From what Tara had observed, he had been there all along, but now it was more of a commitment. Sevilla wore the sapphire ring that Kadar was bound to on her left hand, and it no longer glowed. Tara often wondered if she had made her final wish, and if so, what it would be. Whatever it was, perhaps it gave them both a happily ever after.

Zilla and Erebos came around to help with harvests and building new structures, but for the most part, kept to themselves. Theo had made an effort to get to know him better and would often take him fishing in the pond where Brooke first met him all those years ago. She had told Tara the stories, about how he had tricked her into thinking he was Will and how he had tried to keep the two of them apart for the longest time. Erebos was working hard on earning his forgiveness, but Brooke would be a hard sell.

James had moved to Wisteria permanently and spent his time with Fate in a small cabin in the woods. Tara was right, there had been something between them. Fate promised she would tell her the story one day. Aleck's dog Max, who had been adopted by James after the babies were born, stayed at the cabin with them. Taksi had grown very fond of him, and she would often take both Max and Misty along with her on animal adventures. They had plenty of places to roam in the woods near Theo's estate, and Tara had gotten really good at communicating with them over long distances. Especially, with the help of the Ents.

Tara had just changed into her dressing gown and was removing her jewelry when Theo came in to see her. He looked amazing in his suit and sash, but she knew that he was itching to change. He didn't like the pomp and circumstance, merely did it for his people or sometimes for her. Tara didn't mind it. She had met some amazing people and knew now why she had never felt like she belonged before. Her roots had always stemmed from Wisteria, it all made sense now.

"You look gorgeous tonight," he said as he kissed her neck. He pulled in a breath and she smiled. She had worn the vanilla musk just for him. He removed his jacket then loosened his cravat.

"And I couldn't get up here quick enough after what you whispered in my ear down there," she grinned. "I am liking this naughty side to you."

He tugged off his shirt and dropped it to the floor before standing behind her and leaning down. "You mean the thing I said about how hungry you made me?"

"Mhmm." She held her breath as he leaned down and nibbled her neck. He took another deep pull of her scent into his lungs. "And about what I wanted to eat?"

His tongue licked the curl of her ear and paused on her newly formed points. They were still extremely sensitive, and he had a habit of nibbling on them. A moan escaped her lips, and she felt his mouth curl in a smile. "Yes, that," her whisper was throaty. He was definitely being naughty.

He turned her chair and got on his knees, running his hands up her legs and pooling her sheer negligee fabric up on her upper thighs. He looked up her, with anticipation gleaming in his eyes, and she gave him a wink before quoting the book they had read until they knew the words by heart.

"It is a truth universally acknowledged, that a single man in possession of a good fortune, must be in want of a wife."

Theo grinned, knowing full well that she was aware of how he first felt about that line. But so much had changed since then, their lives weren't close to resembling what they were before they had met. Most of all, he had changed. All his seriousness and stress had disappeared.

"Ms. Austen knew what she was talking about," he said as he slid back on his heels and reached into his pocket. "Now's as good of time as any," he remarked, holding a ring out in front of him and taking her hand with his other. He kissed it gently then looked into her eyes. Eyes that were a little misty now with his actions.

"Would you do me the honor of taking my hand and never letting go? Of being the last person I see at night and the first as I wake? Of being the queen of my heart, and my people, from this day forward?"

Her heart swelled with love. "Of course, Theo. I will." Tara held her fingers out, and he slid the ring onto her hand. It was amethyst in a silver setting, clearly chosen to match her hair and wings. It fit perfectly. "I love you so much."

"You make me unbelievably happy. I'm so glad you came into my life."

Tara slid down in front of him, kneeling and taking him into her arms. She could hardly put into words what she was feeling. It was as if all her dreams had finally come true. So, that was precisely what she told him, in more ways than one.

Fate's blindness doesn't prevent her from seeing the future, but her visions don't always agree on the way to get there.

The spirits who once guided Fate are silent while dark energy leaches across Wisteria. She once had control over all destinies, but now is helpless as mystical creatures die. Without the internal voices to guide her, she is afraid of her own path for the first time in her immortal life.

She and her two sisters represent Past, Present, and Future. They struggle to maintain the balance in a land intrinsically connected to Earth. Their magick must be combined to defeat a growing evil that transcends time, but at what cost to the nature than binds us?

Loyalty to the men they love battles their divine purpose. In a universe where all energies are connected, the corruption of one can spell devastation. Fate's blindness mustn't prevent her from finding the light. It will be the only way the earth will survive the darkness.

Desperate to find the source of his power before it falls into enemy hands, a powerful Jinni must accept help from a widow, whose caution might eclipse even his. Will they discover that trust in each other is the biggest risk of all?

If you liked *Twist of Fate*, you'll love *The Jinni's Wish*! Get your free copy today by following this link: https://bookhip.com/TWLTXJ

Book 1: Sea of Dreams

In a land that parallels ours, a great evil lies in wait. To defeat it, Brooke must face her greatest fears.

Just when Brooke Fisher thought she had a handle on her anxiety, strange things start to happen. In addition to her hair turning green, she's had nothing but cold showers and iced coffee for weeks. When the man starring in her nightmares walks into her reality, she fears what their connection truly means

The beautiful woman Will Engel has met is complicated in a way that speaks to him. As he helps her unravel the clues in a mysterious journal, he finds that their pasts are intertwined in a way that defies all logic.

As the threat of the Shadowman grows stronger, their journey takes them to a magical land that parallels their own. What they find there not only confirms Brooke's destiny as the element of Water, but Will's role in her future as well.

Book 2: Winds of Change

Amie must unlock the secret to her destiny. One in which she embodies the element of Air.

A persistent ex-boyfriend is the least of Amie Petridis's concerns. After a cryptic tarot reading, winged creatures start to show up more noticeably in her life. Their energy is especially prominent after a sexy U.S. Air Marshal breezes into her life.

Although Aleck has a painful secret that had kept him from getting close to anyone in the past, his attraction to the feisty pilot can no longer be denied. During a romantic getaway to the land of her heritage, they stumble upon a portal to a magical world. Amie's connection to the element of Air is brought to light and her destiny is sealed.

They have both been dealt a hand by Fate which they will have to embrace. They will also learn they aren't the only ones who have had to make sacrifices. Amie is the second element that has been found, and what they do next will determine the fate of the others. Balance must be restored.

BOOK 3: PLAYING WITH FIRE

Sera is the element of Fire and is as unpredictable as the flame she represents. Logan has waited his entire life for her, but has he met her in time?

Sera Cardoso's thistle tattoo generally warns her away from danger, but this time it's different—she's seeing visions and hearing voices in the flames she fights. A younger man with whiskey eyes haunts her and when her abuela disappears, Sera returns to Italy and is pulled into a magical world by the man in the flames.

If Logan Blackwood is unable to find his soul mate by the end of three moon cycles, his life will be altered—forever. When the fiery woman with the temper to match enters his life, he can hardly believe his luck. She is empowered, strong and will make the perfect bride for him. But the choice must be hers, and she clearly doesn't feel the same connection.

As Sera connects to the element of fire; the volatile nature of her energy has her seeking help. The other elements help with her transition, and it becomes clear there will be much expected from them all in the battle that lies ahead. Her decision to accept Logan into her life is one of many she will have to face as the evil in Wisteria grows stronger.

Acknowlegements

It is surreal to be writing the acknowledgements in the final book of this series. When I started this journey, I only had an idea and the support of my friends. Thankfully, both are still with me. As always, please forgive my memory if you have helped me in some way but I forgot to thank you here.

As always, thank you to my wonderful family for putting up with my crazy dreams. Your steadfast belief in my abilities is entirely the reason this series has seen the light of day.

To the Muse Crew, Judy Bobrow, Madelyn March, Sharon Quiroz, Linda Grischy, Kathy Wheeler and Judy Waggoner. Thank you for being my Alphas and for keeping me honest when I toss too many commas and "ings" into my manuscripts.

To my content editor, Jennifer Melzer, holy cow! We did it! Thank you for challenging me on each and every book. Thank you for pointing out the opportunities where I can dig a little deeper. Your instinct has proven to be spot on each and every time!

To my line editor, Alexa Nussio who took a complete manuscript and polished it to a shine! Your attention to detail is amazing! To my book designer, Jen Sumeracki at Sumo Design, you rock so much! I am so incredibly proud of what we have created together! I look forward to so many more projects with you!

To my BFFs, my sisters, my cohorts, Nettie McHugh and Barb Thompson, who continue to support me in every way imaginable. I couldn't possibly have done this without you both. Thank you for being my obsidian tree.

To all my GDRWA peeps, you are truly the best group of people I have the honor to know. You inspire me to keep my fingers on the keyboard and my head in the story each and every time we get together!

And, last but not least, I want to thank the Oscoda Writer's Weekend crew. The weekend in September is one I look forward to for the entire year, and it has been so amazing wrapping this series up while sharing each of your writer journeys. I count myself fortunate to be in such talented company and look forward to the day we can celebrate your stories going off into the world. Keep on Writing!

While it hasn't always been part of her occupation, writing has always been part of D.A. Henneman's life—poetry and song lyrics through teenage angst (no, you won't get to read any of them), short stories in college classes (perhaps you will get to read some of them), and random marketing materials during her stint as a flower shop owner. Even with all of that writing in her life, ten chapters of a book stayed buried in her file cabinet until she closed her flower shop. The timing was finally right, and the Power of Four series was born.

Most days she can be found on her blog posting about her writing journey. You can find her at www.dahenneman.com. You can also follow her on multiple social media plaforms.